POWERS OF DARKNESS

POWERS OF
ᴅARKNESS

THE LOST VERSION OF *DRACULA*

BRAM STOKER
VALDIMAR ÁSMUNDSSON

TRANSLATED FROM THE ICELANDIC, WITH AN
INTRODUCTION AND ANNOTATIONS BY
HANS CORNEEL DE ROOS

FOREWORD BY DACRE STOKER
AFTERWORD BY JOHN EDGAR
BROWNING

OVERLOOK DUCKWORTH
NEW YORK • LONDON

This edition first published in hardcover in the United States and the
United Kingdom in 2017 by Overlook Duckworth, Peter Mayer Publishers, Inc.

NEW YORK
141 Wooster Street
New York, NY 10012
www.overlookpress.com
For bulk and special sales, please contact sales@overlookny.com,
or write us at the above address

LONDON
30 Calvin Street
London E1 6NW
info@duckworth-publishers.co.uk
www.ducknet.co.uk

Translated from the Icelandic, with an Introduction and annotations,
copyright © 2016 by Hans Corneel de Roos
Foreword copyright © 2016 by Dacre Stoker
Afterword © 2016 by John Edgar Browning

Cataloging-in-Publication Data is available from the Library of Congress

Design concept by Yellowstone Ltd.
Design augmentation and typeformatting by Bernard Schleifer
Manufactured in the United States of America
ISBN US: 978-1-4683-1336-9
ISBN UK: 978-0-7156-5127-8

FIRST EDITION
10 9 8 7 6 5 4 3 2 1

Dedicated to Petre Tutunea, Pienette Coetzee, Lounette Loubser, Amanda Larasari, Marsha Maramis, Sarah Mawla Syihabuddin, Susannah Schaff, Joyce Georgewill, Aïda El Hani, Andreea and Teo Vechiu, Shantal Jeewon Kim, Shiva Dehghanpour, Dian Risna Saputri and Yofina Pradani, who all volunteered as assistants in my creative studio and over the past three years shared my enthusiasm, my questions and my worries about this book project.

CONTENTS

FOREWORD *by Dacre Stoker* 1

INTRODUCTION *by Hans C. de Roos* 13

A ROOM WITH A VIEW: *The floor plans of Castle Dracula* 45

POWERS OF DARKNESS 59

AFTERWORD *by John Edgar Browning* 291

ACKNOWLEDGMENTS 295

REFERENCES 301

FOREWORD

by Dacre Stoker

"There are mysteries which men can only guess at, which age by age they may solve only in part."
—BRAM STOKER, *Dracula*, 1897

I T IS AN HONOR TO WRITE THIS FOREWORD FOR MY FRIEND and travelling companion Hans de Roos, who has bravely delved into the newest of the *Dracula* mysteries. I remember well the phone conversation in which Hans first told me there were significant textual differences between the English and Icelandic editions of *Dracula*. Once I realized *Makt Myrkranna* was not simply an Icelandic translation of *Dracula*—that this was a unique story—I wondered: How could this go unnoticed for so many years? As I shared my enthusiasm and initial thoughts with De Roos, I was eager to read the English translation of the Icelandic text and begin to make my own sense of this new development. Moreover, I was prompted to reflect anew on the enduring legacy of my great granduncle's most famous work.

I lecture regularly at literary and film events—on the subject of the history and mysteries which surround *Dracula*—and always find that fans of the novel and of the subgenres it has inspired are genuinely interested in any background information about Bram and the circumstances associated with the novel. *Dracula* is considered a classic—in part because more than a century after its initial publication, speculative material keeps readers and researchers searching for answers to some of the mysteries surrounding the novel's origins. The translation of *Makt Myrkranna* and the uncertainty about the text's source present more than enough fodder for another generation to wonder and speculate about.

With de Roos's discovery, another significant mystery is added to the list of unresolved questions about Bram Stoker's Gothic classic. For example, how did 124 pages of author's notes for *Dracula* survive such a circuitous journey before finding a home at Philadelphia's Rosenbach Museum? And where was the one known typescript of *Dracula* during the years between its arrival in Philadelphia and its eventual possession by Paul Allen of Microsoft fame?

It appears that shortly after *Dracula*'s publication, Bram gave the only known typescript of the novel to Col. Thomas C. Donaldson, Esq. of Philadelphia, a close friend and biographer of Walt Whitman who handled the affairs of many writers. After Whitman's death, according to his wishes, Donaldson gave Bram the original notes from Whitman's 1886 lecture on Abraham Lincoln. During one of Bram's visits with Whitman, the men discussed their mutual interest in Lincoln; Bram later quoted Whitman's exaggerated personal account of the night Lincoln was shot in his own presentations about Lincoln. Donaldson passed away in 1898, and the next year, Henkel's sold his extensive collection of manuscripts and letters. Yet it was nearly a century before the *Dracula* typescript was found in a Pennsylvania barn amongst the Donaldson family possessions. The typescript changed hands a few times, and then in 2002, after being offered with great fanfare by Christie's, failed to meet the reserve bid and was subsequently bought by Paul Allen.

On July 7, 1913, fifteen months after Bram Stoker's

death, Sotheby's sale of his personal library included a book written by Col. Donaldson and inscribed in 1898 by his son Thomas Blaine Donaldson to Bram, "as a remembrance." At the same Sotheby's auction, James Drake, a New York book dealer, purchased lot # 182, 124 pages, "Original Notes and Data for his 'Dracula'" for the price of two pounds. The "Notes" surfaced again in 1946, pictured in a *Life* magazine article about rare manuscripts, having been purchased for Scribner's collection for $500; then in 1970 they were bought by the Rosenbach Museum in Philadelphia from an antiquarian bookseller, Charles Sessler. It was not until the mid 1970s that—thanks to Raymond McNally and Radu Florescu, two Boston College professors—attention shifted to Bram's preparatory work for *Dracula*. While researching a famous pamphlet, *Dracole Waida*, Nuremberg (c. 1488), which included a woodcut of Vlad Dracula lll, McNally and Florescu visited the Rosenbach Museum in Philadelphia. To their great surprise, the archivist suggested they might also be interested in Bram Stoker's research notes for *Dracula*, which had been purchased by the Museum a few years before and were still in the archives in relative obscurity. Thus, they gained new insight into Bram's research and writing process, which they referenced in their book *The Essential Dracula* (1979). However, in another of their works, *In Search of Dracula* (1972), they drew a close connection between Bram's Count Dracula and the Wallachian leader Prince Vlad Dracula, essentially transforming Vlad Dracula lll into a vampire—much to the dismay of historians and the Romanian people. Other scholars followed McNally and Florescu, and to this day, a pilgrimage to the Rosenbach provides a unique and important opportunity to form conclusions based on Bram's source notes. Alternatively, those who are interested can consult the excellent annotated facsimile edition created by scholars Dr. Elizabeth Miller and Robert Eighteen-Bisang in 2008.

Unfortunately, apart from the typescript and the notes, Bram left us very little firsthand information about *Dracula*. In the void, a private family joke relayed by Noel Stoker, Bram's only son, to Harry Ludlam, author of *A Biography of Dracula: The Life Story of Bram Stoker* (1962) and *My Quest for Bram Stoker* (2000), has been quoted over and over as the gospel truth: flippantly, Bram "attributed the genesis of *Dracula* to a nightmare he had after a surfeit of dressed crab at supper one night."

To date, only one interview given by Bram on the subject of *Dracula* has been found: written by Jane Stoddard of the *British Weekly*, it appeared within five weeks of the novel's publication and spans a mere 896 words. Additionally, there is only one known letter in which Bram discusses *Dracula*—addressed to former British Prime Minister William Gladstone in 1897, it reveals precious little about Stoker's personal thoughts on his work, except that he hoped it would "cleanse the mind by pity and terror."

Other than this small reservoir of "canonical texts"—the Donaldson typescript, the Rosenbach notes, the crab joke, the Stoddard interview and the letter to Gladstone—we have only the opinions of others to explain the possible inspirations and motivations behind Bram's writing.

The rediscovery of *Makt Myrkranna* provides us with new information and new riddles. Unfortunately, we may never know the full details of Bram Stoker's arrangements with Valdimar Ásmundsson, who transcribed the story to Icelandic and published it in his newspaper, followed by a book edition about six months later. Bram's 1897 agreement with Archibald

Constable, the publisher of *Dracula*, "does not include any place or country other than the United Kingdom of Great Britain and Ireland and the British Dependencies (Canada being excepted from such British Dependencies) and the said Author shall be free to license others than the said Publishers to publish the said work . . ." with no specific mention of translations. The Stoker family no longer has copies of Bram's publishing contracts, but Bram's agreement with Archibald Constable clearly left him free to sell *Dracula*—or any version of *Dracula* for translation.

Until evidence to the contrary is presented, it is safe to say *Makt Myrkranna* (1900) was among the very first literary translations of *Dracula*, second only to a Hungarian edition of 1898. The preface to *Makt Myrkranna*—which surfaced in 1986—is notably different from the preface to the original 1897 Constable edition of *Dracula*. This Icelandic preface was long assumed by researchers to be the only difference between the two editions; no one noticed the entirely new plot elements and characters waiting to be revealed in the body of the text. It took a devoted researcher like De Roos to organize a team and translate the complicated Icelandic language back into English and uncover this conundrum—one that has been sitting on the shelves in front of many of us for over 100 years. I believe Bram would have loved the irony of this situation. He knew the best place to hide something was in plain sight—just as he hid his vampire Count as another face in the crowded streets of London. *Makt Myrkranna* was published in 1901; and now, more than 100 years later, we are surprised to learn that it is not at all what we imagined.

Additionally, De Roos's discovery spotlights the translation process, which in the case of this Icelandic edition

1 McNally and Florescu, *Dracula, Prince of Many Faces* (1989), p 233, and *In Search of Dracula* (revised edition, 1994), p. 85.

appears in conjunction with significant differences between the two texts. This begs the question of whether all the other translated editions of *Dracula* should be examined for major differences as well. While such further comparisons exceed the scope of Hans's endeavor—certainly of this foreword—and must be addressed by future efforts, the metamorphosis from *Dracula* to *Makt Myrkranna* is of particular interest to me.

Having had two texts translated for publication in multiple languages, I know from personal experience that literary translation is not simple, and there is a considerable amount of work involved in doing it well. Even today with the accessibility of highly advanced language software, the human element is indispensable to the translation process. It is crucial that the translator understand the genre and the historical time period in which the novel is set. The translator must ensure that the intended meaning, emotion, and atmosphere from the original language survive for the reader of the target language, especially as word-for-word translation of literature is very seldom effective. Poor translations could have affected the work of all but the most determined and diligent authors. In relation to the *Dracula* novel, the mistranslation of a fifteenth-century poem dramatically changed the poet's intent and led to a misleading interpretation of Bram's intentions. In describing the cruel actions of Vlad Dracula III against Saxon traders in Transylvania, Michael Beheim, court poet for Holy Roman Emperor Frederick lll, wrote that Vlad washed his hands in the blood of his enemies. A portion of the poem was translated incorrectly, telling of Vlad dipping his bread into a bowl and drinking the blood of his dead enemies, thus labeling him as a vampire.[1] The poem was later translated within the proper context, the difference between a blood drinking vampire and a bloodthirsty tyrant being very significant.

Was *Makt Myrkranna* the result of translator errors, creative license taken too far, or was this Icelandic edition simply another version of the story that Bram had been working on for years? I certainly lean towards the latter.

I believe during the seven years commonly accepted as the span of time Bram worked on *Dracula*, there was more than one version of the story—multiple drafts, and story lines were added or subtracted. Probably the best-known example is *Dracula's Guest*, which was published as a short story after Bram's death. Although widely disputed now, Florence Stoker claimed that during the editing process, this section was removed because the book was too long.

In the (Rosenbach) notes, Bram used calendar pages to establish the correct timeline for the movements and correspondence in *Dracula*. The pages begin with Jonathan Harker leaving Paris and stopping off in Munich for six days en route to Transylvania, yet these first elements of the story were not included in the 1897 publication. There are enough similarities between the *Dracula's Guest* story line and that of *Dracula* for it to be at least regarded as an early treatment of the novel. The typescript given to Donaldson begins with page 102, *Dracula's Guest* is less than 20 pages, so there seem to be 80 pages of the typescript unaccounted for.

Indeed, the 529-page typescript given to Col. Donaldson bore the title *The Un-Dead*. On the pages, Bram and/or an editor made additions and deletions in ink, the most significant change being the title change from *The Un-Dead* to *Dracula* and the deletion of three paragraphs—which completely changed the ending. Instead of Count Dracula's castle being demolished by an erupting volcano, as in the original typescript, the scene in the Archibald Constable edition suggests a much more ambiguous ending.

Bram's brother Thornley, a surgeon who lived in Dublin, made editing notes on the same Donaldson *Dracula* typescript. Did that one typescript travel between London and Dublin, and back to London, with Bram, and then to editors in London to be refined further before becoming the final 1897 Archibald Constable version, only to be rediscovered in a Pennsylvania barn?

Others may find it intriguing that Bram's work would be translated into Icelandic, but considering the fascination with Vikings and "the Old North" in the literary circles of his day, it makes sense to me. Schoolboys read translations of the heroic sagas; growing up near Clontarf, Dublin, site of a battle in 1014 between a Norse-Irish alliance and the king of Ireland, Brian Boru, Bram's connection with the Vikings was personal.

In the years preceding the publication of *Dracula* and *Makt Myrkranna,* travel to Iceland was in vogue. "Travel" was a popular recreation listed in *Who's Who: An Annual Biographical Dictionary*, and artists, scholars and writers of the day were fascinated with Iceland's folklore, language, history, and untamed landscape. Rev. Sabine Baring-Gould, archeologist, folklorist, and songwriter, taught himself Icelandic and translated Norse sagas. He wrote that Icelandic literature gave insight into the origin of worldwide superstitions, and three years after he traveled to Iceland he published his *Book of Werewolves* (1865), one of Bram's sources for *Dracula.* In the only direct reference to Iceland made in *Dracula,* the Count describes his bloodlines as including the fighting spirit of Icelandic berserkers. In the *Book of Werewolves,* the Icelandic superstition, "to be *eigi einhamir*, not of one skin," described

2 *The Westminster Review* vol 81, 1864, pg 117.

3 Magnússon, *The Saga Library*. Vol. VI, 1905, p. ix.

one aspect of Count Dracula's power: "men who could take upon them other bodies, and the nature of those beings whose bodies they assumed," who "acquired the strength of the beast in whose body he travelled, in addition to his own" . . . "only to be recognized by his eyes, which by no power can be changed." Baring-Gould's account, *Iceland: Its Scenes and Sagas* (1863), was used as a guidebook by Icelandophiles making the pilgrimage north, and offered "the minute particularity of each day's journey and of the means of accomplishing it."[2]

Bram was a close friend of Thomas Hall Caine, Manx author and Icelandic enthusiast. *Dracula* (1897) was dedicated "To my dear friend Hommy-Beg", Caine's nickname (Little Tommy) in the vernacular of the Isle of Man. Caine's popular novel *The Bondman* (1890), partially set in Iceland, was completed and published in serial installments before Caine spent two months in Iceland in 1889. He would return fourteen years later to study the details he was to describe later in *The Prodigal Son* (1904). Another contemporary in direct contact with Bram Stoker and Hall Caine who also traveled to Iceland, H. Rider Haggard, was a prolific writer of adventure fiction including the Viking epic *Eric Brighteyes* (1890).

An associate of Hall Caine, well-known writer/artist /designer William Morris, traveled to Iceland twice in the early 1870s. Morris taught himself Icelandic, as did others fascinated by its linguistic purity, and collaborated with Eiríkr Magnússon in translating many of Iceland's tales into English, including *The Saga Library* (1891). The work of Hans de Roos and his team of native speakers harkens back to Magnússon's description of Morris's care in proper translation, "he would on no account slur over them by giving in the translation only *what they meant* instead of *what they said*."[3] Publications of Morris's Icelandic to English translations were regularly reviewed—with literary critics generally quite complimentary of Morris's skill as a translator. According to Caine biographer Vivien Allen, "Morris was important to him, not least in introducing him to Icelandic sagas."

Because for years Bram traveled extensively in the British Isles and America with Henry Irving's Lyceum Theatre company, he likely had few opportunities for personal adventure travel. But anecdotal evidence and circumstantial connections lead me to believe he could not have been immune to the influences of the Icelandophiles who surrounded him.

I feel safe in saying Bram was not only aware of the differences between *Dracula* and the Icelandic edition, *Makt Myrkranna*—I believe he orchestrated them. The deviations from the 1897 Constable edition cannot result from translation errors or even from a liberal interpretation of the original alone: the changes are too significant. The Icelandic preface and the modified plot are interconnected in a way that points towards Bram writing both. In my opinion, *Makt Myrkranna* is another version or draft of *Dracula*, written by Bram sometime during the 1890s. I don't believe it was originally written for the Icelandic market, but I can well imagine that Bram used the translation process as an opportunity to make *Makt Myrkranna* unique and more relevant to Icelandic interests. *"Powers of Darkness"*—a different title for a different book. Not *"Dracula,"* or *"Drakula."*

It is a pity that for whatever reason *Makt Myrkranna* comes across as raw—an unfinished project. It seems as though Bram (or Valdimar, or both) drew out Part I—the details of Harker's travel to and ordeals in Dracula's Castle—but never fleshed out the story in Part II. Part II reads like an outline of the characters' movements and conversations on stage, left undeveloped as the author(s) hastily brought it all to a conclusion. Bram's outline in the Rosenbach *Notes for Dracula* shows the story's balanced division into four "Books": "Transylvania to London," "Tragedy," "Discovery," and "Punishment," each with seven chapters. Why was *Makt Myrkranna* published in what seems to me to be an unfinished state? Sadly, we may never know. But, the revelation that *Makt Myrkranna* is not *Dracula* warrants a fresh look at other early translations of Bram's work.

The future may well hold further significant discoveries relating to *Dracula,* but I believe De Roos's efforts will stand as a milestone in the never-ending succession of curious and well-directed inquiry on the subject. Admittedly, his discovery of the unique character of the Icelandic edition of *Dracula* creates more questions than can possibly be answered at this point. But regardless of its history, the story as such— now accessible to English-speaking readers for the first time—has a great literary appeal of its own. Let us enjoy the fruit of Hans's labor, revel in the challenges it presents, and allow this work to inspire and illuminate further endeavors. The depth of mystery surrounding Stoker's Gothic thriller increases through every age, and the resurrection of *Makt Myrkranna* illustrates another example of *Dracula*'s immortality.

INTRODUCTION
MAKT MYRKRANNA:
THE FORGOTTEN BOOK
by Hans C. de Roos

1. BRAM STOKER AND VALDIMAR ÁSMUNDSSON

FOR MORE THAN A CENTURY, THE LANGUAGE BARRIER between Iceland and the rest of the world has prevented readers from enjoying the unique work presented here—an early and significant variation on Bram Stoker's world famous *Dracula*, rather more than just a translation into Icelandic by one of the country's foremost literary talents, Valdimar Ásmundsson. Partly due to the rarity of the book, it has remained hidden to even the most versed scholars. Valdimar's[1] life and work are virtually unknown outside of Iceland. And even in his home country, no one ever studied how Stoker's vampire story, only a few years after its first publication, made its way to the Far North.

Jóhann Valdimar Ásmundsson was born in 1852 and grew up with his parents in Þistilfjörður[2]—a remote bay in the very northeast of Iceland. He was largely self-educated and taught himself English, German and French, aside from Norwegian, Swedish, Danish, and some Latin and Greek. Bram Stoker, by contrast, had the privilege of studying at Trinity College in Dublin from 1864-1870, but after receiving a B.A. with honors in mathematics, he had to enter work life as a civil servant at Dublin Castle, where his father worked as well: three of

[1] In Iceland, the second part of a name is not a family name but a patronymic. Therefore, Icelanders would expect to be referred to by their given name, in this case Valdimar.

[2] The Icelandic letter "þorn" ("Þ" or "þ") can be transliterated as "Th" or "th"; the letter "eð" ("Ð" or "ð") as "D" or "d."

3 *Norðanfara* appeared 1862-1885. *Ísafold* was founded in 1876, as the voice of the Icelandic Independence Movement, headed by Jón Sigurðsson (1811-1879), publisher of *Ný félagsrit* (since 1841) and President of the Icelandic Literary Society. Björn Jónsson was its president from 1884-1894.

4 Founded in 1877 as a primary school, it became a lower secondary school in 1882, when Valdimar worked there.

Bram's brothers studied at the Royal College of Surgeons, and Bram's income was needed to support the family. Despite these different backgrounds, both Valdimar and Bram started out as journalists in the 1870s. Valdimar wrote his first articles for *Norðanfara,* a newspaper in Akureyri in the north of Iceland, published by Björn Jónsson, who would become publisher/editor of *Ísafold*,[3] while Bram volunteered to write theatre reviews for the *Dublin Evening Mail*, co-owned by Joseph Sheridan Le Fanu, the author of *Carmilla*. After writing a rapturous review of Henry Irving's performance as *Hamlet* at the Theatre Royal in Dublin in 1876, Bram met with the actor —a meeting that would change his life and career. In 1878 Irving invited him to come to London and become the manager of the Lyceum Theatre, which the actor intended to lease. Some years later, Valdimar also moved south: in winter 1882 he became a teacher at Flensborg School in Hafnarfjörður— one of the oldest schools in Iceland still in existence today.[4] During these early years he created a very popular and widely used grammar book, *Ritreglur*, just like Stoker, during his years at Dublin Castle, had written *The Duties of Clerks of Petty Sessions in Ireland* (1879), a detailed professional handbook that also would become a standard in its field. And just like Bram, Valdimar finally moved to the "big city," to Reykjavík— although London had quite different dimensions than the Icelandic capital.

In the 1880s, London, the political and cultural center of the global British Empire, already had a population of 4 million, with another million inhabiting its outskirts. Reykjavík, by contrast, had only 3,000 to 4,000 residents; its center was tiny, with only one main street, so that the paths of the local officials, teachers and other intellectuals must have crossed every other day. But just like Bram Stoker started meeting people of the

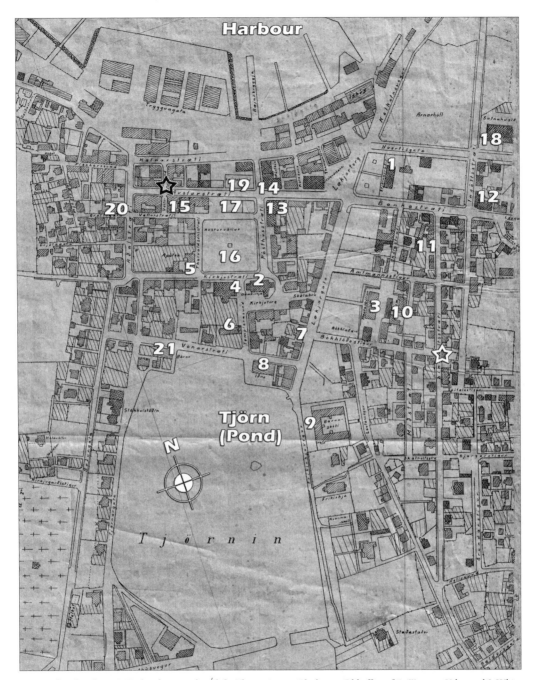

Center of Reykjavík in 1915 (detail)—map by Ólafur Thorsteinsson. Black star: Old office of *Fjallkonan* at Veltusund 3. White star: Thingholtsstræti 18. Nr. 1: Government House. Nr. 2: Dómkirkja. Nr. 3: Latin School. Nr. 4: Alþingishús + National Library 1881-1908. Nr. 5: Reykjavík Pharmacy. Nr. 6: Good Templar House (promoting abstinence from alcohol and cursing). Nr. 7: Police Office. Nr. 8: Iðnó Theatre, built in 1897. Nr. 9: Children's School, after 1898 (formerly in Posthússtræti). Nr. 10: K.F.U.M. = Kristilegt félag ungra manna =Y.M.C.A. Nr. 11: Gutenbergprentsmiðja. Nr. 12: Félagsprentsmiðja (where *Fjallkonan* was printed in the 1890's). Nr. 13: Nathan & Ólsen (store). Nr. 14: Post Office. Nr. 15: Ísafoldarprentsmiðja. Nr. 16: Albert Thorvaldsen Statue. Nr. 17: Hotel Reykjavík (burnt down in April 1915). Nr. 18: Sáfnahús (National Library and Museum, after 1908). Nr. 19: National Bank, rebuilt after the fire of 1915. Nr. 20: Gamla Bíó (cinema, 1906-1925, before moving to Ingólfsstræti 2a). Nr. 21: Bárubúð or Báruhús: Meeting House.

5 The poet Bjarni Thorarensen first used the word around 1810, in his work *Eldgamla Ísafold*. The character quickly became popular in poetry and in 1866 was depicted for the first time by Johann Baptist Zwecke, as a frontispiece for the last volume of *Icelandic Legends* (London: Longmans, Green, and Co., 1866).

6 For the political programme of *Fjallkonan*, see its issue of 12 January 1899, pp. 1f.

7 See *Lifið í Reykjavik—Næpan og Helgi sæm* in *Alþýðublaðið* of 11 August 1969, p. 8.

highest London circles, who came to admire the Shakespeare plays revived by Irving, the most celebrated actor of his time, so Valdimar set up shop in the local center of power. In February 1884, he founded the newspaper *Fjallkonan* ("Lady of the Mountains"), referring to a mythical figure symbolizing the Icelandic nation.[5] *Fjallkonan* focused on political and cultural news, summarized the foreign press, reviewed books and published obituaries, boat schedules, and advertisements. It became one of Iceland's leading newspapers, with around 2,000 subscribers. It positioned itself as the champion of farmers and traders, supporting Iceland's independence, free trade, better education, and technical progress.[6]

In 1888, Valdimar married Bríet Bjarnhéðinsdóttir, one of Iceland's first women's rights activists and founder of *Kvennablaðið*, the first Icelandic women's magazine. Internationally, voting rights and public education for women were among the most controversial political issues of the day; in Dublin, Bram's mother Charlotte had been fighting for the same goals.

In November 1890, Valdimar and Bríet bought a two-story stone house at Thingholtsstræti no. 18, somewhat farther away from the new House of Parliament (built 1881-82) but nearer to several printing companies. While Bram had his workplace in the London Strand and lived in the fashionable Chelsea area, Valdimar and Bríet were now settled in the "Fleet Street of Reykjavík."[7] Business was not the only reason for the relocation, though: in 1890, their daughter Laufey was born, followed by her little brother Héðinn in 1892. Bram Stoker and Florence Balcombe, who had married already in 1878 before moving to London, only had one child, Noel, born on the last day of 1879. Noel would be boarded at Summer Fields School and later at Winchester College in Oxford, while Laufey and Héðinn remained with their parents and attended the Children's School, later the Latin School, just a few footsteps from their home.

Although both Valdimar and Bram successfully climbed the social ladder, the men also had a certain modesty in common. In a letter to the American poet Walt Whitman, Bram wrote: "I am equal in temper and cool in disposition and have a large amount of self-control and am naturally secretive to the world."[8] Irving's stage partner Ellen Terry noted that in the voluminous *Reminiscences of Henry Irving*, Bram Stoker "described every one connected with the Lyceum except himself."[9] And some of Stoker's biographers remarked that the author of *Dracula* seemed to be overshadowed by his own creation.[10] Similarly, Valdimar is often only remembered as the husband of Bríet, or as the editor of *Fjallkonan* at the most; his private life remained in the background. In his obituary, Valdimar's intimate friend Jón Ólafsson wrote:

> He was a very reticent and reserved man, and sometimes almost seemed shy. And many who only knew him superficially thought that he was no emotional person, because he showed only little of his feelings. But those who were closer to him knew that this shy and distanced man was most entertaining in the small circle of his friends, cheery, playful and funny, and that his cool appearance as a closed individual was just a mask concealing a warm and sensitive heart— sensitive to all kinds of suffering, sensitive in his friendships, but above all things sensitive against all injustice and oppression and baseness.[11]

Ólafsson also stressed that Valdimar had acquired all his knowledge on his own, from a true desire to learn and un-

8 Letter to Walt Whitman dated Dublin, 18 February 1872, in the Walt Whitman Archive.

9 Terry, 1909, p. 182.

10 See especially Belford, 1996, and Murray, 2004.

11 From *Reykjavík* of 26 April 1902, p. 2.

Valdimar Ásmundsson, Bríet Bjarnhéðinsdóttir and their children Laufey (l) and Héðinn (r), around 1900

12 An expression used in the obituary on the front page of *Fjallkonan* of 25 April 1902, probably authored by Bríet.

13 First appearing in 1891. For a history of the Icelandic printing press and the publication of Icelandic sagas, see Ólafsson, 2002. See also Haugen, 1992, p. 343. The effect of the introduction of the printing press by Gutenberg, making the copying of manuscripts by hand superfluous, was delayed in Iceland. The Icelandic Catholic Church and later the Lutheran State Church, controlled by the Danish King, used to have the monopoly of printing, until in 1773, the first independent press was founded on Hrappsey. In 1795, it was bought by the Educational Society led by Magnús Stephensen (1762-1833), who thus had a monopoly on printing secular books. Kristjánsson obviously saw a gap in the market and had some of his saga books printed with an initial print run of 4,000 copies. See Magnússon, 2010, pp. 157ff., Karlsson, 2000, p. 172, and Jakobsson & Halfdanarson, 2016, p. 215.

14 See Valdimar's advertisement for his expert services in *Fjallkonan* of 28 March 1888, p. 39.

15 See Valdimar's advertisements in *Fjallkonan* of 10 and 23 November 1900, both on p. 4.

16 In 1900, Iceland's currency was the new Danish Crown, introduced in 1875. The value of 2,480 new Danish Crowns was equivalent to that of one kg of fine gold. A million crowns would thus be worth the price of 403 kg fine gold, today approximately 13 million Euros or 14 Million USD. One Crown would thus be equivalent to 1.30 Euro or 1.40 USD (Status: 23 January 2016). As the prices of gold, Euros and Dollars are fluctuating every day, you may want to check the most recent equivalent on www.goldprice.org.

derstand. According to Ásgeir Jónsson, to a certain extent he always remained "the farmer boy from the North," a "self-made man,"[12] and did not seamlessly fit in with the Icelandic scholars of his time. Still, Valdimar became a recognized specialist for old Icelandic manuscripts, and in their obituaries of him, Jón Ólafsson and Bríet agree that he was believed to have no peers among his contemporaries. For the publisher Sigurður Kristjánsson he prepared an illustrated edition of Icelandic sagas in 38 volumes;[13] these low-priced books secured a still wider spread of these old tales and eliminated the need to copy them by hand, as had been the tradition for centuries. Moreover, Valdimar became an expert for property border issues for lands that had been settled hundreds of years earlier. Because many of these official rulings had sunk into oblivion, Valdimar's knowledge of old manuscripts was crucial in reconstructing the earlier decisions from ancient documents.[14] From 1887 on, he also received a modest grant from the Icelandic Parliament to reorganize the government archives. Finally, he was a Trustee of the Icelandic Archeological Society (Hið íslenzka fornleifafélag, founded 1879) and edited its yearbook in the 1890s, and co-founded the Icelandic Association of Journalists (Blaðamannafélag) in November 1897, together with Bríet, Björn Jónsson, Jón Ólafsson and others.

Although his tasks in the Society and the Association probably were unpaid, the other activities brought him some extra income, just as trading with old books did later.[15] In 1895, he explained to his readers that producing a weekly newspaper with costs of 60-70 Crowns[16] per issue—fees for writing and editing, not included—plus around 600 Crowns yearly for postage, was certainly not making him and his family rich, especially as the income from advertisements was lower than it was for comparable newspapers in the UK.[17] The price for the house had been 7,000 Crowns and, starting on 14 May 1901, ten yearly mortgage payments of 320 Crowns were due to the previous owner, Arnbjörn Ólafsson. After that, there still were the old debts on the house that Valdimar had taken over.[18]

On the other side of the Atlantic, Bram Stoker's financial situation was not very rosy either. Although he had an extremely busy job as Irving's manager, in 1890 he entered a partnership in The International Library, an imprint of Heinemann & Balestier Ltd. The enterprise failed; Stoker lost his invested capital. His investment in 20 shares of Paige Compositor Manufacturing Co., a technology to which his friend Mark Twain had bought all rights,[19] also turned out to be a financial disaster. In June 1896, Bram was forced to borrow £600 from his best friend, Hall Caine, and was only able to pay him back by signing over a life insurance policy.[20] Some time later, the golden times of the Lyceum Theatre seemed to come to an end. In December 1896 Irving badly hurt his knee and could not perform for ten weeks; this killed the winter season. In February 1898, the Lyceum storage at Bear Lane in Southwark burned out; the fire destroyed countless stage sets and props that were needed for the theatre's regular productions. "But the tide must turn some time—otherwise the force would be not a tide but a current," Stoker noted in his *Reminiscences of Henry Irving* some years later.[21] In 1899, Irving fell ill with pleurisy, and the same year, he transferred the lease of the theatre to a consortium headed by Joseph Comyns Carr—without consulting Stoker. By this time, Irving's manager hoped that a literary career might offer a financial safety net.

Earning money with novels seemed not at all unrealistic at that time. Stoker's American friend Twain had made a for-

17 See *Fjallkonan* of 13 November 1895, front page.

18 Sæmundsson, 2004, p. 142.

19 See letter of Clemens of 4 March 1894 to Henry H. Rogers, in Twain/Leary, 1969, p. 40.

20 Skal, 2004, p. 33f. In 1896, the purchasing power of £600 was equivalent to the purchasing power of £62,000 today (status per January 2016).

21 Stoker, 1906, Vol. II, Chapter LXXII, p. 322.

Makt myrkranna.

Róman.

Eftir

Bram Stoker.

Formáli höfundarins.

Lesarinn getur sjálfur séð, þegar hann les sögu þessa, hvernig þessum blöðum hefir verið raðað saman, svo að þau yrði að einni heild. Ég hefi ekki þurft að gera annað en að draga úr þeim ýms óþörf smáatvik og láta svo sögufólkið sjálft skýra frá reynslu sinni í þeim sama einfalda búningi, sem blöðin eru upphaflega skrifuð í. Ég hefi, af augljósum ástæðum, breytt nöfnum manna og staða. En að öðru leyti skila ég handritinu óbreyttu, samkvæmt ósk þeirra sem hafa álitið það stranga skyldu sína, að koma því fyrir almenningssjónir.

Eftir minni sannfæringu er það ekkert efamál, að þeir viðburðir, sem hér er lýst, *hafi sannarlega átt sér stað*, hversu ótrúlegir og óskiljanlegir sem þeir kunna að sýnast, skoðaðir eftir almennri reynslu. Og ég er sannfærður um, að þeir hljóti jafnan að verða að nokkuru leyti óskiljanlegir, þó ekki sé óhugsandi að áframhaldandi rannsóknir í sálfræðinni og náttúrufræðinni geti þegar minst varir skýrt bæði þessa og aðra leyndardóma, sem hvorki vísindamenn né njósnarlögreglan hafa enn þá getað skilið. Ég tek það enn á ný fram, að þessi dularfulli sorgarleikur, sem hér er lýst, er *fullkomlega sannur að því er alla ytri viðburði snertir*, þó ég eðlilega hafi komist að annari niðurstöðu í ýmsum greinum en sögufólkið. En viðburðirnir eru ómótmælanlegir og svo margir þekkja þá, að þeim verður ekki neitað. Þessi röð af glæpum, er mönnum enn úr minni liðin, röð af glæpum, sem virðast óskiljanlegir, en út leit fyrir að væru af sömu rót runnir, sem á sínum tíma slógu jafnmiklum óhug á almenning sem hin alræmdu morð Jakobs kviðristara, sem komu litlu seinna til sögunnar. Ymsa mun reka minni til hinna merkilegu útlendinga, sem misserum saman tóku glæsilegan þátt í lífi tignarfólksins hér í Lundúnum, og menn muna eftir því, að annar þeirra að mínsta kosti hvarf skyndilega og á óskiljanlegan hátt, án þess nokkur merki hans sæist framar. Alt það fólk sem sagt er að viljandi eða óviljandi hafi tekið þátt í þessari merkilegu sögu er alþekt og vel metið. Bæði Tómas Harker og konan hans, sem er valkvendi, og dr. Seward eru vinir mínir og hafa verið í mörg ár, og ég hefi aldrei efað, að þau segðu satt frá; og hinn mikilsmetni vísindamaður, sem kemur hér fram með dularnafni, mun líka vera of frægur um allan hinn mentaða heim til þess, að mönnum dyljist hið rétta nafn hans, sem ég hefi ekki viljað nefna, sizt þeim, sem af reynslu hafa lært að meta og virða snild hans og mannkosti, þótt þeir ekki fremur en ég fylgi lífsskoðunum hans. En á vorum dögum ætti það að vera ljóst öllum alvarlega hugsandi mönnum að

„harðla margt er á himni og jörðu,
sem heimspekina dreymir ei um.“-

Lundúnum, — stræti, ágúst 1898.

B. S.

tune with writing, before he lost everything with the Paige bankruptcy in 1894 and had to start all over again.[22] Through an international lecture tour about his work, Twain was able to generate fresh income and pay off all his debts by 1898. Hall Caine was also successful, especially with *The Bondman*, a novel set in Iceland, which Stoker had managed to bring to Heinemann as its first publishing project in 1890.

2. *DRACULA* AND *MAKT MYRKRANNA*

From 1890 on, Bram Stoker worked on *Dracula* and when the book was finally published on 26 May 1897, it was well received by the international press.[23] While Stoker prepared an American edition (1899), then an abridged edition (1901) of his novel, in Reykjavík Valdimar Ásmundsson worked on the Icelandic version, to be serialized in his newspaper *Fjallkonan* as "*Makt Myrkranna*, by Bram Stoker." It was only with the book edition published in August 1901 that the credit "translated by Valdimar Ásmundsson" was added.

Dracula only turned into a real hit after the 1931 movie with Bela Lugosi was released by Universal Pictures. Until then, it generated only a modest income for Bram and his family. After Bram's death, Florence was confronted with *Nosferatu*, Werner Murnau's unauthorized movie version, and bitterly pursued lawsuits against its production company Prana Film until it went bankrupt.

Despite his legal background, Stoker failed to send a copy of his work to the United States Copyright Office in time to have his rights duly registered;[24] when Universal started to negotiate with Florence Stoker about a second Dracula movie, *Dracula's Daughter*, the material turned out to be unprotected. *Dracula* fell into the public domain in the U.S. and every script

Preface to *Makt Myrkranna* in the first installment
in *Fjallkonan*, 13 January 1900

writer, film producer or theatre manager was free to make money with Stoker's characters—an ironic twist of history, given how little money Stoker himself saw.

But perhaps Stoker's very mistake helped *Dracula* reach global fame; the many unauthorized screen adaptations made Stoker's vampire character known to an ever-growing international public. More than 200 movies featuring the undead Count have by now been produced. Today, the secondary literature about Stoker's creation is extensive enough to fill a small library. The Icelandic version, by contrast, was reviewed only once in the Icelandic press, in 1906, by Benedikt Björnsson (1879-1941). Björnsson was of a younger generation than Valdimar and feared that the translation of "cheap" sensational fiction from abroad might replace Iceland's own literary production, including his own:

> "Without doubt, for the largest part it is worthless rubbish and sometimes even worse than worthless, completely devoid of poetry and beauty and far removed from any psychological truth."

> "Fjallkonan" presented various kinds of garbage, including a long story, "Powers of Darkness." That story would have been better left unwritten, and I cannot see that such nonsense has enriched our literature. [25]

Valdimar, on the other hand, promoting the liberalization of trade relations with England,[26] hoped to connect his readers with the newest literary trends from the U.K. and attract more subscribers to his newspaper. Publishing *Makt Myrkranna* was part of Valdimar's strategy to offer more quality content to his readers, at the same time raising the subscription price from 3 to 4 Crowns.[27]

After Valdimar's early death at age 50, in April 1902, Bríet

22 Twain's own publishing company Charles L. Webster & Co. failed the same year.

23 For decades, the publication of *Dracula* was surrounded by the myth that the novel had only received a "mixed response" from the critics. As John Edgar Browning recently found out, however, the majority of the 230 reviews and responses he was able to locate turned out to be outright positive.

24 Email correspondence with David Skal of 29 December 2013.

25 From *Nokkur orð um bókmentir vorar*, in *Skírnir*, 1 December 1906, p. 344 and p. 346. In 1934, the same Benedikt Björnsson was the translator for *Slunginn þjófur, og aðrar sögur* (A Cunning Thief and Other Stories), by Edgar Allan Poe. In fact, none of the five stories was written by Poe; all were taken from the 1865 novel *Mrs. Carew* by the British author Amelia B. Edwards. See Eysteinsson, 2014, p. 105f. So much for Björnsson's enrichment of Icelandic literature.

26 The Danish government obstructed free trade with the UK, Iceland's nearest trade partner; independence from Denmark would boost the import/export traffic with the UK.

27 See announcement on the front page of *Fjallkonan* of 13 January 1900.

28 I only know of about 20 surviving copies worldwide, of which four copies are in private hands; two of them in mine.

took over the management of *Fjallkonan*. The first edition of *Makt Myrkranna*, originally planned as a bonus present for new subscribers, was sold off; copies of this book are extremely hard to get today, as most of them are in the hands of universities or public libraries.[28]

Despite the lack of positive reviews, *Makt Myrkranna* seems to have penetrated the Icelandic cultural consciousness. When Tod Browning's *Dracula* was shown in Reykjavík in 1932, a newspaper announced the movie as "based on the fiction story of 'Makt Myrkranna' which has been published in an Icelandic translation that will be familiar to many people." Similarly, *Vísir* of 18 December wrote under the title *Dracula*: "Nýja Bíó has recently shown a movie with this name, which is based on the story 'Makt Myrkranna,'" a comment suggesting that the story of the bloodthirsty Transylvanian count was originally invented in Iceland and that the Americans had copied it. Over the decades, "Makt Myrkranna" has become

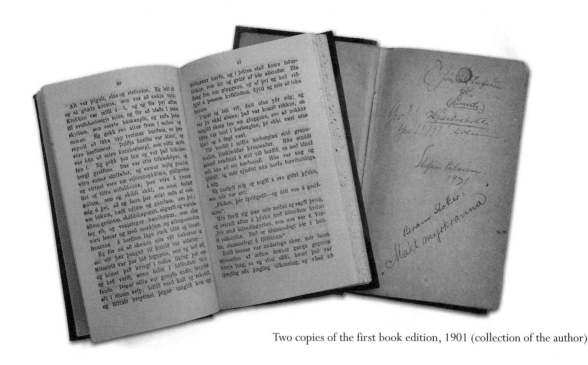

Two copies of the first book edition, 1901 (collection of the author)

in Iceland the standard nomenclature for all sorts of *Dracula* films, showing that Valdimar's book was much better known than can be judged from Benedikt's single review. Maybe due to the general recognition of the title, Hogni Publishers launched a second edition in 1950.

In 1975, Halldór Laxness, the Icelandic Nobel Prize winner for Literature who was fascinated by the Dracula myth, urged:

> And do not forget *Makt Myrkranna* (Bram Stoker) with the famous un-dead Count Dracula in the Carpathians, which was not less popular than today, and one of the best pens of the country was engaged to translate the novel: Valdimar Ásmundsson (ed. 1901).[29]

But: was Valdimar Ásmundsson really only the translator of the story? Until Ásgeir Jónsson, the editor of the third Icelandic edition, in 2011 addressed the deviations from the text of *Dracula,* only two scattered lines in the Icelandic press indicated that anyone had noted a difference between English and the Icelandic plot lines at all.[30]

For those who know *Dracula*, *Makt Myrkranna* awaits with some major surprises. The most obvious one is that the account of Harker's trip to Transylvania has been expanded from approx. 22,700 words in *Dracula* to approx. 37,200 words in *Makt Myrkranna*—a 63% increase in length. The rest of the story, on the other hand, has been cut down from 137,860 words to only 9,100—a 93% reduction. This massive shift of proportions alone forbids calling *Makt Myrkranna* an "abridged translation" of *Dracula*. The Transylvanian part has not been shortened at all, while the rest of the story has shrunk to a mere *coda*. We can only speculate about the "why." Maybe Valdimar was working from a proto-version of *Dracula* that Stoker never worked out to the end. Maybe he

29 From *Í túninu heima*, part I, Reykjavík: Helgafell, 1975, p. 208. In an excerpt from *Og arin líða* (1984), published in *Lesbók Morgunblaðsins* of 7 January 1984, pp. 4-7, Halldór called *Makt Myrkranna* "one of the best Icelandic novels imported from abroad."

30 In *Pabbi, mamma og börn* (an article about family life and raising children) in *Alþýðublaðið* of 8 December 1974, p. 4, an unnamed father reported that he once spent a whole weekend reading *Dracula* to his children, "not *Makt Myrkranna* but *Dracula*, complete and unabridged." In her article *Blóðþyrstir Berserkir* in *Lesbók Morgunbladsins* of 21 April 2001, pp. 10f., Úlfhildur Dagsdóttir acknowledged that *Makt Myrkranna* was rather a modification than a translation of Stoker's novel.

31 See Haining, 1987, and Leatherdale, 1998 b.

lost his patience with Stoker's lengthy story, which had been filling his magazine for over a year, and thus decided to speed up the final part. We know that in the 1980s, the 1897 typescript for *Dracula* was found in a barn in Pennsylvania, with the first 100 pages missing;[31] it has been speculated that these contained a more elaborate start of the novel, eventually worked out as the short story *Dracula's Guest*, published by Bram's widow in 1914. There may have existed other, still earlier, drafts for *Dracula*, based on the notes Stoker made from March 1890 on.

The second major difference between *Dracula* and *Makt Myrkranna* is that in Part II, the epistolary format—which often has been considered *Dracula*'s outstanding characteristic—has been abandoned. In *Dracula*, the story unfolds through a series of diaries, newspaper reports, and letters, usually penned by the novel's main characters. But in the Icelandic version, we are guided through the story by an all-knowing narrator. This is a major deviation from Stoker's initial concept, and also from the Icelandic preface, which states "otherwise I leave the manuscript unchanged"—which can only mean that the author merely wishes to introduce a *manuscrit trouvé*, written by the people playing a role in the story, without giving up the epistolary structure. Although for the understanding of the plot, this change of format does not matter much, it forces the reader to wonder whether Stoker stepped away from the diary format himself, or if Valdimar was responsible for this.

The plot of *Makt Myrkranna* also contains new elements, while large parts of the Whitby and London episodes have been omitted and the chase of the whole party across Europe, through Moldavia and Transylvania, has been cut out completely.

In *Dracula*, Harker's only company during his visit to Castle Dracula is the Count himself, except for a short interlude with three provocative female vampires. In *Makt Myrkranna*, the young lawyer (here named Thomas) is welcomed to the castle by a mysterious old woman acting as the Count's housekeeper. Soon after, a seductive blonde vampire girl starts to play a major role in Harker's desperate existence; their repeated secret meetings become ever more intimate and the prudish Englishman proves to be more than just a passive victim. Moreover, the Count shows Harker a gallery with family portraits, granting insight to the Transylvanian's social-Darwinist philosophy and providing a rich sub-plot of intrigue, passion, adultery, and revenge—seemingly inspired by the life of Joséphine de Beauharnais, Napoleon's wife. During his explorations of the castle in *Makt Myrkranna*, Harker discovers a murdered peasant girl and a secret passageway leading to a hidden temple, where he witnesses an archaic sacrificial ceremony headed by the Count himself. Instead of being a mere solitary relic of medieval war times, as was Stoker's Count, Thomas Harker's host not only commands a large crowd of ape-like devotees but also finances and masterminds an international diplomatic conspiracy, aiming to overthrow Western democratic institutions. In the London part of the story, the Count, acting under various pseudonyms, also entertains a large number of high-ranking guests in his lavishly furnished Carfax residence, where he is always surrounded by the most stunning and elegant young women.

Intriguingly, the end of the Icelandic story almost runs parallel to the later stage and movie versions. This also applies to the more elegant public appearance of the Count—vampire cape included. More research would be needed to understand how *Makt Myrkranna* could anticipate changes made by play-

32 Leatherdale, 1998 a, p. 389, fn. 99, asks if Mina's night dress, after she was forced to drink Dracula's blood, was ripped or pulled up, but even this vague possibility is immediately redressed by Van Helsing, drawing a coverlet over her body.

wright Hamilton Deane and screenwriter John Balderston a quarter of a century later. Despite the shortened ending, the second part of *Makt Myrkranna* also introduces a series of new characters, including Lucy's uncle Morton, Hawkins's agent Tellet, and the police detective Barrington. Various foreign aristocrats, such as Prince Koromezzo, Countess Ida Varkony and Madame Saint Amand, also make an appearance, while *Dracula*'s Renfield character and Mina's "blood-wedding" with the Count are eliminated.

But even more than the changed format, the added events, and the extra characters, the altered style of the novel seems the most significant innovation to me. In the Icelandic text we find no legal discourses nor lengthy sentimental dialogues; instead, it features a number of virtually denuded young girls, absent in Stoker's *Dracula* and other texts.[32] Moreover, there are several elements added from the Icelandic sagas, with which Valdimar was far more familiar than Stoker; I suspect that Valdimar included these references himself and some of them are so subtle that only someone familiar with Norse literature would recognize them. The overall change of style is so obvious, however, that we may safely assume that Valdimar must have shaped the Icelandic narrative to a high extent, instead of merely translating.

An extra bonus in this translation is the chapter that was published in *Fjallkonan* of 13 October 1900 but left out of the 1901 book printing and its second and third editions. This episode focuses on Harker's emotional dependency on the nameless blonde vampire girl who occupies the castle's top floor. We do not know why it was omitted later—or why it was even written in the first place: it has no equivalent in *Dracula* and more or less interrupts Harker's account of the legal studies he has taken up in the Count's library. More than any other chapter, however, it shows Harker's feelings and his strong attachment to his fiancée, named Wilma here, while he is being drawn toward the indescribably gorgeous girl against his will. In this sense, *Makt Myrkranna* is a stronger love story than *Dracula*, where vows and prayers replace real intimacy. Although in Stoker's original, Jonathan Harker is initially thrilled by the vampire ladies, after his first encounter with them he is only disgusted, and he sees the Count as his savior for interrupting their seductive advances. His counterpart Thomas in the Icelandic version, however, constantly longs to be reunited with the fair-skinned temptress and allows her to embrace and kiss him time and time again, and even sit on his lap; in these and in other scenes, the women in the story seem to be attractive to the point of being irresistible— there are no traces of the physical revulsion expressed in *Dracula* and in Stoker's later novel, *The Lair of the White Worm* (1911). A strange complicity unites Thomas and the slender sylph in their joint resistance against the Icelandic Count, who appears as a punishing father figure separating the romantic couple. Physically, the King of Vampires seems to be no direct threat to Thomas—at least not a willing one.[33] The acts of biting and drinking blood are undertaken by the ape-like minions, whose violence lacks the sophistication and discretion of their aristocratic overlord. We never surprise the Count with his teeth in someone else's neck and after Lucia (*Makt Myrkranna's* version of Lucy) dies (no bite marks having been noticed), he does not come after Wilma. The Count and his conspiracy seem not to aim at a bloody killing or two, but at overthrowing the democratic governments of Europe. The terror, in the Icelandic version, is less personal.

33 More than *Dracula*, *Makt Myrkranna* employs the concept of a split personality or "subliminal self," as observed by hypnotists and psychic researchers of that time, or as described in Stevenson's *Dr. Jekyll and Mr. Hyde* (1886): the Count only threatens Harker when he is "not himself."

3. THE HINT AT THE RIPPER MURDERS

The preface to *Makt Myrkranna*, signed with Stoker's initials "B.S.," seems to confirm that the author of *Dracula* generally approved of this alternative edition and was familiar with at least some of the major new plot elements. The comment about remarkable foreigners playing a dazzling role in London's aristocratic circles, for example, does not match the plot of *Dracula*, but exactly fits the—modified—Icelandic version: it points to the foreign guests involved in the Count's political conspiracy, driving around town in eye-catching carriages, showing off their jewelry and enjoying amorous liaisons in the highest circles of power.

The part of the *Makt Myrkranna* preface that received the most attention from *Dracula* scholars is the remark about the Ripper murders. In Dalby's translation:

> But the events are incontrovertible, and so many people know of them that they cannot be denied. This series of crimes has not yet passed from the memory —a series of crimes which appear to have originated from the same source, and which at the same time created as much repugnance in people everywhere as the murders of Jack the Ripper, which came into the story a little later. Various people's minds will go back to the remarkable group of foreigners who for many seasons together played a dazzling part in the life of the aristocracy here in London; and some will remember that one of them disappeared suddenly without apparent reason, leaving no trace.

These words have puzzled *Dracula* experts for decades, as *Dracula* never mentions the Ripper. In fact, it describes no coherent series of crimes that—as this preface suggests—might have caused widespread concern, as the Ripper Murders did. In Whitechapel of the late 1880s, women were warned not leave their homes alone after dark; vigilante troops patrolled the street, inspecting the narrow alleys, which were not gaslit, as today's movies might have you believe, but simply dark and deserted. Newspapers competed to present the grisliest details, the latest drops of blood splattered on the walls of London's East End, and launched ever-new speculations about the "butcher" terrorizing "women of the unfortunate class."

In *Dracula,* we are confronted with the demise of the Demeter crew and with the deaths of Mr. Swales, Renfield, Lucy and her mother. But in the eyes of the police and the general public, these events all seem completely unrelated.[34] Why, then, would Stoker have added this puzzling reference to the *Makt Myrkranna* preface?

Dalby's translation suggests that the Ripper Murders appear in the novel "a little later," that is, somewhere after the preface. As a result, many *Dracula* scholars have started to search for obscured references to the Ripper Murders in the text of *Dracula*. But Dalby's translation is incorrect, and moreover, to understand what the Icelandic preface hints at, we should read the text of *Makt Myrkranna*, not that of *Dracula*.

Instead of "the murders of Jack the Ripper, which *came into the story* a little later," the preface speaks of "the murders of Jack the Ripper, which *happened* a little later." This means that "this series of crimes [that] has not yet passed from the memory" is a series of slayings that started *before* the Ripper Murders, and in *their* time (not "at the same time"—another error in the Dalby translation) also caused terror with the public, and in the imagination of the London population seemed to be connected with the Whitechapel homicides. Which crime series can be meant here?

34 The way Professor Van Helsing kills the three vampire ladies at Castle Dracula could be understood as an allusion to the Ripper's methods, but in England, no one was informed about Van Helsing's measures in Transylvania and therefore, they cannot have caused "repugnance" in the London public.

35 Spicer, n.d. (minor spelling errors corrected). See also Gordon, 2002, p. 35: "The old sacking was made of a common, coarse canvas." Rainham is a suburb in the East of London, 22 km east of Charing Cross.

In *Makt Myrkranna*, Harker's Journal of 8 May describes how the Count discusses a London crime spree and refers in particular to "these crimes, these horrible murders, those slaughtered women, found in the Thames, drifting in sacks; this blood that runs—runs and flows—with no murderer to be found." Beyond a reasonable doubt, this highly specific reference can only point to the unsolved "Thames Torso Murders" (1887-89), also known as the "Thames Mysteries" or "Embankment Murders":

> Evidence that a killer was at work first showed up in May of 1887, in the Thames River Valley village of Rainham, when workers pulled from the river a bundle containing the torso of a female. Throughout May and June, numerous parts from the same body showed up in various parts of London – until a complete body, minus head and upper chest, was reconstructed. (….)
>
> The second victim of the Thames series was discovered in September of 1888, in the middle of the hunt for the Whitechapel Murderer. On September 11, an arm belonging to a female was discovered in the Thames off Pimlico. On September 28, another arm was found along the Lambeth-road and on October 2, the torso of a female, minus the head, was discovered.[35]

Bottom left: The first trunk of a young woman found in the Thames near Rainham, on 28 May 1887. Further body parts were found in the course of 1887. **Right:** On 2 October 1888, during construction of the Metropolitan Police's new headquarters on the Victoria Embankment near Whitehall (Westminster), a worker found a parcel containing human remains. Newspapers suggested a connection to the Whitechapel Murders, but the police linked the crime with the Rainham Mystery.

These "Thames Mysteries" indeed triggered as much public unrest as the Ripper Murders were to cause one year later. And when female torsos were found at the construction site of Scotland Yard(!) in October 1888 and under a railway arch in Whitechapel in September 1889, some newspapers suggested that one and the same perpetrator could be responsible for both series of crimes. Although no more details of the Thames Torso Murders are given in the London part of *Makt Myrkranna*, it is not hard to imagine that

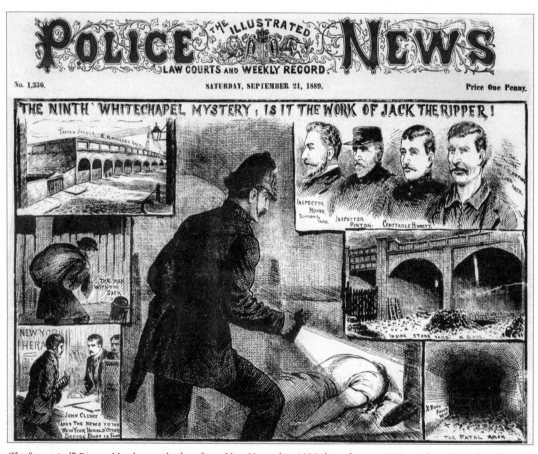

The "canonical" Ripper Murders took place from May–November 1888, but when on 10 September 1889 a female torso, wrapped in some sacking, the belly cut up, was found under a railway arch in Pinchin Street, Whitechapel, about 1,000 meters from the Thames, it was speculated that the Ripper had returned, although the police categorized the crime as one of the Thames Mysteries. Some newspapers speculated that the Whitechapel Murders and the Thames Mysteries might have been committed by the same murderer, using different ways to dispose of his victims. This is the basis for the remark in the Icelandic preface about the discussed murders seemingly stemming from the same root as the Ripper Murders.

36 In the novel itself, the Count's story hinting at Napoleon's jealousy also suggests Stoker's personal contribution: Irving loved to talk about Napoleon and from 1894 till 1898, Stoker was intensely involved in preparing the production of *Madame Sâns-Gene*; he was also familiar with the novelized version by Lepelletier, expressly discussing the love affairs of Joséphine de Beauharnais with the handsome lieutenant Hippolyte Charles.

37 "Saint Amand": Holy Love; "Rubiano": Ruby; "Morton": Death. "Koromezzo" is probably derived from the Hungarian town Körösmez (French: "Koromez") in the Carpathian Mountains, 125 km north of Bistritz, with a population of approx. 9,000 around 1900 (Purfleet: approx. 7,000; Bistritz and Whitby: approx. 12,000; Exeter approx. 35,000). See also footnote on Prince Koromezzo in Part II, Chapter 14, The Evening Party.

the Count's London vampire coven, abducting fresh victims for their satanic rituals, disposed of the dead bodies by dumping them into the river—especially if the Count's Carfax house was located in London-Plaistow (as in Stoker's original concept), not far away from Rainham, where the first Torso Murder victim was found. If nothing else, the fact that the murderer could not be found seems to comfort Valdimar's Count, who apparently relishes the idea that in the darkness and fog of London's streets, his own crimes may go unsolved.

Last but not least, the preface's mention of the secret police only makes sense in the context of the international political scandal that must have followed the uncovering of the Count's machinations—a plot point unique to *Makt Myrkranna* and another indication that Stoker was aware of the planned innovations.[36]

4. THE NAMES OF THE NEW CHARACTERS

A further clue that seems to confirm that Bram Stoker actively participated in reshaping his vampire novel lies in the names of the newly added characters. Some names could easily have been created by Valdimar, inspired by wordplay or geography.[37] The names of the police detective, Barrington, and Hawkins's assistant, Tellet, however, seem a bit too particular to have been randomly invented by an Icelandic author. My guess would be that, like other names appearing in *Dracula*, these designations may have been borrowed from people Stoker knew.

Sir Charles Burton Barrington captained Trinity College's rugby football team from 1867 till 1870; Stoker studied there 1864-1870 and played on the rugby team. Benjamin Barrington was one of the Trinity students linked to a nighttime shooting that killed a professor in his own house at the Trinity Campus, in March 1734. This Barrington became notorious for influencing witnesses during the trial and his name still belongs to Trinity's campus lore.

For "Tellet," an extremely rare name occurring only five times in the 1891 census for England, Wales, and Scotland, I also found a plausible link. On 23 April 1837, the comedy actress Clarissa Anne Chaplin married Daniel John Tellet at St. John's Church in Liverpool and became known as "Mrs. C. A. Tellet" or—for the stage—as "Miss Clara Tellet." In *Fifty Years of an Actor's Life* (1904), her colleague John Coleman described her as "Miss Clara Tellet, who was a perfect pocket Venus, and one of the brightest and most vivacious of soubrettes. This fairy-like creature ultimately became Mrs. Sam Emery and mother of the charming Winifred of that ilk (Mrs. Cyril Maude), who has inherited no small share of her mother's charm."[38] Samuel ("Sam") Emery performed in *Not Guilty* at the Queen's Theatre (1869) together with Henry Irving, Stoker's later employer. Sam and Clara's daughter Winifred Emery played female lead roles at the Lyceum Theatre next to Ellen Terry from 1881 to 1887 and toured America twice with Irving and Stoker.

38 Coleman, 1904, Vol. I, p. 326.

Right *The Morning Advertiser* of 14 Nov. 1848

Below: Charles Burton Barrington (center, with the ball) and his rugby team

OLYMPIC THEATRE.

Last evening the *Eton Boy*, which has for a long time been a great favourite among our minor houses, was re-produced at this theatre, for the purpose of affording an opportunity to Mrs. C. A. Tellet of appearing in the character of *Fanny Curry*, the heroine of the piece. As this lady had never before attempted the representation of the character, considerable anxiety was felt by her friends to learn how she would acquit herself in the part of *Fanny Curry*. Those who were most sanguine in their expectations of witnessing a most effective representation of the heroine of the *Eton Boy*, were not disappointed. Mrs. C. A. Tellet at once prepossessed the audience in her favour, by her accurate conception of the ideas of the author, and the manner in which she embodied her conceptions in the personation of the part allotted to her. The more humorous points were brought out with an effect which convulsed the house with laughter, the best of all proof that the part of *Fanny Curry* was acted as the principal character in the piece ought to be represented. The only drawback to the success of Mrs. Tellet, as the heroine of the *Eton Boy*, was to be found in the circumstance that the spirit with which she enacted the character was not uniformly sustained. It is right, however, to observe that this may have been quite as much owing to the nature of some of the incidents in the piece, as to any defects in the personation of the actress. The part where she shows off to her would-be spouse, and that in which the young Etonians perform their college duties—racing, fishing, hunting, boxing, &c., were very effectively played, and obtained for her much applause. Mrs. Tellet was ably supported by Messrs. Compton (whose humorous acting caused the house to be kept in a continued roar of laughter from the time he entered the stage till he made his exit), Leigh Murray, and Turner.

39 For the Taaffe family and the double wedding, see Debrett, 1840, p. 712 and p. 813; Burke, 1832, Vol. II, pp. 516-518; Burke, 1869, pp. 1089f. Antonia was a daughter of Antal Amadé de Várkony and thus the first cousin of Thaddaeus, the only son of Antal's brother Ferenc and the last male descendant of the Amadé Varkony line. Lodge, 1832, p. 387, mentions 1790 as Antonia's birth year. In musical history, Thaddaeus is known for sponsoring the young Franz Liszt (later befriended by Henry Irving) and Heinrich Marschner, composer of the opera *Der Vampyr* (1828).

The name of Varkony, which appears only in the Icelandic version, may also have sounded familiar to Stoker, from stories his mother told of her home county, Sligo. On 11 April 1811, the aristocrat Francis Taaffe married Antonia Amadé Varkony of Hungary, while Taaffe's sister Clementina on the very same day married Count Thaddaeus Amadé Varkony, Antonia's cousin.[39] Taaffe bore the title of "Baron of Ballymore" in County Sligo. Perhaps, Bram's mother reported on the curious double wedding.

The most intriguing connection, though, concerns the character—again new to *Makt Myrkranna*—of Holmwood's sister Mary. Possibly, Stoker took it from the writer Mary Singleton (whose name already appeared in Stoker's early notes for "a psychical research agent, Alfred Singleton"), famous in London literary circles for her beauty and witty conversation. She played a prominent role as the unhappily married Mrs. Sinclair in W.H. Mallock's *roman à clef*, named *The New Republic* (1877). Mary Singleton was unhappily mar-

Count Thaddaeus Amadé Varkony

Mary Singleton, née Montgomerie Lamb (Violet Fane)

ried indeed: after being rejected by her lover, she married the elderly Henry Sydenham Singleton, but in the early 1880s exchanged secret vows with Philip Lord Currie of the Foreign Office, and also had an affair with Philip's cousin. In well-informed circles, to which also Stoker belonged,[40] her liaison with Sir Philip became a public secret—especially as she hinted at her luckless situation in *The Edwin and Angelina Papers*[41] and in her novel *The Adventures of a Savage* (1881). The latter dealt with a young woman bored with her elderly husband and betraying him with a younger lover; the story had a happy ending when the "old squire" died and the heroine was reunited with her "young squire." Appropriately, Henry S. Singleton died in March 1893 and within ten months Mary had married Sir Philip Currie, the newly appointed Ambassador to Constantinople. The couple moved to Constantinople only a few days after their wedding.[42] The similarities between Mary Singleton's story and the plight of *Makt Myrkranna*'s Mary Holmwood are striking and unique.[43]

5. BRAM STOKER'S PREPARATORY NOTES FOR *DRACULA*

Still another point suggests Stoker's active contribution to the Icelandic version. In what will come as a surprise to every *Dracula* scholar, plot elements that were described in Stoker's early preparatory notes for the novel, but did not appear in the book, are found in *Makt Myrkranna*:

- The notes feature a deaf and mute housekeeper woman acting as the Count's servant. Exactly such a woman is described in *Makt Myrkranna*.
- The early notes indicate that the Count visits the diseased Lucy as a regular guest. Such visits are reported in the Icelandic version, while in *Dracula*, the Count enters Lucy's house only stealthily or by force.

40 Mary Singleton often met with artists around James Abbott Whistler; Oscar Wilde and Bram Stoker also belonged to this group.

41 Collected essays, published as a book in 1878.

42 See *The Standard* of 25 January 1894, p. 5, reporting on the wedding.

43 Intriguingly, in December 1892 Professor Max Müller's son Wilhelm Max Müller also left for Constantinople as an attaché—see Müller, 1902, Vol. II, p. 289. In summer 1893, before the Curries arrived there, the Müllers visited Constantinople to see their son. They were received by the Sultan; Mrs. Müller later published her *Letters from Constantinople* with Longmans, Green & Co., London/New York, 1897. See also the article *The Turk's Town* in *The New York Times* of 10 April 1897.

- In Stoker's original plan, the Carfax house and Seward's asylum were located in London itself—just like in *Makt Myrkranna*. Only in the 1897 typescript version of *Dracula*, these buildings were removed to Purfleet, 20 miles east of Piccadilly.

- The notes repeatedly mention a blood-red secret room in Count Dracula's residence. In *Makt Myrkranna*, Harker discovers a secret temple in the castle, where bloody rituals take place. The Carfax house also contains a hidden room. In *Dracula*, no such secret space is mentioned.

- Originally, Stoker planned for the appearance of a police detective, Cotford. In *Dracula*, the police are not active at all. In *Makt Myrkranna*, however, we find police detective Barrington, assisted by his colleague Tellet. The murder of Lucia's housemaid is also actively investigated by the police.

- The Stoker notes mention a dinner for thirteen people at Dr. Seward's house, where the Count arrives as the last guest. In *Makt Myrkranna*, an evening party takes place in Carfax with Seward as the only English guest. Although the Count is the host now, he again enters last.

- In his notes, Stoker refers to Dr. Seward as a "mad doctor," so that the editors of the facsimile edition had to ask themselves whether or not Stoker intended Seward to be as mad as his patient Renfield. In *Makt Myrkranna*, Dr. Seward—of all characters—actually loses his mind.

If we are not prepared to accept these seven similarities between Stoker's notes and the new plot elements in *Makt Myrkranna* as a mere coincidence, Bram Stoker must have passed his early plot ideas to Valdimar.

Count Dracula.

Dracula   **Historiæ Personæ**   Dracula

- Doctor of mad house ~~Seward~~ Seward
  Girl engaged to him Lucy Westenra Schoolfellow of Miss Murray
- Mad Patient (theory of getting life – instinctively goes for Count & follows
                up idea with mad cunning.
- Lawer ~~Arthur~~ ~~Abbott~~ ~~John~~ Peter Hawkins Exeter
- His Clerk ——————— Jonathan Harker
- Fiancee of above ~~Kate Reed~~ Wilhelmina Murray (called Mina)
- ~~Lawyer~~
- ~~his sister~~
- ~~Auctioneer~~
  Friend & schoolfellow of above ——————— Kate Reed
  The Count ——————— Count ~~Wampyr~~ Dracula
  A Deaf Mute woman ⎫ Slight
  A Silent Man   ⎬ Servants of
                    ⎭ the Count
- A Detective ——————————— Cotford
- A Psychical Research Agents ————— Alfred Singleton
- ~~An American Inventor from Texas~~
- A German Professor ——————— Max Windshoeffel
- A Painter ——— Francis Aytown
- a Texan ——— Brutus M. Marix

  mem
    o notes dinner of 13
  secret room – cleared like box

44 At the end of *Makt Myrkranna*, for example, Seward turns mad and dies. But the preface mentions him as a friend of the author, in present tense. The hint in the preface about the Thames Torso Murders almost runs empty, as the novel barely fleshes it out. The preface states that the remarkable foreigners played a dazzling role in London "for many seasons on end" (also incorrectly translated in Dalby's text), but this cannot apply to the Count himself, who arrived in London in August and was terminated by the end of October/start of November of the same year.

45 We know that Stoker lived at Leonard *Terrace* at that time. But Stoker was a master at camouflaging real addresses and replacing them by fake denominations; this applies to every single key address in *Dracula*. The use of a long dash already indicates that the novelist's private address should not be disclosed under this preface; the use of "Street" may have been part of this cover-up. Moreover, Stoker may have written this preface at his office at the Lyceum Theatre, located at 21 Wellington *Street*. An even simpler explanation would be that the Icelandic language does not know the use of "Terrace" to signify a street; it merely uses "stræti" or "stígur" for streets in a town, "gata" for other streets lined with houses, and "vegur" or "braut" for paths or roads without houses. The Icelandic equivalents for "terrace" refer to the banks of a river or stream ("árhjalli" or "malarhjalli"), or to an elevated garden terrace ("verönd," cf. German "Veranda"). For an Icelandic translator, it thus would be logical to translate "——— Terrace" as "———stræti," what in the retranslation to English results in "——— Street."

6. THE MYSTERIES OF THE PREFACE

How can we be sure that Bram Stoker wrote the preface himself and thus was aware of at least some of the changes to his story?

One important authorship clue is that the preface highlights Van Helsing as a "real" person, appearing under a pseudonym. If Valdimar wrote the preface on his own account, he must have read an interview with Bram Stoker in *The British Weekly* of 1 July 1897—the only known document describing Van Helsing as "based on a real character." The chances that Valdimar ever came across this interview are small, however: in the Icelandic press, the magazine was only mentioned in 1912 for the first time and the National Library of Iceland in Reykjavík never had a subscription to it. Moreover, the author of the preface must have known about the rumors in the London newspapers that the Thames Torso Murders and the Ripper Murders might stem from the same root. Bram Stoker, living in London and forced to cancel the performances of *Dr. Jekyll and Mr. Hyde* at his Lyceum Theatre due to the general Ripper panic, was likely to be familiar with such theories. By contrast, neither *Fjallkonan* nor the rest of the Icelandic press ever mentioned the Embankment Murders. And even if Valdimar had studied the Torso Murders, why should he confuse his Icelandic readers with an obscure hint that they would never have been able to understand? The *Hamlet* quote also reeks of Stoker: Irving performed the role of the Danish prince hundreds of times and *Dracula* contains several allusions to the play. All in all, it seems apparent that Stoker gave the Icelandic project his blessings and was informed about the new direction the story would take, but did not know all the details.[44]

Another important indication is that the preface is dated and signed: "Lundúnu, ——— stræti, Ágúst 1898, *B.S.*"[45]

It would have been a severe—possibly criminal—act of fraud for anyone else but Stoker to sign that way. Up till 1947 Icelandic publishers were not bound by the Berne Convention.[46] Stoker thus had no legal means to enforce his copyright in Iceland and prevent an unlicensed translation or even a modification of *Dracula* there. But fabricating a phony preface and signing it off with Stoker's name—but without his endorsement—would add a whole new dimension of literary piracy: Valdimar would not only damage Stoker, but also hoodwink his own readers and impersonate another writer—no trivial offense in Iceland, where literature plays a central role and straightforwardness is a highly valued virtue.

A last clue is the assessment by Ásgeir Jónsson, the editor of the 2011 Icelandic edition, with whom I exchanged ideas about Stoker's and Valdimar's role in *Makt Myrkranna* in early 2014.[47] In Ásgeir's opinion, the Icelandic of the preface deviates from the style of the novel; it is less fluent, as if Valdimar had translated a text from a foreign language:

> Valdimar Ásmundsson had a way with words and an extremely good command of his mother tongue. Our Nobel laureate, Halldór Laxness, has called him the "best pen in the whole of Iceland in the beginning of the twentieth century." The translation of *Dracula* itself, although not loyal to the original text, is written in an extremely vivid and skillful way—that is why I decided to republish it. However, the preface is very clumsy, the sentences are very un-Icelandic and unlike Valdimar—they have much more of an English character.[48]

This assessment by a native Icelandic speaker and author supports the idea that the preface was written by Stoker and then translated, instead of being concocted by Valdimar.[49]

46 Denmark ratified the Berne Convention in June 1903, but Iceland was not included in this treaty—see *Le droit d'auteur*, Paris, of 15 July 1903, p. 73. Iceland as an independent state ratified the Convention in 1947. Already on 8 May 1893, Denmark signed a bilateral copyright treaty with the US, but it is unclear if this treaty included Iceland.

47 The third Icelandic edition was published by Bókafélagið, Reykjavík. The text was based on the 1950 edition by Hogni, which shows small deviations from the original text. Ásgeir Jónsson wrote an afterword—the first (Icelandic) text clearly stating the differences between *Makt Myrkranna* and *Dracula*. In this afterword, however, Ásgeir expressly left it to other researchers to find more about the nature of Stoker's and Valdimar's cooperation. The purpose of my research was to fill this gap.

48 Email from Ásgeir Jónsson of 1 February 2014.

49 In January 2016, I discussed this issue again with leading translation experts from the University of Iceland, the University of Reykjavík and the Árni Magnússon Institute for Icelandic Studies. With various linguistic arguments, the participants in this debate convincingly supported Ásgeir Jónsson's opinion.

50 Allen, 1997, p. 296 mentions a banquet hosted by the Governor on 1 September. *The Advertiser* (Adelaide) of 9 October 1903, p. 4, wrote: "Mr. Hall Caine was present on August 26 at the Parliamentary dinner at the close of the session of the Iceland Alþing as a guest of the Governor of that island." This is probably more accurate: *Ísafold* of 26 August 1903, p. 223, reported that the 1903 Alþing "was closed today at 5 p.m., after passing the budget." See also *The Pittsburg Press* of 3 October 1903.

51 In 1884: *Edward Mills And George Benton: A Tale* (1880). In 1885: *The Man Who Fought Cats*, published by John C. Hotten in *Practical Jokes with Artemus Ward* (1872). In 1886: *How Hyde Lost His Ranch*, from Chapter 34 of *Roughing It* (1872).

52 *Blucher's Disastrous Dinner*, from Chapter 5 of *The Innocents Abroad*, in *Fjallkonan* of 20 September 1893.

53 *Miljónarseðillinn* started in *Fjallkonan* of 17 February 1894 and ran until 8 May of that year (pages 27-75).

7. WHO CONNECTED VALDIMAR AND BRAM STOKER?

In the foreword to this book, Dacre Stoker mentions the possibility that Bram Stoker's friend Hall Caine had been instrumental in connecting Stoker and Valdimar. Caine wrote two novels set in Iceland and visited the country twice—in 1889 and again in 1903; the second time he was invited to an official dinner organized by the Icelandic government.[50] He admired William Morris's renderings of the Icelandic sagas and may have been in touch with Valdimar, a specialist on this topic.

It is also possible that Mark Twain established the link. Although Twain never was in Iceland himself, in 1884, 1885 and 1886 respectively, three of his short stories were translated and published in *Iðunn*, a literary magazine run by the poet and teacher Steingrímur Thorsteinsson, the journalist Jón Ólafsson and by Björn Jónsson, the editor of *Ísafold*;[51] all three were friends of Valdimar. In 1893, *Fjallkonan* published a fragment from Twain's *The Innocents Abroad* (1869)[52] and in 1894, it serialized *The Million Pound Banknote*.[53] During his trips to

Thomas Hall Caine (painted by Robert Edward Morrison)
(Painted by Robert Edward Morrison)

Mark Twain
(Photo: Associated Press)

America with the Lyceum Theatre, Stoker and Twain had become good friends. From early October 1896 till June 1897, Twain and his family lived just a stone's throw away from Stoker's house at St. Leonard's Terrace.[54] In spring 1898 Stoker offered to act as Twain's dramatic agent in the U.K. and look through his play *Is He Dead?*[55] From June 1899 until October 1900, Twain and his family lived in London again. It therefore would not be unlikely that Twain passed his Reykjavík contacts to Stoker.[56]

It may also be that Frederic Myers, the secretary of the Society for Psychical Research, had given Stoker a hint. The S.P.R. had been founded by scholars gathering around Henry Sidgwick, a Cambridge philosophy professor since 1874. Their goal was to perform scientific research on paranormal phenomena. Spiritism was *en vogue* in Victorian London and many honorable citizens spent their evening around a table while a— usually female—medium apparently received messages from beyond through the Ouija board or table-lifting. As the society's researchers found out, many professional mediums had devel-

54 The 1891 Census shows that by that year, the Stokers had already moved from Cheyne Walk to 17 St. Leonard's Terrace. In 1897, they moved to Nr. 18 (see chronology in Browning, 2012, pp. 318f.). Twain lived at 23 Tedworth Square.

55 Twain/Fishkin, 2006, p. 229, various footnotes. Like *Makt Myrkranna*, *Is He Dead* is a "forgotten work," which only recently received fresh attention through Shelley Fishkin's efforts to republish and stage the play.

56 Twain was a good friend of Professor Willard Fiske of Cornell University, who visited Iceland in 1879 and remained in contact with its leading intellectuals and newspaper publishers, Thorsteinsson, Jónsson and Ásmundsson included.

Frederic William Henry Myers
(Painted by William Clarke Wontner)

Daniel Willard Fiske
(Painted by Cei Cipriano)

57 Palladino even managed to let two examiners, who were supposed to hold her hands for control, hold hands together, so that her own hands were free.

58 1886, with Edmund Guerny and Frank Podmore.

59 Stoker and Irving knew Dufferin already since July 1892 at the latest, when Irving was made Doctor of Literature *honoris causa* at Trinity College, Dublin, and Dufferin formally proposed a toast to Irving during the subsequent banquet. See Stoker, 1907, p. 394.

60 Stoker, 1907, pp. 395f. In the 1906 two-volume edition: Vol, II, p. 248.

61 Still other links can be found if we start mapping the personal networks connecting London with Reykjavík. I plan to publish these results in a separate paper.

62 The idea of Count Dracula personally leading such group rituals only showed up in the Dracula films of the 1960s and 70s, e.g. *The Satanic Rites of Dracula* (1973) with Christopher Lee. The Count as the leader of a larger group of vampires can be found (as a parody) in *The Fearless Vampire Killers* (1967, Roman Polanski) and in *Sundown: The Vampire in Retreat* (1989, Anthony Hickox).

oped ingenious tricks to move tables with sophisticated mechanisms or sheer body control. In 1895, for example, Frederic Myers, Oliver Lodge and Richard Hodgson exposed the celebrated medium Eusapia Palladino, proving that she had been manipulating furniture with her feet during her séances.[57] The Society counted as many as 1,400 members and reported on their experiments and meetings in their famous *Proceedings*. Stoker was friends with such prominent S.P.R. members as Alfred Tennyson, John Knowles, William Ewart Gladstone, and Arthur Conan Doyle. On 9 September 1890, Valdimar dedicated the complete front page of *Fjallkonan* to the S.P.R. and extensively discussed Myers's book *Phantasms of the Living*.[58] In June 1898, Stoker and Irving lodged at Myers's house, along with Lord Dufferin,[59] the author of the international bestseller *Letters from High Latitudes*, recounting Dufferin's visit to Iceland.[60] Is it possible that Myers, entertained by Dufferin's adventures, mentioned the leading Icelandic newspaper that had shown so much interest in his paranormal research—a most suitable platform for Stoker's supernatural novel?[61]

As long as no letters between Bram Stoker and Valdimar Ásmundsson (or manuscript versions or notes etc.) are found, the debate about the Irishman's personal contribution to *Makt Myrkranna* will continue and maybe even split the field of *Dracula* scholars—like the mysterious identity of Count Dracula once did.

For the outstanding quality of the novel, however, this makes no difference; in the pages that follow, the reader can enjoy the story, including such vivid scenes as the tribal ceremonies in the Count's hidden temple.[62]

It is the combination of Stoker's original ideas—as documented in his notes—with original contributions by Valdimar Ásmundsson and daring innovations antici-

Lord Dufferin
(Painted by George Frederic Watts)

pating later movies and screenplays, that makes *Makt Myrkranna* such an intriguing literary work. Regardless of the mysteries attached to its creation, the novel can now be read by readers all over the world, who may make their own discoveries in the text.

Hans C. de Roos
Munich, March 2016

A ROOM WITH A VIEW:

THE FLOOR PLANS OF
CASTLE DRACULA

TWO-THIRDS OF *MAKT MYRKRANNA* IS DEDICATED TO Harker's stay in Castle Dracula and his desperate attempts to find a way out. While translating the novel, I followed Harker's explorations tour in my imagination and started wondering if the Transylvanian part of the story was based on a logical plan of the building—and if yes, if it would be possible to reconstruct such a plan from the text. Here are the results.

1. A FIRST ORIENTATION:
A RECTANGULAR SHAPE WITH FOUR WINGS

The first thing we learn about the castle is that the calèche arrives in a large courtyard, surrounded by old, high walls. The simplest sketch of the castle's floor plan would thus show a quadratic or rectangular shape, consisting of four wings, with this courtyard in the middle. We would expect towers to be placed at the corners. Starting from this most primitive sketch, we can try to fill in the rest.

To get into the building, Harker has to walk up a staircase leading to an ornamental gate, which means that the entrance hall of the building is on a raised ground floor. Later we will learn that the underground crypt has high-set windows to let some light in—these two facts agree with each other: The basement or souterrain is partly below, partly above ground.

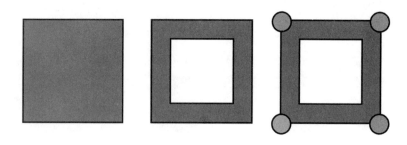

Entrance gate

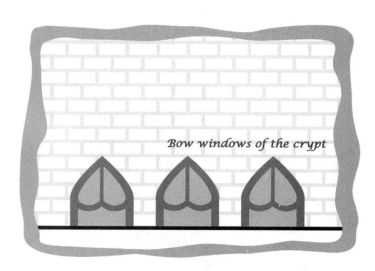

Bow windows of the crypt

This gives us some first façade views, seen from the court-yard, with the entrance in the east wing and the crypt in the west wing.

2. HARKER'S HOME BASE: THE FOURTH FLOOR

Harker follows the Count to the living room or dining room. Here, a number of rooms are grouped together. Adjoining the dining room is the small octagonal cabin that leads to Harker's bedroom. Moreover, the dining room has one door to a corridor, and another door to the library. As these are the rooms where Harker sleeps, eats and studies, thus spending most of his time, we might call this group of rooms his *home base*.

During his explorations of 10 May, Harker learns that the dining room is also connected to the Count's personal rooms: a private study and a bedroom. Behind these two rooms is the large hall with the oaken floors and old chairs; this hall, in turn, opens up to a corner tower, where the Count stores his gold. The hall also has a door to a staircase. Harker believes this door to be locked, but some mysterious person opens it for him.

Because Harker states that the Count's gold is stored on the fourth floor, all these interconnected rooms must be on the fourth floor.

3. ROUTES LEADING AWAY FROM THE FOURTH FLOOR

From this fourth floor Harker can access the other parts of the castle. Together with the Count, he goes up from the corridor next to the dining room and arrives at the portrait gallery. After seeing the murdered peasant girl, he runs down the stairs, arriving in the entrance hall, but finds all the doors locked, and notes that the way up to the gallery is the only alternative (10 May). Only much later does he discover the third vertical route leading away from the fourth floor: the secret staircase, leading to the underground temple (21 May). Later, he uses this secret staircase again to reach a tunnel to the west wing and the crypt. Here are the details:

A) THE ENTRANCE HALLS

On the elevated ground level with the entrance gate, Harker finds another hall, but there too, all the doors are locked. I imagine these two halls to lie in an L-shape, leaving enough room on this level for the chapel, and stables for the horses (which of course must have their floors on the ground level).

I assume that the entrance area consists of a high, impressive hall; in combination with the raised ground level, this would mean that the first floor would be where normal houses have their second floor ($\frac{1}{2} + 1\frac{1}{2} = 2$).

B) HARKER'S TOUR OF 10 MAY

Because our hero finds no exit from the elevated ground level, Harker goes up to the portrait gallery. From here, he has access to

(i) the tower room from which he will later watch the sunset;

(ii) the west wing with its many deserted chambers;

(iii) the tower the Countess was locked in (he goes in there only on 16 June);

(iv) the room with the diamond floor patterns, and from there—through still more rooms—the gate tower, where he finds a steep staircase leading down.

The room with the iron chains in the gate tower gives access to another staircase, which Harker describes as a "deep well." Here he is attacked and finally lands in the basement: Through a tunnel and a domed space he reaches the room with the rotting bones and then the crypt with the stone coffins. After the crypt, Harker climbs up again, to a balcony overlooking an old chapel (that is, the floor above the crypt with the stone coffins), and from the balcony up to the hall with the oaken floors—from where he gets into the treasure room and the Count's private rooms—and finally back to the dining room.

Harker's tour of 10 May thus leads him to the highest and to the lowest floors of the castle, making a full circle through all four wings—but on different levels.

C) DOWN THE SECRET STAIRS

When Harker goes down the secret stairs for the first time, he arrives at a second balcony, which overlooks the sacrificial temple with the altar and the burning torches.

Later, he will use this staircase again and find a vestibule, with tunnels leading to the east and to the west. Following the latter, he arrives in the same staircase where he has been before, coming up from the crypt with the stone coffins, and then from the balcony overlooking the chapel. Harker uses this path to take another look in the crypt, where he discovers the transport boxes; the Count is lying in one of them.

These are all the places mentioned in the Transylvanian part of the story: The floors between the entrance hall and the fourth floor are never described, nor are the floors between the fourth floor and the top floor.

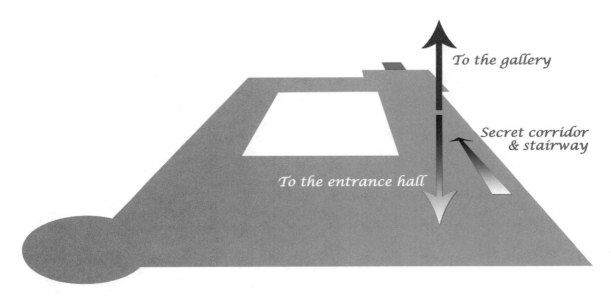

To the gallery

Secret corridor & stairway

To the entrance hall

The novel contains enough hints, however, to make a rough plan of the parts Harker has seen—but we still need a more precise orientation.

4. THE FOUR TOWERS

The towers are ideal clues for improving this orientation, because they mark the corners of the castle and connect the four wings with each other.

The southwest tower: When Harker comes up from the crypt and the chapel-balcony, he notes that he is in the southwest corner of the castle. The Count's treasure room is a rounded tower room, evidently in the southwest tower, which we can now pinpoint on a provisory map of the fourth floor.

The gate tower: Similarly, when Harker arrives in the gate tower, he notes that he has through countless detours arrived at the north part of the castle.

The southeast tower: Again, we have a clear hint, because the Count calls the tower where the Countess was locked in "that little tower room in the southeast." We may assume that this was the highest room in this tower, so that to drop from the window meant a sure death. Harker notices that this room is rounded, like the treasure room in the southwest tower.

A fourth tower: There are no further towers mentioned, but the underground room where Harker finds the rotting bones and the skulls is round, so that we may suspect that it forms the base of a fourth tower.

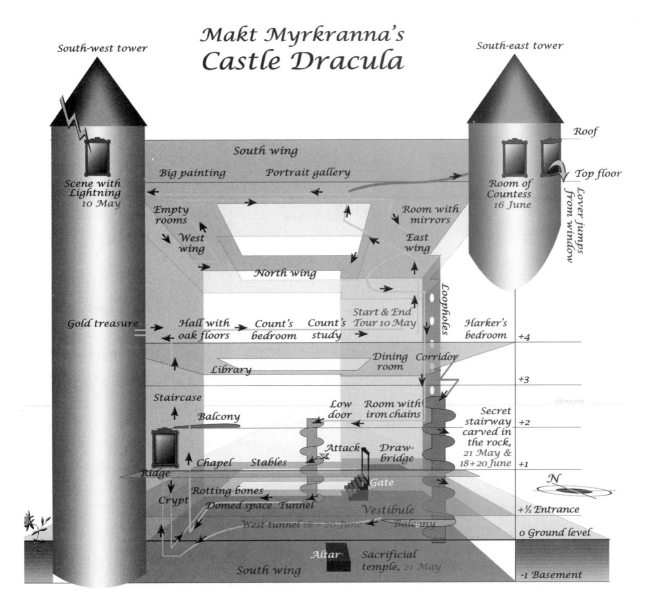

Makt Myrkranna's
Castle Dracula

South-west tower

South-east tower

Scene with Lightning 10 May

Gold treasure

South wing

Big painting   Portrait gallery

Empty rooms

West wing

North wing

Room with mirrors

East wing

Roof

Top floor

Room of Countess 16 June

Lover jumps from window

Hall with oak floors   Count's bedroom   Count's study   Start & End Tour 10 May

Loopholes

Harker's bedroom   +4

Library

Dining room   Corridor   +3

Horizon

Staircase

Balcony

Ridge

Chapel   Stables

Crypt

Rotting bones

Domed space   Tunnel

West tunnel 18 + 20 June

Low door   Room with iron chains

Attack   Draw-bridge

Gate

Vestibule

Balcony

Secret stairway carved in the rock, 21 May & 18 + 20 June   +2

+1

N

+½ Entrance

0 Ground level

Altar   Sacrificial temple, 21 May

South wing

-1 Basement

5. THE FOUR WINGS

The south wing: Like the fourth floor, the portrait gallery plays a vital role in the story. Before Harker discovers the secret staircase, the gallery is his only way to access the rest of the castle. We may assume that it is on the highest floor, as it connects the highest tower room on the southwest corner (where Harker watches the sunset) with the highest tower room on the southeast corner (the room of the Countess): Harker can reach both tower rooms starting from the gallery without climbing further stairs.

The gallery itself must thus be part of the south wing. When Harker goes in there during the day, the paintings are bathed in sunlight.

The west wing: When Harker enters the gallery on 10 May, he sees two doors at its far end, where the large portrait hangs. One leads to the southwest tower, one to a series of rooms which Harker calls the west wing.

The east wing: Because the west wing turns out to be a dead end, Harker returns to the gallery (the south wing) and at the side where he first entered finds a door to a room with a rhombic floor pattern and high windows. He runs through them and a series of other rooms, feeling half-sick, before he arrives at the gate tower, that is, the north side. We can also conclude that he has passed through the east wing.

The north wing: The description of this wing mostly concerns its underground part. In the room where the iron chains are, Harker finds a low door and then goes down the "deep well," walks through a tunnel and a space with a domed roof, then arrives in the round room with the foul-odored skeletons. If we assume that this round room is part of a tower (the northwest tower), then the north wing ends here and Harker continues—still underground—in the southward direction through the crypt, until he arrives at the staircase in the southwest corner.

Both the crypt and the chapel above are thus part of the

west wing, but are located much lower than the deserted rooms Harker reached from the gallery.

6. A PLAN OF THE FOURTH FLOOR

Now we can try to fill in the floor plan of the fourth floor, where Harker lives. Again, the easiest way is to start with the corners.

We already know that the treasure room with the gold is in the southwest corner. When Harker looks out from the window of the southwest tower (on 10 May), he notes: "I saw that I was in the southwest corner of the castle, and from there I could see its east side, where my room was. I also saw the windows which I had left open there." Since Harker cannot look around corners or through walls, the only logical possibility is that his bedroom is in the southeast corner. The room of the Countess is in the same corner, but much higher up: The Count mentions that Harker can view the same ravine as the young lover did, but that the drop from the room of the Countess is much more dramatic.

The next corner, counter-clockwise, would be occupied by the gate tower. This fortification must be quite a massive structure; Harker can see it both from his own bedroom, and from the dining room, which has windows to the courtyard.

In the northwest corner, finally, must be the library: When Harker first enters it (around 5 p.m.), he notes it is a large corner room, where the sun shines in. After his long trip of 10 May, he sits there and watches the sunset, before he decides to go up to the highest room in the southwest tower, to have an even better view. The library thus must have windows to the west.

Harker does not state that the library would have a round

corner; it seems that the northwest corner is only round at its base. Harker's bedroom is not round either; the round tower room of the Countess may be part of a bowfront tower that projects from the façade, only higher up.

From all of the above, we can conclude that the dining room should be in the east wing of the fourth floor. It borders both the library in the north wing and the Count's private rooms, which must be in the south wing. It also gives access to the corridor and its staircase (leading downwards to the entrance hall and upwards to the gallery). Finally, via the octagonal cabin, it links to Harker's bedroom in the southeast corner. All these criteria define its shape and location.

The secret corridor leading to the secret stairs starts directly opposite Harker's bedroom door. It receives some light through two windows, thus it must run along a wall.

The following sketch matches all this information in the most simple way I could conceive of; in fact, I did not find another logical solution.

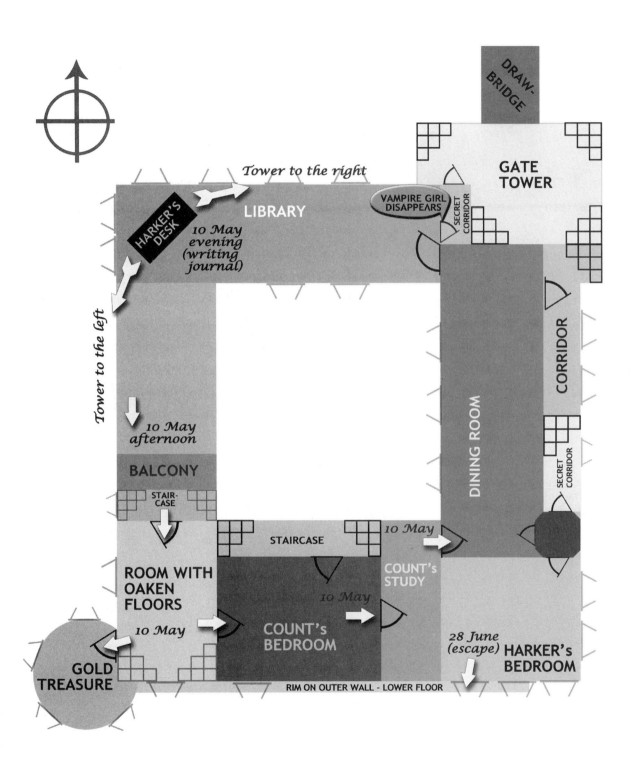

Tower to the right

LIBRARY

HARKER'S DESK

10 May evening (writing journal)

Tower to the left

10 May afternoon

BALCONY

STAIRCASE

ROOM WITH OAKEN FLOORS

10 May

GOLD TREASURE

STAIRCASE

COUNT's BEDROOM

10 May

VAMPIRE GIRL DISAPPEARS

SECRET CORRIDOR

GATE TOWER

DRAW-BRIDGE

CORRIDOR

DINING ROOM

SECRET CORRIDOR

10 May

COUNT's STUDY

28 June (escape)

HARKER's BEDROOM

RIM ON OUTER WALL - LOWER FLOOR

7. THE LEDGE ALONG THE SOUTH WALL

Looking out from his bedroom window, Harker can see two different persons crawl or walk on a ledge along an outer wall. Harker describes how these human shapes move between the "west tower" and the "east tower," meaning the tower on the southwest corner and the one on the southeast corner, where his own bedroom is. Just like in *Dracula,* the ledge thus runs along the south façade, which Harker calls the rear side of the castle. The front side is the north façade, where we find the gate tower and the drawbridge across the waterfall—the regular entrance to the castle.

The ledge can be accessed through a window in the southwest tower. Apparently, this is not the window Harker looks out from on 10 May, when he watches the peasant family: After this event, he is still searching for the right window. He only finds it when he goes down the secret stairs, follows a tunnel to the west and then arrives in the same staircase—but at a point underneath the balcony overlooking the chapel.

8. THE CHAPEL AND THE CRYPT

I assume that the chapel (in the west wing) is on the same level as the entrance hall (in the east wing): an elevated ground level. Underneath is the crypt with the stone coffins, that receives light through high-set windows; its floor is below ground level. The chapel itself could be quite high, so that the balcony overlooking it could be on the third floor; from there, Harker follows the staircase to the fourth floor, arriving at the hall with the oaken floors. The window opening to the ledge could thus be between the second and the third floor, so that Harker missed it when he scaled the stairs from the balcony to the fourth floor.

9. FILLING IN THE DETAILS

Now we can fill in the remaining details. For example, Harker suspects that the blonde girl slips out through a secret door in the library; I created an extra secret exit for her, that is hidden from Harker's sight when the Count opens the door to the library.

The corridor next to the dining room runs across the east wing, while the portrait gallery runs along the south façade. Because there are several floors in between, we have a myriad of possibilities to imagine a route between the two spaces.

The sacrificial temple is underground; I imagine it to be in the south wing, still leaving places for tunnels to the west and the east starting from a vestibule connected to the secret stairs. But if we assume more than just one underground level, the possibilities multiply.

10. LEFT OR RIGHT?

So far, it seems possible to create floor plans of the basement, the elevated ground level, the fourth floor and the top floor without getting caught in logical contradictions. Therefore, I suspect that the author(s) of *Makt Myrkranna* had a consistent model of the castle in mind while the novel was written; maybe, there even were map sketches, like the ones I deducted from the text of the story just now.

A single point kept marring me: When Harker looks out from his bedroom, on 10 May in the morning, he notes that he sees towers to the left and the right; the tower to his left would be the tower where the mysterious shape came from, crawling along the ledge like a cat. We already know that this must be the southwest tower; if Harker looks out from his bedroom window, this southwest tower must be on his right-hand, while the gate tower is at his left hand.

This could be a simple slip of the pen—but there may be a more elegant solution: Harker writes his diary of 10 May while he sits in the library in the north wing, watching the sunset, before he goes up to the top room of the southwest tower. Sitting in this position, the southwest tower is indeed on his left hand, while the gate tower is on his right hand: Harker's description is logical and consistent from the perspective he had while taking down his notes.

11. TAKE A LOOK AT THE FLOOR PLANS AT OUR WEBSITE!

Whatever the case, the Transylvanian part of the novel is much more enjoyable when we can follow Harker's adventures in our imagination, through the three dimensions of space. Even with the help of this essay, though, the reader may have difficulties building such a virtual model in his mind. For this reason, I have worked out the floor plans for the four levels discussed here. Pienette Coetzee, a young Munich artist who studied Graphic Arts at the University of Stellenbosch, South Africa, has re-created them in a style that would fit the dilapidated, medieval structure Harker describes. They can be viewed online on my project website www.powersofdarkness.com.

Enjoy.

POWERS OF DARKNESS

AUTHOR'S PREFACE[2]

WHILE READING THIS STORY, THE READER CAN SEE for himself how these papers have been combined to make a logical whole. I had to do no more than to remove some minor events that do not matter to the story, and so let the people involved[3] report their experiences in the same plain manner in which these pages were originally written. For obvious reasons, I have changed the names of people and places.[4] But otherwise I leave the manuscript unchanged, in accordance with the wish of those who have considered it their solemn[5] duty to present it to the eyes of the public.

To the best of my belief, there is no doubt whatsoever that the events related here *really took place*,[6] however unbelievable and incomprehensible they may appear in light of common experience. And I am further convinced that they must always remain to some extent unknowable, although it's not inconceivable that continuing research in psychology and the natural sciences may all of a sudden[7] provide logical explanations for these and other such strange happenings, which neither scientists nor the secret police[8] have yet been able to understand.

I emphasize again that the mysterious tragedy described here is *completely true as far as the events as such are concerned*, although

1 *Fjallkonan* was the name of the newspaper owned and edited by Valdimar Ásmundsson. The Icelandic version of *Dracula* appeared here as a serialization from 13 January 1900 until 20 March 1901.

2 As discussed in the Introduction to this book, Stoker's preface is the only part of *Makt Myrkranna* that has been translated before. The first translation was commissioned and published by Richard Dalby in *A Bram Stoker Omnibus* (1986), and reproduced in *Bram Stoker Journal* #5 (1993). It gave rise to manifold speculations about a possible link between *Dracula*, the Ripper Murders, and the life of Bram Stoker. A second translation by Sylvia Sigurdson was commissioned by *Dracula* expert and book collector Robert Eighteen-Bisang in Canada in 2004. It was published in Storey, 2012. Because most *Dracula* experts are familiar with the Dalby translation, the following notes will highlight the most important differences between his translation and mine.

3 *Fjallkonan* and the 1901 book edition use "sögufolkid," literally "the storypeople" or "the people of the story." The 1950 and 2011 editions replace "sögufolkid" with "sögunnar," lit.: "storytellers."

4 "For obvious reasons": an elegant formula to skip the vital weakness of the truth claim staked out in this preface. If the dangers described in this novel were real, it would—for obvious reasons—be much wiser if the survivors would step forward to take the lead in a public campaign, aiming to completely eradicate such threats. For a further analysis, see my article *Dracula's Truth Claim and its Consequences* in the *Journal of Dracula Studies,* October 2014, pp. 53-80.

5 Dalby's translation omits the Icelandic word "stranga," which in this context can mean "solemn," "strict," "grave," or "serious." Cf. German and Dutch "streng."

6 The italics, emphasizing the authenticity of the novel's events, appear in the *Fjallkonan* serialization only, not in the 1901 book edition and later republications.

7 Dalby gives "in years to come." The Icelandic expression "þegar minnst varir" means "without any warning," "when we least expect it," "suddenly" or "unexpectedly."

8 A first hint at an altered plot, because in *Dracula* neither Scotland Yard nor the secret service perceives an inter-related pattern of crime.

9 Again: "sögufolkid."

10 Dalby proposes "at the same time," but in the Icelandic expression "á sínum tíma," "sínum" ("their") points back to the mentioned crimes, which took place *before* the Ripper murders. See also next footnote.

11 Dalby's translation states "… which came into the story a little later," suggesting that the Ripper murders will be featured—a little later—in this very novel. The Icelandic expression "ad koma til sögunnar," however, means "to occur," "to take place," or "to come into existence." Stoker's preface simply states that the Ripper murders took place *after* this incomprehensible series of crimes discussed in *Makt Myrkranna*, that is, the Thames Torso Murders. Bram Stoker was much more likely to be familiar with these Thames murders than Valdimar. Even if Valdimar knew that they were rumored to stem from the same root as the Ripper murders, it is highly improbable that he would insert a reference that his Icelandic readers would not be able to understand; the preface thus appears to be written by Stoker himself. See Introduction.

12 Dalby's translation gives "group of foreigners," although "group" is not mentioned in the Icelandic text.

13 In Dalby's text, the Icelandic "saman" is translated as "together," but "saman" relates to the seasons ("on end," "in a row"), not to the foreigners.

14 Icelandic: "annar þeirra," lit.: "the other one of them." Ásgeir Jónsson points out that this refers to the other of a *pair* (i.e. two), not to one of a *group*, and he suspects that a line articulating what this pair is may have been dropped from the preface.

15 Icelandic: "… án þess að nokkur merki hans *sæist* framar," lit.: "so that no signs of him was ever seen again." The 1950 and 2011 editions change "sæist" to "sæjust" ("were seen"). The final meaning stays the same.

16 Icelandic: "Allt það fólk, *sem sagt er*, …" Dalby's translation omits the relative clause.

17 The end of this novel mentions Dr. Seward's death; the preface—supposed to be written *after* the pictured events—does not match the plot in this point. See my Introduction essay.

18 Dalby's translation "… will also be too famous" could be understood to mean that this scientist is not famous yet, but will be so in future. The Icelandic auxiliary verb "munu" can express a probability in the future, in the present or even in the past. I have opted for the present

in certain points, of course, I have reached a different conclusion than the people who are recounting it here.[9] But the events as such are irrefutable, and so many people are aware of them that they will not be denied. This series of crimes has not yet passed from the public's memory—crimes which seem incomprehensible, but appear to stem from the same root and have created in their time[10] as much horror within the public as the infamous murders by Jack the Ripper, which occurred a short time later.[11] Some will still recall the remarkable foreigners[12] who for many seasons on end[13] played a dazzling role in the life of the aristocratic circles here in London, and people will probably remember that at least one of them[14] suddenly disappeared inexplicably, and that no trace of him was ever seen again.[15]

All the people who are said[16] to have played a part in this remarkable story—willingly or unwillingly—are widely known and well respected. Both Thomas Harker and his wife—who is an extraordinary woman—and Dr. Seward are my friends,[17] and have been so for many years, and I have never doubted that they would tell the truth; and the highly regarded scientist, who appears under a pseudonym here, may[18] likewise be too famous throughout the educated world for his real name—which I prefer not to mention[19]—to remain hidden from the public,[20] especially from those people who have learned firsthand[21] to appreciate and respect his brilliant mind[22] and masterly skill, though they no more adhere to his views on life than I do. But in our times it should be clear to all serious-thinking men that

"there are more things in heaven and earth
than are dreamt of in your philosophy."[23]

London, —Street, August 1898[24]

B. S.

here, because the word "likewise" places the famous scientist next to the Harkers and Dr. Seward, that is, in the category of people who are—presently—"widely known and well respected."

19 In his 1897 interview with Jane Stoddard, Stoker had already stated that the character of Professor Van Helsing was based on a real person (Stoddard, 1897, p. 185)—again an indication that this Icelandic preface was authored by Stoker himself, not Valdimar. Various role models have been proposed over the years: Dr. Gerard van Swieten (1700-1772), personal physician of Empress Maria Theresa of Austria; the Flemish physician and alchemist Johan Baptista van Helmont (1580-1644); Prof. Arminius Vámbéry from Budapest; Prof. Max Müller from Oxford; Prof. Moriz Benedikt from Vienna; and John Freeman Knott, a physician married to the sister of Florence Balcombe, Stoker's wife. Knott was a friend of Bram's brother Thornley, a highly renowned brain surgeon and a possible role model himself.

20 The interjection "which I prefer not to mention" is confusing and may lead readers to believe that this scientist is "famous for his real name"—just like Paris is famous for its Eiffel Tower. In fact, the text states that this scientist is *so* famous *that* his real name cannot remain hidden from the public.

21 Icelandic: "af reynslu," lit.: "from experience." This again indicates that the real Van Helsing is a friend, a personal acquaintance or at least a contemporary of Bram Stoker, like the Harkers and Dr. Seward, and thus excludes the long-deceased Van Swieten and Van Helmont—the only candidates who actually speak Dutch. In 2012, the biography of the Dutch filmmaker Tonny van Renterghem drew my attention to his grandfather, the psychiatrist Dr. Albert W. van Renterghem, whom his grandson claimed to have been the true role model for Stoker's protagonist. Together with the physician and writer Dr. Frederik van Eeden, Dr. van Renterghem had opened a clinic for hypnotic treatment in Amsterdam in 1887, which soon became internationally famous. I indeed discovered a whole network of interconnections, which makes it highly probable that Stoker was familiar with Van Renterghem's work and reputation. See my article in *De Parelduiker* of October 2012.

22 Icelandic: "snilld." Dalby's translation gives "genius," which is the first translation listed in modern dictionaries; Cleasby/Vigfússon, 1874, gives "masterly skill, eloquence" and "excellency of art, skill" as translations, referring to acquired skills or knowledge or great intellect rather than to the romantic concept of genius.

23 A quote from Shakespeare's play *Hamlet*, in which Prince Hamlet addresses Horatio. Instead of retranslating the Icelandic, I have reinstated Shakespeare's original text. Stoker's friend and employer, the actor Henry Irving, was famous for his performance as Prince Hamlet, so Stoker must have known these words by heart.

24 The date of August 1898 suggests that some of the most significant modifications of the novel must have been discussed between Bram Stoker and Valdimar Ásmundsson more than a year before the first installment was published in *Fjallkonan*: the appearance of "remarkable foreigners" in "London aristocratic circles," the reference to a series of horrible crimes causing public concern and finally the involvement of the secret police.

PART I

The Castle in the Carpathians[25]

25 *The Castle in the Carpathians* (*Le Château des Carpathes*) is also the name of an 1893 novel by Jules Verne, which may have inspired Stoker's description of Castle Dracula.

CHAPTER ONE

Thomas Harker's Journal[26]

(written in shorthand)

BISTRITZ, 3 MAY

FINALLY I ARRIVED HERE AFTER A SPEEDY JOURNEY ACROSS Europe by express train. Left Munich at 8:30 p.m. on the 1st of May, arrived in Vienna the next morning. From there to Budapest, a strange city, although I only saw a little of it. There it felt as though I were saying goodbye to the West and Western civilization, as Eastern culture came to the fore. I spent the night in Klausenburg; got there yesterday evening after dark and continued with the mail coach to the Borgo Pass this morning.[27] Today I have gone over hilly country, very different from the plains of Hungary. Here and there I could see a village or a castle on the hilltops, and, occasionally, the road crossed gushing rivers. At the coach stops I saw many rural people gathering, clad in all sorts of attire— I wish that I could have drawn some sketches of life here around me. Oddest of all do the Slovaks seem to me. They wear wide trousers with shirts overtop, and belts around the middle. Their hair falls to the shoulders and their eyes are black and fiery, which makes them look like bandits. Other than that, however, they seem harmless.

26 Stoker borrowed the surname "Harker" from Joseph Cunningham Harker, a set designer at the Lyceum Theatre.

27 The first deviation from the original story: in *Dracula*, Harker takes the train to Bistritz, not the mail coach.

WHILE I WAITED IN LONDON FOR ORDERS FROM MY employer, I did not forget to visit the British Museum to gain some knowledge about Transylvania from books and maps, as up to this point I knew next to nothing about it. I learned that my destination was in the eastern part of the country, somewhere up in the Carpathian Mountains, close to the borders between Transylvania, Moldavia and Bukovina[28]—in other words, in one of the wildest, least-known corners of Europe. As the maps they make in Transylvania cannot be compared to those created for the War Office[29] back home in England, I could not locate Castle Dracula on any of them. The post town is called Bistritz,[30] and the castle is close to the Borgo Pass.[31] Transylvania's population is a colorful mixture of varied nations, just like in Hungary—at least according to the experts at the British Museum. They say that the country is a melting pot of Germans, Vlachs, Magyars, Czechs, Slovaks, Gypsies, Slovenes, and God knows how many other diverse peoples.[32] Religions are nearly as numerous as ethnicities, and apart from that, the semicircle[33] of the Carpathians, so to speak, harbors all the superstitions and backwoods beliefs[34] of this world, along with plenty of obscure tales, archaic myths, and customs passed down over centuries.[35] Here the tribes met in ancient times, when they were still moving from place to place, and today, Western culture and the occultism of the East still intersect here, like two rivers meeting, forming a vortex where much of what has elsewhere long ago sunk deep into oblivion still

28 Between 1867 and 1920, Transylvania was a principality within the Hungarian empire, which had controlled it since medieval times. Bukovina had been annexed by the Habsburg Empire in 1775; only in 1918 was it reunited with Moldavia, of which it had been a part since the 14th century. Moldavia and Wallachia united under the name "Romania" in 1859. Following the defeat of the Ottomans in the Russo-Turkish War, Romania proclaimed sovereignty in 1877. The territory of modern Romania was formed only in 1920 (Treaties of Trianon and Paris), when Wallachia, Moldavia, Transylvania, Bukovina, and Bessarabia were united. During World War II, Romania was compelled to leave a part of the northern territories to the Soviet Union.

29 Icelandic: "herstjórnarráðuneytið." Up till 1964, the British Ministry of Defence was called "War Office." In 1855, the Board of Ordnance, traditionally in charge of Ordnance Survey mapping services, became a part of this War Office. In *Dracula* this sentence reads: "I was not able to light on any map or work giving the exact locality of the Castle Dracula, as there are no maps of this country as yet to compare with our own Ordnance Survey maps." In fact, the military maps of the Austro-Hungarian Empire, including Transylvania, were highly detailed, but not available to the public.

30 "Bistri a" in modern Romanian, a city in the northeast of Transylvania ("Nösnerland"), fortified and inhabited by Saxon (German-speaking) settlers after 1200.

31 From Bistritz, the road to the Borgo Pass (today known as "Tihu a Pass") went in a northeast direction. After the village of Maros-Borgo, the road continued up the mountain past the customs post of Tihucza where the Borgo Pass began, and gradually turned north until the border of Bukovina was reached at M gura Calului at a height of 1,117 m.

32 Transylvania was dominated by the Saxons, Magyars, and Szeklers, who in 1437 had proclaimed the Union of the Three Nations (*Unio Trium Nationum*). Although the Romanian-speaking people (named "Vlachs," "Wallacks," or "Wallachians") constituted the majority of the population, they were deprived of political rights; in *Dracula*, they are hardly mentioned. For an analysis of Stoker's "mythical Transylvania," see Cri an, 2013.

33 Reflecting the overall shape of the Carpathian Mountains, like *Dracula*'s term "horseshoe."

34 Icelandic: "*hjátrú og hindurvitni,*" a first example of alliteration in this novel. Alliterative rhyme had a strong tradition in the Old Icelandic *Poetic Edda* (13th century), a text that Valdimar was very familiar with.

35 Stoker knew about these topics from the article *Transylvanian Superstitions* by Emily Gerard, July 1885; other important sources on local traditions and history were the books by William Wilkinson, Charles Boner, Major E. C. Johnson, A. F. Crosse, and Elizabeth Mazuchelli (see list of references).

36 Icelandic: "*allur í lögfræðinni*"—this can also translate to "completely the lawyer." Perhaps coincidentally, in *Dracula* Harker calls himself "a full-blown solicitor" (Chapter 2, Journal of 5 May) while he is waiting in front of the gate of Castle Dracula.

37 Similarly, in *Dracula* the hotel is named "Golden Krone," which Stoker may have derived from *Baedeker's* description of Salzburg; the story originally was set in Styria. See Klinger, 2008, pp. 22f., note 42.

38 *Baedeker's Travel Guide for Austria*, 1896, tells us that the distance from Bistritz to Kimpolung (Câmpulung Moldovanesc) was 126 km, and could be covered by post coach in 17 hours. Klinger, 2008, p. 33, note 81.

39 This archaic sign-off is rarely used today, but we can find several examples of it in the letters of George Washington.

40 Stoker took the name "Dracula" from a book by Wilkinson about the history of Moldavia and Wallachia, but understood it as the denomination of a whole dynasty or clan. The Drăculeştis, named after Vlad II Dracul (a member in the Order of the Dragon), ruled over Wallachia. From the 1970s on, Professors Raymond McNally and Radu Florescu propagated the idea that Stoker had heard of the cruel reputation of Vlad III Dracula the Impaler, the son of Vlad II, and, with this in mind, had picked him as the model for his vampire character. In their book *Prince of Many Faces* (1989) they even presented a mistranslation of a medieval poem by Michael Beheim, who, according to them, describes Vlad III as drinking the blood of his enemies (see my article *The Great Dracula Swindle*, www.vamped.org of 26 May 2016). While the Count in his conversation with Harker actually refers to a voïvode whom we recognize as Vlad III, Stoker neither knew the name "Vlad" nor his bloodthirsty reputation. In Chapter 25 of *Dracula*, Van Helsing and Mina identify their enemy as "that other of his race who in a later age again and again brought his forces over the great river into Turkey-land." This might be a reference to Michael the Brave, on whom Stoker took notes from Wilkinson's book. In the novel itself, however, it appears as if Stoker preferred this "other" to remain anonymous (see my article *Bram Stoker's Vampire Trap*, Linköping University Electronic Press, 19 March 2012).

swirls near the surface—emerging when we least expect it. This is all very interesting, but unfortunately I am too much the lawyer,[36] and thus engaging in such studies—whether national or historical—is not my innate strength. Who knows, perhaps the Count could enlighten me on this subject?

The Count had sent me detailed instructions about how to organize my trip, recommending the *Golden Crown* guesthouse to me, which he believes to be the best place to stay in this area.[37] I followed his directions and soon found that they had been expecting me, for at the very entrance I was met by an old woman with a kind face, wearing an ordinary peasant dress. She bowed low and asked in more or less understandable German if I was "Mr. Englishman." I said that I was and told her my name. She looked at me closely and then said something to a man in the next room. He came at once with a letter in his hand, and I immediately recognized the Count's handwriting, which is very queer. It was written in English, just as were his letters to the lawyer's office in London where I work, and it read as follows:

"Dear Sir!
Welcome to the Carpathians. I am anxiously expecting you. At seven tomorrow evening the mail coach will leave from Bistritz for Bukovina, and I have booked you a fare on it.[38] I will have my carriage wait in the Borgo Pass to bring you to my home. I hope that you have not strained yourself too much during the journey, and that you will enjoy your visit to our beautiful country as you are bound to stay here for both our benefits, and am your friend,[39]

Dracula."[40]

All of this sounds fine. I am growing curious, as it's not every day one meets a Hungarian—or rather, Transylvanian—nobleman[41] who lives in an old castle in some deserted mountains at the end of the civilized world, yet writes letters in flawless English with all the urbanity of cultivated scholars, while negotiating with solicitors and real estate agents to buy a house in the heart of London.[42] Such a man must be remarkable.

41 Both in *Dracula* and *Makt Myrkranna*, the Count calls himself a Szekler and claims that the blood of Atilla runs through his veins; the Szeklers lived in the eastern part of Transylvania and spoke Hungarian. There are at least three different theories why Stoker introduced a noble with a Wallachian name but a Ugric origin. See also note 134.

42 Stoker's notes of 14 March 1890 also mention "the purchase of London estate"; in the typed manuscript (1897), Plaistow (eastern suburb of London) was replaced by Purfleet in Essex, 20 km farther east. See Klinger, 2008, p. 483, note 8. *Makt Myrkranna* shifts the action back to London itself—maybe based on Stoker's original ideas.

BISTRITZ, 4 MAY

I COULDN'T SLEEP LAST NIGHT, AS I WOULD HAVE NEEDED to after such a trip, because it was as if all the town's dogs had agreed to meet under my window and howl, letting all hell break loose. Eventually I became so tired that sleep overcame me, but I awoke shortly thereafter when I heard something scratch at the window. I raised the curtain and saw that a bat had landed on the window sill, but it flew away just as I approached it.[43] The barking and howling were no better than before, so I couldn't peacefully sleep again before dawn.

When we sat down for breakfast, the hotel owner told me he had received a letter from the Count requesting he see to it that I get the best seat in the carriage. He had included money for the ticket, too. I tried to ask the owner and his wife about the Count, but they were more than reluctant to tell me anything about him, except that he was rich—or was said to be rich—and that they had only seen him in passing, but he rarely came into town, and so on. To be honest, I barely understood the poor German they spoke.

When I told them about the barking dogs and the bat, I noticed that they glanced at each other and crossed themselves furtively. Superstition is deeply rooted in this country and I regret not being able to learn more about these people and their way of thinking. It would be interesting to explore the simpleminded beliefs that are so alive around here, although modern people—like myself—would just call them old wives' tales, as they are remnants of pagan thinking, attesting to the customs of a bygone era.

43 In *Dracula*, bats only appear in the Whitby, Hillingham and Purfleet scenes, representing the vampire Count in disguise. "The early bat catches the worm," the author(s) of *Makt Myrkranna* must have thought.

45 Icelandic: "hefði verið ættfylgja," lit.: "had been the ghost of the family." In Old Norse mythology, "fylgja" is a spirit attached to a person or family, influencing their fate or fortune; it may appear in the form of an animal, mostly during sleep. A related concept is that of the "hamingja" (Old Norse: "luck"), which also personifies the luck or fate of a person or family.

Later on I met a Saxon teacher who spent part of the day showing me the town. When I asked him about Count Dracula he was surprised to hear that I was going to meet the Count and stay with him for a fortnight, because—he told me—the Count was known to live in seclusion, avoiding all people, and never had he heard of the Count inviting anyone to his home. "There will certainly be many stories about him," I said, "as men tend to taunt those who don't tie their bundles the same way as their fellow travellers."[44] He said it was true that much was rumored about the Count, but no reasonable person would put trust in such blathering. Other than that, he had nothing to say about the Count, except that he was born of the greatest and oldest family in the country, of which—due to the innate qualities of their kin[45]—the men were the bravest and the women the most beautiful, throughout the centuries the subjects of poetic lore. He didn't know whether the Count had children, but he had been married three times and had lost all of his wives.[46]

When I returned to the guesthouse to prepare for my departure, the landlady, who seemed very distressed, came to me and said,

"Are you seriously going?"

She was so upset that she completely forgot what little German she knew and jabbered away in another language of which I didn't understand a single word. When I told her that I had to go because I had an important business deal to finalize, she stared at me before asking solemnly,

"Then you don't know what day it is today?"

I said that it was the fourth of May—as it was—but she shook her head, saying,

"Yes, I know that, too, but do you know what *kind* of day it is?"

I had to tell her that I didn't understand her point, at which she answered me with urgency, saying,

"But what part of the world are you from, you poor young man, that you don't know it is the eve of St. George's Day,[47] when all the evil spirits are at large!"[48]—and now she crossed herself—"Do you know where you are going . . . and what could happen to you there? Believe an old lady who wishes you well. Don't depart until morning; it's a sin to tempt God and throw yourself into perdition." Tears streamed down her cheeks, and in an instant she was down on her knees, gesticulating before me and begging me in the name of the Holy Virgin Mary—and a number of other holy men whose saintly deeds I am actually not familiar with—not to leave within the next two days. To tell the truth, I was beginning to feel uncomfortable while she carried on like this, but I don't believe in such prattle, of course. I got her to stand up, wiped her tears and then told her sternly that I had to go—it was my duty. When she got ahold of herself she took a rosary from her bosom and handed it to me. I didn't know what to do; like any English Churchman,[49] I have been taught disdain for such holy toys since childhood, but I didn't want to offend this dear old woman. When she saw that I was wavering, she ended the discussion by putting the rosary around my neck, and with a quivering voice she said, "Do it for your mother's sake."

Having said this, she left.

Superstition is contagious like the plague. I do not feel well. I have now been writing this to compose myself while I wait for the mail coach, as it is delayed. It vexes me that the Count's horses will have to wait, too. I will now write a letter to my Wilma,[50] which will probably surprise her. — — —

47 Harker does not suspect that he is travelling during the Romanian St. George's Eve. Because the Eastern Orthodox Church in Transylvania still used the Julian Calendar, its St. George's Day (23 April) would coincide with the date of 5 May in England (Gregorian Calendar). Stoker took notes on these calendar differences. See Eighteen-Bisang & Miller, 2008, p. 25; p. 121; p. 93, footnote 200.

48 Icelandic: "leika lausum hala," lit.: "play with a free tail," derived from the *Poetic Edda*, *Lokasenna* (*Loki's Wrangling*), verse 49: "Lightly said, Loki! | But too long it won't last | That your tail freely plays | As on this peak, with the guts | Of your own ice-cold son | The gods will bind you." (my translation). Like the evil spirits the landlandy fears, the god Loki represents malice and deceit in Scandinavian mythology; in many aspects, he resembles the suave but spiteful Count Dracula in *Makt Myrkranna*.

49 Icelandic: "rétttrúuðum," lit.: "of the true creed," which would translate to "orthodox." To avoid confusion with the Roman-Orthodox religion practiced by the Vlachs in Transylvania, I have deferred to Stoker's original term "English Churchman."

50 Like *Dracula*'s "Mina," the name "Wilma" (Icelandic: "Vilma"), is derived from "Wilhelmina," the full name of Harker's fiancée. According to the 1891 census, "Minna" was the name of a governess living in the household of Bram's brother George at 14 Hertford Street in London.

CASTLE DRACULA, 5 MAY,
IN THE MORNING

I T'S BROAD DAYLIGHT OUTSIDE AND IT IS FOUR O'CLOCK in the morning.[51] I haven't gone to bed yet but am wide awake; I wouldn't be able to sleep now, so I might as well write instead, as the Count has said that I can rest as long as I want after my travels.

When I stepped into the mail coach that was to take me to the Borgo Pass, the driver had not yet come to his seat, as he was palavering with the landlady and some of the other villagers. It seemed as though the people were talking about me, and they were looking at me with expressions of surprise and compassion. As I only caught a few scattered words, I took my dictionary out of my pocket and looked up the ones I could make out best. They were not very pleasant: words such as *devil, hell, monster* and other such "nice" expressions were thrown around, and I suspected they related to my prospective host, the Count. When we departed, a crowd of people had gathered at the guesthouse, making the sign of the cross with two outstretched fingers and pointing to me, me who—innocent as a child—had done nothing wrong. I asked one of my fellow travellers who spoke German the reason for this, and he said that the people meant me no harm. Quite the contrary: they meant me well and were praying for me! Then the coachman struck the horses and I soon forgot all their blessings and ill-forebodings as I began to watch the scenery. The hills spread out before us, everywhere grassy and wooded, and on the slopes we saw farms with their windowless

51 An observation perhaps based on Icelandic daylight hours: On 5 May, twilight starts before 3:00 a.m. in Reykjavik (natural local time). In Bistritz, dawn would have come at 5:30 a.m.

52 In *Dracula*, Stoker explains that the Transylvanian rulers would abstain from repairing the roads too quickly, to avoid suspicion that they were preparing for war.

53 Stoker's dramatic description of the Borgo Mountains was actually derived from the travel journal by Major E. C. Johnson, reporting on his trip through the much steeper Bicaz Pass, approx. 60 km south of the Borgo Pass.

gables facing the road. Along the coach route, which lay in countless curves between the hillocks, I noticed an apple tree in bloom and many other fruit trees. The driver maneuvered the horses as if his life depended on it, over rocks and through potholes; road repairs, which are always to be done in spring, hadn't yet been made, leaving the track in bad condition.[52]

Beyond the hills the rocky peaks of the Carpathians towered over the dark woods.[53] They were soon surrounding us, glowing in the sunlight with the richest of colors, while in the distance we could discern blue-white glaciers. We came across farmers in motley attire, and I witnessed many sights I had never seen before, such as haystacks being put up in the treetops to dry.

With darkness drawing near it was getting much colder. We even caught glimpses of snow in the ravines and passes. Sometimes the road was so steep that I wanted to get out and walk, as we would in England, but the driver flatly refused, saying, "No, by all means, do not step out of the carriage, it's not safe here—wild dogs," and so, except for when he turned on the carriage lights, he didn't stop once. The darker it became, the greater the apprehension that seemed to engulf my travel companions as they spoke to the coachman, and from what I understood, they were asking him to make haste— which he did, brutally snapping his whip at the horses like the worst butcher and whistling very high from time to time, hurrying them on even more.

UDDENLY THE SKY CLEARED AHEAD OF US, AS IF THE mountains had opened up, and yet they became even steeper on both sides. My fellow travellers now became even more tense than they already were. The road was better here and the ride continued at an even more tearing pace than before, such that I had to hold myself in order not to be thrown around in the carriage. I am no coward, but it seemed crazy to rush on like this in the dark. I was then told that we were galloping up the Borgo Pass, and as if to make this event more ceremonious, my travel companions started giving me odd gifts, such as rose tree branches, rowan twigs, white flowers, crucifixes, and other small trinkets. I didn't have the heart to refuse them, but little by little I tried to get rid of most of them, as I could not see how they would be of any use to me. I did, however, understand that they were meant to protect me against the attacks and cunning tricks of the Evil One. The carriage rushed forward with the same breakneck speed as before, and all the while my companions wriggled in their seats as if sitting on hot coals, looking around us in all directions, which eventually made me nervous as well. I asked them if there was anything to fear, but they answered me with some balderdash, or muttered phrases I didn't understand. As the road began to descend from the pass, the driver pulled on the reins and we stopped. Although it was still behind the mountains, the moon had risen, illuminating our surroundings.

I started to worry whether or not the Count had even

54 As carriages were rare in ancient Iceland, the word "vagn" covers all kinds of vehicles. In *Dracula*, Stoker uses "calèche," a word borrowed from Wilkinson, 1820. I have re-introduced this term here, to distinguish the Count's lighter vehicle from the heavy stagecoach or the transport carriages later used by the Slovaks.

55 In *Dracula*, it is one of Stoker's fellow travellers who quotes Burger's *Lenore* in German by saying: "Denn die Todten reiten schnell" ("For the dead travel fast"). The same quote is used in *Dracula's Guest*, engraved on the tomb of Countess Dolingen-von Gratz.

56 In *Dracula*, the coach driver tells his passengers that they had covered the distance to the agreed meeting point in "an hour less than the time"—obviously, he had been speeding in order to arrive well before the Count's driver so as to offer the Englishman an excuse to continue to Bukovina.

sent his carriage for me, as the coachman insisted that no one would come. He advised me to go back to the village with him and to return tomorrow or some other day.

While we were discussing this, the horses became skittish and began to prick their ears, whinnying and rearing, and the coachman struggled to keep hold of them. My companions shouted, called for the saints, crossed themselves and grabbed their crucifixes.

In the midst of this chaos, an antiquated calèche, drawn by four splendid pitch black stallions, drove up to us.[54] Their harnesses were adorned with silver and seemed as though they belonged in a history museum rather than on those magnificent animals. The driver was tall and had a large black beard. He was not in uniform, but in some sort of national dress, and wore a wide-brimmed felt hat on his head, so that only the lower part of his face was visible. I noticed, however, that his eyes seemed red in the lamplight. I have seen such eyes on other people, but it always makes an eerie impression. As I already felt rather beat up after the tiresome journey and conversation with my companions, I would have preferred this new escort of mine to be less peculiar.

"You have been travelling fast this evening, my friend," the stranger said to our driver in German.[55]

"The English gentleman was in a hurry."

"And so you have advised him to return with you; I hear well and am not easily fooled. Besides, I have swift horses."[56]

He laughed out loud, so that his teeth shone white as snow.

"Give me the luggage of the gracious lord," he said, and with the help of all my travel companions, my baggage was transferred to the other carriage in the wink of an eye. Then I stepped out of the mail coach and the driver lifted me up into the calèche, rather forcefully. In an instant, the man got in his seat and grabbed hold of the reins, and we dashed off. I looked back and saw that my fellow travellers had stepped out of the carriage to see us better—still crossing themselves.

When they were out of sight, some sort of horror struck me, and I felt all alone—as if I had left the civilized world and entered a realm of darkness, where anything could happen. The superstitions of my companions had unduly impacted me, and I had to employ all my common sense and self-control to pull myself together. I kept telling myself that I was no adventurer wrestling with ghosts and demons but the steady Thomas Harker—a candidate for the bar with good testimony, currently an assistant at the law firm of Peter Hawkins, Esq.,[57] who had sent me to Count Dracula in Transylvania to finalize his real estate purchase in London. I was also thinking about my fiancée, Wilma; I had just written her a letter, and as I brought her and our home life to mind my mood improved and I became composed once more. I began to look forward to exploring unknown paths at the Count's place. As I lit a cigar, the calèche suddenly stopped. The driver left his seat, came over to me, and spread a fur over my feet and knees. He also wrapped me in a pelt coat above the waist and said in good German:

"It's chilly in the mountains tonight, and the gracious Count told me that I should make sure you would not be cold. There is a bottle of plum liqueur under the seat, if you need to warm yourself."

I thanked him, and he went back to his seat to steer the horses.

I was about to doze off when it felt as though the carriage suddenly turned around. This was probably just my imagina-

57 In the Icelandic text, Mr. Hawkins is mostly referred to as "Hawkins málaflutningsmaður." Zoëga, 1922, lists "lawyer; solicitor, attorney; barrister." As already described in *Hrafnkels Saga* (10th century), "mála-flutningur" pertains to the conduct of a suit, originally before the General Assembly at Þingvellir. After 1873, the title would thus more specifically translate to "Solicitor of the Supreme Court of England and Wales." In the rest of the story, I have avoided repeating Mr. Hawkins's title. According to Davies, 1997, p. 133, the name "Hawkins" was borrowed from Anthony Hope Hawkins, author of *Prisoner of Zenda* (1894).

tion, but it felt very real to me. A short while later I lit a match and looked at my watch—it was a few minutes to twelve. I began to remember some of the things the landlady at the inn had told me, but I laughed it off, tightened the mantle around me, and tried to sleep.

But as soon as I closed my eyes I heard dogs barking from a farm nearby, and some time later from another direction, and then again from the distance, until the whole air, near and far, resounded with whining and barking, growing louder as the winds grew stronger. I could not sleep now, the more so as the horses were beginning to stir. The driver calmed them by speaking to them in a soothing voice, saying something to them that I didn't understand. The wind was growing more violent, and nothing could be heard but the rushing of the forest and the occasional hooting of owls in the treetops. Then the barking came again, followed by a ferocious howling that instantly terrified me.

"What is that?" I asked the driver.

"It's wolves, sir; wolves here in the mountains," he said. "They are out tonight, but you can rest easy. To *us*—they do nothing."

The horses, however, seemed to be of a different opinion, as they were now becoming unruly, kicking back as if they were afraid. I saw that the driver had to muster all of his tremendous strength in order to keep them under control. The calèche nearly tipped over, which would have thrown me out into the gorge that I suspected was beside the road. I was prepared to jump out to safety, but the driver finally managed to settle the horses so that he could dismount the calèche and get to them. He stroked them and whispered to them, like horse tamers do, and soon they were meek as lambs. The driver took his seat again and we continued.

Not much later we came out of the woods and were moving alongside enormously high cliffs. There we were sheltered from the gale, but I noticed that the storm was still building up, and it was not long before the weather became murderous.[58] The barking from the valley we had crossed was faint now, but the sound of wolves was much louder than before and could be heard all around us.

I was not scared, but I was not at ease either. I wished I had some rifles with me, as I would have liked to give my Wilma two or three wolf furs as a wedding present. I had to laugh to myself when I thought of the hunters I knew, who would have been grateful to be granted a month's stay in this area.[59]

Suddenly I noticed that the driver was scanning the forest in all directions, and as I watched more closely I saw something like a bluish flame flicker not far from us in the woods. The driver had obviously noticed it too. He jumped from the carriage and took off into the forest. It seemed that this glimmer was close to the road, and I could clearly see what the driver was doing: he was building a cairn.[60] – – –

It felt as if I had fallen asleep for a moment when I realized that the calèche had halted.[61] The driver was away, longer than he had been before, and after a few moments the horses became restless. This puzzled me, especially as there was nothing to be heard from the wolves. Soon the horses were so unruly that I took hold of the reins myself and was about to leave the carriage to better handle them—but then the moon came out, and all of a sudden I saw four, five, six large *wolves* sneaking down the road with gaping snouts and sagging tongues. In a flurry, I reached into my pocket for my revolver, but I had put it into my carpetbag that morning.[62] I had nothing to defend myself

58 Icelandic: "aftakaveður," mostly translated as "violent storm." The literal meaning: "murder-weather."

59 Actually, the Borgo Pass region was very popular for bear hunting during Stoker's time — see Tsérnatony, 1902, pp. 256ff, and the hunting statistics given by Boner, 1865, p. 155.

60 A pile of stones used to indicate a border, a path or a certain spot. The Icelandic expression "hverfa út í" is mostly used when someone dissolves or vanishes into the night, into the fog, into the blue, etc. It is curious that Harker could still see clearly what the driver was doing in the forest.

61 In *Dracula*, all characters driving to Castle Dracula from the Borgo Pass fall asleep during their trip, such that their route cannot be exactly reconstructed from their diaries. Perhaps, Stoker wished to obscure the castle's true location, which I contend is on Mount Izvorul C limanului, ca. 25 km (beeline) southeast of the Borgo Pass (see my book *The Ultimate Dracula*, 2012). *Makt Myrkranna* omits the last part of *Dracula*, in which the vampire hunters pursue the Count through Moldavia back to his stronghold, so that decisive clues about the castle's location are missing in the Icelandic version.

62 In *Dracula's* Transylvanian episode, Harker is unarmed; later he fights with the kukri knife.

63 Icelandic: "við erum bráðum komnir heim," lit.: "we will soon be back home." The Icelandic text repeatedly uses "að koma heim" in the sense of "to arrive."

64 See footnote 61.

with but the whip, which I could hardly use, as I was having enough trouble handling the horses. Unwilling to sit idle, I yelled "Hello" as loud as I could, so that it echoed through the forest; the wolves didn't seem to like it. Then I heard the driver saying something I didn't understand, and when I looked to the side I saw him gesture to them, at which they shamefully crept away with drooping tails.

"How could you leave the carriage in a situation like this?" I shouted to the driver. "We nearly had an accident. I could hardly cope with the horses much longer."

"I told you there was nothing to fear, even if the horses are young and inexperienced—I am an old hunter. The wolves will do *us* no harm. You saw how I drove them away. I know how to deal with them, they do not dare attack me. There are, however, much worse things in the woods when it's dark like this. Try to sleep; we will soon be at the castle."[63]

I let this be a lesson and I am sure I must have fallen asleep.[64] When the calèche halted once more, the moonlight had become clear and I saw that we had arrived at a large courtyard, fenced in by a high wall, which in some places had started to crack.

7 MAY, MORNING

I WILL CONTINUE WHERE I LEFT OFF WRITING ABOUT THE events of the last few days.[65]

Although I have not yet seen it in daylight, the courtyard of the castle seems unusually large to me.

Upon arrival here at the castle, the driver helped me out of the calèche, and again I saw what a hellishly large fellow[66] he was. I am more than six feet tall[67] and of matching build, but I felt as though he could toss me away like a glove. He took my luggage from the calèche and put it down beside me. Ahead of me was a stone staircase leading up to an ornamental gate.

The driver tugged on the bell rope and the sound reverberated in the distance. Then he jumped onto the calèche, struck the horses, and in an instant disappeared through some passageway in the walls.

From the castle no sound could be heard, nor could light be seen in the windows. As I stood there kicking my heels, I considered waking up the residents by banging on the door when I heard footsteps on the stone floor inside, and then the gate opened.

An old woman appeared, wearing what seemed like national Hungarian dress—or the attire of some other nation found in this region. She bowed, looking at me with a strange smile, which gave me the impression that she was deaf and dumb—as was later confirmed.[68] But I didn't take too much notice of her, as I soon spotted the man behind her—who drew all my attention.

65 In *Dracula,* the following events are still part of Harker's Journal Entry of 5 May (continued).

66 Icelandic "heljarmaður" literally means "a man from Hell": a brute, a strongman, a muscleman.

67 Lit.: "full three ells high." Since the 13th century, the Icelandic ell ("alin") had been identical with the "lögalin" ("law-ell," approx. 49.2 cm). By the beginning of the 16th century, the Hamburg ell (57.8 cm) was adopted, until it was replaced by the Danish ell (62.5 cm) in 1776, so that Harker was at least 187.5 cm (6 ft 1 in) tall. In this novel, I have converted all ells to feet.

68 This character is unique to the Icelandic version, but in Stoker's preparatory notes, there is also mention of a deaf and mute female servant of the Count.

69 Galloons are woven trims, mostly used to decorate uniforms. The German equivalent is "Tresse," related to the English word "tress" ("braid," "lock of hair").

70 In *Dracula*: "Welcome to my house! Enter freely and of your own will!" and later: "Welcome to my house. Come freely. Go safely; and leave something of the happiness you bring!" The Icelandic version condenses these formulas. Stoker introduces the idea that a potential victim must enter the vampire's territory voluntarily.

71 Icelandic: "hvíldar og hressingar," another alliteration.

He was tall and old with white hair and a long white moustache. He, too, was wearing some kind of folk costume, dark and trimmed with galloons.[69] He held an old silver lamp in his hand, and even before I had reached the top of the staircase, he greeted me very politely in fluent, slightly accented English, saying,

"Welcome to my house! Enter freely and merrily."[70]

As I stepped over the threshold he grasped my hand tightly. His grip was so forceful that it made me wince, especially because his hand was so cold, and the chill shot right to the bone. He then welcomed me again, and although I presumed that this was my prospective client, I felt compelled to ask,

"Count Dracula?"

He nodded and replied in a friendly tone,

"I am Dracula. Yes, please be welcome, Mr. Harker; I have eagerly been awaiting your arrival. But you are tired and cold—you have travelled a long way in the night and you are not used to such journeys. You could do with some rest and refreshments."[71]

He motioned to the old woman and she rushed out to fetch my luggage.

AMP IN HAND, THE COUNT LED ME TO AN IRON-SHOD door, which he opened wide. We entered a well-lit living room, where the table had already been set and a fire was burning in the fireplace.

The Count went into a windowless octagonal chamber, where he opened a further door, inviting me into a large room—this would be my bedroom. On the table stood two lit wax candles in silver candlesticks, while another fire was crackling cosily in the open hearth.

"You are tired," said the Count. "I assume you'll want to tidy yourself up a bit before you eat, so I shall wait for you in the living room."

I did as he said and then hurried back to the living room.

Dinner was on the table and the Count offered me a seat. "Please, eat whatever you like, but you must excuse me for not joining you, for I have had dinner already."

I handed him the letter from my employer, Mr. Hawkins. He read it and handed it back to me with a genial smile. I, too, enjoyed the letter, as it stated:

"Sir Count,[72]
I am terribly sorry for not personally tending to you, but I am suffering from gout, which for some time forbids me to make any journeys. Fortunately, I can send someone else in my place; someone whom I fully trust as a reliable, hard-working and energetic man. He is a young but very promising lawyer whom

72 In *Dracula*, Harker addresses his client simply as "Count." In *Makt Myrkranna*, Hawkins and Harker use "Sir Count" ("Herra greifi")—a phrase found in many 19th century novels (Scott, Dickens). What is quoted here as a complete letter is, in *Dracula*, only a passage from it. I have inserted "for not personally tending to you" to avoid the impression of impoliteness.

73 This phrase combines *Dracula*'s description of the peppered *paprika hendl*, which Harker enjoyed at the *Hotel Royale* in Klausenburg, with the qualities of the "excellent roast chicken" served in Castle Dracula.

74 Tokay (Tokaj) is the center of a famous wine region in northern Hungary, between the rivers Bodrog and Hernád. Louis XV of France praised the Tokay wine as "The Wine of Kings; the King of Wines."

75 Lit.: "was like paradise-food in my mouth."

76 Canines: incisor teeth. For Stoker, these teeth seemed to be a special sign of animalistic power: "Tennyson had at times that lifting of the upper lip which shows the canine tooth, and which is so marked an indication of militant instinct. Of all the men I have met the one who had this indication most marked was Sir Richard Burton." "As [Burton] spoke the upper lip rose and his canine tooth showed its full length like the gleam of a dagger." See Stoker, 1907, pp. 130 and 229.

I have known since he was a boy, and he now works as an assistant in my law firm. I can absolutely guarantee that his proficiency in this field is excellent, and that he is silent as the grave. You may therefore discuss with him any legal particulars regarding the planned real estate purchase. I have informed him well, but to prepare for this journey he has also acquired a great deal of the necessary knowledge himself. Therefore, I highly recommend him, and am yours with humble respect,

Peter Hawkins."

The Count lifted the lid of the tray on the table and again invited me to sit down. I didn't need to be told a third time, and without further delay I began to eat. Although it was quite peppered, it was the best chicken fillet I have ever had.[73] There was also a good salad, cheese, bread and butter, and an old bottle of sweet Tokay wine,[74] which all tasted ambrosial[75]— as famished as I was. The exhaustion lifted from me, and when my client, presenting me with a cigar, offered me an armchair by the fireplace, I became so comfortable that I could have talked with him all night.

The Count sat right up against the light, directly in front of the fireplace, giving me a good vantage point to observe him. With eyes that lay deep beneath his beetle-brows and a nose like a vulture's beak, his features appeared very harsh. He had a domed forehead peering out from the grey hair that ran down onto his shoulders; a white moustache that covered his mouth, in which I detected a hardness, or even cruelty, that disappeared when he spoke or laughed; impeccable teeth, except for his unusually long canines;[76] and white and elegant hands, though hairier than any man's I have ever seen.

We talked about anything and everything,[77] including my journey to the castle and current political issues, about which he was very well informed. We also briefly touched upon the purpose of my trip, but he said that we would discuss it the next day.

There was a pause in our conversation, and when I cast a glance out the window I saw that dawn was breaking. All was quiet, until suddenly I heard the rushing sound of wolves. It was as though a streak of lightning flickered in the Count's eyes, which glistened like a carrion bird's.

"Hear, hear," he said, "the children of the night—what tuneful tones!"[78] I thought the sounds were horrible, but he laughed gently and said, "Oh, dear Sir! You city dwellers cannot understand the sentiments of an old hunter."[79]

Then he stood up, saying, "You must be tired; I beg your pardon for keeping you awake this long. Your bedroom is ready and you may go to bed whenever you please. Feel free to sleep until after noon—you must rest yourself. It just so happens that I have to leave the castle and will probably not return until evening. You may be at ease. Sleep well and have pleasant dreams."

He opened the door and bowed courteously, and I bid him good night, but I didn't sleep until the sun had already risen high.

After waking up rather late in the day,[80] I reviewed what had happened the day before and chuckled at how adventurous my travel story would sound to Wilma when I came home.

I began looking around the bedroom. The bed curtains were made of heavy old silk and there were very expensive-looking tapestries on the walls. As for the furniture, one couldn't get by with less than what was present; nevertheless, all the

77 Icelandic: "um alla heima og geima," lit.: "about all worlds and spaces," about things that are within reach and things which are out of reach.

78 Icelandic: "Þvílíkir tónar!"—an alliteration.

79 The Count calls himself "an old hunter," just like the driver of the calèche. In *Dracula*, Harker soon suspects that they are the same person.

80 In *Dracula*, Harker's Journal of 7 May starts here.

81 In *Dracula*, this paragraph points to the absence of mirrors, as vampires do not cast a reflection in the mirror: "There are certainly odd deficiencies in the house, considering the extraordinary evidences of wealth which are round me. The table service is of gold [...] but still in none of the rooms is there a mirror. There is not even a toilet glass on my table, and I had to get the little shaving glass from my bag before I could either shave or brush my hair."

82 The shortened form "D-a" might point to a hastily jotted, almost illegible signature.

83 Icelandic: "gullgerðarlist," lit.: "the art of goldmaking." The secret art of alchemy dealt with turning worthless materials such as lead into gold.

furnishings appear to be precious and antique. The wash-bowl, for example, was unusually small but made of solid gold.[81]

When I was dressed and ready I went into the room where I had dined the night before. It was a big hall with more tapestries on the walls. Cold food and wine were on the table, and as I came nearer I saw that it had only been set for one person. The Count had left me a note on the table, reading,

"I will be away from home for most of the day, but hope that you shall kindly forgive me for this impoliteness, which I cannot help. If you could arrange all your documents, we can talk upon my return.

Much obliged, your D–a"[82]

After I had eaten—the meal was good, though seasoned and cooked in a different way than I'm used to—I looked for a bell to call the servants but found nothing of the sort. I then tried to open the door to the corridor and was surprised to find it locked. Strange are the habits of this house.

All was silent as the grave. I looked out the window and saw the old woman from the night before fetching water. It was between four and five o'clock, so I went back to my bedroom and began looking through and sorting the papers relating to the property purchase. Then I returned to the dining room and tried to open two of the other doors, but they were also solidly locked. The third door, however, was unbolted and led to a large corner room where the sun shone in. As I entered, I saw that it was the Count's library. There were large shelves with books—some still handwritten, and some very old—that seemed to cover topics such as astrology, alchemy[83] and magic of the Middle Ages; they were written in various languages that I didn't understand, but what surprised me most was the large collection of English volumes I found—old and new, covering a variety of subjects, from poetry, old tales and sagas, to scientific publications and ordinary reference books. Markings and reader comments showed that all of them had been read. On the table lay English newspapers and magazines.

I began to entertain myself with the books and sat with them until the sun went down. The sunset was the most glorious I have ever seen—incomparable to any I have enjoyed in other places, except perhaps in the Highlands of Scotland.[84] But when the sun sank beneath the horizon, everything changed in a heartbeat; the air became cold and moisture-laden, while the colors faded under the pale shimmer of the rising moon. The swallows disappeared and in their place came bats, which are plentiful around here. One flew in through the window, and as I am disgusted by these creatures I hurried to close it.[85]

When I looked back from the window I was startled—I was not alone. It was dusk now, and although it was not as bright as day, the moon shone through the window, casting light onto the scene.

At the table in the middle of the room stood a woman, slender and dressed in light colors. She rested one hand on a chair near the table, and with the other she held a shawl to her shoulder. She was young and fair-skinned, and she seemed to be looking at me with curiosity.

I bowed and said in my best German,

"Please forgive me, Miss—I was expecting the Count."[86]

As I said this, she moved closer to me and replied in German, with traces of an exotic accent, "You are the foreigner we were expecting. Be welcome. It is lonely in the castle; lonely in these mountains."

Her voice was curiously clear. It felt as though the sound of her words pierced my every nerve, but I was not sure

84 In *Dracula*, there is no reference to sunsets in Scotland, but while preparing his novel, Stoker and his family used to spend holidays in Cruden Bay, near Aberdeenshire; Stoker's *The Mystery of the Sea* (1902) was set here.

85 In *Dracula*, there are no bats in or near the castle. *Makt Myrkranna* seems to anticipate the 1931 Universal Pictures movie *Dracula* (Tod Browning, dir.), in which a large bat hovers outside the open window of the castle.

86 In all conversations, the honorific form "þér" ("ye") is used. Today, this form is as good as extinct in Iceland—as in Britain. To avoid an archaic rendering, I have used the modern "you" (which originally also was honorific).

87 The original text uses "feber," in quotation marks—the word is used in Danish, Swedish and Norwegian, not in Icelandic. The 2011 text uses "hitasótt."

88 In *Dracula*, Harker meets with three vampire girls, the blonde, blue-eyed one being the most provocative; *Makt Mykranna* singles her out from the group and assigns her a major role in this Transylvanian episode.

89 This could refer either to Joséphine de Beauharnais (1763-1814), the wife of Napoleon I, or to her eldest granddaughter, Joséphine of Leuchtenberg (1807-1876), Queen consort of Sweden and Norway. The dresses of their time would show more skin than those of Victorian England.

90 Icelandic: "skygðum" (1900 and 1901) or "skyggðum" (2011). In modern dictionaries, the verb "að skyggja" is translated as "to darken" or "to overshadow," but both the 1874 and the 1922 dictionaries still give the meaning "to polish." Accordingly, the 1874 dictionary lists "skyggðr" as "bright, polished, transparent, so as to throw a light." Similarly, the 1922 dictionary lists "skygður" as "polished, bright" and "óskygður" as "not polished."

91 Icelandic: "það kemur sér […] betur," the comparative form of "það kemur sér vel" ("that comes in handy"), is used to indicate a preferable situation. Unfortunately, the text does not explain why or for whom Harker's good looks are advantageous. Maybe a double entendre is meant: "að koma sér vel" means "to make oneself popular," especially with the other sex.

92 The plural "our" might be a *pluralis majestatis*, also mentioned in *Dracula* with regard to the Count: "Whenever he spoke of his house he always said 'we,' and spoke almost in the plural, like a king speaking." The girl starts her sentence with "I," however. Moreover, the *pluralis majestatis* is hardly ever used in traditional Icelandic. The "our" could either refer to the girl and the Count, both inhabiting the same castle, or to possible "vampire sisters," or it could suggest an unmentioned partner.

whether it was a pleasant or unpleasant feeling. All I knew was that she caressed some strings within me that before had been untouched, and it flustered me quite a bit. I felt my heartbeat quicken, as if I had a fever.[87]

I'm not quick to be overcome by women—in fact I'm considered rather impassive and reserved, and since I was a boy I have never loved anyone else but my Wilma. But as I watched this woman while she spoke to me, I couldn't take my eyes off her.

She stood in front of me in the moonlight, and I couldn't recall ever seeing a girl of such breathtaking beauty. I won't provide a detailed description, as words can do her no justice, but she had golden-blonde hair, which was bound in a chignon. Her eyes: blue and large.[88] Her dress resembled those worn by beauty icons from the turn of the century—like Queen Josephine[89]—with her neck and upper chest revealed. Around her neck she wore a necklace of glittering[90] diamonds.

"You admire the view," she said. "They say that our mountains are beautiful. Indeed they are. But they are so barren, so barren. Here one lives like a prisoner, wanting to go out into the world—to the big world . . . to men. There are no men here, and I am so fond of men." She reached out as she said this, as if overcome, and her eyes appeared to flash in the moonlight.

"I am glad that you have come here," she said. "You look so handsome and masculine—that is an advantage[91] here in the Carpathians. It will be our pleasure to get to know you."[92]

I didn't know how to respond, as I was completely beside myself—my foremost desire was to take her in my arms and kiss her. I moved closer to her, but she disappeared when the Count suddenly entered the room with a lamp in his hand. She must have snuck out behind him, or gone through a secret door in the room.

Y DEAR MR. HARKER, I AM TRULY DISTRAUGHT THAT I wasn't able to be here with you today. You must think poorly of the hospitality in this old house. Unfortunately, I could not come sooner and now I find you here in the dark. I sincerely ask for your forgiveness—my servants are not used to guests. Please excuse how primitive things are here in the Carpathians." He lit the candles and closed the shutters. "I hope that you have now recovered from your journey. I am glad that you have found your way in here, for there is a lot here that may interest you. These books," he said, pointing out the English volumes, "have been my friends for years; ever since I began to think about going to London—should I have the opportunity. It is thanks to them that I know about England, your pretty and powerful country. I long for London with its crowds and its commotion, its infinite activities, all that makes that big city what it is. I have lived alone for long enough. I want to get to know people."

It was almost exactly what the mysterious girl had said, yet I felt a kind of cruelty in his voice. For a moment, it was as if I was looking upon a beast stalking its prey, and it sent shivers down my spine. The Count seemed to have noticed that I was a bit unnerved, because his strange eastern eyes[93] looked up at me from beneath his brows before he said in a changed tone,

"And how have you been during my absence?"

I said that I had slept for most of the day, at which he nodded and reassured me that it had been a good idea to sleep off my exertions.

93 Icelandic: "austurlensku augum," lit.: "Eastern eyes." This might point to the Count's descendance from the Huns or to the genetic influence of the Tatars—as mentioned later in the novel—or simply to his Transylvanian homeland.

94 A first indication of the Count's aspiration for power. In *Dracula*, Harker's host is portrayed as a former military leader, but doesn't show public ambitions; in the Whitby and London episodes he remains hidden, unless confronted by surprise.

"But what have you been doing since then?"

I told him truthfully that I had arranged my documents and found that the doors were locked. It had been mere chance that I had come across this reading room, and I hoped that he was not angry with me for entering.

"No, not at all! Here you are always welcome, and I hope that you will spend most of your time in this room while you are in my house. This is my usual place as well. I beg you to excuse me for locking the door to the corridor—I always do that out of old habit. You are, of course, welcome to look around our castle as much as you'd like. Unfortunately, most of the rooms are empty now and have been so for many years, while dust falls on a heap of relics from ancient times. Some of the rooms are locked, however, for reasons that no one needs to know. Old houses like this contain many things that outsiders are not meant to see, and I hope that you will respect that. Transylvania is not England—there is much here that British people will not understand."

I bowed, so as to show my consent, but noticed that he was observing me persistently.

"I live here now," he said, "like an old hermit in the house of my ancestors. I live in hoary memories, but I also observe what happens in the outside world—hearing merely the echo of it, here in this deserted corner of the earth. You might find it surprising that, although my hair is white, my heart is young, and it wants to take part in life outside these castle walls, where the destinies of nations are forged and the wars of this world are fought. I once played a role in this game and pulled quite a few of the strings." His voice grew cold. "To *rule*, my young friend, to rule—that is the only thing worth living for, whether it be over people's wills—or their hearts."[94]

He was silent for a moment, and then he spoke again.

"So you have been here most of the evening? It shortens the hours to read my books—but you had to wait for me in the twilight. I hope that you have managed to get some sleep?"

It was as if he was trying to find out whether I had noticed something unusual, and as I suspected it would be best[95] not to conceal anything from him, I told him the truth.

"I was admiring the sun setting over your mountains, as I have never seen anything more magnificent. And the air—the fragrance of the forest—was like a heady wine, intoxicating. I couldn't step away from the window."

"The window," he said. "You have opened the window. The view is indeed stunning; these mountains are unique. But by Jove, assure me, you did close the window again before sundown?"

95 Now the Icelandic uses "það kæmi sér best," the superlative form of "það kemur sér vel" ("that comes in handy")—see footnote 93.

A FEW MINUTES LATER, YES, I DID. FIVE, OR PERHAPS TEN minutes later—I don't remember so precisely," I replied, surprised by his fervor.

"What the devil!" he said viciously, rising halfway from his chair. The thought flashed through my mind that he might dart at me and bite my throat, so I jumped up, ready to defend myself.[96] But the Count quickly calmed down, and then he said in his usual tone, "Forgive me, dear Harker—I tend to be a little irritable. But please understand this, my friend: There is a rule in this house that must never be disregarded—especially when we have guests. No window shall be left open after the close of day. There are harmful vapors—toxic gasses, or whatever they call them—that make the evening air here unhealthy for strangers. This you must always remember from now on. You may not wander these rooms and hallways once darkness closes in, and, for my sake, do not sleep in the unoccupied chambers, as this could have grave repercussions for the both of us. That aside—I hope nothing bad has happened to you. You are sure that you closed the window?"

"Yes, I did. The air was getting colder and was swarming with bats, the most disgusting creatures I know," I said frankly. "And I must confess—one of these vile things managed to get in through the window. I haven't been able to find it yet, but it must be here somewhere."

The Count sat very still, rubbed his hands together, and looked at me with a peculiar, observant gaze.

96 Harker's intuition is surprisingly exact, given the fact that he seems unfamiliar with the habits of vampires and does not suspect that the Count is one of them.

"I was just searching for it when this woman came into the library."

The Count seemed oddly baffled by this, and I expected him to flare up again, but instead he just asked me to explain.

"The woman who was in the room when you arrived. You must have seen her," I said. "You came in just after her."

"No, I did not see her," he said, seeming distracted. "I should have expected this—there are indeed things in this house which few people know about. You have experienced one of them. What did the girl look like? Was she blonde?"

"Yes."

". . . and dressed in pale colors, but in somewhat unusual fashion?"

I nodded.

"She had sparkling diamonds on her breast, with a ruby in the center?"

"Yes."

". . . and she must have been, let's say—rather pretty?"

"Very pretty!"

"Very pretty? Ha ha ha! Ravishing! Radiant, like Venus, like Helen of Troy! A wonder of nature one might say. Have you ever seen a neck like that? Such a bosom, such arms, such lips—not to speak of all the rest. My poor boy, my poor, virtuous Englishman, you have probably never seen a woman like that in your whole life." There was something indecent in his voice and laughter. "Excuse me for making fun of you," he said. "You modern young people take everything so seriously, but we laughed about such things when I was a lad. I was really just laughing at your innocent expression, but the truth is that there is nothing to laugh about here.[97] Did she speak to you by chance?"

"As I recall, she welcomed me. I thought that she was living here."

"Yes, she lives here, and she is closely related to me—gorgeous as a goddess, but galloping mad."[98]

My heart skipped a beat.

"That, however, does not mean one has to fear her. She believes she is her own great-grandmother. This is why she always wears the same kind of clothes as seen in her great-grandmother's portrait. Some other evening I will show you the paintings of my relatives, and I am sure you will find that the women are remarkably similar. It is, of course, nothing but innocent folly. Normally one keeps a close eye on her, but every now and then she sneaks out at dusk, wandering through the corridors of the castle. You see, she has been unlucky in matters of love—the poor girl—and thus she is always searching for her suitor.[99] I have now told you everything there is to know about her."

He stared at me with a vacant look, as if thinking to himself. "Any more than that you will most *certainly* not find out." I could have been mistaken, but I was quite certain he was not telling me the truth.

I'm not sure why, but the Count frightens me. It's normal to feel uneasy about someone whom you don't like, but I cannot help being afraid even though the Count is nothing but affable.

"The farmers here in the countryside tell many stories about the castle. One of them is about the white woman, who legend has it roams around the castle, appearing only to those who are in some kind of mortal danger. You must be familiar with tales of such white maidens in old European castles,[100] but here, to a certain degree, the story is rooted in facts. Of course, there's no need to tell everyone about that."[101]

I bowed to show him that I agreed.

"I trust that I do not have to tell you not to believe all the

98 Icelandic: "fögur eins og gyðja, en geðveik" — an alliterative wordplay.

99 Icelandic: "mannsefninu sínu," mostly used in a retrospective sense to describe the man whom a woman will marry someday: her husband-to-be. In *Makt Myrkranna*, it is unclear whether the term refers to a particular fiancé, who may have left the unlucky girl, or to a potential new partner — or to a man she might mistake for her former lover.

100 Grimm, 1854, pp. 914-918 retells a dozen of such legends, the white maidens representing princesses or ancient heathen goddesses. See also the English translation in Grimm, 1883, pp. 962-968.

101 *Dracula* mentions a similar myth, but in a completely different context: The Whitby chapter alludes to the ghost of St. Hild, sometimes appearing in the ruined abbey. Later, the sleepwalking Lucy Westenra is seen at the graveyard as "a half-reclining figure, snowy white"; in London, she turns into the white-clad "Bloofer Lady," wandering about Hampstead Heath and victimizing small children. Davies, 1997, p. 132 points to *The Woman in White* (1859) by Wilkie Collins as an influence.

102 Icelandic: "menningar birtu þessarar aldar." Icelandic inflection allows two translations: "civilizations of light of this age" or "light of civilization of this age." The second possibility sounded more plausible to me.

rumors you have probably heard about me or my home. Here in the mountains people tend to be superstitious, as they say, and often old houses are linked to a host of frightening stories. You may think you have experienced some unusual incidents here in this castle, but I assure you everything stems from natural causes and that you need not have any fear."

"Yes, please be assured that I don't believe in ghosts."

"Perfect. I had figured as much," he said. "England is a land of culture and practical pursuits. Eyes that have cherished the light of modern civilization[102] never see phantoms."

"Of course not," I replied. "Those kinds of beliefs are now regarded as pathological, and as far as I can tell, they are caused by hallucinations and overexcited nerves—nothing more. Could anything be more absurd than imagining the spirits of dead people ghosting around, even dressed in the same clothes as they wore when they were alive—clothes which have rotted and fallen apart by now?"

"That's right," he said with—what seemed to me—a scoffing look on his face. "I like that. That is how young people are supposed to think. We old diehards may cling to our dogmas, but the future belongs to the younger generation. That is why I long for the whirlpool of young life in London. There, people have other things to think about than believing in spectres. Yes, but we should look into business matters now. Will you please get the documents?"

I went to fetch them and came right back. The Count thoroughly examined all of the papers and bombarded me with questions. I was greatly surprised at how familiar he was with the habits and customs of people in London.

"Yes, but as I have already told you, I have spent years studying the heart of England, which I soon hope to enjoy in person. Unfortunately, though, I've had to learn everything from books—including the language. I think I might be able to learn from you now, while we converse."

"You speak English pretty well, Sir Count."

"I still have a lot to learn," he said. "I am familiar with the grammar and can speak so that people understand me, but when I come to London, I know that everyone will hear that I am a foreigner. I want to learn to speak the language like the local people do."

We started looking through the documents.[103] The house offered to the Count was located in the east side of the city;[104] it was a large, old mansion, which no one had lived in for a long time.

The Count said that he was pleased with the property in every way. He loved that it was old and worn out, much like his own house, and he also found the nearby chapel to be an additional benefit. "Here, in this country, people like me cannot forget that we will, one day, be buried[105] together with the crowd of common peasants—the worst earthworms, who have only lived a day's life."[106]

After looking over the documents, my host invited me to dinner. He told me that he had already eaten on the way home, which is why he had been delayed. He took a seat by the oven[107] and we started chatting.

I told him about my travels and what had happened the previous night, on my way to the castle. He said that the driver had acted appropriately when he left the carriage, as the wolves might have attacked the horses but usually shy away from humans. When I asked him about the gleam of light that I had seen in the dark, he asked me whether I had ever heard of grave mound fires.[108] He said it was believed that such fires could be seen on St. George's Night—burning in places where money had been buried.

103 A few lines earlier, Harker already reported that the Count thoroughly examined the documents.

104 Like in Stoker's original typescript for *Dracula*; see footnote 42.

105 Icelandic: "að dreifast," lit.: "to be scattered." The connection with being buried is evident from the corresponding text in *Dracula*: "I rejoice also that there is a chapel of old times. We Transylvanian nobles love not to think that our bones may lie amongst the common dead."

106 Icelandic: "hafa lifað dagslífi." This could mean that the common people – unlike the vampires, who live forever – are like the mayfly, only living for a few hours and dying in the evening. Alternatively, the Count could mean that they have only lived during the day (because they sleep at night, when the vampires are awake).

107 Icelandic: "ofninn," lit.: "oven" or "furnace." Previously, Harker had mentioned a fireplace.

108 Icelandic: "haugeldar," a fire seen on a burial mound. In Norse pagan rituals, a "haug" was a mound erected to honor a buried person. Stoker took his information about flames and treasures from Emily Gerard's article on Translyvanian superstitions: "In the night preceding Easter Sunday witches and demons are abroad, and hidden treasures are said to betray their site by a glowing flame." See Gerard, 1885. Such Transylvanian folk beliefs had much in common with their Norse counterparts: "It was a consequence of their ideas of a future state [=life, existence—HdR], to bury with the dead in the grave, not only useful implements [...], but also gold and ornaments with which they could shine in the halls of Hel, or else splendid armor with which the spirit [...] could make an honorable entrance into Valhalla. These treasures, which, when very rich, were thought to betray themselves by nocturnal fires which burned above the mounds (haugeldar), often allured bold men to break open and rob the graves. But these mound-breakers had to go prepared for a hard struggle with the inhabitant of the mound (haugbúi) or the ghost of the buried man." Quoted from Keyser, 1854, p. 307f.

"There is no doubt," he said, "that there are countless coins hidden in the ground around here. The Turks, Vlachs, Szeklers and Saxons fought in this area for many centuries, and it was customary to bury one's treasures to shelter them from the enemy."

"But how could this money have stayed hidden for so long, when it's possible to find the places where it's buried?"

"Because peasants are, and always will be, cowards. They are parasites, and while they will badger us whenever they can, they lack guts. It is also no easy task to find the money where such flames have been seen. In fact, you may find that there is no money at all, as old tales are not often reliable, but yes, it would be lovely to find a chest of glowing gold; gold—the only thing this world will be ruled by."

It was as if the Count had fallen into some kind of trance as he stared blankly into the distance, scratching the chair with his fingers, like an animal with its claws. I began to believe that he was not entirely sane—at least, not like other men—so I will have to try to keep him in good spirits and make sure that everything is very well handled, as would be expected from a lawyer.

By now dawn was already starting to break. The Count awoke from his trance and apologized for having kept me up for so long. He then wished me a good night and I went to my bedroom.

As before, once I was alone, sleep eluded me. I was overwhelmed by what had happened to me during the day and it made me restless. To ease my mind—and to lock as much as possible in my memory—I began to write. I wrote in shorthand so that my client wouldn't be able to read it; even if he wanted to pry, shorthand strokes would be too difficult for the Count to crack, even with his wolf teeth.

Every time I think of the girl I found in the library, the memory is as fresh as ever. What the Count told me about her may be true, but it felt as if something didn't add up. I am certain that here in this castle not everything is as it seems. But we lawyers tend to be skeptical—as mistrust is our shadow spirit.[109]

I would like to see her again though, preferably in broad daylight.

109 Icelandic: "fylgja," again referring to Old Norse mythology: a spirit or ghost attached to a specific person, defining or influencing his character and destiny.

8 MAY, MIDNIGHT
COMING TO AN END

MUCH HAS HAPPENED SINCE MY LAST ENTRY—SOME OF which is rather suspicious. A large part of the day had already passed before I awoke. When I walked into the dining room food was on the table, but all the doors were locked as usual. There were also some foreign newspapers lying there—and a letter from my Wilma, which had come by mail. That was by far the best spice on the table.

I was ravenous, and I sat at the dining table for a long time—the more so as I couldn't help but look through the newspapers. Later, I went to the library, but as usual the Count was nowhere to be found. Every day he is out and about, which does not surprise me, as he has a big estate to take care of and also happens to be an avid hunter. I sat reading the newspapers until sunset, and then I hurried to my bedroom to shut the window. There I realized that I had forgotten to shave, and as I had nothing better to do while I waited for the Count, I hung my shaving mirror in the window, took off my jacket and vest, then picked up the razor blade and put it to my skin.

I looked out the window, admiring the landscape, and thought about the letter from Wilma. I didn't notice that anyone had come into the room until I heard the Count say, "Good evening, my dear young friend."[110]

He is always so cordial.

110 In *Dracula*, Jonathan Harker explains: "I started, for it amazed me that I had not seen him, since the reflection of the glass covered the whole room behind me."

I was so startled that I gave myself a nasty cut with my razor, but I ignored the blood running down my throat and turned to answer the Count's greeting.

Never have I seen anyone's appearance change so drastically. Suddenly the Count became as pale as a corpse; his eyes, turning red, bulged out of his head, and with his hair standing up like that of an angry dog, he looked like a raging beast. Before I knew what was happening, he seized me by the throat, tearing my shirt, and would probably have bitten my windpipe had my rosary not gotten in the way. He must have been momentarily possessed.

Soon his outburst subsided, and he asked that I forgive him for becoming so frenzied. "But I cannot bear to see human blood," he explained.

"THESE CUTS CAN BE DANGEROUS," HE ADDED. "MORE dangerous than you can imagine, and it is all because of this instrument of vanity: this mirror— away with it!"

He flung the mirror towards the furnace, shattering it into countless pieces.[111] Then he threw the shards into the coal basket and left for the dining room, saying, "I will wait for you there, my dear Harker."[112]

I was uneasy about the Count, as he was clearly not of an entirely sound mind, and even though he was old and white-haired, I surmised that I would be no match for him, neither in strength nor agility, as he boasts of being a descendant of Attila, king of the Huns. It seems that in this castle anything can be expected. I have spotted no other servants here but the deaf and dumb old woman and the driver, whom I haven't seen since I arrived. This manor is so large, however, that it could hide dozens of people and for hours they'd have no knowledge of one another. It's as though the silence of death rules over this castle, and as I have no contact with anyone but the Count, he would quite easily be able to lock me up entirely if it so suited him. I wouldn't even be able to get away through the windows, as the castle is built on a rocky mountaintop with steep cliffs on three of its sides. Looking down, all I can see is a deep ravine where tall trees grow, so unless I could fly like a bird, I cannot escape. In broad daylight, my self-control and lack of exaggerated imagination generally keep me from fearing what darkness may bring, but if the

111 Davies, 1997, p. 133 explains that this scene was inspired by *The Compensation House* (1866) by Wilkie Collins.

112 Previously, Harker mentioned the fire burning in the hearth in his room, now he speaks of an oven or furnace—matching the presence of a coal basket. See also footnote 107, about the fireplace in the dining room.

Count has inherited some nasty tribal character[113] from the Huns, such as an urge to kill or some other sinister trait, it is best to be cautious.

I found the Count in the library skimming through magazines and newspapers. He was composed and courteous, as if nothing had happened in my bedroom. He greeted me kindly and asked how I was, as if he hadn't spoken to me earlier that day. I realized he must not have been fully aware of what had occurred. He then stood up, saying,

"It is not late yet, and I wondered if you would like to see the family portraits upstairs."

I said that I would love to.

"It may not be ideal to look at the portraits by candlelight, but as I have so much to do during the day I am unable to show them to you at a more appropriate time. Later, you can view them again in daylight. If you don't mind waiting for a moment, I will go take care of the light, so that it will be bright enough."

He walked away and I heard his footsteps as he went down the corridor and up the stairs. It seemed to be a long way to the portrait gallery.

Suddenly I grew frightened, so I ran to my room and grabbed my revolver, which had remained in my travel bag, untouched since I'd embarked on my journey.

When I returned to the library I was struck with yet another shock that left me lightheaded. It was getting dark, and before leaving the library the Count had lit all the silver candlesticks. There, in the chair by the fireplace, sat the Count's "niece,"[114] her ivory arms adorning the arm rests.[115] She had opened up her shawl, revealing her breast, which was bare down to her bosom and shining with diamonds, just like the first time I saw her. She turned her head slightly, like a flower on a stem, her bright blonde hair coiled upon her head in a Greek style. I had hoped that I would see her again but was greatly surprised at the effect I allowed her to have on me, for I had promised myself that it would be different next time—especially because the Count had briefed me about her.[116] Nevertheless, everything happened the same way as before. I experienced the same sensations again, a kind of dull and deadly dread, but also a sort of bittersweet pain.[117] I tried to pull myself together to guard against the effect she had on me, and I more or less succeeded, but the moment she turned towards me and locked her incomparable eyes with mine, it felt as though an electric current surged throughout my body. I grabbed a nearby chair and held onto its backrest. She looked steadily into my eyes, and it didn't even occur to me that I should have greeted her, or that my behavior was doltish. But evidently neither did she see a need for salutations. It felt as though we had already known each other for a long time and therefore didn't need to explain ourselves.[118]

"Why do you never come up?" she asked, with the same astonishing voice as last time. I have never heard such a voice before. "I thought that you would come up and visit us. There is so much I would like to discuss with you." I tried to pardon myself and explained that I didn't know what she was referring to. "That's right," she said, not taking her eyes off me. "You will come, you will come. You are expected." Without shifting her gaze away from me, she smiled, almost imperceptibly. The blue glow in her eyes was so striking that it felt as though one of its rays had pierced right into my brain and I could feel it burn.[119]

Then I heard the Count's footsteps in the hallway.

"He's coming," she whispered. "I must go, but remember—" she got up and for a moment stood before me, bathed

116 It remains unclear why Harker puts any trust in the Count's words now.

117 Icelandic: "ljúfsárrar tilkenningar." "ljúfsár" = "ljúfur" ("sweet" or "lovely") + "sár" ("bitter" or "painful"), a combination mostly used to describe nostalgic longing. *Dracula* uses a similar wording: "There was something about [the vampire women] that made me uneasy, some longing and at the same time some deadly fear."

118 In *Dracula*, there is a similar notion: "The other was fair, as fair as can be, with great wavy masses of golden hair and eyes like pale sapphires. I seemed somehow to know her face, and to know it in connection with some dreamy fear, but I could not recollect at the moment how or where." It is speculated that this blonde girl reminds Harker of the Countess Dolingen-von Gratz appearing in *Dracula's Guest* (1914), a story often seen as the deleted first chapter of *Dracula* or a study for the novel.

119 Wilhelm Conrad Röntgen published his research on X-Rays in December 1895 and Marconi discovered the principle of wireless transmission a few months later. Therefore, it is not surprising that by the end of the 19th century, psychic researchers were starting to speculate about "thought rays" influencing the brain.

121 In *Dracula*, Harker's Journal of 7 May mentions that he looks at a map of England in the Count's atlas and discovers little rings marking Exeter, Whitby and the East of London. The Count has planned his arrival in Whitby well in advance, although Harker never mentioned that Mina and Lucy would go on holiday there.

122 While in modern movies, the infamous Whitechapel murders mostly take place in gas-lit alleys swirling with fog, the actual Ripper killings were committed on clear nights, in unlit streets. Typical for London by the turn of the 19th century was a mixture of smoke and fog; in July 1905, the word "smog" was coined at the Public Health Congress in London. Harker must mean this unhealthy combination of humid air, smoke and sulfur dioxide. Normal mist also occurs in the mountains, as described in the following chapters.

in candlelight. She was a sight more striking than any other I had ever seen. She then proceeded to tiptoe past me so quietly that I hardly noticed, and without taking her eyes off me, she put her white hand, glittering with rings, on top of mine and whispered, "—tell him nothing, but come! And beware, beware, beware."[120]

Then she disappeared, but just as before, I didn't see what had become of her. I may, however, have heard a tiny spring click in one corner of the room, where I had never seen a door before.

With much effort, I tried to get ahold of myself again before the Count came in, and I somehow managed to do so, pretending to be absorbed in the map of England that was lying on the table in front of me.[121]

"Come on, my dear friend," he said, "everything is ready upstairs. You must excuse us that everything is so primitive in this place—we do not have electric light here in the Carpathians."

"But you don't have any of the London fog here in the clean mountain air, either," I said.

"Yes, these fog banks," he said with excitement. "I have also read about them in my books. I think they only increase my longing for London. This fog, which turns day into night and lies like a thick blanket over the streets and squares—all over, more obscure than darkness itself—I want to see it."

"I am afraid that you would soon tire of it. Fog is the main drawback of London. It smothers the town like a vampire sucking the blood and bone marrow of its citizens, poisoning the blood and lungs of the children, and resulting in countless diseases. Not to mention all the pernicious crimes committed under its cloak—crimes that would otherwise be quite impossible to perpetrate."[122]

"Yes," the Count said, breathless with excitement, while fire seemed to spark from his eyes.[123] "Yes, these crimes, these horrible murders; those slaughtered women found in sacks, drifting in the Thames; this blood that runs—runs and flows—with no killer to be found." I don't think I wrongly accuse him when I say that he seemed to be licking his lips with lust when I mentioned the murders. "Yes, it is a tragedy," he said, "and these murders will never be solved—ever. Your writer, Conan Doyle, has written many good books about London, and I read your newspapers. According to them, barely two or three percent of all homicide cases are solved. Yes, London is indeed a remarkable city."

"Then perhaps, my good fellow, it would be best if you stayed in police custody once you are there," I thought to myself.

123 Icelandic: "og eldur brann nærri því úr augum hans," an expression repeatedly used between 1820 and 1920, inspired by old Icelandic sagas. See *Fornaldar Sögur Nordrlanda (eftir gomlum handritum)*, 1829, p. 111; *Fjörar Riddersögur*, 1852, p. 19; *Sagan af Starkaði Stórvirkssyni*, 1911, p. 138. Halldór Laxness also uses it in his first novel, *Barn náttúrunnar*, 1919, Chapter 24, p. 217.

E WALKED DOWN THE HALL, THE COUNT LEADING the way with the light. Then we climbed the stone stairs and reached an iron-clad oak door. He opened it and we entered the portrait gallery. When the Count closed the door again, I thought I saw something dart across the other end of the hall—a big, hairy animal of some kind. I was quite startled, and my host noticed.

"What is the matter?" he asked. "Have you suddenly taken ill? I did tell you that the air in these old rooms would be harmful."

"No, there is nothing wrong with me. But what is there at the far end of the gallery?"

"There is nothing—or did you mean the large painting—?"

Now I saw nothing either, but I somewhat sheepishly told him what I believed to have seen. He laughed at me and said,

"I will not say it is just your imagination, dear Harker— no, that I will not say, because you claim it with such conviction. But if you *did* indeed see something, it must have been—a rat.[124] There are plenty of them in these old houses."

"No, I dare say, what I saw was the size of a—"

"A cat," he said. "Many parts of the castle are barely more than ruins, and the cats have multiplied. It is their instinct to hunt rats and mice; natural laws are the same everywhere: the stronger and smarter creatures live off the weak and dumb."

The gallery was unusually large. At the far end hung a large portrait—which at first seemed to portray the unknown

124 Icelandic: "valska." In Iceland, the rat was unknown before the 17th century; when it arrived there aboard of ships, it was called "valska" or "völsk mús," lit.: "Welsh mouse." The word "Welsh" refers to something foreign or strange (originally used by the Anglo-Saxons to denote the Celtic-speaking inhabitants of Wales).

125 In *Fjallkonan*, we find the word "dömu" (cf. English "dame"); in the 1950 and 2011 editions "konunni" ("woman").

126 Although I could find no other mentioning of "dragon jewels" in Icelandic literature, dragons played an important role in Icelandic myths and were also depicted on jewelry. See Cutrer, 2012, p. 17.

lady[125] whom I have now seen twice in the library. It looked so much like her that it was impossible to distinguish: the same eyes and look, the same countenance in all respects, the same hairstyle and the same clothes. The likeness was executed life-size by one of the masters of the beginning of this century.

The woman was reclining on a chair or some kind of divan, with flowery shrubs and trees behind her. The artist's arrangement, although rather pretentious, had some effect. He had also allowed himself to make some changes to her garments, which the ladies of those times would no doubt have considered proper—although they probably would have fainted if they were to see the bicycle garments worn by women today.

At first glance the picture surprised me greatly—she looked like an exact replica of the noble girl I had seen here in the house. But I soon collected my thoughts and recalled what the Count had told me; I knew that this was not *her* in the portrait but some female ancestor of hers. This had to be the reason why they appeared so much alike, especially as the portrait was full-scale. When I took a closer look, I saw that the lady in the portrait wore on her chest the same diamond jewelry with a ruby in the center. She also had a belt around her middle, displaying a brooch with dragon jewels.[126]

I gazed at the portrait entranced, while the Count watched me with eager curiosity.

"Ha, ha, my friend," he said, "you do not have to be embarrassed. You are not the first person she has confused—and you will probably not be the last. But look at her now—watch closely," he continued, raising the candelabra that, although it was very heavy, appeared weightless in his hands, as if it were just a wax candle. "These breasts, which poets would compare to alabaster—your language has no words to express it, you poor bloodless people, neither snow nor alabaster—and that skin, firm and soft as down feathers to the touch . . . and that unrivaled physique."

I looked at him and saw that his mask had now fallen. In that moment, I realized that he was an old libertine.

"And these lips," he said, pursing his own a little, as if he were swallowing up the painting.

Then he shared more pictures with me, such as a portrait of a naked woman being sold by a slave trader, displayed at the last show.[127] The Count introduced each painting with a very indecent description.

"You are not saying anything," he said.

"No, Sir Count, you are so well spoken. I have nothing to add."

"It is the cold blood in you Englishmen; you do not know the power of love and beauty, and still, I have read that English women are among the most enchanting in the world."

"There are quite a lot of handsome girls there, yes," I said.

"Like her, up there?"[128]

I answered truthfully that I had never seen anyone like her, but also that I was generally unfamiliar with women, and that I only knew the fine ladies pictured in magazines and newspapers—some of which are thought to outshine others when it comes to beauty.

"I have seen these illustrations; they are captivating," he said. "I have had some of them sent to me for my own enjoyment, but a picture is just a picture—not the same as flesh and blood."

"Whose portrait is this, then?" I asked.

"A cousin of mine," he said.[129] "The family blood was pure in her veins, as her mother was also of our clan. It has been a

127 The Icelandic text allows two interpretations: either the picture was seen at the latest art show or the woman in the picture is being offered at the latest slave trade show. In Britain, however, slavery was already counteracted by the Habeas Corpus clause in the Magna Carta (1215); it seems very improbable that Harker ever saw a slave market. A few pages later we will learn that he knows "savages" only from pictures. The topic of a nude female slave being presented by a slave trader was popular with 19th century painters such as Jean-Leon Gerome, Ernest Normand, John William Waterhouse and Géza Udvary.

128 Icelandic: "Eins og hún þarna uppi?" The use of "þarna" ("there") suggests that the speaker refers to an object or person already discussed. To introduce something or someone new, "hérna" ("here") would be used. After discussing various other paintings, the Count now speaks of the large portrait of the beautiful woman again.

129 Lit: "the brother-daughter of my father"—the woman portrayed is the Count's first cousin. Since the Count claims that she is the great-grandmother of the blonde girl, Count Dracula's uncle must be the girl's great-great-grandfather, while the Count's father would be her great-great-granduncle; Count Dracula and the blonde girl would be first cousins, thrice removed. The story strongly suggests, however, that the blonde girl is *actually* the woman in the portrait, locked in eternal youth by her vampiric nature.

custom in our family that the men do not marry outside of the clan, as it has usually ended badly when they do. The women have been short-lived and the children rarely reach adulthood."

I was horrified; it was as if there was something triumphant in his voice.[130]

UT SOME OF OUR DAUGHTERS," HE SAID, "HAVE MAR- ried outside of the family, as they have not been able to find a match amongst their relatives. Because our daughters have always been the most beautiful women, distant kin from the noblest clans in Europe have joined our family, although they hardly possess the same rank as ours. She up there—" He arched his head towards the large portrait.[131] "—even from childhood she was one of those women who hold the hearts of men at their fingertips, playing with them as a child plays with grapes before sucking out the liquid."

He slipped his arm through mine and began leading me back around the gallery, saying,

"She married a young Austrian man, a nobleman—the name does not matter, but you can look it up in many books if you want, as she made it famous."

"She understood that each gift of nature bestowed upon man to its fullest extent is essentially the gift of power. Artistry, prowess, wisdom and beauty—all that is *power*! It is passed on from one generation to the next, my good friend; nature is always working, it is constantly trying to produce something more refined; squandering much material selecting and rejecting. That which is inferior contributes its part, and then it is discarded—like trash." He waved his hand, as if he were throwing something away, and his face turned cruel; I could not discern the slightest trace of human feeling.

"But then," he said, "perhaps once or twice in a genera-

131 By repeating "hún þarna uppi" and by the use of the definite article ("towards *the* portrait"), the text indicates that the Count is still talking about his first cousin depicted in the large portrait he showed at the start.

132 These words are reminiscent of the lines Napoleon wrote to Joséphine de Beauharnais in February 1797: "You to whom Nature has given spirit, sweetness, and beauty, you who alone could rule in my heart, you who doubtlessly know all too well the absolute power you exercise over me!" See Bonaparte, 1935 (my translation). Cf. Blaufarb, 2008, p. 40.

132 Icelandic: "fallegu hendurnar hafa haldið . . ." another example of alliteration.

133 The historical Dracula dynasty ruled over Wallachia, but Stoker's vampire Count lived in the northeast corner of Transylvania. The mountaintop on which I contend Stoker imagined his Castle Dracula to be located, Mount Izvorul C limanului, actually belonged to a district with a 63% share of Szeklers in the population, vs. 2% in the Bistritz region. See population map in Boner, 1865. In *Dracula*'s typescript, the Count speaks of throwing off the "Austrian yoke"—which would match the view of both Magyars and Szeklers. In the printed book, however, the Count refers to "the Hungarian yoke," although the Szeklers were Hungarian allies. With this last-minute switch, Stoker may have tried to restore the Wallachian ancestry of his "Dracula race."

135 The Scythians were semi-nomadic Iranian tribes living in the Central Asian plains since 700 BC.

tion, the hard work pays off and the family flourishes; the elite among them are revealed." Although the Count has a remarkable number of English words at the ready, he had a hard time coming up with these last ones. He always tends to be at a loss for words when enthusiasm seizes him. "She up there," he said. "She had the power, and that is why she had the right to rule. She was blessed with everything: beauty, as you can see, intellect and eloquence, nobility and willpower and strength. She held the destinies of whole nations in her hands, though few suspected it. Heads of state, kings and emperors, lay at her feet—or in her arms.[132] She knew very well that such a woman, possessing all these qualities, could not be bought for all the gold in the world, and thus, she could make everyone her slave—the most humble slaves, whom she could wrap around her finger because they imagined that they possessed her, when in fact *she* was the one holding the reins in her beautiful hands.[133] Everyone danced like a puppet beneath her fingers. She knew how to rule, and she knew that such is the supreme goal of life.

"She became a widow early," he said. "Her husband withered up. The poor devil had been a weakling since childhood, although he was from a noble line." He laughed contemptuously. "It was said that she cared for him—he was a good-looking lad, his portrait is there—but the love of *our* women is like a consuming flame, and he . . . he melted from it, like a wax candle thrown into a blazing bonfire. We of the genus Dracula, a primary line of the Szeklers[134]—we believe that our kin descends from the ancient Huns, who once swept across Europe like wildfire, destroying nations and their people. As the story goes, the Huns were descendants of the Scythian witches,[135] who had been banished to the woods, where they commingled with the demons. These tales, of course, are like any other of their sort, but it is known that no demon or wizard has ever been greater or more powerful than Attila—our ancestor.[136] Therefore it is not surprising that we, his descendants, hate and love more passionately than other mortals. But I have now come a long way from our story.

"She became a widow, but as you might guess, such a trivial incident did not matter to such a woman. No historian has ever suspected how much power she held, and that is why some things will never be fully explained. The few who know—I could mention names, but it is not necessary—can prove that there was hardly a political event at that time in which she did not have her pretty finger in the pie. In fact, for most of these occurrences, some sort of planning can be traced right back to her bed chamber—for there she was a queen, and it is from *there* that she reigned in secret.[137] What a grand life! No law but love and free will! This picture was painted in Paris, two years before Napoleon was crowned.[138] It was a few years later that she met a man in Vienna, who, like her, was of the Dracula family. He was younger than her in years, but women like her never age. She was more beautiful than ever, and he was unlike anyone she had ever fallen for, a man cut from the same wood as her.[139] It was as if two fires had met. Oh, you cold, rational children of the West— you do not know *this* kind of love. A love as biting as the bitterest hatred, with kisses that burn like glowing iron, and embraces. . . but no more of that! She married him and moved here with him, to the ancient family estate—which was, of course, not as decrepit as it is today—and here they lived together as one fire, both created to rule. If these old walls could talk, they would tell many stories that your cool English virtue could never dream of—although even I can appreciate that virtue, as it is also a form of power. Yet we, Attila's children,

136 The lines in *Dracula* mentioning the battles of the Dracula dynasty with the Turks are omitted in *Makt Myrkranna*, eliminating possible associations with historical persons, that is, the anti-Turkish campaigners within the Dracula clan.

137 This is another possible allusion to Joséphine de Beauharnais, who was said to rule the world from her bedroom.

138 Napoleon I was crowned on 2 December 1804.

139 The only male member of the Dracula family mentioned so far who would qualify is Harker's host himself, the first cousin of the lady in the portrait. This would explain his surprisingly intimate knowledge of the story that is about to be told.

140 This mirrors the biblical words: "All flesh is grass, and all the goodliness thereof is as the flower of the field: The grass withereth, the flower fadeth: because the spirit of the LORD bloweth upon it: surely the people is grass. The grass withereth, the flower fadeth: but the word of our God shall stand for ever" (Isaiah 40: 6-8, King James Bible). This thought is reiterated by Thomas à Kempis in his *Imitation of Christ* (around 1420): "This life is short. It is like the flower in the field, it springs to life in the Spring, flowers in the Summer, begins to fade in the Fall and dies in the Winter." The same idea is also worded in the *Dance of Death* from the Preacher Churchyard in Basel (around 1440): "O Mensch betracht | Und nicht veracht | Hie die Figur | All Creatur | Die nimpt der Todt | Früh und spot | Gleich wie die Blum | Im Feld zergoht." [Oh Man, behold | how here unfold | On graveyard's wall | The fates of all | Who soon or late | To Death must yield | Like on the field | The flowers fade." (My transcription from the German). See also Job 14:2 and Psalm 103:15.

141 Still another possible reference to Joséphine de Beauharnais (1763-1814), who in 1779 married the young Alexandre, Vicomte de Beauharnais (1760-1794). Joséphine indeed made the name "de Beauharnais" famous. After Alexandre was executed during the Reign of Terror, the young widow had several amorous affairs with leading politicians, until she married Napoleon Bonaparte in January 1796, being his senior by six years. Still the same year, while Napoleon led military campaigns abroad, she started a liaison with Hippolyte Charles, a young good-looking Hussar lieutenant (1773-1837). The affair was reported to Napoleon; in his rage, he decided to divorce her, but his letter with instructions to his brother Joseph was intercepted by Admiral Nelson, thus adding ridicule to shame when it was published by the London and Paris newspapers. Josephine dumped her lover in order to save the marriage, although Napoleon had several mistresses himself and in 1809 demanded divorce all the same, when she could not produce an heir. During their marriage, Napoleon presented her with various sets of exquisite jewelry, which—through her grandchildren—were inherited by the Norwegian and Swedish royal families.

have a nature truly different from yours. Oh, you are going to hate the ending of this story.

"I have read about eternal love from your English books, but perhaps I will come to understand its meaning when I arrive in London, as I do not yet fully know what it means—or rather, I do not understand the meaning *you* attach to it. Love has its lifespan, like the flower in the field: once in full bloom, it quickly withers away.[140] Then spring returns, but not the same flower, nor one of the same root. This is a law of nature. Once passion has blazed at its peak, it is more likely to be extinguished. This love of theirs eventually burned out, as love usually does—or hers at least . . . she was one of those women." He lowered his voice to a mysterious whisper. "I will tell you, my friend. She was one of those women whose life is *too* rich to have just one man. Yes, such creatures do exist—but no more of that! She got herself a lover, a pretty boy from the mountains here; a country bumpkin, as you would call him, although we Szeklers are all aristocrats. For her it was no disgrace, and her husband should have understood that and let her live her life the way she needed to, but he did not, and that was a major mistake on his part. She was his dutiful wife, nevertheless, and she managed the castle's household as was expected of a noble lady. Simply put: as his spouse, she paid him proper respect and performed her duties to him. Her personal affairs were none of his business."[141]

"None of his business?" I blurted out, unintended.

"Certainly not, dear friend; love is free. It is detached from all other commitments and circumstances. In our clan this has always been the applicable law. His refusal to accept this, as I said, was a great and punishable mistake. Perhaps the fire of love had not yet been extinguished in him, as it had been in her. It could be that a few glowing embers still survived within him—which would explain his actions, but not excuse them, for he certainly did not act in the honorable way of a nobleman. Instead, he acted like a lowly commoner. He belittled himself by spying on her and her lover. One evening he burst in on them and, without even realizing how ridiculous it was, began to play the role of the betrayed husband, which was far beneath his dignity.[142] Then he let himself have his revenge. And how do you think he accomplished this, my dear friend? Plain and simple, and undeniably funny as it was, he had the door to the Countess's chambers nailed shut, letting them stay in there by themselves. But it was not his intention that they should starve to death, for they lacked neither food nor drink; it is said that he saw to that himself. All the servants were dismissed, except for the most loyal and reliable one. The castle, then, was as quiet as a dead man's grave. Can you imagine, with your mind's eye, the lovers living there in that room? In the beginning, I would imagine, they lived as if they were in paradise: she was too proud to know the meaning of fear, and he, the poor boy, must have considered himself richer than the king, having her all to himself. The Count, however, knew very well how he would have his requital. Knowing the Countess and the devouring flame of her emotions, he sensed that her lover, being one of life's wax candles, would melt at such heat, as her first husband had done. Some people die, others go mad—poor useless devils—and so the Count just bided his time. It took several months, until one evening, when the moon was waxing, the window of the locked room—that little tower room in the southeast—was opened. It was said that the terrible sound of insane, anguished cries could be heard: 'Help me! Help me! She is killing me!' The next moment, it seemed as if someone had stepped onto the window sill and plunged out, head first.

142 The disdain with which Harker's host describes his first cousin's second husband here casts doubt on our suspicion that both Counts might be the same person.

Have you not seen the abyss out there? You can see it outside your window, but here, at the top of the tower, the drop is several hundred feet. When he was found down there among the cliffs, there was not much left of him for her soft arms to embrace."

CANNOT DESCRIBE THE IMPACT THAT HIS STORY HAD ON me, as it seemed to be absolutely free of any human sentiment. He lowered his voice, as if noticing my reaction to what he was saying.

"No one knows what she had been up to, but the window was shut again and all was quiet once more. The Count waited a few days before he went to her, after her lover had leapt to Heaven—or Hell.[143] Nobody knows what came to pass between them, but it is said that he kept going to her every night, at the same hour. This probably was a joyful time for him, though perhaps not quite so much for her—but who knows! No one saw or heard anything more, but a few months later he had women picked up from the village to provide the death service.[144] She was lying dead in her bed; any more than that, people did not know. She was dressed in a garment similar to the one shown here in the portrait and placed in her coffin by command of the castle's master. She rests here in the chapel, along with her family members. But as you see, my friend, she is still as beautiful as ever."

"How awful to hear this," I said, trembling with such distress that I could barely manage to shake it off. Had I been a woman, I would have believed I was going hysterical.[145] I had never felt like this. Had I suddenly caught a glimpse into the bowels of the earth, with all its demons and blazing brimstone down below—as medieval people believed—I would not have reacted worse.

"Yes," he said, "it was a major mistake on *his* part. The

143 Icelandic: "hlaupið fyrir ætternisstapann," lit.: "jumped over the Family Cliff"—a bitter mockery, referring to *Gautrek's Saga*. Upon getting lost in the woods during hunting, King Gauti of West Götaland meets with a dull-witted family; the eldest daughter, Snotra, explains to him: "There is a steep bluff near our farm, it is called Gilling's Bluff, and it has an overhanging cliff, which we call "Family Cliff." It is so high and the drop so deep that no living creature can survive falling down from it. We call it "Family Cliff" because we use it to reduce the size of our family when something very wondrous happens; there, all our elders can die without suffering any illness, and fare straight to Odin. This way, they become no burden for us and we do not have to endure their stubbornness, as this blissful bluff has been open to all members of our kin alike, and therefore we do not have to put up with lack of money or food, nor with any other strange marvels or miracles that may befall us." (my translation). At the start of the saga, the unknown writer already warns his readers that this is a "merry story": The ideas and behavior of this family are obviously foolish. According to Norse beliefs, Odin and Freya will only receive those who have died an honorful death in battle. Those who have died from sickness and old age would go to the realm of Hel; those who had committed suicide (especially for such trifling reasons as later occur in the saga) probably to a particularly gruesome section named Náströnd, the Shore of Corpses, where snake poison endlessly drips on murderers, oath-breakers and adulterers. According to Christian beliefs, the boy (guilty both of suicide and adultery) would also go to Hell (a name derived from the Norse "Hel"). In the theme of forbidden love, ending with a fatal drop, lies a still deeper parallel between the Count's story and Snotra's words; cf. Milroy, 1966-69, and Grimm's tale of Rapunzel.

144 Icelandic: "að veita nábjargir." In the old Norse tradition, this means the service of closing eyes, nostrils and mouth on a dead person. See Boyer, 1994, p. 56.

145 Icelandic: "taugaveikur." Today, "taugaveiki" is translated as "typhus." The first typhus epidemy reached Iceland only in 1906, however. Here "taugaveikur" refers to a state of nervous agitation ("tauga-" means "nervous," while "veikur" means "ill"), as mentioned in *Nordri* of 30 April 1856: "sjúkdóma [...] kallada Taugaveiki (Hypocondrie og Hysterie)." While hypochondria could also befit

men, hysteria was believed to be an exclusive women's disease. Dr. Jean-Martin Charcot—mentioned in *Dracula*—treated large numbers of women diagnosed with this mysterious illness in the Salpêtrière Hospital in Paris; he claimed it was a defect of the brain. The School of Nancy, on the other hand, maintained that hysterical behavior had psychological, not physiological causes. Shortly before his death in 1893, Charcot had to admit that his views had been wrong; the number of "hysterical" patients dwindled dramatically. See my article on Bram Stoker, Dr. Van Renterghem and hypnosis in the Victorian Age in *De Parelduiker,* October 2012.

146 An allusion to Christian views: "take no account of it if they do thee wrong" ("virð einskis við þá er þer gora í mein"), from the Icelandic *Book of Sermons* (12th century); in 1872, a much-acclaimed Swedish edition of this handwriting was published: Wisén, 1872.

147 The Count now speaks of himself in the third person and refers to his planned relocation to England.

people in the region—Czechs, Tatars, Vlachs, and all the ragtag and bobtail who have swarmed to this country that we Szeklers are born to rule—have always feared and held a grudge against us, particularly us members of the Dracula family. Now they had found new gossip to enrich their chatter. And though we ignore the serpent that creeps on the ground, it will bite nonetheless.[146] I have learned this the hard way. That is why I now live like a recluse, with owls and crows nesting in the towers of my forefathers' castle. Perhaps people have also tried to smear my name while talking to you, dear friend. Come out with the truth now, what have they told you about Dracula before you came here?"

"Nothing worth mentioning," I said candidly, "but—"

"But they insinuated all the more," he said. "Oh, these slaves! These vagabonds! They fear Dracula, and for good reason! Vengeance and curses shall bite them long after he has found himself a new homeland![147] Come on, my dear friend," he said, slowing down and changing his tone, "on another occasion, let us look at this picture again in daylight."

He held up the candlestick, illuminating the portrait one last time, and then he showed me more paintings, telling me something about each of them.

It was a strange collection of family portraits, spanning over centuries. Many of the paintings were amateurishly executed and some poorly made, though others were masterpieces. What intrigued me most was the unbroken perpetuation and gradual perfection of the two or three human likenesses that consistently emerged, generation after generation. It seemed as though the clan had reached its greatest bloom with the Count and the ravishing noble lady in the magnificent portrait he had described. The same facial features as possessed by the Count could be seen in paintings from different eras, three or four of which looked so much like him that I was taken aback.[148]

"It is exactly as you say," said the Count. "I am a true Dracula."

The reoccurring features—big head with black hair, short neck, unusually broad chest, low forehead, and brown, wrinkly skin (even in the young men)—looked very different from modern, civilized people. Not even pictures I'd seen of savages had looked less appealing to me.

I praised the Count's family for its continuously heightening beauty. Although he clearly appreciated the compliment, he changed the subject all the same.[149]

"Yes, my friend," he said, "that is just more proof of what I always say—that the strongest must prevail and conquer the world. Those who are weak are only created to satisfy the needs of others more powerful. The person who knows how to exert his strength will gain supremacy and have everything at his command—beauty, prudence and knowledge—in the same way that the small seedling, growing in the graveyard, will gradually become a tall tree with the life force of a thousand generations, all contributing their strength, comeliness and other good qualities."[150]

As far as I could follow, it was Darwin's law fluttering vaguely through the Count's mind, but he had adapted it in his own way.[151]

While we were discussing this, he doused the lights in the portrait gallery with a long extinguisher, and we left the room in the faint moonlight. I had managed to regain my full composure and was in a serene mood when we came down the stairs and entered into the courtyard, but then I clearly heard someone walking close to us. I turned, but the sound of footsteps seemed to move farther away, and I saw no more than a

148 This either hints to a strong hereditary trait, possibly reinforced by the practice of inbreeding, or to Dracula's and his cousin's centuries-long existence chronicled in the paintings.

149 Icelandic: "fór út í aðra sálma," lit.: "started to read from another psalm."

150 Icelandic: "... úr afli, fegurð og öðru atgervi," echoing *Egil's Saga* (13th century), Chapter 8: "About Þórólf and Bárð people said that they were equal in handsomeness, stature, strength and all other good qualities." ("Þat var mál manna um Þórólf ok Bárð, at þeir væri jafnir at fríðleik ok á vöxt ok afl ok alla atgervi." (my translation).

151 In 1859, Charles Darwin published *On the Origin of Species*; despite resistance from clerical side, within the next 20 years it was broadly accepted as an explanation of the variation and selection of species in their struggle for existence. The Count's presentation of Darwin's mechanism of natural selection is accurate, but Harker obviously dislikes his host's conclusion that the stronger have a "natural" right to rule and exploit the weak—a normative judgement not included in Darwin's theories.

152 This is another character that only appears in *Makt Myrkranna*.

153 "Natra gamla" must refer to the old housekeeper woman. Perhaps the text plays with the word "naðra," meaning "adder," "viper," "serpent," or "snake" (Old High German "natra"). The *Völuspá*, the first and most famous poem of the Older Edda, tells how Thor fights with the World Serpent Jörmungandr, guardian of Midgard; deadly wounded, Thor still manages to walk away: "Nine steps still strode | Earth's son in pain | struck by the snake | fearing no sneer." ("Gengr fet níu | Fjörgynjar burr | neppr frá naðri | níðs ókvíðnum." (my translation). As we will see later, the old woman actually acts as a guardian, keeping an eye on Harker when he tries to find a way out. Another option is that Valdimar played with the name of a well-known church ruin in Sweden, "Nätra gamla." Today, "natra" is propagated by Icelandic language purists as the native word for "stinging nettle," mostly called "netla."

glimpse of a short, stocky man suddenly disappearing through one of the doors to the corridor.[152]

The count was walking ahead of me, holding the light. "What is wrong, my friend?" he asked. "Why have you stopped?"

"It's nothing—just that I heard footsteps behind us," I said, "and I thought I saw someone slip through the door over there, by the corridor."

It occurred to me that although my bedroom faces the direction of the corridor, I had never heard anyone enter or wander around in it.

"A man walking *here?*" he asked. "You must be kidding. No one is here. It was probably just the echo of our footsteps and your own shadow."

"But I saw it with my own eyes . . ."

"I can assure you, my friend, that no living creature sets foot in here at this hour—unless it was old Natra, but she never comes this way.[153] You said yourself that you do not believe in ghosts."

"Yes, but *here* one might be led to believe differently," I said.

"What you saw was nothing more than a trick of the senses," said the Count.

When we reached the living room, everything was prepared as usual: The candles were lit and the dishes were set on the table. The Count invited me to dine, but he said that he himself didn't have an appetite, as he usually does not sup so late. I haven't seen him touch any food since I arrived, but as the master of this estate he should be able to have his meals whenever he wants, and it would be consistent with his usual manners that he would prefer to eat by himself.

"With your permission, I will sit here while you eat," he

said, taking a seat by the fireplace. "I would like to practice my English."

Yes, that would explain why he is so talkative with me. His English has progressed a great deal in these past few days. I've noticed that he has an unusually sensitive ear for languages, as he corrects his pronunciation as soon as he hears that mine is different.

When I finished my dinner I seated myself in the chair opposite him.

"What you said earlier in the hallway reminded me of something," he said. "The superstitious cowards here in the surrounding countryside maintain that this castle I live in is full of spectres and evil spirits, because of how rich its history is—because here, there is much to remember from the past that the general public does not get to know. I struggle to find workmen, even if I offer higher pay, because they are simply too frightened. These poor wretches. I know that in the big city of London such superstitious views are not adhered to, but I still feel that it is best for your health to always stay inside after dark. The evening air is detrimental to you, and you may see or hear things that you don't understand. I only hope that you are comfortable and well here and that you will stay with me for a few weeks—as I have said before. I wouldn't take it kindly if you were to leave before I feel it is time for you to depart. I hope that you stay here with me for one more month, from this date on."[154]

Staying here for so long didn't suit me at all, but I didn't have the courage to say so. So instead I mentioned my employer, Mr. Hawkins.

"I will let him know. In fact, I have asked him for his permission already," he said sternly. "Yes, you will stay. There are many things to be found in my library, including works of

154 The following scenes, spread out over two days, correspond to Harker's Journal entry of 12 May in *Dracula*, but the conversation about the blonde girl only appears in *Makt Myrkranna*.

155 Like "frænka," the word "frændkona" can refer to different kinds of female relatives, except mother, daughter or sister.

156 A strange apprehension for a libertine who has just explained that passion is not bound by any conventions. Considering the girl's hunger for a romantic partner, the Count's concern is not unrealistic, but it remains to be seen, who in the end would be the victim, and who the perpetrator.

art—but no ghosts," he said, laughing heartily. "As I have told you, these superstitious people talk about a white-clad woman wandering about the castle, but it is none other than the poor young girl whom you've already met, living upstairs"—he pointed up to the ceiling—"and she is rumored to appear when danger lurks. Still, I ask that you remember if you ever see any glimpse of white that it is no ghost, only her. She truly is dazzling enough to be dangerous, but not to you. She has, as I have told you, bats in the belfry, believing she is the noble lady whom she resembles in the portrait. She wanders around the castle looking for her cavalier. It is sad, but then again, it is also amusing."

He spoke with such arrogant airs that I could barely stand to listen to him, so in an effort to say something I asked him whether his mentally disturbed relative[155] would accompany him to London.

"No, no! Don't even let that idea cross your mind. As captivating as she is, she could easily end up in the claws of a Casanova, as you call them—I have read about them in your books as well.[156] It would be a risk to take her to London. It's more suitable for her to stay here at home, in this secluded place. Don't you think so?"

I said something to the effect of him knowing what the best arrangement would be in regard to this matter.

"Of course," he said, "but now it is nearly twelve o'clock. I can no longer rob you of your sleep and also have a few letters to write. Good night, my friend, sleep well and long."

THE NEXT EVENING[157] THE COUNT ASKED ME,

"Have you not written to your employer, that fine old gentleman Mr. Peter Hawkins, or anyone else since you came here?"

I told him truthfully that I had not done so, for I didn't know how I would send such letters.

He shrugged and stroked his moustache, saying,

"Yes, we here in the mountains lack many of the luxuries that you have in your splendid London. It is a long way from here to Borgo,[158] and unfortunately I do not have many servants to run errands for me, but if you write them this evening—I also happen to have many letters to write—I will take care of them all in one go. Please write, my friend," he said, resting his hand firmly on my shoulder. "Write to Mr. Peter Hawkins and anyone else you like. Tell them that you feel comfortable here, as I hope you do, and that you are going to stay here for the period we have agreed upon."

I made a final attempt to escape sooner from his custody.

"You trouble yourself too much for my sake," I said. "Do you really want me to stay for so long? I am afraid that you will be bored to death having me here." I tried to sound as if I were making a joke.

"I have already told you, and so it still stands," he replied in such a steely tone that it felt useless to make any further objections. "When your employer made his arrangement with me regarding your trip here, the intention was, of course, to have my interests taken care of—and that my needs would

157 Icelandic: "í kveld," lit.: "In the evening." This must be the evening of 8 May, because the Count later refers to the agreement about Harker's prolonged stay, discussed the night before.

158 Probably meaning Borgo-Prund, the largest of the villages between Bistritz and the Borgo Pass. See K. & K. Spezialkarte, 1876-1907, Zone 17, Columns XXXI and XXXII.

159 The alliterative expression "að sér hitnaði um hjartaræturnar" literally means "to become warm around the roots of the heart" and mostly refers to a sudden sympathy or enthusiasm. Cleasby/Vigfússon, 1874, also gives the negative variant "to be alarmed"—the only logical reaction to the Count's arrogance.

160 Like in *Dracula*, the Count has planned his arrival in Whitby in advance, although Harker never told him that his fiancée and her friend intended to spend their holidays there—see also footnote 121.

161 In *Dracula*: "Herr Leutner, Varna"—"Seutner" may be a transcription error. In *Dracula*, it is to be from Varna that the *Demeter,* with the vampire aboard, starts her journey towards Whitby.

162 This ignores Stoker's inside joke: *Dracula* mentions "Coutts & Co., London," the bank of Stoker's wealthy friend Angela Burdett-Coutts (see Davies, 1997, p. 133f). In the 2011 republication of *Makt Myrkranna*, we read "Corsets bankastjóra," meaning: "the bank director of Corset's Bank"—maybe a typographer's joke.

163 In Stoker's *Dracula*: "to Herren Klopstock & Billreuth, bankers, Buda-Pesth."

come first and foremost. As you will come to see, I don't ask for favors that I would not readily return."

I bowed in silence. I hadn't heard him speak in this fashion before, and I cannot deny that I was growing irritated.[159] But then he immediately changed his demeanor, saying,

"I did not expect that my friend's assistant would be so much to my liking, as you have turned out to be. You will have to excuse my stubbornness and grant me the pleasure of your stay."

I bowed again. How could I protest? I was—and am—convinced that although he is a man of great intellect, he must be a bit unhinged, and perhaps even dangerous when something is done against his will. Given my current circumstances, I better avoid disobeying him. It would also be in my employer's best interest for me to give in to his wishes.

I wrote to Wilma, my fiancée, telling her more or less that I felt comfortable here, and that the Count's castle was pleasurable. I also told her that the Count had asked me to stay with him for a few more weeks.

I wrote another letter to my boss, informing him that the Count seemed happy with the real estate purchase and that he wanted me to stay with him at the castle for a while longer.

When I finished my letters the Count sat down at the table in the chair I'd been sitting in and began to write his own, while I read a book. However, I couldn't help but glance to see whom the Count's letters were addressed to. I found that the intended recipients included Samuel Billington in Whitby,[160] Seutner's shipping company in Varna,[161] Coret's Bank in London,[162] and Klopstock's Bank[163] in Vienna. When he was finished writing the Count collected all the letters and set off, bidding me farewell.

"I have several things to take care of tonight and hope that you will excuse me for saying good night earlier than usual. I hope that you have enough here to keep yourself entertained until you go to bed," he said, pointing to the bookcase. "The food is on the table, but I am in a hurry."

From the way his eyes flickered and his lips trembled, I could tell that he was excited about something. This surprised me, as until then he'd seemed to be in such a balanced mood.

10 MAY

LOOKING THROUGH MY JOURNAL ENTRY FROM YESTERDAY, I realize that I have been long-winded. Thercfore I'm determined to be more concise from now on.[164]

I went to bed early last night, extinguishing the lights not long after midnight. It felt as though I had just drifted off to sleep when it started growing light out and I was suddenly awoken by a sound from outside. It was like the sound of a dying person; a loud cry at first, but then it gradually got weaker. Fully awake now, I sat up in bed and a cold sweat broke out all over my body. I could still hear the scream echo in my head. In one sweep, I threw on my clothes and rushed to the window. I had forgotten to let the shutters down the night before, and when I opened the window the cool air flowed in.[165]

I could vaguely make out the first trace of early sunrise in the east, but fog lay over the ground, so nothing could be seen. I peered out the window as far as I could and listened. The air was cold and damp, and through the thick brume I could just make out the outlines of the castle walls a little farther away. After standing at the window for nearly half an hour, I heard a shuffling noise out in the darkness. It sounded as though something was creeping along the outside of the castle wall—perhaps on a ledge,[166] which had either been built for decoration or simply marked the transition between the lower and upper levels of the castle. As it moved closer, I saw that it was a human form, wrapped in a long grey coat,

164 In *Dracula*, we find the opposite observation: "I began to fear as I wrote in this book that I was getting too diffuse; but now I am glad that I went into detail from the first, for there is something so strange about this place and all in it that I cannot but feel uneasy." See *Dracula*, Chapter 2, Harker's Journal of 8 May.

165 Icelandic: "að setja hlerana fyrir"—"to let the shutters down." Cleasby/Vigfússon, 1874, defines "hleri" as "a shutter or door for bedrooms and closets in old dwellings, which moved up and down in a groove or rabbet, like windows in Engl. dwellings, and locked into the threshold."

166 Icelandic: "stétt." In Icelandic communities, the "stétt" was the heightened pavement running in front of the houses. In this scene, it obviously is a kind of ledge or rim horizontally set along the outer wall.

167 In *Dracula*, the Count crawls along the wall like a lizard, face down, which rules out any kind of natural explanation. *Makt Myrkranna* leaves this possibility open here.

with a sort of hood over his head. He crawled on hands and feet, like a cat, along the narrow ledge, but after some time he disappeared, as if he had slipped through a crack in the wall or climbed into a window.[167]

In a desperate hurry I closed the window and let down the shutters.

After lighting the candles in my room, I was able to steel my nerves and calm down a bit. I shivered from the cold, so I went straight for my hip flask and took a mouthful of cognac. It wouldn't be funny if I became ill here. Then I checked whether the door was locked and made sure that the revolver was loaded. I laid it on the bedside table and got back under the blankets.

If I'd seen something like this in London—a strangely dressed man creeping cautiously along a gutter—my only thought would be to fetch the nearest police officer and, with his help, find out whether this was some unfortunate sleepwalker or an unconventional burglar, and then make sure he be taken into custody. But as a stranger here, I have no idea what to do. I don't know my way around the castle—in fact, I don't even know where the Count sleeps! I also suspect that, save for the two of us, not a single living soul would be found in this part of the house. I considered the risk of making a commotion to wake the Count, so that I could tell him what I'd witnessed, but I wasn't certain he'd take kindly to such a disturbance. I decided it was wisest to try to keep myself safe with the means I had at hand and to pretend that everything was fine—keeping hold of my emotions.

INTENDED TO KEEP WATCH AND NOT FALL BACK ASLEEP, but I dozed off all the same and didn't wake up until ten o'clock, when the sun was already shining brightly outside. I opened the window and inhaled the refreshing spring air with its forest fragrance; with daylight's arrival, the terror of the previous night had vanished. I could have told myself that what I'd seen in the night was all a dream, had the burned-down candle and revolver on the table not been silent witnesses. I leaned out of the window to get a better look at the surrounding landscape, and it became even clearer to me that the castle was built on a large rock, with nothing but cliffs reaching up all but one of its sides. This would have made this stronghold impenetrable in former times.

I saw that there were towers on the right and left sides of the castle. The tower to my right was in good shape, but the one to my left was dilapidated. Many of its walls are covered with cracks and its roof has collapsed. The human figure I saw the night before had come from this part of the castle.[168]

I leaned even farther out the window and saw large rocks on the ground down below. They had probably plummeted from the surrounding cliffs. Farther out from the rocks I could see shrubbery and forest, but in the distance beyond the trees there were only bare mountains. I spotted two or three solitary farms farther away, but otherwise there was no human habitation or signs of civilization to be seen.

I sheltered my eyes from the sun with my hand so that it wouldn't hinder my sight. Then my eyes fell upon something

168 Harker will later describe that the ledge runs between the southwest tower and the southeast tower (where his bedroom is), and so the human figure must have come from the tower on the right, not on the left—unless Harker, writing this diary entry in the library, adapted his description to the perspective he had in the library.

169 Another character unique to *Makt Myrkranna*. In *Dracula*, the Count hands the vampire women a bag with a "half-smothered child." Later, the lamenting mother is devoured by wolves.

white in the bushes to my left. I thought it might be laundry spread out to dry and I took out my pocket telescope to get a better look. But then I saw that it was a human being! He or she was lying on their back, hands and feet stretched out, and seemed to be sleeping there in the bushes. As I hadn't seen a living soul outside the castle since I arrived, I was glad to see another person here. I lifted up the spyglass and looked again—but then I sank down in the chair next to me, shivering with horror. I didn't want to see more.

It was a woman—still a young girl, in fact. I saw her as if she had been right next to me. She had a pleasant face and a shapely figure. She was dead. Her head was bent backwards and was halfway sunken into the moss. Her black hair was loose, as if someone had torn at it, and her mouth and eyes were wide open—her expression reflected nothing but great fear. Her clothes had been ripped open across the breast, so that her neck and bosom were bare, and there on her throat was an open wound. Blood had flowed from it down her shoulders, drenching her clothes. She was wearing coarse white woollen garb, like the women in this country do. Her arms were stretched out, as if she had dug her hands into the moss in agony.[169]

After a few minutes, I looked through my monocular again to make sure that I hadn't been mistaken.

Everything was as just described.

This must be the reason for the cry of distress I had heard. But how could this horrible thing have happened? I wondered if the wolves had done it, as there are so many of them in the woods. But the Count had told me that they don't attack humans—especially not at this time of year, when they have enough prey to catch in the forest.

Or had this girl been murdered?

Wolves would hardly have left her like that, but a murderer might have.[170] She was half hidden in the bushes, and there were no real roads nearby.

I grabbed my hat, put the revolver in my pocket, and made to rush out to where the body lay; there had to be some path along the rock that would lead me there.

I ran down the stairs to exit the building, but as I reached the entrance hall, I remembered that I hadn't placed a foot outside the castle walls since my arrival here. Because I had slept so much during the day and the Count had spent so much time with me at night to improve his English, I hadn't once been outside the castle's enclosure.

I tried opening the gate but it was closed shut and there was no key in the lock. I looked around for the key, but it was nowhere to be found. I tried to force open the gate, but to no avail.

The entrance hall is large and there are doors leading in many different directions. I tried opening every one of them but they were all firmly locked.

As a free man, I'm not accustomed to having my movement restrained. But now I realized I was a prisoner in this castle.

Already earlier I'd wanted to roam the castle grounds, with no plan as to what I'd do outside. But now that I had seen the girl's body, I could think of nothing else but to get to her and—if possible—try to help, call for assistance, and with the support of the authorities seek out the murderer. That is: I wanted to do what any civilized man would do in my situation. But only now did I realize what that situation actually was. I thought back on everything I had seen and heard here, and now my fate looked bleaker than ever.

Of course, I knew there had to be many other exits, but

170 Meaning that wolves, if they were hunting for prey, would have guzzled their victim. The way the girl is ravaged reminds of werewolves, but as we will see later, the castle houses still other creatures.

171 Icelandic: "varla hálfvöxnu tungli": the moon in the fifth or sixth night after new moon, shortly before reaching the first quarter.

when I found another entrance hall, all of its doors were also locked.

There was no place else I could go but to return to my room, where—if anywhere within these glum walls—I felt secure. I stood there restlessly, and my face flushed with agitation, because as I thought about the Count's behavior since my arrival, it dawned on me that he'd deliberately prevented me from getting out of the castle! Every night he had kept me up till cockcrow, so that I would sleep through most of the day, and—for courtesy's sake—I have barely left my room until he returned. And so the time has passed, and I've hardly had a chance to take stock of how many days I have been here. It's clear that the Count is quite strange. His behavior, at least, is like no one else's. Perhaps by keeping me here he is taking advantage of my help—especially as he has seen that I am rather pliant—but I simply cannot accept being locked up like a criminal.

I looked around and saw no other exit from my room, nor from any of the other rooms I dwelled in, except down the stairs that I had ascended on the first night, or into the hallway leading through this wing of the castle. But in this hallway, too, all the doors were locked.

Next I tried going up the stairs leading to the portrait gallery. When I took hold of the handle to the big oak door, I was amazed to find it unlocked.

The sun shone in through the windows of the long gallery, and the portraits seemed to have a different aura about them than they did when I saw them at night, lit by the weak glow of a still young moon,[171] and with the help of candlelight. Nevertheless, the images still had an effect on me. I suddenly started feeling rather sick, on the verge of breaking down. I took only a brief look at the paintings, even though it felt as if the stately portrait at the end of the hall was pulling me towards it with almost irresistible force. But I was determined not to let anything delay me until I had examined the castle as widely as I could.

On the opposite side of the gallery, two doors were standing wide open.

THE DOOR ON THE LEFT LED TO A ROOM IN A LARGE, round tower with several windows, but there were no doors in this room other than the one from the portrait gallery. Next to this door was another open door in the side wall of the gallery, leading to a long series of rooms of various sizes; they all faced west, and I guessed that they made up a large part of the castle's west wing. I had no time to examine these apartments more closely, but I judged by the look of things[172] that there were no staircases leading to the other living areas in the building. I assumed that such a set of stairs was somewhere to be found, but the last door in this series of rooms—which probably lead to a hallway or exit— was securely locked, so I couldn't open it.

All the rooms were furnished in the typical way of old castles, with furniture originating from different periods, but nothing in present-day style. Everything was old, faded and worn, though not rickety. I wanted to inspect the furniture more thoroughly later, as I didn't have time to do so at that moment. Realizing I wouldn't be able to get out this way, I hurried back to the portrait gallery. At its other end—the same side as the entrance—there was one more door. It was unlocked, and I entered a large, richly ornamented hall with three windows through which the sun shone in. Between the windows hung mirrors with black and gold frames,[173] and the floor was painted in a grey and white rhombic pattern. Everything was in a style known to be fashionable among highborn people at the beginning of the century, with pink, blue, grey

172 Icelandic: "ég (. . .) þóttist ganga úr skugga um." The expression "ganga úr skugga um" means "to ascertain," "to verify," "to check." The mediopassive form "þóttist" followed by an infinitive is mostly translated as "to pretend to . . .," but here it is used in the original meaning of "to think to oneself." In his rendering of Mark Twain's *The Million Pound Banknote*, Ásmunddson used exactly the same phrase to translate "I (. . .) judged by the look of things." See Twain, 1893, p. 34 and *Fjallkonan* of 1 May 1894, p. 71.

173 Maybe these mirrors date back to a time when the Draculas were still mortal people? In Stoker's 1897 novel, no such mirrors are mentioned.

174 This description matches Harker's Journal of 15 May in *Dracula*: "At last, however, I found one door at the top of the stairway which, though it seemed to be locked, gave a little under pressure. I tried it harder, and found that it was not really locked, but that the resistance came from the fact that the hinges had fallen somewhat, and the heavy door rested on the floor." The same method to build suspense will be repeated twice in the Icelandic version.

and white colors—all pale with age. Then I found another series of rooms, and I raced through them as if in a dream: I had grown ill now—I felt faint and unwell—so I hurried as fast as I could. These rooms have probably been deserted so long that the air in them may be unhealthy—especially at this time of year, when the sun's warmth has not yet penetrated the thick walls. But it appeared as though these living quarters had been inhabited not too long ago. Most likely they had been ladies' quarters; neither arrows nor other enemy fire could reach them, and the windows were larger and much higher than those in the rooms beneath.

After I had gone through several of the rooms, I found another door on the wall opposite the windows. I tried to open it, but it wouldn't budge. However, upon closer inspection, I saw that it was not locked; the wood was merely swollen.[174] At last I managed to open it. I came to a dilapidated corridor, and through some loopholes in the walls I could look straight into the ravine lying east of the castle, where a river fell to form a waterfall. The rooms on the other side of the corridor were all securely locked, but when I reached the end of the corridor, I finally came upon a downwards staircase. It was narrow and steep, with small embrasures in its massive walls.

I was starting to feel better, as the air in the stairwell felt fresher and healthier, relieving me of my nausea. But at the same time, the implication of what I had seen last night and this morning became clearer to me: I had to get out of this prison as soon as possible.

The staircase led to another corridor, longer and even more dilapidated than the one before. I suspected that I was now standing in the north wing of the castle, which—more than the other parts of the castle—seemed designed for self-defence and resembled a fortress.[175] At the end of this corridor I found a large iron-clad door. The key was in the lock, and I barely managed to turn it. When I came through the door I entered a rectangular room resembling a cellar. The walls and floor were constructed from unevenly carved rock and everything was covered in spider webs—it was evident that no one had been there for years. Light was falling through two windows, and between them were iron chains and screws, for which I could not determine the purpose. A set of stairs led up to one of the windows, so I rushed up the steps to see what I could find there.

175 Throughout the novel, the Icelandic text uses the word "höll" ("hall" or "palace") to describe Castle Dracula; in this sentence, "kastali" ("castle," "fortress") is used to set the gate tower apart from the rest. Because Castle Dracula is not a palace (associated with elegance, luxury, located in a park or garden), I have used "fortress" here to describe the gate tower and kept to the term "castle" in the rest of the novel—as also used in *Dracula*.

HEN I LOOKED OUT THE WINDOW, I SAW THAT I must have made countless detours on the way here to finally arrive at the building's north side. The window was small, so I couldn't see far to the right or left, but again I saw that we were near the ravine, with a misting waterfall below. I had often heard the rushing water in the silence of the night, but I didn't think it was so close. From the main gate the bridge led over the cataract, but now it had been drawn up, so that the castle could not be entered this way. I now understood the function of the chains I had seen by the windows: they were used to pull up the bridge. I also realized that even if I were able to exit the entrance hall, I still would not be able to escape. Quickly, I went back down the steps and took a good look around the room. I saw that the tools for pulling up and lowering the bridge had recently been repaired and that fresh footprints had disturbed the dust on the floor. I surmised that the drawbridge was moved gradually, and that the people who operated it had to move about this room to do so. It was hard to believe that they had to go through all the corridors and suites I had passed through in order to access this room, so there had to be another exit nearby. Then I spotted another door opposite the one I had entered, but it was much smaller—barely head-high—and had no lock, only a simple handle, like the ones seen on old farms in England. The handle could be pressed down easily, but the door itself was rigid and heavy. When I pushed it open my face was met with a waft of foul odor, and I found four or five steps of a winding staircase leading down into murky darkness. Had I been less wrought-up, I no doubt would have hesitated to go down there, but all I could think of was forging ahead. I propped the door wide open with a log lying in a corner. Then I slowly went down the stairs . . .

At first I could see by the little light from the doorway, but soon stygian gloom took over, so that I had to reach ahead of me to find my way. It was a great distance between each step, which were so narrow that only one person could walk them at a time; it was as if I were descending into a deep well. Running my hand along the damp wall, I cautiously moved ahead. I must have gone down at least fifty steps and was beginning to think of turning back, but curiosity drove me forward; I wanted to find what must be hidden in this castle—as the Count's words had implied—although I suspected that whatever it was, it must be something no honest man should go near! If this is the case, I must warn Mr. Hawkins, my employer, of the Count, who would undoubtedly be best kept exactly where he is.

Suddenly, it seemed something was behind me on the stairs! I heard nothing, nor did I see anything, but I felt that someone was right on my heels. My hair stood on end, and I felt shivers running down my spine. I couldn't bear it, and so I turned to the side, backing up against the wall and placing one foot onto the lower step.

And just then I was attacked! Something—man or animal, I do not know—grabbed me. Not from behind, for then I would have been a dead man, but from the front and side, so that it was easier for me[176] to defend myself.

Something enormously heavy weighed down on my left shoulder and started strangling me. I could feel a gaping snout touch my ear, cheek and mouth with its thick lips, releasing its rank breath. Then a leg—or something like it—was wrapping itself around my right foot, but luckily I had both hands free and could brace myself against the stair. I couldn't get to my revolver, but I grabbed the arms that were coiling around my neck and found that, although very hairy, they were definitely human! I yanked at them with all my strength, but they wouldn't give way. I felt something scratching at my neck, and it seemed as if my attacker was trying to get his lips to my throat. I had just grabbed his head with both hands when he suddenly released his grip and pushed me away, and I fell a great distance — — —

I don't know how much time passed before I came to life again, but it took me awhile to get my head straight. I was lying on the ground in front of a narrow doorway, and behind me, in the darkness, I could see the staircase. Ahead of me was a long tunnel with some light coming from windows high up by the ceiling. Luckily I had landed on a soft dirt floor, so I was not badly hurt.

I considered the possibility that I might simply have panicked[177]—became dizzy and fell down the stairs, hitting the door I now lay in front of and smashing it open—and that everything else had just been my imagination . . . But why would my shirt and its collar be torn and my necktie be gone, while the rosary with the iron cross—which I carried in memory of the landlady I had stayed with—had pressed itself so tightly into my neck that it left bruises? There was also this burning sensation in my throat.

Suddenly it occurred to me that I would have to go back up the same way I had come, and the mere thought of it nearly killed me. It felt like I was stuck in a trap, so without thinking I continued my journey, half limping.[178]

When I came to the end of the corridor, it opened up into

177 In the 2011 edition, this paragraph starts with "I do not know how much time passed until I truly realized what had happened to me," almost verbally repeating the first line of the previous paragraph. In *Fjallkonan* and in the 1901 edition, there is no such repetition.

178 In *Fjallkonan*, this line ends with "hálfhaltur" ("half limping"), omitted in the 1901 edition.

a windowless vault. Exiting the other side of it, I reached a round space with a dirt floor and three or four windows up high on the wall. The walls were constructed out of very large stones, and I guessed that I'd reached one of the deepest rooms of the castle. I could hear the waterfall better here than from anywhere else. The floor slanted downwards by the wall, like a trench.

I stood for a moment, finding my bearings. The windows were open and a breeze was blowing through the spiderwebs hanging from the ceiling. Even so, the air in the room was rancid. It didn't take me long to discover where this stench was coming from.

At first I thought I was standing in a food cellar—it seemed as if heaps of produce were stockpiled along the walls. It also occurred to me that an exit should be nearby, to make it easier for the residents to access the room. I then noticed a kind of shutter or hatch on the wall right next to me. I managed to open it. When I saw I might get some air and light in the room, I looked deeper into the opening, but just as I leaned against the wall to peek through the hole in the stonework, two skulls rolled down—one pale and shiny, but the other one with hair and skin still sticking to it!

I was aghast by what I was seeing, even more so when I found that the trench by the wall was largely filled with human bones, moldy and half decomposed. I could see a ribcage still connected to a spine, arms and legs with their tendons still intact, and skulls with hollow eye sockets, all tangled together. The stench coming from this pile of horror—magnified by the increased airflow—was so putrid that I nearly flung myself out through the opening in the wall. Fortunately, I managed to remain composed enough not to do so; otherwise it would have been my very last step. Below the window was the abyss with its sharp cliffs and the sweeping waterfall!

I looked again to make sure: This was no exit for any living human. It was meant for the dead!

Panic struck me when I envisioned the trip back to my room. In my frustration I ran right across the heap of bones, rattling beneath my feet, while I hastened to the other end of the room. There was another door and I managed to open it.

What on earth would emerge from behind this door?

Hesitantly, I opened it—and slipped through.

I had come to some kind of church or temple, though there were barely any of the icons found in Christian churches.

The room was gloomy inside, with high-set bow windows. There were repulsive, half-primitive pictures on the walls, and I also detected strange symbols on the floor.[179] I saw stone coffins, and towards the end of the room was an oversized sarcophagus made of yellow and multi-colored marble.

Suddenly I came across a doorway with a staircase behind it, leading upwards.

I hesitated before ascending, vividly recalling what had happened to me on the other staircase, but still I decided to proceed.

When I reached the top of the stairs I was standing on some kind of balcony; from there I could see down into an old, decrepit chapel. I realized that the room I'd just come up from functioned as an underground crypt and must be connected to this sanctuary, but I could find no way down from this platform to the chapel.[180] What I *did* find, however, were stairs leading up from the balcony, and I decided to climb them. I could tell by the condition of the steps that they

179 In light of the occult books in Dracula's library, this is perhaps another indication that the Count is engaged in witchcraft and occult practices. In *Dracula*, a reference to such signs in the castle's crypt is absent. Like most folk beliefs, Icelandic folklore knows a number of magical symbols. These magical runes or staves include, among others, "ægishjálmur" (protection or invisibility in battle), "vegvísir" (a magical compass), "óttastafur" (to induce fear in the enemy), "lásabrjótur" (to open locks and escape from custody), "þjófastafur" (protection against thieves) and "stafur gegn galdri" (to protect against the magic of others). The use of magical runes is described in *Sigrdrífumál*, a part of the Poetic Edda.

180 In *Dracula*, this whole trip is described in only a few words; after climbing along the outer wall to the Count's room, Harker quickly arrives in the chapel: "I descended, minding carefully where I went, for the stairs were dark, being only lit by loopholes in the heavy masonry. At the bottom there was a dark, tunnel-like passage, through which came a deathly, sickly odour, the odour of old earth newly turned. As I went through the passage the smell grew closer and heavier. At last I pulled open a heavy door which stood ajar, and found myself in an old, ruined chapel, which had evidently been used as a graveyard." See Jonathan Harker's Journal of 25 June. See also footnote 191.

were used often. As I ascended the staircase, I saw sunbeams dancing on the wall above me, which greatly lifted my spirits: There was a window! I was so relieved that for a moment I forgot that it was still uncertain whether I would ever get back to my room. I leaned out of the window and looked around.

I saw that I was in the southwest corner of the castle, and from there I could see its east side, where my room was. And then I saw the windows I'd left open. If only I had wings, I would have flown there!

SUDDENLY, I SAW SOMETHING ELSE THAT GAVE ME PAUSE.[181] Along the wall beneath the window I was looking out from ran the ridge I had observed the night before. It seemed as though a shadow had been cast upon it in the night. Whether this shadow was caused by a human or not, I do not know, but it could only have come from this window, for there were no other doors or windows nearby to cast light.

I'd had more than enough on my mind in my attempts to escape the castle, and so I'd almost forgotten about the body of the young girl I'd seen not far from here. But then something happened to remind me.

I saw an elderly woman wearing peasant clothes suddenly appear between the bushes and the place where the corpse was lying. It was evident from her movements that she was trembling with fear, and upon reaching the body her lips parted as if to let out a scream. But instead she steadied herself and gestured to someone else, whom I couldn't see, to come closer. I now saw that she was standing on a narrow path on the other side of the castle that led along the foot of the cliffs.

A group of people from the countryside—both men and women—came walking up the trail, the same apprehension in their demeanor. When they reached the elderly woman they crowded around her, and it was clear she was reporting something to them. I had no doubt what it was. The people spoke in low voices, but they were plainly upset. Then they all walked up to the dead girl. I could see everything: her pal-

181 While in the 2011 edition, this line ends with "sem olli mér óhug" ("which scared me"), in *Fjallkonan* of 11 August 1900 we read "sem fékk mér íhugunarefni," lit.: "which gave me material for reflection"—which better matches the depicted events.

182 "Mountain ash" is another word for "rowan tree" (*Sorbus aucuparia*). We remember that Harker was handed rowan twigs in the mail carriage, to protect him from evil. In *Dracula*, Harker's Journal of 15 May informs us that mountain ash was growing on "the sheer rock" around the castle. Incidentally, mountain ash was the only tree growing in Iceland during the Settlement, next to the dwarf birch; it was dedicated to Thor.

183 In *Dracula*, neither the murdered girl nor her mourning family is described; instead, there is a desperate mother looking for her abducted child. Harker's patronising words about the family's "ignorance" demonstrate that he still does not realize he is lodging in a vampire's lair.

lid face in the sunshine, the wound in her throat, and the blood-stained clothes on her dead body.

Among these people was an old man who appeared to be in charge of the others; he seemed to tell them something that they were hesitant to obey. But they finally nodded their assent. A young man—who seemed even more grief-stricken than the rest—went into the bushes and fetched a limb from a mountain ash, which he handed to the old man. The elder then drove the branch into the corpse's chest, mumbling a great many prayers, and then the crowd carried the body away. [182]

It was obvious that this ritual originated from ignorant superstition. [183] I sat down and looked at my watch. It felt as though I had been wandering around the castle for a very long time, but now I saw that it had only been three hours. Though I had expected the day to be coming to an end, the sun was still high up in the sky.

I knew that I had to continue my tour. These stairs would lead to the upper part of the castle, and surely somewhere up there I would find its inhabitants. She had to be there, too—the glorious girl I had met, and then had seen once more—and she could not be alone: Somewhere there had to be handmaids, occupied rooms, and doors that could be passed through without hindrance, although, until now, I had only managed to find my way to the abandoned parts of the castle.

"Carry on," I said to myself.

I ran up the stairs, which were no longer pitch dark, and soon I came upon a sturdily built door. I was so jittery that I could hardly catch my breath. I suspected the door would be locked and that I would have to go back the same way I'd come—or else perish here.

The windows were somewhat farther off, so there was not much light and I had to feel for the lock. The keyhole was open; the door must have been fastened.

I felt light-headed and nearly keeled over, so I sat down at the top of the stairs, leaning against the wall. I was exhausted, and I don't know how long I sat there, when suddenly I thought I heard someone moving about. I straightened up and listened as closely as I could. Yes! I heard it again! It sounded as if someone was carefully unbolting the door.

Could it be? I jumped to my feet and stepped towards the door, discovering that it was indeed unlocked![184]

I grabbed the penknife from my pocket and squeezed its strongest blade between the doorframe and the door until it opened.

A spacious hall with oak floors and wall tapestries spread out before me. There were also heavy, oldfangled chairs, like the ones in my bedroom. The blinds were half drawn, dimming the light.

Without making a sound I entered the room.

On the other side of the hall, two doors stood ajar.

I guessed that the door on the left would lead me towards my room and to that of the Count,[185] but before I headed that way I wanted to make sure that no danger awaited me from behind the door on the right, so I tip-toed across the floor and peered inside. I soon realized that I was in the corner tower I had noticed earlier.[186] It was a large, round space without a door, except for the one through which I entered the room. The windows had been partially bricked up; the rest were barred with iron grates. There was no decoration on the walls, save for the spiderwebs. A wooden fence ran along the wall, and between it and the masonry lay heaps much like the corn piles I'd seen in tillers' barns. At first I thought this room

184 Was the door really locked before or did Harker simply assume so? If the sound he heard was real, then who was the person opening the door for him—and then quickly disappearing? Until now, only one of the characters we have read about would qualify as an accomplice, ready to assist Harker in undermining the Count's rules.

185 A logical error: in the morning, Harker had complained that he did not know where the Count was sleeping.

186 This he did while watching from his bedroom window, in the morning. Harker had also entered this tower, some floors higher, when he explored the gallery and went through the door on its far side.

187 In 1900, Iceland's currency was the new Danish crown, introduced in 1875. The value of 2,480 new Danish crowns was equivalent to that of one kg of fine gold. A million crowns would thus be worth the price of 403 kg fine gold, today (March 2016) approximately 14 million Euros (16 million USD). Accordingly, "many millions of crowns" would mean several tons of gold.

188 Icelandic: "fáguðum gimsteinum." Today, "fágaður" mostly describes someone sophisticated in manners or something in impeccable order. Here it is still used in the original sense of "polished," meaning that the stones were cut and reflected the light.

might be used for grain storage, but this seemed highly unlikely as it was on the building's fourth floor. Out of curiosity, I put my hand on one of the piles and felt hard, small, round objects that were cold to the touch. I took a handful and carried them to the window. I found it was something quite different from what I'd thought: they were gold pieces—dusty, old gold coins, as was evident by their weight and metallic sound.

I walked quickly around the room and examined the heaps. They all looked the same to me. Some coins were flawless, as if freshly minted, but some had blackened. I found none from our time—some of them I didn't even recognize, while others were Greek or Roman. I am no numismatic expert and therefore cannot judge the antiquarian value of this coin collection, but the price of the precious metal alone would certainly have amounted to many millions of crowns. But that was not all I found.[187]

I was becoming more curious and started snooping around more when I saw two chests with iron fittings in the middle of the floor. They were not locked, so I was able to peek under the lids. The chests were filled with myriad finery made of gold, silver, jewels and pearls. There were golden drinking bowls, a large casket full of glimmering gemstones,[188] and other such valuables.

I also noticed compartments in the walls containing even more precious goods—no less sumptuous than those in the chests—but I had no time to examine them now. I came to realize that people hadn't exaggerated when they told me the Count was as rich as Croesus, for I had never seen anything like this.

Somehow I felt relieved that nobody had cared to *lock* the door—even though it was ironclad on both sides—and secure this room, although it contained such immense treasure.

BELIEVE I NOW HAVE A CLEARER UNDERSTANDING AS TO why the Count is in so many ways extremely cautious: he must expect robberies and thefts in the house when he's not around, and thus locks all the doors so carefully.

Next I opened the door on the left. It was a bedroom, slightly larger than my own. By the wall opposite the window stood a four-poster bed with heavy bed curtains. From the bedroom I could see into another room with bookshelves and a large desk in the center. I was quite certain I was now standing in the Count's private rooms, which matched the other rooms in the castle where I had lodged and moved about thus far.[189] I hardly dared to look around, as I suspected the Count or someone else would discover me, and I was unsure what would happen to me if they did. There were two doors in the room and I walked to the largest one. At first I thought it was locked, but when I put more pressure on the handle the door opened, and I was suddenly standing in the large dining room where I usually eat. Now these rooms felt pleasant and welcoming—I felt as if I were coming home, and yet, just a while earlier, I'd felt incarcerated and could think of nothing else but to escape from this place. It seemed many months had passed since I'd been here, though it had only been a few hours. Everything looked as it had before. I went to the window and looked out over the courtyard. To my right side loomed the gate tower,[190] where the stairs had led down into the depths of the castle. I realized now that I'd returned here alive by a hair's breadth.[191]

189 Icelandic: "sem *svöruðu til* herbergja þeirra annars vegar í höllinni," in which the expression "svara til" means "to match" or "to correspond to," from the From Old Norse "svara" = "to answer." Compare Anglo-Saxon "and-swarian," Old English "andswaru," Middle English "answere" and the later English "an-swer." In this case, Harker must mean that the Count's private rooms are the—thusfar unaccessible—counterpart of the already known rooms: his own bedroom, the dining room and the library. Either Harker must have an excellent orientation to know that the Count's private rooms are on the same floor level as the dining room, or the furnishing in all rooms must look similar.

190 Harker arrives at the dining room coming from the private rooms of the Count, which are on his *left* side when he leans out of the dining room window; the gate tower is on his *right* side. See the essay at the end of this book, and our online floor plans.

191 In *Dracula*, Harker makes this tour in reverse: First he crawls along the outside walls into the Count's room and finds the gold; from there, he descends a narrow stairway and ends up in the dilapidated chapel with the Count's coffin. See also footnote 180. There is no door connecting the Count's room with the dining room—Harker has to climb back along the castle's walls.

I felt a weight lying over me and I needed to wash off the dust, spiderwebs, mould and dirt I was covered in.

I noticed a sore on my throat, just above the artery—and I found bite marks! The rosary had obviously protected me, as it had pressed its shape into my flesh.

No matter how thoroughly I cleaned myself, the mark on my throat could not be erased.

I was becoming ravenously hungry so I returned to the dining room, where I had noticed a cloth on the table when I entered from the Count's room. Now the old mute woman was there, setting the table. I don't think I'm mistaken when I say that she startled upon seeing me, as if she was both frightened and surprised; apparently, she didn't understand how I could have got there. She must have been in my bedroom just moments before to make sure I was not present. She looked at me with fright and glanced at the door I'd come through, and then at the door to the Count's quarters. When everything was prepared, she invited me to sit down and I happily obliged.

I vigorously began to eat, filling my wineglass and emptying it in one stretch. But then suddenly something so shocking happened that the glass dropped from my hand and shattered on the floor.

I heard the key to the Count's room turning from the inside. Someone had locked the door.

This incident would have been insignificant to me had circumstances been different, but in this house, everything seems to be pregnant with foreboding.

As far as I knew, this door had been locked from the inside since the day I'd arrived here.

But today it had been unlocked, which was a stroke of luck for me; now it was fastened again, which meant that someone had been behind me or had seen me when I came in from the Count's room; *or* the Count had arrived to his room and bolted the door; *or* the old woman had realized I'd ventured this way and rushed to lock the door so that I wouldn't enter those chambers again—where I doubtless should not be.

I'd presumed the Count didn't want me in his chambers, as he'd never offered to show them to me and always kept them locked.

I hadn't entered these rooms on purpose, but neither can I erase from my memory that I'd been in them all the same.

Should the topic arise, I intend to tell the Count forthrightly what had happened—that I got lost in the castle and found my way back to my room by sheer luck—but I would not let him know the things I'd chanced upon.

HEN I GOT UP FROM THE TABLE I LIT A CIGAR AND walked towards the window. I found it rather chilly inside, so I opened the window to enjoy the warmer air that had been heated by the sun and which had settled between the walls of the courtyard.

As I stood smoking, I heard something like a lock being bolted shut and turned around. The mute old lady had entered, but where had she come from? I'd been so tired and absentminded when she first came in that I hadn't noticed which way she'd come. I could tell that she hadn't entered through the door to the corridor that runs along the castle.

I was convinced she must have entered another way, and that somewhere there had to be a secret door that she regularly used.[192] I had often tried in vain to talk to her with gestures; she simply could not understand me, staring at me in bewilderment, almost as if she were afraid. The only way to find out was to watch precisely whence she came, and where she went.

I saw her peering at me from the corner of her eye, but I pretended not to notice. Turning to the window, I glanced over my shoulder to watch what she was doing. I was sure somewhere in this dining room was the door to the exit I'd sought for so long, hoping to escape my imprisonment.

Quickly and skilfully, she took the cloth off the table and put the tableware into a wall cabinet I hadn't noticed before. After picking up the pieces of glass lying on the floor, I saw her hesitate, not moving. She looked in my direction, and I

192 This matches the Count's remark that "old Natra" never uses the corridor, but always takes "another path." In Stoker's preparatory notes for *Dracula,* a secret room in the Count's residence is mentioned, but this idea did not show up in the 1897 publication. Like the presence of the deaf and dumb housekeeper woman, this suggests that *Makt Mykranna* may be based on early ideas for *Dracula.*

could tell she was suspicious of me. I pretended not to notice anything but observed her all the more closely. However, a moment later, I happened to look out the window at the swallows flying over the courtyard, and I heard the same whistling sound as before. When I looked back the old woman had vanished . . . This time, I clearly heard the sound coming from the small octagonal room between the dining room and my bedroom. I had left the door to the dining room open.

The secret door had to be there.

Quickly, I charged into the tiny cabin to examine the room.

I checked it as thoroughly as I could but found nothing. As the space is without windows and a shimmer from the adjoining rooms is its only light source, it was very dim. I decided to have another, more thorough, look later and stopped groping around for now.

I was also quite tired from wandering about the castle earlier in the day, so I went to bed and fell asleep at once, but I woke up again after an hour, feeling well and rested. I expected the Count to be home by now, so I went into his library, but he was not there. To pass the time I started writing in my journal, and it all seemed so unbelievable—more dream than reality—were it not for the tangible evidence, which cannot be contested. I hardly know what to believe, but worst of all I cannot trust the Count. Why is he buying himself a house in London and moving there? My employer is a thoroughly honest person, and it would damage his reputation were he to facilitate the migration of shady scoundrels to London—there are enough of them in the city already.

The Count should arrive any moment now. The sun is

setting, and that lovely valley is fraught with evening scent and the same gentle beauty as the first time I saw it. I should go up to the top floor, as there must be an even more captivating view from the portrait gallery and the tower. Shouldn't I . . .?[193]

193 Icelandic: "Ætti ég ekki – – –" The subjunctive form of "að eiga" mostly precedes an infinitive, describing something one should do ("eiga að gera"). As the question is left unfinished, the possibilities are myriad.

GOD SAVE ME! I HARDLY KNOW WHETHER I AM AWAKE OR asleep! Why do I see and hear things that are not real? Is it the solitude? Is it because everything here is so different from what I am used to? It was probably just a dream, but God grant that I never have such a nightmare again.

The Count told me that he found me fully clothed and fast asleep in my bed when he came home, and that it seemed as if I'd had a nightmare. He said that I'd been mumbling and tossing wildly around in my sleep, so he had woken me up. My first thought was to believe he would report correctly,[194] for I had indeed woken up in the middle of the night, lying on my bed, fully clothed, with a light burning on the table and the Count standing next to me, glowering at me with his black eyes. I was exhausted, as if I'd drunk sleeping medicine, so I silently obeyed him when he told me to take off my clothes. I must have fallen asleep directly thereafter, as from that point on, I was dead to the world around me until quite late the next day.

194 Icelandic: "mundi herma rétt frá." The phrase "að herma rétt" means "to report correctly." The verb "mundi" ("he would") indicates a probability or uncertainty: Harker doubts if the Count has told him the whole story. Curiously, this exact expression was used only a single time in the history of the Icelandic press, in *Fjallkonan* of 12 August 1889: A certain Mr. Lárus Blondal from Kornsá had complained that the newspaper had reported inaccurately about the meeting of a trade association in the north of Iceland. As *Fjallkonan*'s editor, Valdimar replied that the article was based on a letter from a local gentleman, of which the newspaper had assumed "that he would report correctly about the meeting."

But one thing is sure: When I woke up, I clearly remembered everything that had happened the day before and into the night, but it doesn't at all match what the Count would have me believe. He maintains that he found me in my bedroom. However, I cannot understand why he does not just tell me the truth. He had previously warned me not to dwell in the empty rooms on the higher floors after sunset, but last night I had totally forgotten about that.[195] I have to accept—as he told me—that the air in this old castle is not healthy, though it may be difficult to identify the afflictive agents. People speculate about contagious mental diseases, but why shouldn't they just as well imagine mental infections that weaken one's mind and disposition in the same way that cholera and diphtheria bacteria weaken the body?[196] And nothing speaks against the possibility that such germs can be in a dormant state for years or even centuries on end.[197] I am neither a psychologist nor a doctor, but I can give my opinion. I am unable and uneager to put it into words, but I can feel it clearly: In the same way that various external factors can make one ill, so have I been affected. Whether these causes are mental or not, they have provoked visions and emotions in me that I've not had before—and which are of a rather nocuous sort!

The Count says that I have only dreamt things, and that would be the most logical explanation. I was tired that evening, my nerves were on edge, and my imagination was sickly after all that had happened to me since noon. I had

195 In *Dracula*, Harker is simply defiant: "The Count's warning came into my mind, but I took a pleasure in disobeying it." See Chapter 3, Harker's Journal entry of Later: the Morning of 16 May.

196 The presidential address to the Hastings Health Congress of 30 April 1889 dealt with contagious mental diseases such as the dancing mania of the 14th century, mental epidemics on the Shetland Islands (1817) or a suicide wave in Napoleonic times. See *Longman's Magazine* of June 1889, pp. 145-163. Until today, the causes of the medieval dancing mania could not be identified with certainty; for all three phenomenons mentioned, imitative behavior would be a more probable explanation than infectious germs.

197 By the end of the 19th century, the modern germ theory of disease superseded the old miasma theory, which had maintained that "bad air" was the cause of epidemic illnesses — a view fittingly worded by the reactionary Count. Researchers such as Louis Pasteur and Robert Koch studied the life-cycles of micro-organisms causing cholera, diphtheria, dysentery, smallpox, scarlet fever, tuberculosis (consumption), typhus, typhoid fever, malaria, syphilis and the plague; many of these diseases feature a dormant state, during which the symptoms disappear, although the germs survive and wreak havoc in a secondary or tertiary stage.

The alliterative expression uses two near-synonyms ("leg"
and "limb") to amplify the statement; they serve as a *pars
pro toto* for the whole body.

199 Icelandic: "að verða […] heitt um hjartaræturnar,"
lit.: "to become warm around the roots of the heart," this
time in a positive sense. See also footnote 159.

200 Again, this may be a hint that this line was created
in Reykjavík, where the summer nights never are truly
dark. But also in London (51°31' North), the nights
would be somewhat lighter than in the Borgo Pas (47°16'
North), additionally, the Victorian metropolis would
show the first signs of light smog.

fallen asleep with all my clothes on. No, I shall swear that I
had not!

I was sitting at the table, in the library, just as I am now,
when I suddenly felt the urge to go up to the top floor to have
a better view of the sunset. I threw my pen down and took
my book with me to the bedroom; then I ran up the stairs.
When I came to the tower next to the portrait gallery, the
sun had not yet set. The view from up there truly is better
than from any other place in the castle. I went to all the windows and finally stood by the one that gave me the best view,
and—as there are benches in all the alcoves—I sat down,
opened the window, and completely immersed myself in the
beauty of nature. I lit a cigar and leaned back.

The air was sultry and I expected the night to bring thun-
derstorms. I was tired and didn't feel like lifting a finger;[198]
instead, I felt called upon to enjoy the splendor of the scenery.
After the sun had set, a glowing evening redness spread across
the heavens; it was as if the whole sky was ablaze! Then, with
black-blue and reddish misty streaks in the east, goldish clouds
came dashing in, high up in the sky, driven by the upper air
streams. I started to feel curiously thrilled,[199] as if anticipating
something, but I didn't know what. Never in my life have I
felt like that before. I cannot describe it, but it was as if I was
half drunk. Darkness slid over, yet the same stifling heat remained, filling the air with a floral scent from the valley. I
arranged the pillows on the bench to be more comfortable,
stretched myself out even more, and stared steadily into the
distance, wondering why the tempest hadn't broken yet.

I must have fallen asleep, because I clearly remember
waking up to a feeling as though an electric current were passing through me, and I sensed that I was not alone. It was growing
as dark as it can on a summer's night in this region.[200] The

windows were hardly visible, and I could barely distinguish any of the furniture around me. At first I couldn't figure out where I was. I thought I had arrived in some kind of unknown world, and that a voice was whispering to me, "Love, which burns like bitter hatred, and hatred that burns like love!"

Those were the words the Count had used when he was showing me the paintings, but now they were being spoken by an utterly different voice—some seductive voice. Half unconscious, I sank back into the bench.

At that same moment, two flashes of lightning burst forth, casting their light into the room. In this light I saw *her* right next to me. She was just as she had been the first time I met her. When the light vanished I lost sight of her, but I could feel her coming closer and bending over me. I turned feeble, unable to move—

Lightning struck again, and I saw her face right next to mine; she stared straight into my eyes, her lips parted. I saw the necklace around her neck, which was bare right down to her bosom. I could see that she'd sank down on her knees by the bench on which I sat.[201] Then unbroken blackness surrounded me once more and I seemed to be tumbling down somewhere into the deep, half unconscious. The flowery fragrance had half numbed me, but I could still feel her soft feminine arms wrap around me; her breath on my face and her lips pressing to my throat—

I don't know how much time had passed, but suddenly I woke up with a shock. It felt as though she were slipping from my arms and a great grief engulfed my body. In that moment I saw a light flare up—not from a lightning bolt, but from a lamp carried by the Count as he entered the room. He shouted something—it sounded like a curse in a language I did not know. He came straight to me and lit up my face.

201 As described in the previous paragraphs, Harker is lying, not sitting—otherwise the girl, kneeling next to the bench, would not be able to reach his throat.

202 In *Dracula* there is no such dialogue: Harker faints after seeing the Count hand a bag containing a wailing child to the three vampire women.

"What by all the devils are you doing here? Why do you not obey me?" he barked at me in German, trembling with anger despite his efforts to control himself. "Here, at this hour! You should know that Dracula is master of this house."

He closed the window. He had left the lamp on the floor, and from below it cast a ghostly—or rather, demonic—hue onto his face. His hair stood up on his head like that of an angry lion.

I rose—about to stammer some excuse—as he stood, staring at me, as if considering something.

Then he said in a commanding tone: "Lie down."

Automatically, I obeyed and lay back on the pillow.

He took the lamp and examined my face and neck carefully. Then he laughed a cold laugh.

"Good friend," he said, his voice suddenly gentle, "you should have remembered that I warned you against being up here when it starts to get dark. This you have forgotten, of course, but in this matter I must caution you again. You have put yourself at risk, falling asleep in front of the open window. Have you been attacked in your sleep?"

He stroked my forehead and the top of my throat.

After that, I cannot remember anything before waking up in my bed, fully clothed and with the Count standing next to me, saying he'd woken me because I'd had a bad dream; that it was past bedtime and that it would be best to undress.[202] I obeyed him and didn't wake up again until much later in the day.

I HAVE NOW WRITTEN DOWN EVERYTHING THAT HAS HAP-pened to me, and although it's but a few words, it's clear enough to convince me that this was no dream—or at least no ordinary dream. To be certain, I went to the top floor in broad daylight and had a look around. I went into the tower room and everything appeared just as it had the night before. The furnishings were untouched and nothing had been moved. The pillows on the window-bench were in a pile, exactly as I recall arranging them so that I would be more comfortable, and I no doubt recognized the silk that the benches were lined with. It was all exactly as I remembered it to be. I found cigar ash on the window sill, which I had left there while smoking. I also saw footprints in the dust on the floor, which apparently had not been swept in a very long time, and traces left as if by a light dress. Thus I have no doubt that my memories are accurate. I know that I was up there that evening, although the Count denies it. But I cannot understand why he does so. It would be more understandable were he to reproach me for violating his instructions not to go up there.[203] Perhaps then I might accept the idea that everything I believe has happened to me may have been but a dream.[204]

When we met last night the Count had already arrived in the library, quite contrary to his habit. He was most amiable in manner and had taken a number of English and Austrian lawbooks from the bookcase to show me, to help make my evening as pleasant as possible. It is truly amazing how much

203 The Icelandic text seems to be elliptic here; I inserted the words "were he to reproach me" to arrive at a logical statement. See next footnote.

204 The last two sentences in Icelandic: "Hitt væri skiljanlegra, að ég hefði brotið móti boði hans með því að vera þar uppi. Ég gæti þá fremur skilið í því, að allt, sem mér þykir hafa borið fyrir mig sé draumur − − −" The expression "Hinn/Það væri skiljanlegra, að ..." is often used to describe the arguments or wishes of another party, in a conceding sense, "skiljanlegra" meaning "more understandable," "more than understandable" or "perfectly understandable." I assume that Harker describes here how he would have reacted *if* the Counted had spoken frankly with him and had reproached him for being upstairs, instead of pretending that he had found Harker in his own bed. In this case, Harker might have been willing to consider the possibility that his last encounter with the blonde girl had merely been a dream. Because he notices, however, that the Count is lying about this one point, he concludes that his host must also be lying about the other points.

205 In *Dracula*, it seems as if the Count's highest goal is to remain inconspicuous and merge with the crowd. After the present Transylvanian episode, however, *Makt Myrkranna* deviates from this concept and assigns the Count a more public role, entertaining international diplomatic guests at his Carfax house. Intriguingly, they all communicate in French, not English!

his English has improved in such a short time. He must have a keen ear, as he catches on to pronunciation at a staggering pace. By now it's hardly possible to hear that he isn't an Englishman, save for single words in which the intonation is too difficult for him. I praised him for this, and it appeared he'd appreciated the compliment.

"I'm glad to hear that, dear Harker," he said with great enthusiasm. "Do you think that in a few weeks, let's say—or a month—I could speak your beautiful language like an Englishman? Don't you think that Londoners will immediately hear that I am a foreigner? I owe you a lot, my friend, and I will repay the favor, you may count on it."

I said that he would learn the language best—or the pronunciation, rather, as he can already build perfect sentences—once he is in London. Once there, he would hear other people speak as well and get to know the various dialects.

"No, it must be as I say. I do not want to risk drawing attention to myself or being laughed at when I come to London.[205] What do you think? I am buried in work and I'm willing to pay for some proper help. There are, however, certain things that cannot be paid for with money, and such is the case with the favor and the pleasure that you have bestowed on me. I hope you will enjoy staying with me here for the time being, and you should be able to rest here after a hard day of work. There are plenty of law books in my library, and among them are many rare publications that you will not easily find in larger collections. There is a treasure trove here for an intelligent lawyer, and I know with certainty that this castle has a good deal to offer you—far more than you suspect . . . I am sure you will not be bored."

I didn't know what to think. I thought I detected a sarcastic undertone in his words, and throughout our conversation I considered telling him all that I had chanced upon, asking him to speak to me openly—but I dropped the idea, and it was probably for the best. Instead I merely mentioned that my employer might dislike it if I were to stay here much longer, potentially for weeks on end.

"I have *told* you that you will be my guest for now. You must inform your employer—and in any case, a few more weeks will not make any difference. We will speak no more of it."

He gave me such a dark look as he said this that I realized it would be wisest not to mention another word about my wish to leave. I am to be imprisoned here, willingly or not.[206] Yet I still don't understand why he keeps me here; he pretends that he needs my English lessons, but that is nothing but pretext. He must have another reason that I cannot figure out.

I have now decided not to stay here, though he wishes to keep me. I will not be granted permission to leave, on neither good nor bad terms, so there's nothing else I can do but try to escape secretly.

When I embarked on this journey—like on any other business trip—I expected to complete it within a few days, but now I have become a captive, fearing for my life under the power of an Oriental tyrant.[207]

No. I have to get out of here. Staying here will be unbearable. I can already feel that I've lost my normal sense of composure. I have always been known to be an impassive person and have aimed not to let others unduly influence me. This is the first time that I've felt seriously compelled to bow to someone else's will.

If only I had some task at hand, so that I would not feel so restless.

206 Icelandic: "ljúft eða leitt," another alliterative standard expression.

207 With the threat of "Oriental tyranny," Herodotus referred to the clash between the Greek democratic city-states and King Xerxes of Persia in the Battles of Marathon (490 BC) and Thermopylae (480 BC). In the 1850s, Karl Marx used the term "Oriental despotism" to describe the "Asiatic mode of production," characterized by state control over land ownership and irrigation systems. Friedrich Engels set forth this thought in his *Anti-Dühring* (1878). Valdimar, familiar with socialist theories, may have introduced this vocabulary, which is not used in *Dracula*.

I am now starting to write an essay for the *Law Journal* on the legal procedures of Hungary, past and present. The Count was right when he said that his library is an inexhaustible treasure for a lawyer. It could have been of great use, had the circumstances been different. It is always better to know than not, and in such a situation as I am in now, idleness can be very harmful, so I work intensively and immerse myself in the books.

OVER THE LAST FEW DAYS THE COUNT HAS BEEN IN THE best of moods, spending more time at home than usual. He sat with me all evening—like he did on the first night I was here—and tried to entertain me; he may partly have done so to improve his English. He has told me many stories about his family and most of them were so obscene and lewd that they are not to be repeated, neither in speech nor in writing. Certainly we English folk are no angels,[209] but nevertheless—thankfully—we consider certain moral principles to be our laws of nature, and we believe that our moral aspirations are supported by decency in speech, written word and behavior. Sinfulness may hide beneath an impeccable disguise. Much like dust and dirt, it can be found anywhere, yet it is crucial to society that such behavior is condemned as vicious and damaging. Surely the community that is ashamed of its filth is truly healthier than that in which people are shameless enough to throw their rubbish on streets and crossroads as if it does not matter. I understand that the Count may consider our ideas of morality to be worthless, and that ethical behavior—as we call it—in his opinion is nothing but worldly wisdom that man has learned from experience. I do not pretend to be very strict with morals myself; still, I cannot condone that the only strings constantly struck are those of uncurbed carnal craving.

It's as if the Count believes that the love between a man and a woman—in its basest form—is the only thing that

208 The following episode was published in *Fjallkonan* of 13 October 1900, but omitted from the 1901 book publication and its second and third edition.

209 An Icelandic alliterative pun: "við erum engir englar, Englendingar."

210 Previously, the Count had told Harker that to rule over people is the only thing that counts in life. In his view, power and sex must be closely connected.

211 This may refer to Joseph, the virtuous husband of the Virgin Mary, or to Joseph, the son of Jacob and Rachel. Genesis 37-50 describes how his brothers mocked at Joseph, calling him a "great dreamer," In Egypt, Joseph resisted Potiphar's wife, who tried to seduce him; he became a prisoner, but later rose to power. When his brothers came to Egypt to buy food, they fell on their knees before him, their faces to the ground, and called themselves his servants.

212 Icelandic: "kærleikar kvenna kringsnúa jörðinni," probably an alliterative creation of Valdimar's own making, with "kvenna" being the genitive plural of "kona." An alternative translation would be "Loving women is what makes the world go round." In *Alice in Wonderland* (1865) by Lewis Carroll, we find: "Oh, 'tis love, 'tis love that makes the world go round," spoken by the Duchess in Chapter 9. Sometimes, the phrase is attributed to the dramatist W. S. Gilbert. Bram Stoker personally knew both authors.

counts in this world.[210] Half in jest, I pointed this out to him the other day, and I didn't fail to mention that I cannot subscribe to such a view.

"Oh, you are such a great Joseph, I admire you,"[211] he said and laughed disturbingly. "I respect your principles—for having them is truly a rare virtue nowadays—but believe me, you too will someday prove the saying 'C'est l'amour, l'amour, l'amour, qui fait tourner la terre' to be true (that is, 'The love of women is what makes the world go round'[212]). You will understand me! Look at me!"

He slapped my shoulder, and I felt the blood rush to my head as he looked at me, but I must not have understood him the way he intended, for if I had, I would have been—

18 MAY[213]

I WOULD HAVE BEEN DONE FOR. YES, THAT IS WHAT I CANnot erase from my mind—even as I sit here to read or write—for my thoughts are constantly wandering. It feels as though some current is carrying me to the brink of destruction and I cannot fight it.

My dear Wilma, I call upon you, just like a Catholic man calling to the Virgin Mary at the hour of temptation.[214] There's another image that always crops up before my mind's eye, clouding your appearance so that my spirit cannot see it any longer, and when I try to seek comfort in memories of our happiest times—when we would silently understand one another and look with hope towards the future, with all our plans to live and work together in harmony—another memory surfaces. One that suffocates all else and affects me like a fever, or poison, or drunkenness. And when I open my arms . . . it is not you – – –

Whether I am awake or sleeping, she haunts me—this strange creature. She scares me, and yet she attracts my thoughts, harder and harder. I don't understand how I have changed—how I have become crazed and obsessed.

I have seen her again, although I have sworn a solemn oath—more than once!—that I would never do so again. But what's the use of that? Without the least forewarning, she shows up here.

When I sit here and write in my journal—only about the things I have experienced—she suddenly stands behind me,

213 Starting with 18 May, the Icelandic text changes the date format to "the 18th" etc. and later to "the 10th of June" etc. For clarity's sake I have standardized the date format.

214 These words effectively install Wilma as a saintly or virginal figure, the counterpart of the lascivious blonde girl. Although *Dracula* today is often read as an encoded description of sexual excess, Stoker himself insisted: ". . . the book is necessarily full of horrors and terrors but I trust that these are calculated to cleanse the mind by pity & terror. At any rate there is nothing base in the book . . ." See Stoker's letter to William Gladstone, 24 May 1897. A decade later, the novelist pleaded for censorship in fiction, arguing that "the only emotions which in the long run harm are those arising from sex impulses." The views of Valdimar may have been different. In an article about the United States, he took a critical stance at American Puritanism: "The respect for women takes such a subtle form [in the US], that it is possible to sue a man for hanging his underwear in a place, where a housewife can throw an eye on it. [. . .] Doctors say that the high infant mortality rate [in the US] is due, among others, to the fact that mothers are hindered to breast-feed their babies." See *Fjallkonan* of 10 June 1890. p. 70.

like the other day, when I put down my pen and left my diary. I hear nothing and don't notice anything until I feel an electric shock run through my every nerve, urging me to look up, and then — — —

I will try to describe these personal trials, as that may make it easier to avoid them.

One example: I sat writing in the library after the Count had bid me good night. Suddenly, while writing those last lines on the previous page, I felt the urge to go up to the top floor—to the tower room next to the portrait gallery. Something drew me there against my will. I fought against it with all my might and continued to write, but it felt as though some voice were whispering in my ear, incessantly, "Why do you not come up? I thought you would visit us. I have so much to talk about with you. You will come. Remember that you are expected."

I didn't go up there—*there* I will not go again while I'm still in control of myself—but although I have considered myself tougher than most other people,[215] I am so weak. I can control my body, but my inner man I cannot.

Physically I was not there, but something in my inner man obeyed her and called her to me. I continued to write, but then I suddenly sensed her presence. The pen dropped from my hand—I looked back and saw that she stood behind the chair, gazing at me with those eyes that are like radiant beams, cutting through bone and marrow. — — —

THERE IS A LOT OF DISCUSSION ABOUT HYPNOSIS.[216] I have never tried letting myself be hypnotized, but in my law cases I have seen on more than one occasion a wrongdoing blamed on hypnosis. I have always believed that this so-called hypnotic state is nothing more than a lack of moral endurance or will, and I have never wanted to accept that such an excuse would be honored in legal proceedings. If men of law would acknowledge and use this as an argument, it could lead to a confusion of people's moral compass and accountability. It would, however, be convenient for all weak men, if they could employ this subterfuge to lay blame on some chap whose evil will they couldn't have resisted.[217] As a result, society would plunge into chaos. Although I had to undergo the painful experience myself, that another person was powerful enough to make my will melt like wax—weakening until it dissolved altogether—I feel and I know that it is entirely my own fault. If my soul were purer, and my desire for the good stronger and tougher in the battle, I wouldn't so easily give in to something that I cannot identify—which I cannot even understand with common sense.

She bent over me and I could feel how her eyes sought out my innermost nature, my independence and all my mental strength. I sensed it, although at that moment I couldn't put it into words. I leaned back in the chair and looked at her. A ray of light revealed the ruby heart on her chest and it seemed to me as though blood ran from it. Was I asleep? At first I only

216 This thought seems to come out of nowhere. But as noted in the Introduction, the previous chapter, omitted from the book editions, interrupts Harker's legal studies in the Count's library; here he is picking them up again.

217 At the time that *Dracula* and *Makt Myrkranna* were written, legal and medical circles fervently discussed whether or not criminal behavior could be triggered by hypnotical suggestion. Although many physicians maintained that an intact moral instinct could not be overruled by abusive suggestion, some culprits claimed that they had acted under hypnotic influence, e.g. Gabrielle Bompard in the Gouffé murder case, which the Paris court dealt with in 1890. This debate had a direct relevance for *Dracula* and *Makt Myrkranna*, as the portrayed vampires wield hypnotic powers, forcing their victims to act in an immoral way. Stoker was most likely familiar with these medico-legal discussions, e.g. in *The Nineteenth Century*. The play *Trilby*, based on George du Maurier's 1895 novel and dealing with the abuse of hypnosis, was a huge stage success at the time. See my article in *De Parelduiker* of October 2012. Ironically, the physician who most strongly opposed the idea that hypnotic influence could provoke criminal impulses, Gilles de la Tourette, was shot in the head in 1893 by Rose Kamper, a woman who claimed that he had ruined her sanity by hypnotising her against her will.

218 Previously, Harker had described himself as a man of the "true creed" ("rétttrúuðum"), which I translated as "English Churchman" (see footnote 49). This time, the Icelandic uses "sannlúterskur" ("truly Lutheran"). Like the Icelandic Lutheran State Church, the Church of England follows Lutheran principles. Neither church recognizes the authority of the Pope nor practices a Maria cult, and both churches prefer the simple (empty) cross symbol over the crucifix showing Christ's tortured body.

219 While *Fjallkonan* and the 1901 edition state "finni til hryllings," the second and third editions read "finni til tryllings"—a transcription error.

saw the radiance in her eyes, but then I clearly saw that her bosom was bloody, and I remember how horrified I was. What happened next I only recall as if from a dream in which truth and fantasy merge. She sank down on my knee, and I felt her soft body in my arms as she wrapped hers around me so tightly that I could hardly breathe. I can still feel how she pressed her lips to my neck with a long, quivering kiss. It was as if I melted and lost all awareness, as if time and space dissolved. But then I woke up in pain and she whispered to me impetuously, "Take away the cross—the cross, I cannot stand it—take it away."

I assumed that she meant the crucifix hanging from the rosary I carried around my neck, but it was as if some internal force within me revolted. By no means can I explain it, for I put no belief in inanimate objects—neither in the cross, nor in anything else—and I am such a devoted Lutheran[218] that I cannot ascribe supernatural power to the crucifix, as Roman-Catholics do. I honestly don't know what stopped me from obeying her. It was as though some voice whispered to me that I should pay no heed to her words. I woke up as if from a slumber, and it felt like some invisible string suddenly snapped. She jumped up from my lap like a spring, glancing at me with a threatening look. She extended her arm over my head, gradually lowering it while she stared at me; at the same time, she inched backward towards the door. I stood still, stunned as if struck by a rock, and so I didn't notice how she stole out, though I was curious to find out.

— — — And since then I've felt that she is constantly around me. Even though I'm clearly helpless and horrorstruck[219] when I think of her, I cannot rid myself of the strings she has wrapped around me; those invisible threads that have been spun around me ever since I got here, initially filigree and light like spider silk, but then stronger and stronger—so strong that they practically strangle me.

I have seen her twice since then. Once in the twilight, like the first time I saw her. I stood by the window in the library and looked out, but when I glanced back I saw that she was standing behind me, and before I knew what was happening she had slung her arms around me and pressed a kiss on my throat like before. The second time, she was standing, pale and sylph-like, right under the lamp in the octagonal room, when I opened my door. We looked at each other, but I had enough strength to turn around and slam the door so that it locked between us.

——— But whether I'm awake or asleep, she always hovers before my mind's eye, and if I were to obey that voice that always seems to be talking to me, I would search the whole castle for her.

There is only one desire in me that is stronger: my wish to get away from here, even if it costs me my life. But *how* do I get out?

The gate is always locked and I don't know any other exit. True, the Count doesn't monitor me at all times, but I know for sure he'd soon find out if I tried to flee. It seems he's constantly observing me in his self-satisfied and scorning manner —he hardly cares to cover that up. Sometimes when he speaks to me (always diligent to practice his English) and I'm so lost in thought that I forget to answer him, he pauses and looks at me with an expression that I cannot describe. But it frightens me. I am almost convinced that he knows and understands how I feel, and that he's enjoying it.

The things he said to me during the first days of my stay here often cross my mind, when he talked about his— allegedly moonstruck—cousin; I remember how slyly he

220 Madness (feigned or real) was an essential topic both in Shakespearean and Victorian drama and plays an important role in *Dracula* as well: Both Harker and Holmwood doubt their own sanity, and Seward suspects that Van Helsing is mad, while the latter describes his own wife as "no wits, all gone." Surprisingly, Dr. Seward's mad patient Renfield acts as a learned philosopher in his dialogue with Van Helsing.

peered at me with those eyes of his. Now I wonder whether I am caught in a trap. Is she actually a lunatic—or what then?[220] No. I have to get away from here . . . before I go insane myself.

21 MAY

NO LONGER DOUBT THAT THIS CASTLE IS HOME TO hideous demons—not human beings with hearts and conscience.

I shall now explain in a few words what I have discovered.[221]

I have repeatedly studied the octagonal room, searching for the exit that I was convinced had to be there, although I had yet to find it.[222]

Last night, after the Count had gone to bed—and I assumed he'd be fast asleep—I decided to make one more attempt.

I opened my bedroom door, lit all the candles, and investigated every inch of the small room.[223]

I guessed that the secret passage had to be right across from my bedroom door. In effect, the octagonal room has only four walls large enough for a door, as the diagonal panels at the corners aren't wide enough for passage. In two of the walls were the doors I already knew about—one leading to my bedroom and the other one to the dining room—and as one of the remaining sides backed an outer castle wall, there was only one side left. After a long search I found a triangular button on the floor. I stepped on it. Immediately, and without a sound, a door wide and high enough for me to walk through opened up in the wall.

Now I saw how it was possible for the old lady to disappear in an instant every time she left the dining room.

Cautiously, I shined my light into the doorway and saw a broad corridor, which I assumed during daytime would get

221 The following scenes—a bit more than a "few" words—have no equivalent in *Dracula*.

222 Icelandic: "… þótt mér tækist ekki að finna hann." The second and third book edition replace "tækist" with "takist," which makes little sense, grammatically.

223 Icelandic: "í krók og kring," another alliterative expression.

224 Icelandic: "járnbrautar ljósberanum," lit.: "railway lightbearer." In 1900, Iceland had no railroad system and in my team of native speakers, no one had ever seen this word in Icelandic; even the Árni Magnússon Institute for Icelandic Studies in Reykjavik could not find any reference. In Europe and the US, however, the second half of the 19th century was the heyday of railway development and railroad lanterns played a vital role in signalling. Another option would be that Stoker wrote a text containing the word "train lamp," meaning a lamp fuelled with whale train—just like Van Helsing in *Dracula* uses a candle made of whale sperm. The Icelandic "járnbrautar ljósberanum" would then be a translation error; the correct term would have been "grútar-lampi." In both cases, however, the lantern should have a wick, not a candle.

225 The 2011 edition uses "12"—which made me wonder how Harker could identify the number of instruments so precisely. In *Fjallkonan*, however, we read "tólf" ("twelve") so I assume that Valdimar picked what—in his eyes—was a round number, just like in *Egil's Saga*, where everything comes in dozens: twelve men to make a company, twelve ounces of gold in the spangles, twelve witnesses to swear an oath, twelve people from each folk to act as judges, or like in *Laxdæla Saga*, where twelve women were seated behind a curtain. Up till Christianization, the Icelandic "hundrað" ("hundred") meant 10 x 12 = 120 and only later, the "stórt hundrað" ("big hundred") or "tólfrætt hundrað" was distinguished from the decimal hundred ("tírætt hundrað") by the extra adjective, if needed. Iceland adopted the metric system only in 1900.

226 The Icelandic word "básúna" has the same roots as Dutch "bazuin" and German "posaune" (Latin: "bucina"). Today, trumpets, horns and trombones mostly have piston valves or a slide mechanism, but *Makt Myrkranna* probably refers to a natural trumpet here. The Icelandic sagas frequently mention the use of such trumpets in war.

light from a window above. At the end of the hallway I saw a stairway leading down.

I rushed to my room to fetch matchsticks and my revolver, then lit the candle in my train lantern,[224] before starting my expedition down the stairs. They descended gradually and it was clear they were used often. I felt vigorous and high-spirited—I had finally found the exit I'd sought for so long. I went down the steps and proceeded as cautiously as possible.

I startled and stopped dead in my tracks when I heard the echo of some sound I couldn't identify. This reverberation seemed to come up from deep below the ground. I soon found, however, that it was the sound of trumpets, but then the music slowly faded away. As I stood there stock-still, listening, I thought I could make out a dozen[225] horns or trumpets.[226]

I was so horrified by these sounds, truly terrified for the first time in my life, that I was about to turn back.

I managed to brace myself, however, and continued down the stairs.

I had been circumspect enough to take off the shoes I usually wore and put on slippers instead. I made no more noise than a fly. When I went down another floor, the sound was clearer and I could hear people talking—their voices striking me as primitive and aggressive. I heard many people speaking at once, like when school children are reciting something by heart, as in the old days.

Then I detected a strange smell, and when I lifted my lamp I saw thin streaks of bluish smoke drifting up the staircase.

I was becoming very curious and no longer thinking of the danger that could be—or most likely *was*—waiting for me, should I go any further. At any cost, I *had* to see what was happening down there.

I headed down another stairway, just as careful as before. It was a spiral staircase cut into rock, and I guessed that I was now below the castle's ground level. I wondered if these stairs would ever end!

Finally I saw a gleam of fire down in the deep, while the chords from below grew to a crescendo.

I extinguished my light straight away and froze on the spot.

The glow of a fire shone through a low door at the foot of the stairs[227] and cast its light on the nethermost steps, the smoke obscuring the end of the stairway like a fog. I went farther down the stairs, pressing myself to the darker side of the wall. Finally I made it to the door and reluctantly peeked through it.

I relaxed when I saw that the door didn't lead to the domed space from which the glow came, but instead opened up to a kind of balcony, from which a winding staircase led down towards a hall where the fiery glow and voices originated. I crawled onto the balcony and was able to hide myself behind the lattice.

Even if I live to be a hundred years old, I will never forget the sight I witnessed there.

There was a large arched vault down below, with a very low ceiling held up by two stout pillars supporting the roof. It appeared that the walls weren't made of brickwork but were carved into the rock. They were pitch-black with soot left by the burning torches—the source of the light I had seen—and the waves of smoke billowing up the stairs.

Below me was a mass of people, men and women in separate groups; there might have been 150 people altogether.

Never have I seen faces with such distinct animalistic features. I refer to them as such because they are the kind of

227 The Icelandic word "rim" refers to the rim or rung of a ladder, but as the text speaks of a spiral passage carved into the stone, we must conclude that Harker is still walking on stairs, not on a ladder.

228 In the 19th century, it was commonplace to associate animalistic qualities with people of color; neither Bram Stoker (*The Mystery of the Sea*, *The Lair of the White Worm*) nor Valdimar Ásmundsson were exceptions.

traits we find to be normal in other creatures, but we think them repulsive in humans. It was as though I could, to some extent, recognize the faces, but I couldn't immediately recall where I'd seen them. But after some further thought, I realized I had seen similar features in Count Dracula's family portraits! When I try to recall the impression their appearances made on me, I remember they seemed more diabolical than beastlike.

They were all bare to the waist, and it was horrendous to see their yellowish-brown frames, with muscular structures more like that of apes than humans. When in full harmony, the human body is the noblest work of nature, but here, the combination of their primitive look, build and posture created something more beastly than human.[228]

It seemed as though some kind of religious ritual were taking place.

STARTED LOOKING AROUND. ACROSS FROM WHERE I crouched I saw a kind of altar—for lack of a better word—consisting of a large black stone with a pillar of black marble on top. Behind this pillar—which seemed to replace the cross normally standing on church altars—a mural displayed a disgusting, horrible face with coarse and lewd characteristics. Around it, on a black background, fiery flames were painted.

In front was a large marble staircase, where I saw that six brutes were sitting; they were even more ape-like than the rest. They were perched on their heels and were staring at the wall on the other side. I saw that the hateful characteristics, so evident in the faces of the others, were multiplied in these individuals. Their foreheads were receding, wrinkled, and barely an inch high; straw-like hair grew from their big heads; their necks were like that of a bull and they had very broad shoulders. All six were stark naked, revealing their tan—and very hairy—bodies.

I shuddered at the sight and immediately understood that it must have been one of these brutes who had overpowered me on the stairs when I was attacked in the dark.

The same chord I'd heard while coming down the stairs started up again. The whole vault resounded with the same tones of horror. If the trumpets used by the priests of Israel when they marched around Jericho were akin to these, it's no surprise that the city walls collapsed.[229] The rock began to tremble and I felt myself begin to pass out.

229 In fact, the Israelites marching around Jericho blew ram's horns or *shofarots*, not copper instruments. See Joshua 6:1-20.

230 Stoker's Count only wore black; Bela Lugosi's vampire cape was white. *Makt Myrkranna*'s red cape matches the bloody character of the ritual the Count is leading.

231 This may be another Biblical reference: "Yes, a human being's days are like grass, he sprouts like a flower in the countryside—but when the wind sweeps over, it's gone; and its place knows it no more." See David, Psalm 103, Complete Jewish Bible, 1998.

232 Cf. *Egil's Saga*, Chapter 25: "Men have arrived here outside, twelve men in total—if one could call them such—because they look more than giants in build and appearance than normal men" (my translation). A few moments later, Skallagrim's men split up: Six enter the hall to greet the king, while six stay outside to guard their weapons.

Then I noticed a tall, old man. He had whitish hair and a grey beard, and he wore a red cloak that went all the way down to his feet, though his arms and neck were bare.[230]

It was the Count.

When he rose before the congregation, they all bowed as low as wheat in the field bending in a gushing wind.[231]

He went to stand before the altar.

After various ceremonial procedures, which were of such a nature that they cannot be described, I saw the six men—if one can call them such[232]—enter the room again two by two, each pair leading a young girl with her hands tied behind her back. The girls were all practically naked, of luscious build, and with most lovely looks. They probably would have appeared exceptionally alluring had they not been disfigured by terror.

Then came another group of men who looked like the rest. They carried archaic-looking drums that made a rare sound, which can best be described as resembling the rumble of thunder.

Next, four men came forward who were unlike the others. They carried shiny copper trumpets that were almost as tall as the men themselves. I realized they were the source of the trumpet sounds I'd heard.

Now the whole congregation approached the altar, whereupon the old man dressed in red—the Count, as far as I could see—stepped forward to read some kind of ceremonial invocation. The trumpet players sounded their instruments again, and in the same moment, one of the gorillas grabbed the fettered girl next to him and threw her lengthwise onto the altar. She struggled, as if fighting death itself.

A moment later the red-clad Count advanced towards the girl. He bent over her, staring hard into her eyes. I saw her face begin to change; little by little the fear seemed to fade and, after a while, her deathly pale cheeks were flushing normally again. It was as though she'd given up her resistance, her lips parting in a lascivious smile. She closed her eyes halfway, leaned her head back, and opened her arms.[233] And then she seemed to swoon.

The old man gestured to one of the scoundrels[234] kneeling by the altar, who promptly jumped onto the girl like a wild beast. I could hardly stop myself from crying out.

I saw how he bit her throat, seeming to suck her blood. She struggled for a moment, but all was over in a flash. She was dead.

The trumpets called again while the corpse lay on the altar.

The crowd went berserk upon seeing the blood flow from the wound. The Count went to the girl's body, dipped his hands in the blood, and splattered it all over himself.

I had seen too much and couldn't stay in my hiding place any longer. With great difficulty, I managed to stand up. My legs could hardly carry me, but with great effort I succeeded in getting up the stairs. When I reached the top of the staircase I lit my lantern again. I managed to open the door—and I closed it behind me with great care. On my way back to my room, I could still hear the grisly sounds from below.

I felt weak, as if I had been confined to bed for a long time and had just stood up. I threw myself onto my mattress, quivering with fear.

It isn't mere fabrication by theologists that Hell exists, for it is right here on Earth. I have personally stood at its border and seen the devils carry out their work.[235]

Perhaps next time it will be *my* turn to be slaughtered on that stone slab . . .

———————————————————

233 In *Dracula*, Van Helsing and his men perceive a similar transformation in Lucy: "The sweetness was turned to adamantine, heartless cruelty, and the purity to voluptuous wantonness. [...] When [Lucy] advanced to [Arthur] with outstretched arms and a wanton smile he fell back and hid his face in his hands." See Chapter 16, Dr. Seward's Diary of 29 September.

234 After repeatedly describing these men as "ape-like," the Icelandic text uses "mannhundur" here, (lit.: "man-hound"), maybe as they listen like dogs to their master. Generally, this word means "scoundrel," "villain," "bandit" or "rascal" and had already been used in the Icelandic sagas: *Flateyjar-bók*, *Gísla-Saga*, *Karla-magnus-Saga* and *Stjöran-Saga*. I did not find any connection to animalistic mythical creatures, such as the wolf-man ("vargr," "úlfr" or "úlfhédinn," lit.: "wolf-hide" or "wolf-skin," and later: "varúlfur" = "werewolf") or the bear-man ("berserker"), which are warrior types. See Gudmundsdóttir, 2007.

235 Harker now takes on the role of a Victorian Dante, after descending step by step to the lowest circles of Inferno.

Two days have now passed, but I haven't had the courage to further investigate whether I can use this secret staircase to escape.

Everything still follows the same routine as before. The Count sits beside me in the evenings and is the epitome of benevolence itself—both in words and manners. On the table before me lies the latest home directory of London, and in this library one can find all kinds of books explaining the progress of the nineteenth century.

But down below—underneath this castle—the most gruesome human sacrifices, more horrifying than in any story, seem to be common practice.

25 MAY

HAVE BEEN FEELING SICK AT HEART AFTER WHAT I HAVE seen and heard here.

I don't believe I'm wrong in saying that the Count is becoming more ominous with every passing day. He is certainly very kind when he speaks, but I can feel the mockery in his words, which are becoming all the more ambiguous, and sometimes when I make the mistake of looking into his eyes his expression terrifies me.

Since writing to Mr. Hawkins and Wilma of my need to stay here for a few more weeks, I have not heard from them. And every time I complain that not a single letter has arrived, the Count answers something like,

"Why should I, an old hermit, deal with the outside world? Who would write to me and to whom should I write? Here in the mountains, the land is sparsely populated and the flooding rivers have now broken many bridges, making transportation difficult. You must excuse us, my young friend, if our traffic connections and other facilities—which are sufficient to us—are less advanced than those in the center of the civilized world. I hope, however, that the roads will improve when the snowmelt abates."

I noted that this would most likely be his last word on the matter, and because I'd written to Wilma that the mail connections here were far from perfect, I assumed she wouldn't worry or become restless if she didn't receive a letter from me.

But I personally cannot stay calm; God knows that.

Two days after the Count told me about the communication problems, I found five or six newspapers in his library, both in English and French, including an issue of the *Times*—and all were much more recent than the newspapers the Count had shown me before. It occurred to me that the post deliveries were not all that infrequent, as my host had told me they were. I've also got the impression that he's very familiar with various political events that have only recently occurred. He said that he'd heard about them from his acquaintances in the neighborhood, but it's quite peculiar that any of these neighbors would be so well informed when floods and other natural obstacles are inhibiting the mail connections here.

But there is more.

A few days ago, I forgot my watch in the library when I left the Count and went to bed. When I noticed it was missing I got up and returned to the library, taking the light with me. My watch was lying on the table under some loose letters that had been placed on top of it. When I moved them aside, I saw two or three letters sealed and addressed by the Count. I read the addresses and was surprised to find that the letters were directed to men known throughout Europe for their involvement in political, social and cultural affairs.

I itched to open one of these letters, but I didn't dare do so.

When I laid them back on the table I saw that there were also letters the Count had opened to read. I was flabbergasted to find that these letters were only three days old!

There was absolutely no reason to deplore the slow mail connections. Why had the Count not wanted to tell me the truth?

Now I didn't hesitate to read the letter lying open next to me. It was in French and was signed by a well-known man.

Its author expressed his gratitude for a very high remittance, which he'd received from the Count with the honorable letter of 16 May—that is to say, last week—and he wrote that he'd completed the missions that had been entrusted to him with that message. After various elusive paragraphs—in which several people were named by their initials only—the letter reached its conclusion, reading,

> "With tireless dedication, everything is finally set for the great revolution. Our cause acquires new followers every day. Those of mankind who are 'chosen' have suffered for far too long under unbearable oppression, bigotry, and the shame of majority rule. We have outgrown these slave morals and will soon reach the point where we can preach the message of freedom.
>
> The world must bow before the strong ones."

This is the very phrase constantly repeated by the Count.

The text itself, however, didn't weigh heavily on me; neither did the well-known name it was signed by. What shocked me most was the fact that, as I saw now, the Count had regularly been sending and receiving letters since I'd arrived here!

I wanted to read more of the letters and even saw the name of a well-known Englishman on one of them, but I had the distinct feeling that I should leave, sensing that *she* was on her way to me. I ran back to my bedroom and twice locked the door behind me.

I feel safer this way. — — —

It was several days later that the following incident occurred—the incident that proved to me I'm in a most life-threatening situation here.

236 The following scene matches Harker's Journal entry of 19 May in *Dracula*. That Harker discovers and reads any newly arrived letters addressed to the Count is unique to *Makt Myrkranna*.

237 The Icelandic uses the imperative form to word a request; it does not know the word "please." See also footnote 379.

238 In *Dracula*, the dates are 12 June, 19 June, and 29 June, followed by the exclamation: "I know now the span of my life. God help me!" The Icelandic date of 22 June may be based on a transcription error, because Harker's Journal entry of 28 June makes it clear that he considers this day as his last day in safety. His entries of 20, 23 and 24 June do not mention that his time might be running out.

I sat in the Count's library and wrote, as I often do. He came in and greeted me, giving me the good news that he could now send a man to Bistritz, and that now I could write home, if I wanted.[236]

Although I didn't believe him, I expressed my joy and got up to fetch paper and pen.

"Here is everything you need, my friend," the Count growled. "Time is running out." He opened a drawer and gave me some paper and a pen. Then, with a an innocent expression on his face, he said,

"The mail service here is slow and uncertain, and so it would be best if you write three messages with three dates. I will ask the postmaster to ensure that your letters are passed on in time, so that your friends may know when to expect your return." He could see that I didn't understand his proposal. "You see," he said, "you will write in the first letter that you have finished your work here and that you will be coming home in a few days. In the second letter, please write that you will leave the next day. And in the third letter—well, let's see—yes, write in it that you are on your way to Bistritz."[237]

My jaw dropped and I stared at him, but he returned my look with such an evil glare that I didn't dare utter another word.

It's no use to try and protest against his will, and I'm afraid he suspects that I know too much—and thus will never let me out of here alive.

I gasped a few words, indicating that I would do as he told me, and asked what dates I should put on the letters.

The first letter should be dated 12 June; the second 19 June; and the third 22 June.[238]

It felt as though I'd been sentenced to death but I wrote as instructed nevertheless.

29 MAY

SOMETHING HAS HAPPENED—QUITE A TRIFLE, BUT perhaps it could be helpful.[239] The overwhelming silence, which has loomed over this place since I arrived, was disrupted yesterday. When I came into the dining room, I saw a group of Tatars in the courtyard.

These nomadic people are numerous in Hungary and Transylvania (Siebenburgen), with a population of many thousands. To some extent they live outside the country's laws, clinging more tightly to their old customs and habits here than elsewhere in Europe. Still, sometimes they elect some mighty nobleman as their protector, adopt his name, and assume themselves as his liegemen. They are wild, brave and merciless; they have no known religion, but they are very superstitious.[240]

It occurred to me that I might be able to send messages with the help of these people. To make contact, I greeted them and spoke to them from the window. They looked at me with great respect, but they understood me no better than I understood them. I had finished the letters. I only wrote a few lines to my employer, asking him to speak to Wilma, as she could tell him what he'd want to know. I had written her a long and clear letter, explaining everything about my situation.[241] This letter was coded in shorthand,[242] so that it's less likely to be read by others. I told her that the Count is more or less deranged and that one of his whims is to keep me here for as long as he can, but that staying here is unbearable for me. I urged that my employer make an effort to try and get

239 The entries of 29 and 31 May in *Makt Myrkranna* correspond to Harker's Journal entry of 28 May in *Dracula*.

240 *Makt Myrkranna* describes the Tatars in the same way as Stoker describes the Gypsies.

241 In *Dracula,* Harker worries about his fiancée's tender nerves: "To her I have explained my situation, but without the horrors which I may only surmise. It would shock and frighten her to death were I to expose my heart to her." In *Makt Myrkranna*, there is no such reservation—this may be another indication of Valdimar's influence. Although Stoker's major heroines (Norah Joyce, Mina Murray, Margaret Trelawny, Marjory Drake, Teuta Vissarion, Mimi Watford) are always intelligent and strong-willed, their male partners never forget to protect and patronise them.

242 Icelandic "hraðskrift," lit.: "quickwriting," meaning "shorthand," which became popular in the UK during the 19th century, especially in the form of "Pitman shorthand," developed by Sir Isaac Pitman. The system called "speed writing" was only developed in the 1920s by Emma Dearborn.

me out of here, with the help of the British ambassador in Vienna and the Consulate in Budapest. I expressed confidence in the English Government, which always goes to great lengths to protect its citizens.

I have managed to pass the letters to the Tatars. I tossed them out the window, along with two gold coins. One of the Tatars picked them up, bowed deeply and, pressing the letter to his chest, pointed to the west; apparently, he had grasped my intentions. There was nothing more that I could do. I went back into the library and waited for the Count to return. — — —

31 MAY

WHILE I WAS WRITING THE LAST WORDS OF MY previous entry, the Count entered. He greeted me with his normal courtesy, which I now find disturbing as I know what lies beneath. Then I took a seat on the other side of the table. I remarked something about the unusual guests in the courtyard and added some meaningless comment about what remarkable people the Tatars were.

"They are good people. I wish there were more of them—then a lot would be different. For centuries, they have faithfully[243] preserved many treasures of the occult sciences that otherwise would have been forgotten.[244] When the time has come, their loyalty will not go unrewarded."[245]

I didn't know how to respond to this, for never has the conduct of the "twilight people" been considered exemplary in Western Europe; their doctrines and beliefs are frowned upon as the most wretched[246] sort of superstition, completely worthless. But the Count saved me the worry and continued,

"The chief of the Tatars gave me these letters, which, of course, I felt obliged to accept, although they are not addressed to me, and I do not know whom they are from. What is this?" he said, tearing open one of the letters. "Is this from you, dear Harker, and addressed to our good friend Peter Hawkins? But this other letter," he ripped that one open as well, but upon seeing the strange writing—which he could not read—his face turned black as soot and he looked at me furiously. "It is a dishonest, anonymous letter that mocks trust

243 Icelandic: "trúlega," today translated as "probably," but here in the original sense of "faithfully," "safely," "to be relied on." Hence the mentioning of "loyalty" in the next sentence.

244 Icelandic: "huldu fræða," lit. "hidden sciences," referring to systems of knowledge and wisdom repudiated by modern rationalism: alchemy, astrology and other forms of divination, secrets of healing and eternal life, etc. We remember the collection of esoteric books in the Count's library. In *Dracula*, Van Helsing refers to the Count as an alchemist and a scholar of the Devil himself.

245 While Stoker's Count has helpers but no allies, here the vampire seems to envision some new world order, in which those who have been loyal to him will be rewarded—maybe by eternal life, plenty of blood and victims, gold or political power. The Count's vision might be understood as a satanic counterpart to the Christian expectation of a Last Judgment.

246 Icelandic: "örgustu," superlative of "argur," in old Norse used to ridicule men who were too cowardly to defend themselves, which was despised in Norse culture. Cf. Grimm, 1828, p. 644. The word was considered so abusive, that the mocked person had the right to kill the speaker on the spot. See Wilda, 1842, p. 50, footnote 4.

247 Icelandic: "Örvæntingin getur fundið sér hvíld." In *Dracula,* the corresponding phrase reads: "Despair has its own calms."

and hospitality, but as it is unsigned, it is of no relevance to either of us."

He set the letter on fire with a candle and threw it into the oven.

"Of course, I will take care of the letter to Hawkins, as I see that you have signed it. All letters from you, dear friend, are sacred to me, and you should know that they are in safe hands. I sincerely apologize for opening it. Perhaps it is best if you write the address again." He handed me an envelope and bowed politely.

I had no other choice but to address the letter again and hand it back to him. He walked away with it. A few moments later, when I was about to go to my room, I found that the door of the dining room was locked from the outside. I was unnerved by this and returned to the desk, trying to calm myself as best I could. I wanted to continue my writing but couldn't. I started to walk around, but I wasn't calm enough for this, either. Finally, I threw myself down on the couch, and I must have fallen asleep there because I woke up when the Count came in again, seemingly in the best of moods. When he noticed I had been sleeping, he said gently, "Oh, dear friend, you are tired; you have to go to bed. The blanket is one's best friend. Unfortunately, I will not have the pleasure of your company this evening as I have a lot to do. Good night and sleep well."

I wished him a good night in return and saw the mockery in his face. Then I trudged to my bedroom and fell asleep as soon as my head touched the pillow. Despair can find itself some rest.[247]

3 JUNE

I HAVE NOW DETECTED NEW TRICKERY[248] THAT PREDICTS even worse things for me.

Today when I went through my suitcase looking for my writing utensils—in case I should get the chance to dispatch a letter—I noticed that all the paper was gone: Everything I had written (save for this one book, which I usually carry on me)—my passport, my letters of recommendation, all my notes for this trip, such as train schedules, hotels, etc.—was taken. It will be even more difficult for me to get back now. Curiously, my money and valuables were untouched, and everything else was exactly as it ought to be.[249]

My mind raced as I hastened to the closet where my travel clothes were hanging; I hadn't opened it for days.

Everything was gone—not so much as an umbrella had been left behind!

I stood thunderstruck. How had this happened, and for what purpose? The first thought that came to mind was to hurry to the Count, report the theft, and ask him to take immediate action in pursuit of the thief. But when I considered it further, I thought it wiser not to do so.

No one walks around these rooms without the Count's knowledge and consent; not even the Tatars would dare commit such brazen theft right under the nose of the Master of the House. I don't suspect the old blind woman;[250] neither she nor the Tatars would bother to take my papers, so long as they'd had a chance to steal other things of greater value. My

248 Icelandic: "nýjar vélar." In modern Icelandic: "new machines." In older Icelandic, "vél" or "væl" would mean "artifice," "craft," "device," "fraud," or "trick." The corresponding line in *Dracula* confirms this reading: "This looked like some new scheme of villainy."

249 In *Dracula*, this scene corresponds to Harker's Journal of 31 May.

250 Until now, the old housekeeper was only deaf and dumb but still able to spy on Harker; here the poor lady also loses her eyesight—probably through a mere slip of the author's pen.

notecase contains expensive items made of precious silver and crystals; in my pocketbook, there is still a bunch of Austrian banknotes—a true find for greedy fingers—and an exquisite cigar case lies right next to the place where the now stolen papers had been. All of these items have been left undisturbed, and so it can be deduced that this was no ordinary thief wanting to steal from my suitcase, but someone who specifically wished to obtain my letters of recommendation and the other documents I'd had with me during my journey. Someone who didn't care at all about money or valuables.

I decided to behave as if nothing had happened—but why have these things been stolen?

I doubt that anybody but the Count himself has done this. But it's hard to understand what he should want with my passport or letters of recommendation, for even if he went to England, he could obtain both these things in his own name.

The purpose can only be to prevent me from getting back home or escaping this place.

Even if I manage to get out of the castle, it will be difficult for me to traverse across Europe in my everyday clothes, and without a passport. I will be considered a fugitive or a vagabond! — — —

6 JUNE

GOD ONLY KNOWS WHAT'S HAPPENING HERE. IN THIS part of the castle where I'm detained, a deathly hush always rules; never does one hear even the smallest of footsteps in the corridors, nor any voice resounding in the old vaults. But now the harsh, raw voices of the Tatars boom in from the courtyard, their fires burning into the night. I hear a clamor of shovels and iron picks, seemingly coming from the undercroft. I have asked the Count what's going on, but he only replied with some absurd answer.

Among the group of Tatars I have noticed several men of a different stock—the same I saw in the temple vault: men who are more like apes than humans. But it seems as if the Tatars are on quite friendly terms with these men. The Tatars are rather good-looking;[251] some of the women are even eye-catching. I'm inclined to believe that the Dracula clan can trace its origin to members of both these groups.

251 Icelandic: "laglegasta," lit. "the most beautiful." In Icelandic the superlative is often used to indicate that something is "quite OK."

8 JUNE

THIS MORNING I WAS ROUSED FROM SLEEP AROUND nine o'clock[252] by some raucous noise outside. I leapt to my feet and hurried into the dining room. Looking out of the window, I saw what was happening: four big transport wagons—like the ones used by the farmers in this region—had arrived in the courtyard.[253] They were loaded with large boxes made from whole wooden planks. The Tatars unloaded them from the wagons and stacked them together in the courtyard. The crates appeared to be empty.

There were six strong-looking horses for each carriage, and the drivers were all dressed in the colorful national Slovak attire. They wore wide-brimmed felt hats, high shoes and sheepskin coats, and they held long staves in their hands.

The Slovaks stood a bit aside from the Tatars, and I could see from their faces that they greatly marvelled at the castle and its high towers.

I was glad for their arrival and thought Providence had sent them to me as one small favor. I ran down the stairs as fast as I could, convinced that the gate to the courtyard would be open, but it was locked as solidly as usual. I rushed back up to the window and saw that the Slovaks were still waiting in the courtyard; I signalled them to come closer, trying to convey that I wanted to speak to them. I wanted to give them a letter, which I would go write in the library without delay. At first they looked at me, took counsel, and then asked the Tatars something. The same man who had taken my other

252 Icelandic: "um dagmálabil," lit.: "the time of daymeal," which was between 8 and 9 a.m. in old Iceland.

253 This scene corresponds to Harker's Journal entry of 17 June in *Dracula*.

letters walked up to them and told them something, at which they all started to laugh. After that I couldn't persuade them to speak to me. No matter how I called or beckoned them, they wouldn't even listen, but merely turned away.

After the wagons had been emptied, I saw the very same man—who appeared to be the chief of the Tatars—give the Slovak farmers money, whereupon they took their horses and left. When I realized that it was a lost cause, I gave up any further attempts to make contact.

10 JUNE

Y STAY HERE IS BECOMING INCREASINGLY OMINOUS. This evening the Count and I sat together discussing political news from the outside world, which had come with the arrival of fresh newspapers during the day (although I haven't yet received any letters). The Count has a sound grasp of all events relating to politics, but I struggle to guess which political party he follows. In some aspects he seems to be very liberal, like a downright revolutionary man—but in other points his views are so very outdated that he may well be far more conservative than most other reactionary people. He spends much time thinking about socialists and anarchists, and he often expresses his peculiar views on both of these political movements.

"They are good people; capable people," he said when we recently spoke about an anarchist-organized riot, one condemned and repudiated by the entire educated world.[254] He rubbed his palms together and fire seemed to burn from his eyes.

"I don't see what you are driving at, Sir Count," I said. "The power of the mob could never be something you'd be pleased with."

"The mob—those dull-witted common people—will never gain any power," he said, "and will never be more than an instrument in the hands of the strong, who rule *with* the masses and *over* the masses. But only a very few understand the wisdom that lies in this truth. Oh, you Englishmen are so proud of your political freedom[255] and progress—as you call

254 This may be an allusion to the Haymarket Riot of 4 May 1886, at Haymarket Square in Chicago. *Fjallkonan* reported on the demonstration itself (issue of 18 June 1886) and four years later, in an article about the US (10 June 1890) it commented critically on the subsequent trials and verdicts.

255 Lit.: "governmental freedom."

256 Icelandic: "feigðarsvip." In medicine, this refers to the facial expression of a dying person, *facies hippocratica*. In Norse mythology, it stands for an apparition foreboding imminent death. The Icelandic noun "feigð" signifies a foreboding of death; the English "fey" and the Dutch "veeg" are cognates of the Icelandic adjective "feigur" ("doomed to die"); "svip" means "appearance," "looks," "expression," "resemblance," "apparition" or "spectre."

it—but there are only two or three men among you who fully understand what progress is, and that this freedom for the masses is its worst enemy!" — — —

I have often heard him talk like this, and it has triggered quite a few thoughts in me; yet I have not been able to understand what the gist of the matter is, as whenever I've attempted to delve further into the question, he has always been evasive, giving me answers that make no sense, thus leaving me no wiser than before.

We sat together for a long time, and as he left he wished me a good night. I had a very difficult time sleeping and got up at the crack of dawn, opened the window, and started reading, hoping I would doze off.

The mornings are nebulous here in the mountains, obscuring my view into the valley below. Atop the castle the sun now reddened the towers, yet the fog lay like a thin veil on the walls underneath, becoming denser towards the bottom. I began to observe this phenomenon, when suddenly I saw the same scene I had witnessed the night the young girl must have been slain. But because of the brume, I could hardly discern this monstrous fellow, nor could I clearly see the ledge of the wall on which he was moving.

Soon I saw another person moving along the ledge. He was much smaller, and as he came closer I saw that he was finding his way along the ridge by gradually inching forward—with the gaping abyss right next to him.

I stepped back from the window, trying to watch him more carefully.

The man was wearing my travel clothes! He seemed so similar to me in size and height, and in all other aspects, that it was as if I was looking at my own ghost.[256] Because he was looking downward I couldn't clearly distinguish his face, but I could see he was young and dark-complected;[257] I could tell that he was determined and possessed nerves of steel from the very fact that he traversed this narrow and dangerous path.

I watched him until he climbed through a window at the west tower of the castle.[258]

I now realized that whoever had stolen my clothes must have a specific purpose for them, and I wondered what that could be. It's obvious they have been taken to prevent my escape, but surely there must be more behind it. This man, dressed in my suit, is probably going to appear in my place—or I in his place—in order to create the impression I was somewhere that I wasn't at this or that time. The ridge—which is hardly two feet wide—must lead to an outside staircase, allowing one to descend the castle wall. That way, one could get in and out of the castle from the rear, even when all the doors are closed and the drawbridge is up.

Now I understand why the Count doesn't wish the windows to be open after sundown. He doesn't want to risk me detecting the truth about his goings-on. Had I listened to him, I wouldn't have had the faintest idea about any of this.

What I have discovered thus far appears rather sinister—I don't know what misdeed I may be accused of should someone have impersonated me.

If the Count suddenly decides to get rid of me—and I suspect that I have seen and heard far too much for him to let me out of here alive—then he already has a plan at hand to protect himself against any suspicion and prosecution.

Suppose that Hawkins or Wilma convinced the Foreign Office and the Ambassador in Vienna to look into the matter—and suppose that officials were sent here to investigate—what would be the outcome?

They would learn that a young Englishman, about six feet

257 Icelandic: "dökkur á á brún og brá," lit.: "dark at eyebrow and eyelash"—an alliterative expression, pertaining to the whole complexion. Thus this man cannot be the Count himself, who has white hair and a pale skin.

258 This scene corresponds to Harker's entry of 24 June in *Dracula*; there, Harker only sees the Count himself, wearing Harker's clothes and carrying the bag he had given to the three vampire women. Later he hears a short, suppressed wailing in the Count's room and a desperate mother shows up at the gate, demanding her child back.

tall, of dark appearance and dressed in a greyish travelling suit, had been on a trip to Transylvania during the first days of May, and then took a carriage to the Borgo Pass, where the Count had sent a driver to pick him up. Letters sent by Thomas Harker would have arrived later, saying that he had reached the castle and had been welcomed there in a most friendly manner. The Count would confirm this, and some time later, Harker would have written that he'd decided to depart on a particular day. Finally he would write from Bistritz, saying he is on his way—and then nothing more will have been heard from him. The Count won't know anything. Enquiries into the castle's surrounding countryside will reveal that Harker had been spotted, but other than that, no one has a clue . . .

The only solution is for me to escape, but it's unlikely I will manage it. — — —

13 JUNE

I SAW HIM AGAIN LAST NIGHT, JUST BEFORE SUNRISE. HE went the same way as before, yet I still couldn't see where he came from. Once I find out where he exits I shall try to examine the tower—even though I loathe the idea of wandering through the many corridors of this castle again.

16 JUNE

AT LAST I HAVE SEEN HIM BOTH LEAVING AND RETURNING. I'd decided to stay awake all night if need be, and so I told the Count that I was unusually tired, as I had worked more than normal that day. He had no objections, so we parted after I finished my dinner and I went to my room.[259] There I extinguished the light and sat by the window, which I had opened completely—it was a bright, moonlit night.

I didn't have to wait long. Soon after eleven o'clock I heard a rustling sound, and when I looked carefully out the window I saw a man creeping on the stone ledge outside the castle walls, apparently coming from the western tower and disappearing near the tower to the east. I then wrapped a blanket around me—and bided my time.

I waited for a long time and eventually fell asleep right where I sat. When I woke up at the break of dawn I thought the night had been wasted. It was nearly five o'clock and had become daylight; he must have returned a long time ago. But just as I thought this I noticed something moving down below, so I grabbed my spyglass. Yes, there he was! But even with the help of the lenses, I couldn't see how he managed to climb up the steep wall. There had to be some footholds, slits carved into the walls—but it would also require strong nerves and a calm mind to be able to clamber in such a way. Yes! There are indeed footholds carved into the wall! This means I have now found a way to escape from here—and *that* is the most important thing. He suddenly disappeared at the eastern tower.

259 Icelandic: "Hann hafði ekkert á móti því, *og* við skildum, þegar ég hafði lokið kveldverði, *og* fór ég þá inn í herbergi mitt" (my italics). This is a typical example of how the Icelandic text strings several statements with "og" ("and"), which in English would be considered poor style. I have replaced one "and" with "so."

17 JUNE

ESTERDAY THE COUNT TOLD ME THAT HE WOULD BE away from home all day, and I used the opportunity to explore the eastern tower.[260]

As all the other routes were barred, I had to go up to the portrait gallery. Physically, I haven't been up there since I received that kiss in the flash of lightning, but in my thoughts and fantasies I've visited that floor often, which is why, with all my might, I've avoided actually going up there.[261] I'd concluded that this was her home and that she would be able to overpower me in it.

Still, I've only seen her at dusk or at night. During the daytime I've never met her, nor have I felt the desires that attract me to her.

So I was not afraid to go up to the top floor now.

The sun shone through the dusty window panes, bathing the paintings in the gallery in daylight. But I didn't dare look at them, for at the same moment as I opened the door, I felt as if the lady in the large portrait on the other side of the room were rising up, spreading her arms out towards me. I hurried through the hall and another series of rooms, all decorated and furnished in a style common during the days of Napoleon I. Finally I reached a winged door that I guessed would lead to the tower. It wasn't fastened, but the lock was stiff with rust.

Upon entering I saw a circular room with a bed in the center. It was a large, colorful bed with a canopy over its head-

260 That is, the tower on the southeast corner, where Harker's own bedroom is, and the room where the Countess was locked in with her young lover.

261 Not entirely correct: After his nightly adventure with the blonde girl, Harker visited this room once again to check the evidence of his stay there.

board. Looking up to the baldachin, one could see a portrait of Amor with his bow. The room's ceiling was painted in clouds—like the sky in spring—with playful Cupids peeking out from behind the woolpacks. It was as if I were in the bedroom of the goddess Venus herself.

Wanting to see whether anyone had slept in it recently, I moved towards the bed, but I immediately saw that a thick layer of dust had settled on the silk duvet and that cobwebs[262] covered the headboard. A full lifetime or more must have passed since anyone had slept in this bed. On the yellow pillow was a dark stain that once must have been as red as blood. Surely someone had lost their life here when that blood flowed from the pillow onto the floor—where a black blotch bears witness to a crime committed a long time ago.

I have no doubt that this was where the jealous husband took his cruel vengeance on his beautiful wife, who was completely in his power. "No one saw or heard anything; nobody dared to ask anything. She was lying dead in her bed and that was all that people knew. She was dressed in the clothes she had worn in her portrait, and then placed in her coffin. She rests in the chapel, where most members of the House of Dracula rest, but as you see, my friend, she will always remain beautiful as ever"—the Count once told me.

I thought I could hear the Count's voice saying this, and memories of the things I had experienced since came to mind. – – –

I hurried to a window and opened it. It was hundreds of feet up from here to the ground—and this was probably the window from which the Countess's lover had jumped.

Beneath this window lay a gorge with a foaming waterfall. I tried to calm myself and went to the window on the other side of the room, located next to the rear facade of the castle.[263] From there I could clearly see which way the man had taken to the other night.

I had my spyglass with me, and when I leaned out I saw footholds—barely visible to the naked eye—carved into the wall. I also discovered iron hooks, which were obviously intended to be held on to. By following this route, one could apparently reach the ledge on the wall where I had seen the man make his way. Now I just have to find out how to get to this ledge from the rooms I occupy, and I hope—with God's help—that I will succeed.

263 Icelandic: "framhlið," normally the frontside of a building. Here, however, Harker can only mean the south facade of the castle, previously described as the "back side."

19 JUNE

ONLY GOD KNOWS WHETHER I'LL EVER MANAGE TO GET out of here alive. I can't even put down in writing which of my suspicions is most urgent,[264] but it seems to me that in these past few weeks I've seen the danger that looms over humanity—to which most people are utterly unaware. But this menace is of such nature that all people of goodwill must begin the fight against it, regardless of which creed or country they belong to.

264 Icelandic: "ríkast," superlative of "ríkur" ("rich"), here in the original sense of "powerful" or "important." Harker's suspicions are indeed still vague; the essential characteristic of vampirism—being damned for all eternity to drink people's blood—has not been addressed yet; instead, an anti-democratic conspiracy and barbarian sacrificial rituals are the obvious threats posed by the Count and his followers.

EMBARKED ON A NEW EXPEDITION YESTERDAY. LAST NIGHT when the Count told me that he would have to be away from home again all day, he asked me to sort a number of documents and books he wanted to take with him to London, and to make a directory of all these items. Upon entering the library I found that a large box had been left there for me, and the books that I had to sort and register lay on the couch. Even after everything I'd seen, it seemed very strange to me, because who would imagine Satan with a suitcase and a railway ticket in hand? Seeing the Count's travel things, however, I can't help but to envision such a scene.[265] These Tatars (also called Gypsies)[266] who have spent the last few days here are helping the Count prepare for his departure. I've seen them come and go with the boxes the Slovaks brought here; they seem very heavy to handle. The number of empty boxes is gradually decreasing, as the Count has engaged three or four men of truly gigantic stature, whom I remember having seen in the vault on that memorable evening. They are strong as trolls[267] and handle huge loads as if they are light as feathers.

Today, nobody was in the courtyard and none of the boxes had been moved.

There was absolute stillness in the castle now. I lit a cigar and walked out of the dining room, intending to stroll along the floor for a moment before I started dealing with the Count's documents and books. The old woman had cleared the table long ago, disappearing as quietly as she always did,

265 In fact, Harker's associations are very appropriate, as the Devil—or the lost souls obeying him—is often depicted as wandering about the earth.

266 An incorrect statement, as Tatars and Gypsies are completely different people. In *Dracula*, only the Gypsies ("gipsies") are mentioned, sometimes as "Szgany": "A band of Szgany have come to the castle, and are encamped in the courtyard. These Szgany are gipsies; I have notes of them in my book. They are peculiar to this part of the world, though allied to the ordinary gipsies all the world over." See Chapter 4, Harker's Journal entry of 28 May. It is unclear why Valdimar and/or Stoker decided to replace *Dracula*'s Gypsies with Tatars; a possible explanation would be the destructive role played by the "Tatars" (actually, the Mongolians) in the North-Transylvanian region in the 13th century.

267 In Icelandic pagan beliefs, trolls are the original, giant-like inhabitants of the world, driven out by the gods to make place for humans, and are therefore mostly hostile; they dwell in caves and woods. Comparing men to trolls is common in the sagas: "Hann var mikill vexti, nær sem troll." (*Gisla Saga*, ed. Valdimar Ásmundsson, 1899, p. 55), "hann var mikill vexti sem troll" (ibidem, p. 156) or "Maðr […] mikill sem tröll" (*Egil's Saga*, Chapter 40), all referring to men "as big as a troll."

and I knew from experience that she wouldn't return for several hours. It occurred to me that I would never have a better opportunity to study the secret stairs and find out whether or not it would be possible to discover a way out.

I thought no more of it and began readying myself to go, for had I started to recall the memories of what I'd witnessed down there, I would never have had the courage to go back again.

I checked whether my revolver was loaded, stepped into the octagonal room, and pressed the button—the door opened suddenly and silently. Then I lit my lamp and cautiously went down the stairs. It wasn't as dark now as it had been that night, because this time a dull light shone through two windows.

I paused while going down the stairs, not sure where to go. I had reached some sort of arched vestibule with tunnels leading to both sides, east and west. I decided to take the tunnel to the west, as it lies in the direction of the window I hoped to climb through to get onto the wall ridge.

At the end of the tunnel a closed door appeared before me; I opened it hesitantly . . .

I practically yelped with joy, for I saw that I'd now come to the staircase I'd scaled during my long journey through the castle, when I'd climbed from the chapel up to the Count's room—and in this staircase was the window I was hoping to get out from, should I try to escape.

Warily, I walked up the stairs to make sure I wasn't mistaken. I saw the sun shining through the window and felt a clean, refreshing breeze on my cheek. I saw that the ridge on the wall was broad enough to walk on, although from a distance it seemed to be very narrow. But one need only to be startled or skid a bit on the stone—and death would be inevitable. I shuddered at the thought of having to go this way, but I felt as though a weight had been lifted from me now that I'd discovered a possible escape route. As a safety measure, I took the key from the lock and put it in my pocket. The door was so heavy and its hinges so rusty that it stayed in place even when unlocked; and those who pass through it—whoever they may be—may not notice that the key is missing.

Then it occurred to me that I might look around the chapel and the crypt below for a while.

Everything looked the same as before, except that the floor had been dug up and everything was scattered around. Iron picks, shovels and rakes were still lying about, revealing a job that had been left unfinished.

It seemed to me that the Tatar group had been at work here.

Deep in the dungeon, where it faced the courtyard,[268] I saw two or three boxes reinforced with iron. On two of them the lids had been fastened, but one was left half open.

I became curious, so I climbed over the unearthed stones and dirt heaps, noticing that this cellar was in fact a grave-yard—and not a very old one, as a human skull, barely de-cayed, happened to roll before my feet.

Each of the boxes was made of thick pine planks and had rope handles. The third box had been manufactured with the most care; it also had a few holes drilled into the lid. I ex-pected to find some costly items in it; I remembered well the treasure up in the tower, so I assumed these boxes were also filled with such gold and shiny jewels.

I was shocked when I looked under the lid! The box was filled halfway with soil, and in it, a man was lying length-wise—an old man with white hair and a white moustache. It was none other than the Count himself.

268 Icelandic: "Innst í hvelfingunni, þar sem vissi út að hallargarðinum." The expression "að vita út að" could neither be found in the SNARA Database nor in Cleasby/Vigfússon, 1874, but I found several examples in the translation of the *Arabian Nights* (1857-1864) by Steingrímur Thorsteinsson. Comparing these passages with other renderings, by Jonathan Scott, Richard Burton, Edward William Lane and Dr. Gustav Weil respectively, confirmed the meaning "to face in the direction of" or (of windows) "to look out over." From Harker's diary of 10 May, we know that this crypt was gloomy and had high set bow windows—which probably looked onto the courtyard, the lower part of the room being under-ground.

WINCED AND HID BEHIND THE BOX IN A CROUCHING position, but after a few moments I got the courage to stand and lean over him and have another look.

There could be no mistake. It was the Count, wearing the same clothes as the evening before.[269] He looked stone dead; I couldn't imagine anyone outlandish enough to rest there willingly. The Tatars—who had left earlier today—sprung to mind. Could it be that those wretches had killed my client and run away with as much of his fortune as they could gather? One couldn't deny they'd make good suspects . . .

But from my perspective the Count had been a prison guard for the last few weeks, so I could only feel relief at being free of his custody.

Was he dead or was he just sleeping heavily, as though he *were* dead? And if the latter, why had he chosen *this* place to rest?

He didn't look as if he were truly dead, though. His features were as impressive and harsh-looking as usual, and although he was pale, it didn't seem like a deathly pallor but merely the usual color of his complexion. I didn't dare touch him, for I assumed he wouldn't let me off unpunished for roaming around the castle without his permission.

After a short while I decided to go back to my bedroom and wait there until morning. If the Count had not returned by then, I would have a definite opportunity to try to escape from here.

If the Count were dead, I hoped I could find another

269 This discovery of the Count lying in a transport box matches Harker's Journal entry of 25 June in *Dracula*, when Harker uses the ledge on the south wall to climb into the Count's room then descends a narrow staircase, leading to the chapel and underground graveyard. See also footnotes 180 and 191.

way to flee the castle than take the more daring route I'd already found.

Before turning back, I noticed that the box lid had six strong iron hasps that could be hooked over staples on the inside of the box, closing it from within, so that it would appear as if the lid had been screwed on. This way it could be locked and opened from the inside. I was quite sure that this casket had been designed to conceal a person who wanted to stay hidden.

I went back up to my room but was ill at ease for the rest of the day.

Once twilight arrived I had finished preparing the books, but I'd become restless and unable to sit still. So I walked nervously across the floor, on pins and needles.

"Will he come or won't he?" I thought to myself.

The clock was ticking: eight—, nine—, ten o'clock; nothing was heard.

I was just about to go down to the basement to check on the old man when suddenly the door opened and the Count entered. He was unusually high-spirited and looked as if he'd grown younger.

"Here I am, my friend," he said cheerfully. "I hope you have not been bored today. I myself have been very busy. I am tired now and in need of rest, but first I wanted to find you to see how you are doing, and if you have come along nicely with your work. No—you are done. I thank you very much. If you could do me a favor tomorrow, by making an inventory of everything in that closet over there," he said, "I'd really appreciate it." He pointed out the middle compartments in the closet, where all kinds of tools were stored that seemed to be used for physical experiments. He said he couldn't do the job himself as he had other obligations.

I stared at him, so stunned, in fact, that I didn't answer.

He seemed so unusually youthful to me now; it was as if fire itself sparked from his eyes[270]—or more accurately—they flashed with the ferocity of a beast that knows it has found its prey.

Then, with a deep sigh, I replied that I had no idea what most of the things in the closet were called, and thus could hardly make a list of them.

"Tools, my friend, nothing but tools a scientist uses to bring dead nature to life under his command," he said. "You men from the West still have much to learn; you haven't gotten much further than the antechamber to the sciences,[271] where life and death are still unsolved mysteries.[272] Well then, I shall do it myself, but I still bid you a good night for now. I need to rest. I also have plenty to do tomorrow and probably cannot come to you again until nightfall. May you be blessed—until next time," he said, giving me his hand.

When he left he was still as energetic as when he'd entered. He was more like a young man running off to a *rendezvous* with his sweetheart than an old man going off to bed after finishing a day's work. — — —

270 Icelandic: "og var sem eldur brynni úr augum hans"—an expression already used when the Count spoke about the London murders (Journal of 8 May—see footnote there) and about the anarchists.

271 "Hence, [logic], as a propaedeutic, merely represents *the antechamber to the sciences*, as it were; and when we speak of knowledge, we admittedly presuppose a logic as an instrument to judge it, but the acquisition of knowledge as such can only be accomplished by the sciences proper, that is, by the objective sciences." Immanuel Kant, *Critique of Pure Reason, Preface to the Second Edition* (1787) (my translation from the German).

272 Icelandic: ". . . en í forsal vísindanna, þar sem líf og dauði liggja í efnishrúgum," lit.: . . . "than the antechamber to the sciences, where life and death lie in piles of material." The word "efnishrúga" ("pile of matter") is sometimes used in a metyphysical context to criticize Materialism, which perceives the human body only as a soulless agglomeration of matter. Accordingly, the Count criticizes Western scholars for thinking that life and death have their basis in the material body alone; his view would match that of Van Helsing, who explains the vampire's existence from the workings of a soul that fails to leave the body and ignites new life in it (see Part II). It would also correspond with Valdimar's own interest in the work of the *Society for Psychical Research*, trying to demonstrate the existence of a soul with scientific means. But "liggja í hrúgum" is also a common expression for "to lie in piles," just like the gold coins in the west tower are lying in piles on the floor, so that this phrase could also mean that life and death are "lying around" on the floor of the vestibule of sciences as raw material waiting to be explored or utilized by advanced scholars such as the Count. Whatever the case, in effect the Count claims that Western scientists have not deciphered the true nature of life and death yet. There is no parallel in *Dracula*, except for Van Helsing's suspicions that chemical, magnetical or electrical reactions may have been co-responsible for the Count's prolonged life (Chapter 24).

20 JUNE

I WENT DOWN TO THE CRYPT ONCE MORE.

The Count was there again, and I thought he looked even younger and more alive than he had before, but nevertheless when he came home late that evening I was staggered to see him and found him more terrifying than ever.

He still remains polite in his manners towards me, but I clearly sense the ridicule and contempt lying underneath.

Today he told me,

"Time passes, my friend, and soon the moment will come when we must part ways. You shall return to your beautiful England"—this he said in a strange tone—"and I shall return to my work, which is laid out in such a way that it's very unlikely I shall see you again. It may also happen that I leave here before you do, but even when I am not at home, my calèche can pick you up whenever you please and drive you to Bistritz. I truly owe you for your company."

At first I was beside myself with joy when I heard him say this, for here at least I had his promise that I would get out of this imprisonment, which has almost been the death of me. But something in his words and expression kept me from believing him.

I cannot help but feel that he won't let me leave here alive. *I know too much.*

I said something polite but meaningless in return, but added that, should he leave, I would have to go too—so why not today or tomorrow, if he no longer had use for me?

273 Icelandic: "Það er ekki við lömb að leika sér," lit.: "It is not playing with lambs," an alliterative expression indicating that one is dealing with a tough adversary.

274 In *Dracula*, this matches the scene from Harker's diary of 29 June, where the Count actually opens the gate, but the howling wolves frighten Harker into remaining.

"No, that's not possible, my friend," he said. "My driver and horses are not present at the moment."

"That doesn't matter, I can go on foot and my luggage can be sent for later."

"On foot, my dear friend? Are you in such a hurry?" He stared at me with a scoffing grin, sending chills throughout my entire body. "You do not know the Carpathians; even if I allowed my guests to leave here on foot, that walk would be your last—there are wolves here in the forest." He went to the window and opened it. "Listen to them," he said.

I heard the wolves howling in the woods outside.

"It's not child's play.[273] It is safer for you to wait here at home."[274]

23 JUNE

HE TATARS CAME BACK YESTERDAY AND TOOK UP THEIR work again, which seems to be nearly finished, as most of the boxes are full. The Count has also paid me a brief visit; he seems to be very uneasy and his appearance has changed even more. My eyes don't deceive me—he looks a few years younger than when I first arrived here. It's as if the blood in his veins runs more freely; the color of his skin isn't as waxen as before, his cheeks have acquired a copper-red hue, his eyes are livelier and even have a certain glow . . . and sometimes a strange tinge of red appears in them suddenly. He is impressive to behold, and I find myself shivering upon meeting his gaze.

24 JUNE

God help me — — — with courage and artifice, it's possible for man to defend himself against threats from the outside, but those dangers that come from within—from man himself—are far more difficult to keep at bay. A bastion that has traitors in its garrison is exposed to risk, no matter how fortified it is, and I—I have been struggling against a power too great to fight. — — —

I don't know who she is, but I'm now convinced that what the Count has told me about her cannot be true. When I recall everything I've seen and experienced, I'm at a loss and I cannot come to any conclusion, unless I decide to give up on logic and believe things no one else would.

I shudder at the thought of her, yet I crave to see her. She is like one of the Elven Ladies who enchant men to follow them into their rocky ravines.[275]

For three days now I have been determined to escape from this place. Even though it's dangerous, I now know the way out, and I've had opportunities. Time and again, I've been on the verge of leaving, but then an irresistible desire overwhelms me and I cannot control myself any longer—I have to see her once more.

It's incomprehensible—I cannot believe it, but there's no denying it either—she always comes when I think of her, as if she were beckoned, or as if she were standing right outside the door, ready to enter.

Before I can calm myself she's standing next to me, and I

275 The "huldufólk" ("Hidden People") or "álfar" (elves) play an important role in Icelandic and other Scandinavian folk beliefs. In the legend of Hildur, the Queen of the Elves (*Hildur Álfadrottning*), Hildur rides on the back of a herdsman to Elf-Land on the night of Christmas eve; he follows her into a precipice between the rocks: "Then mounting on his back, she made him rise from the ground as if on wings, and rode him through the air, till they arrived at a huge and awful precipice, which yawned, like a great well, down into the earth [. . .] So he managed, after a short struggle, to get the bridle off his head, and having done so, leapt into the precipice, down which he had seen Hildur disappear." See Stephany, 2006, p. 4, quoting from Booss, 1984, p. 621.

276 In *Dracula*, Harker hangs the crucifix over the head of his bed, to sleep more quietly. See Journal of 12 May.

can't restrain myself. Yet I haven't once yielded to her—and that alone has saved me.

I've never taken off the crucifix the old lady gave me, and anyone who wishes may call it superstition, but I feel this is the only reason the Count did not kill me that evening when he grabbed me by the throat, and I feel I owe it to this same cross that I managed to escape from the loathsome miscreant who attacked me on the stairs.[276]

She has been whispering to me constantly, begging me to take off the crucifix, but I have not done so. — — —

28 JUNE

I WRITE THESE WORDS IN MY JOURNAL LATE AT NIGHT IN my bedroom, the only retreat I have where I can be without fear. I'm now determined to flee from here as soon as we see the light of day. To alert my family of what has happened to me and what it was that drove me to my death, I have written Wilma's name and address on the first page of this book, both in German and English, adding that whoever finds it should please return the book to her at the aforementioned address and explain how the book has come into their hands. I cannot do anything more, and it's perfectly clear to me that there's but a small chance this final greeting of mine will reach its intended destination, should I meet my doom.

Wilma, if I live, let us read these lines together some day[277] and thank God that my life was saved, but if I die—this is my final greeting to you. Once you have read what I've written, you shall know that I've succumbed to forces stronger than I am, and that these forces pose a danger to the whole of humanity—a danger that every person of goodwill must stand up against. Ask the wisest and foremost people, preferably those with much influence in society. I've written a few names on the last page of this book. I don't have time to explain things in more detail. May God give you the strength to make use of my experience. My spirit stays with you, regardless of what may happen to my body.

I will write a few words here about what has happened to me in the last couple of days.

277 In *Dracula*, Mina shows her trust in Jonathan by wrapping his journal in a piece of paper and promising that she will never read the it, unless for some dire circumstance.

278 In *Dracula*, Harker overhears how the Count tells the "three terrible women": "Back, back, to your own place! Your time is not yet come. Wait! Have patience! To-morrow night, to-morrow night is yours!" See *Dracula*, Harker's Journal entry of 29 June. In the first American edition by Doubleday and McClure (1899), the last sentence begins, "To-night is mine."

279 During the Victorian age, elegantly cut glass bells were much in use to call the house staff. In *Dracula*, the voice of the three "weird sisters" is described in a similar manner: "They whispered together, and then they all three laughed—such a silvery, musical laugh, but as hard as though the sound never could have come through the softness of human lips. It was like the intolerable, tingling sweetness of water-glasses when played on by a cunning hand." And when Lucy speaks to Arthur in her tomb, Dr. Seward notes: "There was something diabolically sweet in her tones—something of the tingling of glass when struck—which rang through the brains even of us who heard the words addressed to another."

My handwriting on the previous page reminds me of how I felt while I was taking down my notes—I was aware that she was nearing and drawing me towards her. She whispered sweet words to me; she kissed me and rather affectionately she asked me to remove the crucifix from my neck. My hands lifted, but at the last moment I was able to control myself. — — —

I'm not sure how much time had passed, but I suddenly heard the Count's sardonic voice sneering at her.

"Get out of here! Your work is in vain—the time has not come yet. Wait a few more days. When I no longer need him, you may have him, and then—"[278]

I heard a strange, shrill laugh, like the sound of a glass bell. It was her voice. I still shudder at it; this voice was not human at all.[279]

Soon after I heard the Count saying,

"Good evening, my friend. I see you have fallen asleep with your work." I opened my eyes and saw him standing at the desk in front of me, casting a biting look at me. I was tired and weak, and when he told me to go to bed I obeyed him in silence. Looking back on it all, I can hardly tell whether I'd been dreaming or if I'd been awake during the time I am now writing about. If it was a dream, then it may have been a warning—but I don't think it was a dream.

Some days later, the Count asked me again to sort several documents, books and instruments, to have them ready for his trip. He also had me check, correct and copy two letters he had written in English and which were addressed to Brits, although I didn't recognize their names. The language was obscure and ambiguous, and the message seemed to be about some important issue. Although I didn't quite understand the text, this incident showed me that the Count no longer feared I might betray him—he probably sees me as standing with one foot in the grave already, unable to divulge any of his secrets.

—————————

Yesterday the Tatars finished their work. Early in the morning, two large wagons, pulled by six horses each, drove into the courtyard, where the heavy boxes were placed onto the wagons before they were taken away in separate loads. The drivers were Slovaks, but each trip was escorted by armed Tatars.

When darkness came there were only three boxes left. Most of the Tatars were gone, but there were still some men in the courtyard of the kind I have already described as being more ape-like than human. It occurred to me that this might be my chance to get away, as the gate would probably be open. I slipped out, but as always it was securely locked, and what's more the Count's hideous servants were standing guard. I rushed back inside, hearing someone running and panting behind me. I fled into the dining room, locked the door behind me and leaned myself against it. I felt someone trying to open it, but after a moment everything went quiet.

I now realized that the Count had probably expected I would try to escape and had taken steps to prevent it. I shudder to think of what might have happened had his pack of thugs got hold of me. I am not afraid of death—but I do not want to die *this* way.

The Count came late that night. He was very cheerful, walking briskly around the room, speaking frantically and constantly fiddling with his nails, which were very long. Although it was his habit, I've always disliked this nervous tick of his. Had it not been for his snow-white hair and his equally white moustache, one very well may have guessed he was barely forty.

"Yes, my friend," he said in a gentle voice, "I am almost ready for my journey, but I still have to take care of a few things here around my estate. I shall probably need the whole day tomorrow, and as I do not know whether I shall return in time to say goodbye to you, I am doing that now. My horses and carriage will be available to you tomorrow. When will you be leaving?"

This question came so unexpectedly that I was dumbstruck. I stared at him and stammered something about the departure times of trains, Bistritz, etc. My head was swimming and my heartbeat became so violent that I felt as if I were going to suffocate.

When I caught hold of myself, I saw the Count looking at me with an odd, ironic smirk.

"Are you fine with leaving at twelve o'clock?" he asked. "Then you may be in time for the evening train to Budapest. Well, I shall make sure the calèche stands by the gate at noon, and if possible, I shall also come to wish you a good journey, but should I be delayed—I say goodbye to you now. Be you blessed, my dear young friend." He gave me his hand. "Goodbye now, and I thank you so much for your pleasant company. I can neither express its true value to me nor pay for it with gold, but time is precious to you, and in our family we are not given to receiving presents without giving something in return, therefore allow me—" he opened a drawer in the desk and reached for a small red silk bag, which he handed to me "—to give you this in exchange, and this—" he took something out of his breast pocket "—as a souvenir from your sojourn here, and as a token of Dracula's gratitude. They are small, but they are old family heirlooms that carry a certain value, and I hope they will serve to remind you of your stay with me."

His voice had a strange undertone, and when I looked up

at his face it was twisted in a malignant, mocking grimace, but he instantly altered it to a friendly smile. I saw that the object he took from his breast pocket was an ancient ring with a heart of jewels and a large ruby in the center. The stones shone in the light from the wax candles; its multi-colored rays were so strong and piercing to the eye that it made me dizzy just looking at it. I almost blacked out.

I struggled to keep my eyes off this trinket that possessed such magical power, but when I finally succeeded in looking away, the enchantment was gone, vanished—but I was not the same afterwards. I felt obliged to accept the small pouch, which I discovered contained golden coins.

"You honor me too much," I said, trying not to show any emotion. "I cannot accept these glorious gifts."

"Do not mention it," he said in a firmer tone. "It is my decision, and it is my pleasure knowing this family heirloom is in your possession. Wear it and think of Dracula. Many have worn it before you and regarded it as a lucky charm of sorts. You Englishmen do not believe in such things, but wear it anyway, and I wish you much luck with it. You have yet to enjoy life; you are a handsome man, young and elegant. Goodbye now, dear Thomas Harker. If we do not see each other again—and that may well be—then you have Dracula's blessing. Until tomorrow then, at noon."

He clutched my hand so firmly, it felt as though he had fists of iron; his grip was as cold as ice or polished metal. My hand went numb, and I felt the dullness creep up my arm. I wanted to shove him away from me but managed to restrain myself. Then he walked to the door.

"Wear the ring," he said again. "Do it for me—and think of Dracula." He kissed his fingers according to old tradition and left.[280]

280 In *Dracula*, this particular greeting occurs after Harker, intimidated by the wolves, has hesitated to go through the opened gate: "The last I saw of Count Dracula was his kissing his hand to me; with a red light of triumph in his eyes, and with a smile that Judas in hell might be proud of." See *Dracula*, Harker's Journal of 29 June.

DIDN'T KNOW WHAT TO BELIEVE. WAS IT POSSIBLE I MIGHT get away from here? Were my suspicions all uncalled for? If anything the Count said is to be taken seriously, I should be on the train to Budapest tomorrow night, and everything I have gone through here will remain an incomprehensible dream.

I sat at the table and thanked God that I'd now escaped all danger. Then I began to pack my luggage and prepare for my journey.

The ring was lying on the table and I felt compelled to see whether it would fit me—it was as if some invisible force were drawing me to it. As soon as I picked it up, it felt as though a burning current were streaming through my veins. Half unconscious, I fell onto the chair and threw the ring onto the table. I regained full awareness again soon thereafter.

I lay in the chair until late at night but eventually stood up, walked to my bedroom, and went soundly to sleep. When I woke up, I saw with dread: *it was one o'clock*! I had overslept! I rushed to my feet and dashed off to the dining room windows.

In the courtyard, nothing stirred. The Tatars had all left by now and the luggage that had been there was gone too. The Count's calèche was not there either.

I ran down to the hall to find the driver and tell him I was ready to travel, but the gate was locked with a heavy bar in front of it. There was no hope of getting out.

Upon my return to the dining room I noticed that no food

282 In *Dracula*: "At least God's mercy is better than that of these monsters, and the precipice is steep and high. At its foot a man may sleep—— as a man."

had been served on the table. I hurried into the octagonal room and stepped on the button to the secret door, hoping to escape the castle this way, but here, too, everything was securely locked.

I realized now I was imprisoned all alone inside the castle, like a mouse in a trap.

The whole building looked deserted. The Count's writing desk was empty and the bookshelves mostly bare. The stationery had also been taken away; there was nothing left but the ring.

It turned six–, seven–, eight o'clock. Dusk was approaching. Absolute stillness ruled the castle. I was weak from hunger now. I tried to force open the secret door but failed.

I no longer doubted that the Count had locked me in intentionally, so that I would starve to death in this horrible tomb, or meet a fate even worse.

The darker it became, the more my mental vision sharpened, allowing much to enter my mind that I'm not writing down here. The Powers of Darkness[281] have taken counsel against me—I do not know for what purpose, but I see and know the danger. It seems as though I can hear someone whispering in my ear . . . I know that she is not far away from me . . . white arms, lovely lips. "When I am gone, you may have him," the Count had said—or had it been a dream?

No, I will not sell my soul! I do not hear these false voices—I want to be a man.[282]

If you ever read these lines, Wilma, then you know that I am dead, and that I have always loved you and been faithful to you.

————————————————

I have now decided what I'm going to do. I've torn up my bedsheets and braided them into a rope, which I hope will hold me. With this rope I intend to let myself down from the window once daylight has come, and I'll try to reach the ledge. It's risky, but it might work. If I fail, nothing worse than death can happen to me.

It's getting lighter: dawn is breaking.

I have attached the rope; I am ready now.

And so, a final goodbye, dear Wilma. Please forgive me for all that I may have done to you, and you may be certain that I have always loved you and no one but you.

PART II

CHAPTER ONE

Lucia Western

WHILE THOMAS HARKER HOVERED BETWEEN HOPE and horror in the castle of Count Dracula, his beloved fiancée, Wilma, spent her time at the bathing resort at Whitby, on the east coast of England. Wilma was a teacher at one of the larger board schools,[283] and this year she was staying with her old school friend Lucia Western during her summer holiday. It was Wilma's habit to keep a diary, just like her fiancé, and most of what is told in the second part of this story is taken from her journal.[284]

Wilma's friend Lucia was a delightful girl and everyone loved her, not least of all the members of the male sex. She had a very kind and amusing manner, but there was also a vain side to her, and she particularly wanted *men* to fancy her. Her mother was a widow and wealthy, but she was in poor health, suffering from a serious heart condition, which meant that she had to avoid all strong emotion and turbulence. Lucia was also of a rather frail constitution, as she had unusually sensitive feelings and, ever since she was a child, tended to walk in her sleep, which was blamed on her father being promiscuous.[285]

283 Icelandic: "alþýðuskólum," lit.: "people's school." The nearest equivalent is "board school," an elementary school administered by an elected board, as regulated in England and Wales by the Elementary Education Act of 1870. They were meant to offer education to all classes, without imposing religious indoctrination. In *Dracula*, Mina calls herself an "assistant schoolmistress."

284 Here *Makt Myrkranna* switches from an epistolary novel to the more conventional form of an omniscient narrator, while *Dracula* continues to present diary entries, letters and newspaper articles. In the 1950 and 2011 editions of *Makt Myrkranna*, Part II is titled "Baron Székely," but in the original edition no extra title is given.

285 Icelandic: ". . . mjög laus á kostunum"—an expression not listed in Cleasby/Vigfússon, 1874; it starts appearing in the Icelandic press in 1882 and loses popularity after the 1960s. *Heimskringla* of 23 November 1892, p. 3, uses "laus á kostunum" to translate "fickle-minded" from an English novel ("Waters," 1863, p. 229); Zoëga, 1922 gives "loose, of easy virtue." Icelandic dictionaries list synonyms meaning "dissolute," "unchaste," "promiscuous," "licentious," "libertine," "rakish," "sluttish," "wanton," "orgiastic." Here, like in other places, *Makt Myrkranna* uses a more drastic vocabulary than *Dracula*, wherein the mother explains Lucy's sleepwalking as a simple hereditary trait.

286 In *Dracula*, Dr. Seward's asylum is located in "Purfleet," which is a village in Essex County on the banks of
the Thames, east of London.

287 In *Dracula*, Quincey's wealth is only mentioned in
Chapter 26, when Mina notes that he "has plenty of
money." His character was probably based on that of the
famous Buffalo Bill (William F. Cody), whom Stoker met
through his friend and employer, the actor Henry Irving.
See Warren 2003, and Warren, 2005, p. 331.

288 This means that Wilma till now has only received her
fiancé's first letter from Dracula's castle (mentioned in
Harker's Journal of 8 May); the three letters dated 12
June, 19 June and 22 June obviously have not arrived yet.

289 In *Dracula*, Mina is desperate as well but takes no action herself, except for travelling to Budapest when the
letter from Sister Agatha arrives.

A few weeks earlier Lucia had been engaged to a young
man named Arthur Holmwood, the eldest son and heir of Lord
Godalming. Before this, his friends John Seward—a famous
physician and director of an asylum in Parfleet, one of the sub-
urbs of London[286]—and Quincey Morris, a millionaire from
America,[287] had also proposed to her; they were both madly
in love with the girl, but she hadn't accepted either proposal.
Nevertheless they were still fond of her and remained afterwards close friends with Arthur as before.

The girls read together, worked together and walked together to entertain themselves. Most often they went to the
churchyard together. It was on a hill and offered the best view
of the sea, so they would often sit there around sunset to enjoy
the beautiful panorama.

Wilma was, however, often anxious and agitated; she
was worried about Thomas. She had received but one letter
from him after his arrival at Count Dracula's castle.[288]
She'd written to Thomas's employer, Mr. Hawkins, asking
him to enquire about Thomas with the Consuls in Vienna
and Budapest.[289]

CHAPTER TWO

The Storm in Whitby

O N THE 4TH DAY OF AUGUST THERE WAS A VIOLENT windstorm in Whitby, so furious that no one could remember ever having witnessed such weather. The gale struck at midnight and the sea became like a boiling geyser.[290] Amid the shaft of light from the Whitby lighthouse, a large schooner was observed with all its sails up. People assumed it was the same ship that had been spotted some days before; it had been watched with curiosity because of its strange steering. Along its route into the harbor there were rocks that had already damaged many vessels, and as the wind blew the ship directly towards these cliffs, it became apparent the schooner was doomed to crash. But suddenly the squall settled, and the ship slipped into the harbor—as if it had suddenly regained control—and ran onto dry land. Crowds gathered down by the seaside. And then, in the flash from the lighthouse, they saw that a dead man was tied to the steering wheel, his head rolling to and fro with the rocking of the ship.

290 A fitting image for an Icelandic text, as Iceland is famous for its hot springs. As usual in Iceland, Ásmundsson used the word "hver"—the name "Geysir" was reserved for a single hot spring in Haukadalur, created by volcanic eruptions at the end of the 13th century.

CHAPTER THREE

From the Logbook

WHEN THE SCHOONER WAS EXAMINED, IT WAS found to be a Russian vessel from Varna, baptized *Demeter*. It was loaded with boxes, each filled with earth—according to the freight bill they were being shipped for engineering experiments. Nobody was found on board, except for the dead man at the steering wheel. Both his hands were tied and a rosary was wrapped around them. In his pocket was a bottle containing a slip of paper that proved to be an addendum to the ship's logbook.

The logbook reported:

The moment the ship set sail, the crew had been unusually sullen. The Captain and the first mate tried to find out the reason, but the men wouldn't answer. They did, however, intimate that there was something foul aboard, and they crossed themselves. The ship hadn't sailed very far when one night the watchman disappeared.

The next day one of the crew-members told the Captain that a stranger was onboard the ship, and some other deckhands also believed they'd noticed a stowaway.

The Captain ordered his men to inspect the whole ship carefully, but they didn't find a clue.

The ship passed by Gibraltar and for a few days the stars were merciful—but then another sailor disappeared one night during his watch.

The following day the ship entered the English Channel and two more crew-members went missing.

One night the Captain was awakened by an awful sound. He ran up on deck and found the steersman there, who had also heard the noise. The watchman was gone.

The following night the vessel entered the North Sea, and there, yet another crew-member went missing. The Captain called on the steersman, who came up on deck, deathly pale with fear. He whispered to the Captain, "The Devil himself is on board. I have seen him; he is tall and very thin,[291] pale as a corpse but very dark around the eyes. He stood looking out over the sea. I snuck up on him from behind and ran a knife through his body, but hit nothing but air."

The steersman said he wouldn't give up until he found him, then went with his light and tools into the freight hold to examine the boxes.

Suddenly the Captain heard a terrible sound coming from belowdecks. The steersman came up again, his face disfigured with fear.

"I know how things stand now, but the sea shall deliver me—I have no other way out." Thereon he threw himself overboard, before the Captain could get ahold of him.

The Captain had also written, "I have seen him—the steersman was right to throw himself into the sea—but the Captain cannot leave his ship. Instead, I've decided to tie myself to the steering wheel."

CHAPTER FOUR

Baron Székely

THE MORNING AFTER THE GHOST SHIP STRANDED ITSELF on the sands,[292] an old skipper was found dead on a bench in the cemetery. Judging from the expression on his face, he'd died of fright. He used to talk with the two young ladies, and it was a real blow for Lucia. She grew even more apprehensive than before and started sleepwalking again.

One evening Wilma walked with Lucia along the sea and up to the cemetery, as they often did. There they met Lucia's uncle, named Morton, who was accompanied by a middle-aged foreigner of very peculiar appearance.

Morton introduced him as Baron Székely. He was a tall brawny man, with greying black hair, a black moustache, and black peering eyes. He started up a conversation with Lucia straight off and seemed to enjoy talking to her.[293]

The following night, Wilma was awakened when Lucia climbed from her bed and stepped to the window. She pulled the curtain aside and stood in front of the window in her undergarments,[294] her hair blowing in the wind,[295] saying, "I come, I come, but the door is locked." At that moment,

292 The Icelandic literally speaks of a "shipwreck" ("skip-brot"): Although the schooner made it safely into the harbor, it stranded itself on the sands. In *Dracula* we read: "There was of course a considerable concussion as the vessel drove up on the sand heap. Every spar, rope, and stay was strained, and some of the top-hammer came crashing down." Regarding the Russian ship on which Bram Stoker based his story, a local newspaper wrote: "The Russian vessel *Dimitri* which so gallantly entered the harbour on Saturday in spite of the terrible sea afterwards ran ashore in Collier's Hope. It was supposed that she would be safe here, but on the rise of the tide yesterday morning, the seas beat over her with great force. Her masts fell with a terrific crash, and the crew were obliged to abandon her. She is now a complete wreck."

293 Both Uncle Morton and the Count's conversation with Lucia are unique to *Makt Myrkranna*; in *Dracula*, the Count is always in hiding after his arrival in England and never has regular social contact with either of the girls.

294 Icelandic: "stóð í nærfötunum." In *Dracula*, Lucy wears a night dress, which in Icelandic is called "nátt-kjóll," a word used in Icelandic newspapers since 1885. In *Kvennblaðið*—run by Valdimar's wife Briét—of August 1898, "njáttkjólar" were advertised along with other kinds of women's wear; Valdimar's use of the word "undergarment" thus is not due to a lack of an Icelandic word for "nightgown." See also next footnote.

295 Lucia's loose hair and her impulse to roam about at night in her "unmentionables" already portend the unholy transformation that will take place. In Norse-Germanic culture, loose hair, inappropriate clothing and leaving the house after sunset could indicate that a woman is a witch: "Woman, I saw you riding on a stick, with loose hair and

ungirded, in witch garb, in the twilight." See quoted by Jacob Grimm as a punishable insult from *Vestgötalag* (a Swedish juridical codex, 1281); Grimm, 1883, p. 1054; cf. Grimm, 1854, p. 1007 and Grimm, 1828, p. 646. My transcription to English.

296 This remark about Gypsies is not included in the 1950 and 2011 editions.

297 In *Dracula*, the Count neither engages in polite conversation nor is there any mention of Tatars or Gypsies in England.

she tried to throw herself out of the window, but Wilma had arrived by her side just in time and put her arms around her friend, pulling her back to bed. Lucia didn't calm down for a long time. She couldn't sleep and muttered time and again, "I wonder what he wanted from me." Wilma gave her a small glass of wine, after which she nodded off and slept well for what remained of the night.

The next day the girls found Baron Székely in the cemetery. He appeared to be in a very talkative mood. A group of Tatars (Gypsies)[296] had just arrived in town, and the Baron told the girls several things about the habits of these wandering people in his home country. He said that there are countless natural forces and laws known only to a few, and that the Tatars were familiar with a variety of such secret ways.

He told them that women are endowed with the greatest and most valuable powers of all, and that the Tatar women also know how to wield them. "I am convinced," he said to Lucia, "that you have those talents as well, and it's up to you to use them."

Wilma noticed that Lucia was completely distraught by this remark.[297]

CHAPTER FIVE

The Tatars

MANY THOUGHTS CAME TO THE GIRLS' MINDS, AND THEY became very curious after their conversation with the Baron. The next day they visited the group of vagrants, who had pitched their tents outside of town.

Wilma suspected that the Tatars had expected them, as they were welcomed with much hospitality.[298] But Lucia was treated with the most distinction—the leader of the group even kissed the hem of her dress.[299] He then instructed his interpreter to ask her whether she would like her humble servant to do anything for her.[300] She answered, saying, "I've been told that your people are more knowledgeable in certain fields than people of other nations; it would be my pleasure to learn more about this." The chief went into his tent and returned with a young girl. She was wrapped in a gold-seamed, yellow silk shawl. She handed Lucia a crystal ball and asked her to look into it. Lucia did so, and she saw her fiancé, Arthur, kissing a young woman sitting beside him. The next day Lucia received a letter from Arthur, in which he told her that his sister, Mary, had come to visit him the night before. Mary had just been married to a Romanian man, an assistant to Prince Koromezzo, the Austrian ambassador to London.

298 Icelandic: "með kostum og kynjum"—another alliterative phrase.

299 In ancient cultures, it was a sign of respect to kiss or touch the seam of someone's robe.

300 A chivalric and biblical figure of speech: The Tatar leader refers to himself in the third person.

301 This scene appears to be a loose end, as Mary is not mentioned again in this novel. It gives us some background information, however, about the function and bad reputation of Prince Koromezzo, who plays a role in the last chapters of this novel. It also demonstrates that the Tatars indeed have supernatural powers, although the visions they show in their crystal ball can have a misleading and manipulative effect: Lucia is led to believe that Arthur has a paramour, while in fact, he is greeting his own sister.

Mary's relatives had done everything in their power to prevent this marriage from happening, as the Prince had a ruinous reputation.

Mary and her husband had left for Constantinople immediately after their wedding.[301]

CHAPTER SIX

Lucia's Illness and Death

A FTER THIS VISIT WITH THE TATARS, LUCIA'S CONDITION worsened more and more; she lost her interest in other people and mainly kept to herself. She then travelled to London and began preparations for her wedding. Baron Székely had also arrived in London and visited her often for conversation.[302]

She couldn't sleep at night and became paler with each passing day. When Arthur came to visit her he was shocked at her appearance. He sent for Dr. Seward, but the physician found himself unable to help her. And so Dr. Seward wrote to a professor in Amsterdam, named Van Helsing, who was world-renowned for his research on nervous diseases. The Dutch specialist gave Lucia medical advice, and for a while her health indeed seemed to improve. But it wasn't long before it deteriorated again, and the professor was called on once more.[303] He said that Lucia must be suffering from anemia and that she wouldn't recover unless they could transfuse blood from a healthy person into her veins.

302 Icelandic: ". . . og talaði oft við hana," lit.: ". . . and often spoke with her." Again, this is a major deviation from *Dracula*, where the Count remains almost invisible after Harker's adventures in Transylvania. Stoker's preparatory notes, however, mention the Count as a sickbed visitor, next to "the Texan" (Quincey Morris).

303 To avoid confusion, I have in some cases replaced "doctor" with "professor" to indicate Van Helsing.

304 In *Dracula* the servants are merely drugged with laudanum.

The doctors did so, and with this treatment Lucia recuperated somewhat. Unfortunately, the Dutch professor then had to return home. The following day Dr. Seward drove to Lucia's house and found both the front and back doors shut tightly—even though it was past midday. Suddenly, he heard someone running from the garden side of the house. It was the gardener and one of his workmen. They were breathless with terror and hardly able to utter a word. Finally, the doctor could make out from their stammering that the housemaid had been killed and that her blood-soaked body lay outside, in the garden.[304] Upon further investigation, he saw that the window to Lucia's bedroom had been broken, and he assumed something terrible awaited him. He looked through the window and saw that everything looked as it had before—except for the bed, where he saw Lucia and her mother, both seemingly lifeless. He reached his hand through the broken window, opened it, and wriggled in, but he told the men to wait for him outside. When he came to the bed he saw that Lucia's mother was deceased—she seemed to have died from sheer terror—and Lucia lay motionless over her; he couldn't tell whether or not she was alive. He didn't know what to do, but just then he heard a carriage pull up to the house. He asked the men outside to welcome their visitor: Professor Van Helsing had arrived.

Both doctors examined Lucia and discovered she was still alive. The professor ordered that she be given a warm bath, so they went looking for a maidservant, but all of them were fast asleep and couldn't be wakened, no matter what the men tried. They then sent for the gardener's wife and daughter, who came to prepare a bath for Lucia. After several attempts, the physicians finally managed to resuscitate her. They wanted to give her another transfusion but were faced with a new dilemma: from whom should they draw the blood? Both Seward and Van Helsing had been subject to massive blood loss during the previous procedures.

Just then, Quincey Morris, the young American who had asked for Lucia's hand, happened to arrive. He brought greetings from Arthur and happily volunteered his blood for Lucia's sake.

At last they succeeded in fully reviving Lucia. Her heart and lungs began working again.[305] When the doctors thought it safe to leave the patient alone for a moment, they tended to the other people in the house.

The police had started to look for the murderer. The servant girls had just woken up, reporting that they had gone to bed around the same time as usual but didn't understand why they had slept so long. They knew nothing about the murder of the housemaid but said she was used to going her own way and liked to take evening walks.[306]

The detectives suspected that the murder had been planned and that the housemaid may have colluded with the trespassers, giving the other maids a sleeping draught. Afterward, the criminals had murdered their accomplice, so that no one was left to give away their secrets. What surprised them most, however, was the fact that nothing had been stolen. The band of Tatars had been in the neighborhood for the past few days, and the police thought it likely they'd played a part in this depravity, especially as they had decamped the day after the murder.[307]

The doctors carefully examined the housemaid's body but could only conclude that she'd been bitten in the throat.

Eventually they came across a slip of paper on which Lucia had written what had happened to her that night. It had seemed to her as though someone were knocking on the win-

305 Icelandic: "toku til starfa," lit.: "started working." The text of *Dracula* is more precise: "Lucy's heart beat a trifle more audibly to the stethoscope, and her lungs had a perceptible movement."

306 Again, a suggestion that women who leave the house alone after dark may be witches, criminal or suspect.

307 In *Dracula*, the police play no active role at all in investigating any of the Count's crimes.

308 In *Dracula*, Lucy sees "the head of a great, gaunt grey wolf." It is the Norwegian wolf Bersicker, which had escaped from the London Zoo. During this horror-filled night, he was accompanied by a large bat. See *Dracula*, Chapters 11 & 12. It is curious that the Bersicker episode is left out here. For Valdimar, it would have been an opportunity to link the story with the Norse wolf-skinned Berserker warriors mentioned in Chapter 3 of *Dracula*: "We Szekelys have a right to be proud, for in our veins flows the blood of many brave races who fought as the lion fights, for lordship. Here, in the whirlpool of European races, the Ugric tribe bore down from Iceland the fighting spirit which Thor and Wodin gave them, which their Berserkers displayed to such fell intent on the seaboards of Europe, ay, and of Asia and Africa too, till the peoples thought that the were-wolves themselves had come." Equally, *Dracula*'s description of Arthur as "a figure of Thor" (Chapter 16) is absent in the Icelandic version.

dow repeatedly, finally beating so hard that the window pane broke. After this she could've sworn she saw malicious human faces in the window, whereupon both she and her mother fell unconscious.[308] When Lucia woke up again she saw that her mother was dead. She'd then barely managed to scribble these words on the piece of paper, along with a farewell to her friends and acquaintances, saying that she expected her own death as well.

The following night, past midnight, Dr. Seward also noticed a slow knocking at the window, but he couldn't see anybody there.

The next morning Lucia was so weak that the doctors lost all hope for her. She died that same day, in the presence of the physicians and her love, Arthur. Her final words were to the professor, saying, "Protect him, and give me peace."

Preparations for the funeral were made. The night before the burial, Dr. Seward and Arthur entered the room where the bodies of both mother and daughter lay. Flowers and tall candelabras with burning candles were placed around the bed. The doctor lifted the shroud covering Lucia's body, and immediately both men were bewildered—it was as if Lucia were alive! She appeared even younger than she had in her last moments of life, and no signs of death or decay could be seen on her body!

That night Arthur slept in Lucia's room, and the doctor slept in the room next door. During the night the doctor was awakened by a strange sound. He jumped to his feet and fetched a light. He saw that Arthur's room was dark, and that the door to the room where the bodies lay stood half open. He went in and saw that the lid to Lucia's coffin had been opened, her face visible, and that the flowers were in a pile on the floor. Arthur was lying unconscious next to the casket. The doctor took him in his arms and carried him to his bed, and when he regained consciousness, Arthur insisted that Lucia was alive and that she had risen from her coffin, smiling. He said that he'd been awake in bed, but then he longed to see her so intensely that he'd got to his feet.

He repeated his story so stubbornly that the doctors did everything they could to revive her—but in vain. But for Arthur this wasn't enough and he refused to let the lid be screwed onto the coffin, so the casket was left open in the crypt, where enough air could get to it. Blankets and food for the body were placed nearby, in case Lucia were to awaken.

CHAPTER SEVEN

The Search for Thomas Harker

THE STORY NOW TURNS TO WILMA. SHE RECEIVED A message from Thomas Harker's employer, Mr. Hawkins, saying that he wanted to talk to her. He had enquired about Harker in the surroundings of Castle Dracula, but the only information his agent, Tellet,[309] had been able to obtain was a rumor that Harker had for some time now been wandering the region as a homeless drifter, and more specifically, that he had stayed at a guesthouse in Zolyva,[310] a small town nearby, where he'd been seen with a troop of philanderers and gamblers. Allegedly he'd also had an affair with Margret, the daughter of the innkeeper there. She was later found murdered not far from Castle Dracula, and most people believed that Harker had killed her.

It was said that he'd been seen in the area in early July, but since then nothing had been heard of him. The Count had left his castle at the end of June and it now stood deserted. On 15 July, a large amount of cash had been withdrawn from

309 Tellet neither appears in *Dracula* nor in Stoker's notes. See the Introduction for a possible explanation of the name. He is described as a "sendimaður," in this context an agent or messenger working for Hawkins.

310 Probably a reference to Szolyva, a Hungarian town 185 km north of Bistritz, today named "Svalyava" in Ukraine.

a bank in Budapest under Harker's name. The bankers had described the man who'd collected the money from the bank, and he seemed to have possessed quite a resemblance to Harker.

Wilma asked for all these reports and, with great insistence, finally obtained them. She had no doubt they were wrong and set off on her own journey, making no stopovers until she arrived in Budapest.

There she lodged with English people who were acquainted with Harker's employer. Once she'd arrived and settled in, she accompanied them one day on a trip from the city to a small town near the Danube.

In the town they came across a tavern and recovered from their journey with some refreshment. As they took their break, they noticed a group of Tatars who'd set up camp nearby. Among them, Wilma saw a man who looked so similar to Thomas that it was nearly impossible to tell them apart; soon after, news spread that a man had been killed in town— the very same Tatar man who not only resembled Thomas Harker but was also believed to be the person responsible for the crimes of which Harker was accused.

The English investigator now realized that he'd been on the wrong track and embarked on a new search.[311]

CHAPTER EIGHT

A Visit to Castle Dracula

THE NEXT DAY TELLET AND WILMA TRAVELLED TO Bistritz, and on the way there Tellet—an old police officer—mentioned that he'd called upon one of his leading colleagues from home, Barrington, to help them.[312] It was now certain they'd stumbled upon a complicated conspiracy, and that it was likely the old Count Dracula[313] was one of the criminals holding the reins. It would be a very difficult case to crack, but if Barrington couldn't get to the truth, certainly no one else would.

When they arrived in Bistritz they went to the same guesthouse where Harker had lodged three and a half months earlier. Wilma spoke with the innkeeper's wife, and the old lady remembered well the "fine English gentleman" who had stayed with her. She also mentioned that she'd tried to persuade him to change his mind about going to Castle Dracula, and that she'd given him her cross as a talisman to protect him.

She could not—or would not—reveal anything about the Count himself, but Wilma could tell from her manner that something ungodly was to be expected.

312 Barrington is another new character; he may correspond to Inspector Cotford mentioned in Stoker's early notes. See my *Introduction* for a possible explanation of the name.

313 Icelandic: "gamli greifinn Drakúla." In Icelandic, "gamall" ("old") is frequently used for any older person, without a patronising connotation. In the Icelandic press of the last two centuries, we thus find "Metternich gamli," "gamli Wellington," "Napoleon gamli," "Disraeli gamli," "Gladstone gamli," "gamli Bismarck," "Vilhjálmur gamli," "gamli Kruger," "Roosevelt gamli," "Hitler gamli," "Stalin gamli," "Churchill gamli," "Nixon gamli," "Clinton gamli," etc.

314 Icelandic: "Hawkins gamli málaflutningsmaður"—see previous note.

315 For "spyrja til" + genitive, modern dictionaries only give "to enquire about," but Cleasby/Vigfússon, 1874, still lists "to receive intelligence about," which makes more sense in combination with "believed."

316 Icelandic: "að gamni sínu," lit.: "to entertain themselves." In this context, with Thomas still unheard from and false rumors still lingering about, and with Castle Dracula being deserted, this passage probably refers to their travelling under the pretense of pleasure.

It wasn't long before Barrington arrived in Bistritz, and with him Hawkins, the old solicitor.[314] Wilma was overjoyed at their arrival. After they'd enjoyed a good night's rest from their journey, they all embarked for the town of Zolyva, as Tellet believed the intelligence[315] he'd received that Thomas Harker had come from there—but the stories Tellet had been told turned out to be nonsense. From Zolyva, it was only an hour's trip to Castle Dracula. They settled in a guesthouse in town and pretended to be travelling for leisure. From the inn, they embarked on their first outing to Castle Dracula, as a pleasure ride.[316]

Their driver was very reluctant to take the road to Castle Dracula, which climbed through a landscape of wooded mountains, and when they came to a peak from which one could see the castle, the man refused to go any further.

The drawbridge was down and the gate stood open. When they reached the courtyard, they split up and started looking around, in an effort to see whether any living creature could still be found there.

They found nothing, except Wilma believed she was being attacked when she entered the castle. She cried out, and in the same moment she was hurled to the ground. Upon seeing this her companions came to her side. She had hurt one of her legs.

They decided to leave right away, and on Barrington's advice—he was the only one of the party who understood the local language—the driver was asked to take a different route than before.

CHAPTER NINE

The Nunnery

THEY TOOK A ROAD THAT LED TO A NUNNERY NEARBY, where the sisters had a long tradition of nursing sick strangers.[317]

By the time they reached the convent, Wilma had fallen unconscious from exhaustion and pain. When she opened her eyes, she saw that she was in a small white room, lying on a hard but clean bed. Her leg had been bandaged. Next to her bed sat a girl in nun's habit, but when Wilma spoke to her in German she didn't answer, save for shaking her head.

A little later an elderly nun came to her, speaking French very well. She asked Wilma to feel at home and told her that her leg had been injured so badly that she would have to stay in bed for a few weeks to recover.

Wilma was very upset about this, but the nun comforted her, saying, "It is the will of God, blessed daughter, and His will is always best. Who can tell for what purpose He has brought you here? Nothing in this world happens without reason."

These words greatly relieved Wilma, and she was also glad to know that the two detectives were continuing their search. They were now convinced that Thomas had been mixed up

317 There actually is a nunnery in the Borgo Pass, at Piatra Fântânele, on a hill just opposite of the *Hotel Castel Dracula*. At night, the hotel is lit in glaring red, while the monastery is marked by a gigantic white neon-lit crucifix. In the bar of *Hotel Castel Dracula*, many impious jokes have already been cracked about the sign of the cross having been placed there by the good nuns in order to protect themselves from the forces of evil.

318 In *Fjallkonan*, Valdimar used the word "heilafeber" (in quotation marks), which is the literal translation of Stoker's term "brain fever"—the word "feber" being borrowed from Norwegian, Danish or Swedish. The Icelandic word for "fever" is "sótthiti," while in Faroese, "fepur" is still in use. In the 1901 edition, Valdimar opted for "heilasjúkdómi," meaning "brain disease."

with someone else and that some sophisticated trickery had been pulled to blame him for crimes committed by others. Mr. Hawkins, on the other hand, had to return home, as he had several business matters to look after.

The nuns took care of Wilma as best they could, and although they didn't speak English, many of them could speak German, some French, and others Italian—and Wilma could make herself understood by all of them. She especially liked a nun from Austria, named Agatha. She was a small cheerful girl with dark eyes who often spoke of her patients, of whom she was very fond. The sisters often visited patients in the neighborhood, even if they lived miles away in all directions. There was also a hospital in the convent, and Sister Agatha in particular had a soft spot for those who recuperated there. She often mentioned a man who'd been lying in the monastery for a long time with brain fever, and when he finally began to improve, he seemed to have lost his memory completely.[318] Wilma asked Agatha many things about Castle Dracula, and the girl had a lot to say about it, most of which seemed inconceivable to Wilma. She said that in this area people believed a woman in white wandered through the old corridors of the castle and could sometimes be seen in the moonlit windows. She said there were rumors that anyone who saw her would lose his mind, and that many men who had ventured to find her had disappeared, never to be seen again.

She also said that a band of thugs inhabited the castle, and that their chief was in league with the Archfiend himself.

CHAPTER TEN

Thomas and Wilma Find One Another

NE DAY SISTER AGATHA ASKED WILMA, "YOU KNOW so many languages—can you not tell me what 'mhai löhf' means?"

Wilma answered that she didn't understand these words and asked her why she wanted to know.

The nun explained that her patient would sometimes talk about "mhai löhf," and that it would be sad if she weren't able to understand him.

The next evening Wilma was thinking about this phrase when it occurred to her that "mhai löhf" could be the English words "my love," and that the patient might be talking about his fiancée or wife. The next morning she told this to the nun, and they agreed to go visit the patient to find out if he was from Wilma's country.

The abbess told them this was not a good idea, as Wilma's leg was still too weak, and so they decided that she would write to him instead. Wilma wrote a note, asking him if he was an Englishman. He was so mentally exhausted that he could hardly read, and he spelled out each word like a child, but after thinking for a few moments he wrote back with a trembling hand: "Yes, I am an Englishman; God bless your help."

They began writing to each other every day. At first he could write nothing but incoherent sentences; he couldn't recall anything that had happened to him. When he was asked about something, he would always reply: "Don't remember, all forgotten."

Finally, Wilma went with the nun to visit him.

Wilma greeted him in English, but upon seeing him she became so alarmed that she let out a shriek and swooned—for she recognized her beloved Thomas Harker! Recognizing her in return, he was equally moved, and he too lost consciousness. The moment he awoke, he called out to her, "Wilma, where are you? I saw you, but now they have taken you from me again!"

Wilma saw that Thomas—albeit very weak—was able to think clearly. She sat with him every day and he recovered quickly. Gradually his memory came back as well—that is, he could remember everything he'd done *before* leaving on his long journey, but what he'd experienced *during* the trip remained blank.

Wilma informed Harker's employer of the good news, and a few days later he arrived at the abbey with Barrington by his side.

Barrington said he'd already uncovered some secrets and that he only lacked a few details to understand fully the complex web of deceit.[319] As of now, he'd by and large managed to disentangle it—Thomas Harker would be able to fill in the missing pieces. He was shocked when he heard that Harker had lost all memory of the time he had spent with the Count, and that it would therefore be useless to ask him.

Old Mr. Hawkins, Harker's boss, had a long talk with him. He believed that Thomas had fully recovered his health and thought his memory problem would wear off over time, because of the short period involved. He told Wilma that he'd designated Thomas and her as the heirs to all his possessions and hoped that they would settle down in his house. Most of all, he hoped that they wouldn't postpone their wedding, so he requested an English priest come from Budapest with a lawyer from the English Consulate there, to serve, together with Barrington, as witness to the marriage.

The wedding ceremony took place the following day, after which the couple bid the nuns farewell. They were very sad that Wilma and Thomas were leaving but pleased that old Hawkins had made a handsome donation to the convent.

They travelled back home at a leisurely pace. In Vienna, Wilma consulted a famous neurologist, who said he hoped her husband's health would gradually improve, although it seemed unlikely he would regain his memory of the period before falling ill. The doctor also advised her not to ask Thomas about anything from that episode.

CHAPTER ELEVEN

Returning Home

AFTER A LONG JOURNEY, THEY FINALLY ARRIVED IN England. Once there, Wilma heard about the death of her friend Lucia, and shortly thereafter she received a letter from the Dutch professor, Van Helsing, who had tended to her. Arthur had been ill since Lucia's death and Van Helsing sent Wilma his regards. The professor wrote that he'd like to visit her and could explain more when they met. She replied that he was welcome to stay with her and Thomas. He arrived shortly afterwards and asked many questions regarding Lucia's habits during the last period of time the girls had spent together. He brought Wilma a precious diamond ring, which he said Lucia had worn, but he begged her—for whatever his warning might be worth[320]—not to put it on her finger. He was very curious to learn how Harker was doing and wanted to know all about his health.

A week later, Harker's now retired employer, the old Mr. Hawkins, died of heart disease. He'd long been prepared for his death and arranged a will, in it explaining what was be done with his worldly goods. He'd left everything to the young couple, as he had promised.

Two days later Hawkins was buried in London, as he'd

320 Icelandic: "að gera það samt fyrir sín orð," an expression already found in Eyrbyggja Saga, relating to the events in Snæfellsnes in the 10th century: "Arnkell bað hann gera *fyrir sín orð* og bæta honum heyið" (Chapter 13).

321 Hansom or hansom cab: a light horse-drawn carriage—the Victorian equivalent of a taxi. In *Dracula*, the girl is waiting in a victoria (another type of carriage) and receives a small parcel from Guiliano's, a famous jeweler at 115 Piccadilly. See Klinger, 2008, p. 255, note 37; the "dark stranger" merely stares at her and then hails a hansom in order to follow her; Jonathan and Mina decide to sit down in Green Park, opposite 138 Piccadilly—a property identified as the Count's town house by Bernard Davies, co-founder of the London *Dracula Society*.

stipulated in his will. The young couple attended the funeral and afterwards went for a walk in Hyde Park. On their way back to the hotel where they were staying, the route led along Piccadilly, where they came across a striking young woman. She sat in a brilliant carriage drawn by grey horses, with servants in uniform accompanying her. She was exceptionally beautiful and elegant, though her garments were somewhat pretentious. Wilma looked at her with fascination, but in that moment she felt Thomas pinch her arm, a low growl escaping from his throat. She turned around to find that he'd become deathly pale, glaring with strange frenzy at something ahead of him. She saw him staring at a gentleman who was talking with the woman. He was tall and impressive to behold but of somewhat peculiar appearance.

Wilma was startled, for there she saw Baron Székely, whom she'd met in Whitby. Thinking of Thomas above all else, she immediately hailed a hansom and rode with him to their hotel as quickly as possible.[321]

Thomas was so confounded that he hardly realized what was going on. Little by little, he lowered his head onto Wilma's shoulder then nodded off. He awoke again just before the couple reached their hotel but had forgotten everything that had happened on the street.

The next day Wilma started arranging various things at their new home, which hadn't yet been put in order since they moved in. Among other things, she looked through their suitcase that had accompanied them from Transylvania. At the bottom she found a parcel wrapped in the nunnery's church newspaper. She remembered that when they made their farewells, sister Agatha had said she would put some of Thomas's belongings in the suitcase; on another occasion, she'd said that he only had a few worthless things with him upon his arrival at the convent.

Wilma was understandably curious then when she began opening the package, but it contained nothing more than a rosary with a brass cross[322] and Thomas's journal, written in shorthand, which is presented in the first part of this story. On the first page she read her own name.

In the evening, when Thomas was asleep, Wilma started reading the notebook and was both frightened and mystified by what she found. Even though she believed everything in it to be a product of her poor husband's imagination, she was still struck with apprehension upon reading it.

She also began to suspect that Count Dracula and Baron Székely might be one and the same person.

Thomas was ill the next day, and though he managed to do his work he was very distracted. That night he spoke in his sleep, and Wilma knew through his words that he was dreaming of his stay with the Count.

322 In the Transylvanian part of the story, Harker mentioned an iron cross, not a brass cross.

CHAPTER TWELVE

The Professor and Barrington

WITH THOMAS SUFFERING LIKE THIS, THE DUTCH professor arrived as though he was summoned. Wilma cordially welcomed him, and it wasn't long before she told him all about her journey to Castle Dracula —and about Thomas's journal. This seemed very important to the professor, and he asked if he might borrow the text,[323] which Wilma had transcribed. He promised to come back the next day and spent the night reading the journal. When he returned, he told Wilma that the notebook was worth its weight in gold, as it shed light upon many things that hitherto had been hidden in the dark.

He said that Thomas was so baffled upon seeing the man on the street in London because in that moment some memory of his stay with the Count must have been triggered. This vague reminiscence, however, must have seemed so unfamiliar to him—now that he'd forgotten all about his stay at the castle and didn't even know about his journal—that he'd

323 Lit: "borrowed the text." The Icelandic does not know the word "please" and mostly uses the imperative to make a polite request: "Give me the butter" instead of "Could you please give me the butter?"

324 Icelandic: "að Tómas hefði aftur fengið minnið," lit.: "that Thomas had regained his memory." In fact, this recovery is a gradual process that has only just started—as we will see at the start of Chapter 15.

325 Icelandic: "þar sem þau Vilma áttu heima." This is probably an error in the text, as the pronomen "þau" ("they") corresponds with the plural "áttu eiga" ("they lived"), while "Vilma" is singular. At this point, Wilma and Thomas are already married and live in Hawkins's house together; in the first line of this paragraph, however, only Wilma is mentioned. Maybe Valdimar had noticed that this was awkward and intended to correct it in the second line, but forgot to cross out "Vilma" there.

believed he was losing his wits. Wilma then fetched her husband for an interview with the professor.

The professor and Thomas talked for a long time, and Van Helsing came to the conclusion that Thomas was now regaining his memory,[324] although he couldn't remember the incident at Piccadilly on the day of Mr. Hawkins's funeral.

The professor gave Thomas some healthful advice and asked him to remain quiet for the time being, and to avoid anything that might upset him. He had the journal with him and wanted to show it to some of his acquaintances.

A few days later Barrington came to visit Wilma. He had just returned to London and now travelled to Exeter—where Thomas and Wilma lived[325]—to learn about Count Dracula's real estate purchase in London. She informed him that Thomas was recovering his memory, and that his diary had been found.

Barrington and Wilma agreed that he shouldn't talk with Thomas until he had consulted with Van Helsing, and they arranged to meet again in two days.

Van Helsing and Barrington arrived at the appointed time and had a long talk with Thomas, after which Barrington came to Wilma once more to tell her that he wondered about the professor's views. He respected him highly, but he thought him a religious sentimentalist, prone to superstition. He said that he personally didn't rely on anything other than facts and thought that there had to be a logical explanation for everything that was said about Count Dracula and his accomplices, even though these stories seemed bizarre to many people.

With these words he left their house.

Professor Van Helsing began to explain his research and its results to Wilma, saying,

"The inventions of the nineteenth century are amazing. They have created a new world, teaching us to recognize the forces of nature that our ancestors either had no knowledge of or which they ascribed to the supernatural. Nowadays scientists can hardly dismiss any phenomenon as inconceivable within the limits of physical law. Nature has an infinite range of such laws, but human perception cannot fully grasp them because the sensory organs aren't sophisticated enough.

"There must be powers and principles that our descendants will someday discover, even if we do not know them now. They will learn to understand these forces, and domesticate and control them. Who knows, perhaps there is a world of invisible beings influencing us to act on behalf of good or evil,[326] depending on their intention.[327]

"I—and many other thinkers of our time—have reached the conclusion that such creatures *do* exist and that they obey certain laws which are unknown to us, as they are equipped with an entirely different range of gifts and powers than we are.

"Folklore recognizes many things that science knows nothing about, or which scientists deny. One such thing is the fact that there are creatures wandering about here on earth after they die.[328] Let's consider such a being, as a person, for example, who has lived sinfully in life, as a criminal or murderer. He departs like any other man, but his soul cannot break free from the body, which binds it to the earth. The soul then remains attached to the corpse and—by some law that we do not know—can settle in it again, bring new life to it, and use it, furthermore, to satisfy its natural lusts. In order to maintain this existence, however, this vermin must feed off the blood of living humans—and by virtue will never stop killing.

326 Icelandic: "að Tómas hefði fengið minnið aftur," echoing the words of Professor Van Helsing. See footnote 323.

327 Icelandic: "sem hrífa oss til góðs eða ills." The expression "færa til góðs eðr ílls" is already used in the Gragas, the Grey Goose Laws of the 13th century. Cleasby/Vigfússon, 1874, translates it as "to turn to good or bad account," describing the effect caused by the original actor; in combination with "ad hrífa" ("to affect," "move," "touch," "stimulate," "stir into a passion," "enchant," "inspire") it could also mean that these beings incite humans to act in a good or evil way — an idea picked up some paragraphs later.

328 Icelandic: "eftir því sem verkast vill." A standard expression, meaning "depending on how the situation develops." In this context, it is up to the will of these invisible beings to determine which direction we may be influenced.

329 Icelandic: "þótt þær deyi," lit.: "although they die." This only makes sense in past or perfect tense.

330 Today, "draugur" is translated as "ghost," "phantom," "spectre," "spirit" or "spook," but I assume that the text refers to the Old Norse "draugr." While ghosts today are mostly depicted as pale, semi-transparent apparitions, hovering weightlessly in the air, the revenants from Norse mythology are revived corpses, blackened, decaying and swollen; they have superhuman strength, can increase their size at will and crush humans with their weight. They also kill by drinking their victim's blood or by driving people mad. Like vampires, they can die a "second death" when their bodies are burned or dismembered. The "haugbui" watching over the grave mounds are a special sub-category: They mostly stay in their mound or its immediate neighborhood. See Jakobsson, 2011.

331 As in *Dracula*, the characteristics of the un-dead are only named at the end of the story—albeit here without using the word "vampire"; only Thomas Harker uses the term, once, to describe the London fog. Lucia's neck shows no fangmarks, nor does she ever bite children; Wilma is never bitten nor forced to drink the Count's blood; even Quincey's remark on the Argentinian vampire bat is omitted. During the ceremony in the castle's vault, it is not the Count who drinks the victim's blood but the ape-like brute. In *Dracula*, Harker over time understands that the vampire women follow a special diet: "[. . .] nothing can be more dreadful than those awful women, who were—who are—waiting to suck my blood." See *Dracula*, Harker's Journal entry of 16 May. In *Makt Myrkranna*, however, the intentions of both the Count and his cousin remain obscure—for never are they caught with their fangs in someone's neck.

"So it is said in folklore, to which we may add that these un-dead creatures[329] are, according to popular belief, supposedly able to influence other people—not only the wicked, but also the weak."[330]

They discussed Lucia's death and the professor said,

"I have every reason to believe that this innocent girl was afflicted by the same forces I speak of now—or by a kind of hypnosis, which these enemies of mankind use to turn decent people into their tools, once they manage to gain power over them. She, who was carried to her tomb adorned in the white garments of innocence, now has this same effect on her beloved; she is now trying to pull him into the grave with her.[331]

"I am convinced that the Powers of Darkness are spreading around us. We find many examples in the newspapers pointing to it, but our friend Barrington is of another opinion, claiming he can explain all in a much different way."

He bid farewell to the couple and left, but Wilma placed no faith in his words, regardless of how much she respected him.

CHAPTER THIRTEEN

The People in Carfax

THE FOLLOWING CHAPTER IS BASED ON A JOURNAL written by Dr. Seward[332]—the Directing Physician at the asylum in Parfleet—who was previously mentioned in this story.

The mental hospital where Seward was Director stood directly opposite the Carfax building that Count Dracula had purchased.

Barrington now set off to visit the doctor and find out what was happening at Carfax.

Dr. Seward told him that a lot of work had recently been done to Carfax, and that costly furnishings had been moved in. He saw lavishly decorated carriages arrive there with some regularity—far more luxurious than was usual in this part of the city.

When Barrington asked Seward whether he'd perhaps noticed a carriage that set itself apart from the others, the doctor told him about a particularly extravagant carriage drawn by grey horses, carrying servants in grey uniforms—

332 Icelandic: "sem fundust eftir Seward," a somewhat cryptic phrase: "found by Seward," "found to be written by Seward," "found after Seward's death" are some of the suggestions I discussed with my team. As we know with certainty that Seward wrote these papers (see end of Chapter 14), and that they must have been found by others, I finally opted for "written by Seward."

and a ravishing young woman, whose face indeed had an extraordinarily striking look about it. From Seward's description, Barrington believed her to be the French Ambassador's wife.

"Yet it was not the sight of the magnificent carriages that caught my attention most of all, but rather the strange and suspicious chaps moving about Carfax, especially in the evening."

Before he left, Barrington thanked the doctor for the information and asked him to keep an eye on Carfax and the goings on there.

Later that day, as the doctor sat down for dinner, he was handed a calling card bearing the name of a certain Countess Ida Varkony. The card had been delivered by a servant in uniform, carrying a message from the Countess asking the doctor to call on her as she was suffering a bout of some malady she was susceptible to. She apologized for sending for him at such a late hour but hoped he would come all the same, as she lived right across from him at Carfax.

The doctor was very curious to look around the old house, which had been uninhabited for a long time, so he went along with the servant without delay. When he arrived at the door another attendant welcomed him inside, and as he entered a French maid greeted him and showed him into a grand hall with old embroidered tapestries.

When the doctor arrived a woman rose from a divan and came to meet him.

It was no surprise that the doctor—though well known for being a calm and controlled man, averse to frivolity—was so taken aback that he lost all composure and manner;[333] he'd never before seen a woman of such strange, indescribable beauty. To him, she seemed so different from other pretty women, as if she had come from another world. She was tall and sleek, both graceful and radiant. Her hair was thick and black; her eyes unusually large and deep, with long black lashes.

But despite her being of such exquisite beauty, the doctor felt a pang of alarm upon seeing her, as though he'd laid eyes upon some wonder of nature that might prove dangerous.

After the Countess had greeted the doctor she sat back down on the divan. She spoke French with a foreign accent.

The doctor asked some questions about her health, and she answered them all if rather casually. He soon learned that she had a habit of fainting[334] and was suffering from insomnia, cardiac arrhythmia and convulsive seizures. She said she'd recently recovered from a fit and had a hard time sleeping after that, so she would like to be hypnotized. Dr. Seward knew the technique very well—though he rarely practiced it. This time, however, he yielded to persuasion, but putting the patient into mesmeric sleep turned out to be harder than usual. In fact, he didn't succeed until he took the lady's hand. He then gave her a hypnotic suggestion: after going to bed she would fall asleep and sleep well all through the night, and then she would wake up again in the morning feeling refreshed and revitalized. After the procedure he woke her from her trance, and she thanked him dearly for his help, saying that she hoped he would do this for her again soon.

The hypnotic treatment had an unusual effect on the doctor himself. He felt weary the day after, and he thought of nothing else but the Countess and what had happened between themin the house across the way.

Towards the end of the day, he went to visit her and was escorted to her bedroom.

She was lying on the bed as though she were dead and didn't open her eyes, yet she seemed to be speaking,

334 Icelandic: "að hún var vön að falla í öngvit." This part of the sentence has been omitted in the 1950 and 2011 editions.

335 The phenomenon of people speaking with a voice seemingly not belonging to them was a central element of Spiritism; attending séances where a (mostly female) medium would speak in "voices from beyond" was a popular pastime in Victorian higher circles. Between 1870 and 1900, neuro-physiology, hypnotical experiments and research on telepathy, clairvoyance and spirit communication still belonged to the same scientific field. The *Society for Psychical Research (S.P.R.)*, the *Metyphysical Club* and the *Ghost Club* had numerous high-ranking members, many of them friends with Bram Stoker. Valdimar had an interest in the subject as well: on 9 September 1890, he dedicated his complete front page to the work and writings of the *S.P.R.* See Introduction.

336 Icelandic; "núning," lit.: "friction" or "rubbing." This refers to the act of rubbing the limbs of the patient in order to stimulate the blood circulation. Klinger, 2008, p. 182, note 38, informs us that Victorian doctors avoided visual examination of their female patients, as it was considered inappropriate. Strangely enough, tactile manipulation and massage—underneath the garments or from behind closed curtains—seemed to be consented to, even to the point of stimulating female patients to "paroxysmal convulsions" in order to treat "hysteria," as reported by medical historian Rachel F. Maines in *The Technology of Orgasm* (1998) and the UK movie *Hysteria* (2011, directed by Tanya Wexler).

337 As we know from the Whitby chapter, Prince Koromezzo is the Austrian Ambassador in London with a bad reputation.

338 Prince Koromezzo means here the evening of the *next* day, as the Countess had previously agreed upon with Dr. Seward.

her voice sounding as if it were coming through the ceiling:

"Good evening, Doctor. She is dead now, but you must revive her. Do whatever you can."[335]

He couldn't find any signs of life.

"You must first hypnotize her," said the voice.

After many attempts to revive her and massaging her limbs,[336] he managed to bring her back to life, but it had the same effect on him as before, as if he were losing much of his own life force; as though his blood were seeping away from him, just like when the Dutch professor had drawn his blood for Lucia. He even had the impression that it was Lucia herself resting there in the bed.

Finally he came to his senses, as if waking up from a stupor, and at that same moment the Countess awoke as well. She made him promise to return the next day then asked the parlormaid to show him to her brother in the next room. He introduced himself as Prince Koromezzo[337] and enquired as to how the lady was feeling, but the doctor said he wasn't yet able to judge her condition. Prince Koromezzo asked the doctor to become her personal physician and requested that he do them the favor of returning at nine o'clock in the evening.[338] She would by then have recovered enough to receive him.

CHAPTER FOURTEEN

The Evening Party

T HAT EVENING DR. SEWARD WAS WEARIER THAN USUAL and took chloral before going to bed.[339] He slept deeply and quietly until morning but still felt feeble and tired when he awoke. He had to pull himself together in order to perform his regular duties and took a nap in the afternoon, waking up again at nine o'clock, at which time he felt well enough to visit his patient across the street.

As he exited the asylum he saw a carriage drawn by grey horses arriving at Carfax, and upon entering the hall, he saw an elegant lady being welcomed there. She wore a white coat with exquisite feather ornamentation, and the doctor realized that this was the same lady whom Barrington had identified as the French Ambassador's wife.

The doctor was then admitted to the Countess.

The lights were dimmed, only slightly illuminating the room. There were about 40-50 guests inside, and although there were both ladies and gentlemen present, there were far more men than women. Although the visitors were speaking in French, the doctor suspected that most of them were from

339 Chloral is an aldehyd. Mixed with water, it forms chloral hydrate, with sedative and soporific qualities. Like laudanum (containing opium), it was often used in the Victorian Age. *Makt Myrkranna* copies this detail from *Dracula* but omits Seward's chivalrous qualms: "I am weary to-night and low in spirits. I cannot but think of Lucy, and how different things might have been. If I don't sleep at once, chloral, the modern Morpheus— $C_2HCl_3O. H_2O$! I must be careful not to let it grow into a habit. No, I shall take none to-night! I have thought of Lucy, and I shall not dishonour her by mixing the two. If need be, to-night shall be sleepless…" See *Dracula*, Chapter 8, Dr. Seward's Diary of 19 August.

340 Intriguingly, in Bram Stoker's early notes for the novel, a dinner party at Dr. Seward's house was planned, the Count arriving as the last guest. In *Makt Myrkranna*, Seward takes on the role of a guest. Even though the Count is the owner of Carfax, he still arrives to the party as the last participant. If we do not accept this as coincidence, this means that Stoker's original ideas for *Dracula* show up in *Makt Myrkranna* again.

different countries, as every now and then he would pick up a word from a language he did not recognize. He seemed to be the only Englishman there.

Prince Koromezzo greeted and welcomed the physician as soon as he came in. He took him to the Countess, who sat in a corner surrounded by a handful of ladies and gentlemen. She—like the other women—was dressed in glamorous attire; their necks and arms were bare but sparkling with gems. The doctor noticed in particular the necklace the Countess was wearing. It had a heart of shimmering diamonds, with a large ruby at the center.

She greeted the doctor with a slight nod of the head and in the same moment the young lady who'd arrived at Carfax a few minutes before him entered the room with two gentlemen. The Countess greeted her and introduced her to the doctor as Madame Saint Amand. Soon after, everyone rose to their feet as a tall, impressive-looking man entered the room. It was clear he was master of the house, as he was greeted with signs of great respect and everyone gave way to him.[340]

He spoke a few words with two of the men in the room and then walked up to the Countess. She'd been sitting as proud as a queen, but when the newly arrived gentleman drew nearer, her whole appearance changed and it was clear she was completely under his thumb. They had a brief conversation in some foreign tongue before he headed quickly towards the doctor, thanking him on behalf of the Countess. He said that he'd read Seward's treatise on hallucinations and optical illusions, which had been printed in some medical journal—an article he believed to be of great significance as he personally performed experiments of this kind. He wanted to make a few such attempts tonight and hoped that the doctor, with his scientific acuity, would observe them.

Then he took the Countess by the hand and led her through a curtained entryway. One of the people in the room turned to the doctor. He was a short stocky man[341] with a dark complexion and deeply set black eyes, and he began to talk to the doctor about the upcoming evening program.

"The Countess is one of a kind," he said, "so it's quite an event in the history of mankind when a master like Marquis Caroman Rubiano engages such a natural wonder to collaborate with him. Her gift of second sight is very strong—she can perceive the hidden world[342] and see into the future."[343]

Suddenly most of the lights in the hall went out, and Dr. Seward got the impression that some wondrous things were taking place that were beyond his understanding—as if he were attending some kind of religious ceremony down in a dark cavern. He then had the queer sensation of floating in the air until he lost all consciousness. Finally, he awoke as if from a dream—still sitting in the same chair with the Countess standing beside him, together with Marquis Caroman Rubiano, as he was called.

He suspected his hosts might have used him for hypnosis or some similar experiment.

The Marquis addressed him, explaining that he had fainted. "I hope you get well again soon. Unfortunately, due to your indisposition, you have not learned anything new this evening, but you are welcome another time."[344]

The doctor then said his goodbyes and left. The hunchback[345] accompanied him home, and when they parted he handed Seward his calling card, bearing the name of "Giuseppe Leonardi," which—oddly enough—was the name of a world famous violinist and composer. As he arrived at the hospital the doctor heard a cry of distress from the garden at Carfax.

341 The person whom Harker believed he saw in a corridor of the castle was also described as short and stocky.

342 Icelandic: "sér gegnum holt og hæðir," lit.: "to see through hills and hillocks." People with "skyggn" can see ghosts, goblins and elves that otherwise are invisible ("huldufólk"), and perceive things in the distance or that are otherwise obstructed from normal sight.

343 Icelandic: "Hún […] veit óorðna hluti," lit.: "She […] knows things that have not happened yet." In *The Mystery of the Sea* (1902) and *The Lady of the Shroud* (1909), Bram Stoker extensively dealt with the gift of second sight, which—both in Scandinavian and in Scottish popular belief   included precognition.

344 Marquis Rubiano is here referring here to their previous conversation about the experiment.

345 Icelandic: "kroppinbakurinn": "*the* hunchback." The only character fitting this description is the short, stocky man who previously talked to Seward about the evening programme. The Icelandic "rekinn saman" used for this stocky person literally means "compressed."

346 The reason for this cry is never revealed. Perhaps another sacrificial ceremony, or a snack for the guests?

"What is that?" he asked the hunchback. "It's a woman's voice." [346]

The hunchback paid no attention to his question and quickly said goodbye to the doctor.

A short while later the same man returned for a visit, and after talking to him insistently he finally got Seward's permission to play his instrument for the patients and to allow the ladies from Carfax to accompany him.

(Here is where Dr. Seward's notes end, appearing as though he hadn't been able to finish them.)

CHAPTER FIFTEEN

The Conspiracy

A FORTNIGHT HAD PASSED SINCE VAN HELSING LAST visited Harker and his wife, during which time he'd also not heard from Dr. Seward. Thomas Harker was now recovering well and was starting to regain his memory. He no longer doubted that Baron Székely, whom Wilma had met, was none other than Count Dracula himself.

One evening Van Helsing, Barrington, Tellet and Seward's American friend, Morris, came to the couple's home.[347]

Van Helsing spoke to them, explaining that it was their mission to deliberate and find a way to utterly destroy the public enemy they all knew. It had become clear that a conspiracy had been formed to thwart all that is good in society, and that there was but one man responsible for this: Count Dracula. This Count was—as folklore imagined certain creatures to be—half-man and half-animal, and had probably lived much longer than mortal men were meant to.[348] Van Helsing explained that such beings were endowed with powers and qualities normal people do not know, but were denied other faculties common to ordinary humans. According to old texts: Such beings could not cross running water, their power dwindled in daylight, and although they could move about

347 Previously, Morris has been described as a friend of Arthur Holmwood.

348 In *Dracula*, Stoker's vampire is a human who has survived bodily death, but can appear in animal shape, e.g. the form of a bat. The vampire's predatory behavior also points to his animalistic qualities.

349 Icelandic: "að flytja búferlum": lit.: "take down one's tents (and pitch them elsewhere)", mostly translated as "to move," "to migrate." In this case, I suspect a temporary relocation: Thomas could not simply close down his law firm in Exeter. In *Dracula*, the whole team lodges in Dr. Seward's asylum, next to Carfax.

among humans, every now and then they needed to rest in the hallowed earth in which they had once been buried.

The Count had left behind his ancestral home in the Carpathians to increase the evil among men. It would have been clear to him that the obstacles ahead would be many, but he would have prepared for them. Among other things, he would have brought with him boxes filled with consecrated soil; in one of them he would have rested during the journey. Some of the boxes would likely also contain immense riches, as it would cost millions to effectuate the cunning schemes the Count had in mind.

Finally they had gathered to try and stop the Count and his evil band.

They agreed that the young couple would take up lodging[349] near Carfax to make it easier to keep an eye on what was happening there.

CHAPTER SIXTEEN

The Count Killed

OON IT WAS ESTABLISHED THAT THE MASTER OF CARFAX was indeed Count Dracula, and it was also widely rumored that the asylum run by Dr. Seward was in a state of complete chaos. Van Helsing and Morris made a trip there, but Seward was not present; instead some stranger seemed to be in charge. Van Helsing asked that Morris be admitted to the hospital, as the two of them were determined to find out what was happening there. They suspected that the people at Carfax had been paying the hospital regular visits.

The next day Van Helsing and the others met with Morris and Dr. Seward, their clothes torn from their bodies and reduced to rags. They looked more like ghosts than men. Both men had come from Carfax, where Morris had fetched the doctor who'd gone mad.[350] Morris was hardly conscious and had wounds on his head. They were both admitted to another hospital on the same day Dr. Seward's asylum burned to the ground, and no one knew how it had happened.

The next day the companions put their heads together and decided to pay the Count a visit at Carfax, as they'd

350 In Stoker's earliest notes for *Dracula*, Dr. Seward is typified as a "mad doctor." In *Bram Stoker's Notes for Dracula*, editors Robert Eighteen-Bisang and Elizabeth Miller state that "this discrepancy [between the original 'mad doctor' and the later 'Doctor of a Madhouse'] raises the question of whether Seward was originally as insane as his 'mad patient.'" The fact that, of all characters in *Makt Myrkranna*, Seward is the one to go mad, once more suggests that *Makt Myrkranna* may be based on Stoker's early ideas for the plot.

learned where he was hiding out during the day. It was already late when they arrived there. They picked the lock on the door and went into the house, where they found themselves in a large foyer. Harker saw that the walls were decorated with the same kinds of pictures as in the barbarian temple in Castle Dracula. There were rooms to both sides, but no one was around. The group went through a door straight ahead of them, entering a kind of crypt. There were lights burning inside, and on the floor they could see a stone coffin made entirely of black polished marble. But they no longer had to continue their search, for in this sarcophagus lay Count Dracula, clad in the long red cloak Harker had seen him wearing at the sacrificial ceremony under his castle.

They all drew nearer to the coffin. Van Helsing, clenching his dagger in his hand, stared at the man in the casket—but the Count didn't move.

All of a sudden the Count jerked—it was sundown! He opened his eyes and sat up, looking not at Van Helsing but directly at Harker. In a flash he jumped out of the coffin and attacked him, hacking and slashing at his chest. All became dark before Harker's eyes, but in the same moment the Count fell lifeless, swimming in his own blood: Van Helsing had stabbed him through the heart with his dagger.

They left the body in the stone coffin, but immediately afterwards they saw the corpse began to change. It now looked as though the Count had been dead for several days. Then, nothing remained at all in the coffin, nothing but a small heap of dust.

CHAPTER SEVENTEEN

Epilogue

ROUND THE SAME TIME, MARQUIS CAROMAN RUBIANO —who'd recently arrived in London and had dealings with people of the highest rank—disappeared. Not long after that, Madame Saint Amand, who'd been the darling of various noblemen in London, committed suicide. And also at this time, several foreign ambassadors in London were called home.

The cause of the fire at the asylum couldn't be determined, but the doctor's diary was found in his fireproof cabinet, and it was from this diary that the part of the story about Dr. Steward is derived.[351] The doctor lived for a while longer after these events but never regained his sanity.

Morris told the police that he'd killed the Count, and the matter was investigated behind closed doors, leaving him acquitted.[352]

No trace was found of the Countess or the others who lived in Carfax with the Count. The house was left abandoned; when it was inspected, only the furniture remained. With the exception of three crates, the Count's boxes were all retrieved—filled with gold coins and precious stones worth millions.

The premises still stand deserted; however, the possibility cannot be ruled out that the Count's followers may still be hiding somewhere.

351 This echoes the burning of the diaries by the Count in Chapter 21 of *Dracula* while the Count is raiding Seward's house. Holmwood reports: "He had been there, and though it could only have been for a few seconds, he made rare hay of the place. All the manuscript had been burned, and the blue flames were flickering amongst the white ashes; the cylinders of your phonograph too were thrown on the fire, and the wax had helped the flames." Here I interrupted. 'Thank God there is the other copy in the safe!'" See *Dracula*, Dr. Seward's Diary of 3 October.

352 In confessing to protect Van Helsing, Morris, as in *Dracula*, takes on the role of the martyr—in Stoker's original he is killed in the final battle with the Count's men. That the police accept a confessed murder without consequences could mean that they have also been informed about the supernatural goings on of late. This also lends itself to the preface, which alludes to the police and secret service being confronted with irresolvable, supernatural riddles.

AFTERWORD

by John Edgar Browning

ANS DE ROOS'S BOOK FURTHERS THE CONVERSATION about—nay, breathes life anew into an increasingly dated subject that time and time again has proven unfailingly capable of invigorating the hearts and minds of peoples, nations, and cultures everywhere. Speak *his* name: *Drácula*. It's a curious little three-syllable word, in particular for all it should arouse in us but *doesn't*, and all it shouldn't arouse in us but *does*.

Hardly three years after *Dracula*'s publication, *Powers of Darkness*, a text that lay hidden for over a century, anticipated the myriad of ambiguous feelings we would all come to share for the Count by inviting him to leave the periphery of Bram Stoker's original text behind and take centerstage in Valdimar Ásmundsson's version. *Powers of Darkness* is even curiouser still, however. *Dracula* has been much like a family recipe, shared among storytellers and handed down with each passing generation who add or leave behind in its scenes a little something of itself. Even still, *Powers of Darkness* reads like no other text in English that has come before or since; here we find perhaps two chefs simultaneously—Bram and Valdimar—in a kitchen that is scarcely big enough to contain both of their disparate tastes. Yet, where Bram's voice ends and Valdimar's begins is hard to discern and, perhaps, remains the true mystery in all this.

In this new version, there are now cats in Castle Dracula, and at one point Thomas Harker, our would-be hero, talks of bicycles, references that will leap off the page at Stoker enthusiasts. (Bram was, of course, fond of both cats and bicycles.) And there are times, as when Thomas talks of sketching the differently attired peasants in Bistritz, that one wonders if it's Bram (a sketcher himself) that we are getting, or Valdimar. Yet, at other times, as when we read of Thomas's encounter with the Saxon teacher in Bistritz who uses Icelandic expressions (a theme that continues throughout the text), or further still as when we learn that Valdimar's Dracula is, among other things, an avid hunter, the two authorial voices become more distinct.

Valdimar's text acquires its own voice in several other ways as well. Among some of its more conspicuous differences is Thomas himself (his name aside). Thomas is in many ways more imbecilic than Bram's Jonathan ever was, yet Valdimar's protagonist is apt enough to carry a revolver and a pocket telescope; he even carries a flask of cognac, items which would prove indispensable to anyone unlucky enough to stay at the Castle Dracula of Valdimar's (arguably more macabre) creation. Deep beneath its stone floors are fell scenes that, at times, combine elements of the Scholomance (*Solomonanță*) from Bram's original narrative with that of Mephistopheles and the Witches' Carnival on the Brocken in W. G. Wills's *Faust*, a play Bram helped to revise and produce and one which Valdimar would certainly have been familiar during its combined 792-performance run in England and America.

More still, Valdimar's version metamorphoses, and "remasculates," Bram's more feminized Dracula into a more brazen warrior, a man adorned in gallooned, military-esque garb who uses an old deaf-mute Hungarian woman to do all his cooking and cleaning. Valdimar's Dracula is also an old libertine. This, combined with the material concerning the Count's "niece," gives us a much more free, sexually uninhibited text, one doubtless impossible under the British censors (of which Bram was a staunch proponent). The dirty old man we can only surmise in Stoker's original text is unabashedly so in the Icelandic version. So full of character is this new Count, this *politicist*, that he even uses Darwinian theory to justify his place both in society and in the new world order he conspires to create.

There are even, at times, certain moments—*meta*-moments, let's call them (as when Thomas is already conveniently well-versed on the topic of vampires and openly engages the subject with Dracula when he arrives at the castle, or when Dracula remarks on such contemporary figures as Arthur Conan Doyle), in which some of the characters behave as if they are self-aware of the novel in which they are appearing, like actors in a play. Indeed, Valdimar's text leaves much to contemplate. Who knows—perhaps Bram didn't know about *all* the revisions made to his novel; he was certainly a stickler when it came to adaptations of his works—he wrote, and testified, on copyright law, and he staged dramatic readings for no less than three of his books that we know of (*Dracula* [1897], *Miss Betty* [1898], *The Mystery of the Sea* [1902]) to safeguard their dramatic copyright. But if we've learned anything about Bram, it's that he never ceases to surprise us or keep everyone guessing, even a century after his death. We can all agree on that at least, particularly in the case of *Powers of Darkness* and the editorial prowess Hans shows in its pages.

Unearthing translations like *Makt Myrkranna* may become the next cottage industry in *Dracula* scholarship and entertainment, wholly thanks to Hans and his indomitable character, something he and the indefatigable Bram had in common.

ACKNOWLEDGMENTS

ITHOUT THE SUPPORT OF MANY PEOPLE, THIS TRANSLATION project would not have been possible. From Dublin, Brian Showers sent me back copies of the *Bram Stoker Journal* with Richard Dalby's 1995 article on *Makt Myrkranna*. Unnur Valgeirsdóttir at Reykjavík University Library, Sigurgeir Finnsson at the National and University Library of Iceland, Katrín Guðmundsdóttir and Einar Björn Magnússon at Reykjavík City Library all helped me to locate the first book edition of *Makt Myrkranna* and were so kind to send me scans of Stoker's preface. Ásgeir Jónsson, the editor of the third Icelandic edition (2011) was of great support in learning more about Valdimar Ásmundsson's background; together, we speculated about *Dracula*'s way to Iceland. Bragi Thorgrímur Ólafsson and Erlendur Már Antonsson at the National and University Library of Iceland and Gísli Baldur Róbertsson at the National Archives of Iceland informed me about the Ásmundsson letters archive.

Petre Tutunea from Bucharest, Amanda Larasari from Jakarta and Pienette Coetzee from Stellenbosch, South Africa—all working as interns or volunteers in my studio—helped with structuring the text files and dividing them among a number of Icelandic native speakers, who assisted in improving the first translation attempts. More about this remarkable group of highly qualified helpers can be found on the next pages and on our project website *www.powersofdarkness.com*.

Pienette's sister Lounette Loubser, a young linguist and journalist, offered to come over from South Africa and spend a month with us to make the English text sound more natural. She proved to be an invaluable and indefatigable transcriber and co-editor; after she returned home by the end of June 2014, she continued to exchange editing proposals with me till the end of October 2014.

Further research into the Icelandic idiom and the backgrounds of the story was undertaken from November 2014 till April 2016. Denyse Sturges at the Chester Fritz Library, University of North

Dakota; Ole Henrik Sørensen at the Royal Library in Copenhagen; Debs Furness at UCL Library, London; and Patrick Joseph Stevens at the Fiske Icelandic Collection at Cornell University, New York, all supplied images of the copies of *Makt Myrkranna* in their collections. Patrick also gave insight into the correspondence of Willard Fiske with Valdimar Ásmundsson and Mark Twain.

Information on Joseph Comyns Carr's translation of *Madame Sans-Gêne* was provided by Carrie Marsh and Tanya Kato at the Claremont Colleges Library, California; Susannah Mayor at House Steward, Smallhythe and Helen Smith at the Henry Irving Foundation.

The City of Reykjavík provided high-resolution maps of Reykjavík from the period 1876-1920.

For an in-depth discussion about the preface of *Makt Myrkranna* I am greatly indebted to Andrew Wawn, Professor of Anglo-Icelandic Literature at Leeds University; Ásta Svavarsdóttir, Haukur Thorgeirsson and Ari Páll Kristinsson, Research Professors at the Arní Magnússon Institute for Icelandic Studies, Reykjavík; Jón Karl Helgason, Professor for Icelandic Language at the University of Iceland; Gauti Kristmannsson, Professor for Translation Studies at the University of Iceland, Faculty of Icelandic and Comparative Cultural Studies; Professor Ástráður Eysteinsson, Professor of Comparative Literature, University of Reykjavík and Dean of the School of Humanities at the University of Iceland; Ragna Eyjólfsdóttir, winner of the Icelandic Children's Book Prize 2015; translation specialists Eva Dögg Diego Thorkelsdóttir and Magnea Matthíasdóttir, and again to Ásgeir Jónsson, who provided most valuable arguments.

My friends Dacre Stoker and John E. Browning showed an early and enthusiastic interest in this project and agreed to contribute to this book with a preface and an afterword respectively. Our agent Allison Devereux of Wolf Literary Services, New York, did a fantastic job while guiding us through the whole publication process and actively helping edit the text before and after its submission to Overlook. There, editors Allyson Rudolph and Tracy Carns were a great support in preparing the text for final publication.

I also thank my family and the young talented people who shared my life, work and thoughts at my Munich house over the past few years—Marsha Maramis, Sarah Mawla Syihabuddin, Yofina Pradani and Dian Risna Saputri from Indonesia, Joyce Goodwill from Nigeria, Aïda el Haini from Morocco, Susannah Schaff from New York, Andreea and Teodora Vechiu from Romania, Jeewon Kim from Korea and Shiva

Dehghan Pour from Teheran. Last but not least, my good friends Alida Kreutzer, Daniela Diaconescu and Magdalena Grabias were a never-failing source of support and motivation.

ENGLISH-LANGUAGE TEAM

LOUNETTE LOUBSER (22) is a young writer with a degree in Linguistics from Stellenbosch University, South Africa. She worked as a journalist for Shout Factory and for *Glamour South Africa*; now she studies entertainment journalism at the College of Media and Publishing. In June 2014, she came over to Munich to help us change the literal translation to a more fluent English. Until the end of October 2014, she supported the project as a transcriber and co-editor of the English text.

SUSANNA SCHAFF (21) studied English and international literature at Marymount Manhattan College and publishing at Pace University, New York. In June 2015, she helped us with another round of editing.

ALLISON DEVEREUX (29) graduated from the University of Texas and works as a literary agent at Wolf Literary Services, New York. She not only represents our book project but also engaged in giving the English text a further polish from Summer 2015 till April 2016.

ICELANDIC-LANGUAGE TEAM

ALDÍS BIRNA BJÖRNSDOTTIR (40) comes from Skútustaðir and studied literature and languages at the University of Iceland; she also studied at the Technical College in Akureyi. She now lives near Munich and works at an Icelandic travel agency; together with her husband and children, she regularly spends her holidays in Iceland. She already translated four English books to Icelandic and tells Icelandic fairly tales to children in the local library.

ANJA KOKOSCHKA (30) is the only member of this team who is not a native Icelandic speaker. She studied ophthalmic optics in Munich and worked in Iceland on various horse farms, and later as an optician, for altogether eight years. After a longer stay in Bavaria, she now lives in Iceland again, in Egilsstadir.

ARNA SIF THORGEIRSDOTTIR (23) is from Akureyi in the north of Iceland and graduated there from junior college in 2011 with language as her focus; she speaks Icelandic, English, Danish and Swedish. She studied dance in Munich at Iwanson International School of Contemporary Dance and now has returned to her hometown to instruct dance there.

Ásdís Rut Guðmundsdóttir (24) studied German as a Foreign Language in Siegen, Germany. She now continues with ethnology as a distance learning course offered by an Icelandic university. She has translated a book about Icelandic fairy tales to Icelandic; she is also a successful handball player. She was born in Reykjavík.

Hafrún Kolbeinsdóttir (20) comes from Húsavík on the northern coast of Iceland and went to high school in Garðabæ. She now works at a hotel in Bremen, but plans to continue her studies in Iceland. A gifted singer, she creates cover versions of English songs and puts them online. In Autumn 2014, she participated in the *Voice of Germany* talent contest and made it to the A-Team.

Ingibjörg Bragadóttir (21) also comes from Akureyi, where she focused on social sciences. She now lives in Paris, where she studies French at the *Cours de Civilisation Française de la Sorbonne* and will also take up studies in journalism and communications. Since age eight, she has been training, performing and coaching other people in figure skating.

Hans Ágústsson (47) was born in Reykjavík but has lived in Germany for 25 years now. In Mallersdorf, Bavaria, he breeds and trains Icelandic horses and acts as a riding instructor.

Herbert Pedersen (44) is the father of Lára Kristin (see below) and assisted in deciphering the Whitby chapter—a fitting choice, as he is currently working on a ship. He studied at the University of Reykjavík and specialized in aviation business Administration at Embry-Riddle, Daytona Beach, Florida. He worked for Icelandair and at a company designing software for the retail business.

Hildur Lofts (45) is another helper originating from Akureyri. She studied music at the Reykjavík Conservatory and creative writing at the University of Iceland. She lived in Sweden and later studied in Marseille. She now teaches at the Scandinavia House in New York.

Hjörtur Jónasson (25) is from Reykjavík and studied at the King Abdullah University of Science and Technology in Saudi-Arabia; he graduated in September 2014. Previously, he studied chemistry at the *Politecnico di Milano*.

Lára Kristín Pedersen (19) spent a year in New York, where she studied psychology at St. John's University. By now, she has returned to Reykjavík to continue her psychology studies there. Moreover, she is celebrated as a soccer player in the Icelandic Women's Premier League.

María Skúladóttir (21) also is from Reykjavík and studied at the Reykjavík Conservatory. Currently, she and her boyfriend live in New York, where she happens to study Psychology as well; previously, she studied at Parsons School of Design in New York.

Sigrún Birta Kristinsdóttir (18) is the youngest participant in this project; she attends the Commercial College in Reykjavík. Like Lára Kristin, she is an enthusiastic soccer player, occupying the center back position in her team, which recently won the cup in its league.

Sigrún Ósk Stefánsdóttir (22) also attended Iwanson International School of Contemporary Dance in Munich, and like her good friend Arna she also has a strong interest in languages. Before coming to Munich, she studied dance at Listdansskóli Íslands in Reykjavík.

Sædís Alda Karlsdóttir (25) studied at the University of Iceland and then moved to Dresden, to study business administration and corporate management—and to enjoy the splendid historical city, together with her friend Chaman from Syria.

Tinna María Ólafsdóttir (22) from Hafnarfjörður lives in Paris and works as a flight attendant for Icelandair, at the same time preparing herself to be admitted to medical school in Iceland. In the meantime, she also studies French.

Vilborg Halldórsdóttir (35) from Mosfellsbær near Reykjavík holds an M.Sc. degree in pharmacy from the University of Iceland and is a licensed pharmacist both in Iceland and Germany; during the time of this translation project, she lived and worked in Mörfelden-Walldorf, Hessen, with her husband and their baby daughter.

Vildís Hallsdóttir (69) is a friend of Dacre Stoker and through this connection, we became acquainted as well. Already at age 18, she read *Dracula*—one of her many ongoing interests, beside her family life with two daughters and six grandchildren. She was born in northern Sweden, with a Danish mother and an Icelandic father, and in 1945 came to Iceland with the first ship after WWII. She graduated from college in 1964; after that, she lived in Denmark, then Scotland, before moving to Denmark again, at age 22. She worked in office administration and correspondence, but has retired now.

The age given for the participants is the age they had upon joining the project.

REFERENCES

Writings & Interviews by Bram Stoker
Quoted in this Book

Eighteen-Bisang/Miller, 2008 — Eighteen-Bisang, Robert and Miller, Elizabeth, eds. *Bram Stoker's Notes for Dracula: A Facsimile edition*. Jefferson, N.C.: McFarland, 2008.

Stoddard, 1897 — Stoddard, Jane. *Mr. Bram Stoker: A Chat with the Author of Dracula*, in *British Weekly*, 1 July 1897, p. 185.

Stoker, 1897 — Stoker, Bram. *Dracula*. London, Westminster: Archibald Constable, 1897.

Stoker, 1907 — Stoker, *Personal Reminiscences of Henry Irving*. London: Heinemann, 1907, one-volume-edition.

Stoker, 1908 — Stoker, Bram. *The Censorship of Fiction*, in *The Nineteenth Century and After: A Monthly Review*, Sept. 1908, New York: Leonard Scott, p. 158.

Recently rediscovered writings
by Bram Stoker

Browning, 2012 — Browning, John Edgar, ed. *The Forgotten Writings of Bram Stoker*, with a foreword by Elizabeth Miller and an afterword by Dacre Stoker. New York: Palgrave Macmillan, 2012.

Stoker & Miller, 2013 — Stoker, Dacre & Miller, Elizabeth, eds. *The Lost Journal of Bram Stoker: The Dublin Years*. London: Biteback Publishers, 2013.

The official sequel to *Dracula*

Stoker & Holt, 2009 — Stoker, Dacre and Holt, Ian. *Dracula: The Un-Dead*. New York: Harper Collins, 2009.

Biographies of Bram Stoker

Belford, 1996

Belford, Barbara. *Bram Stoker—a Biography of the Author of Dracula*. New York: Knopf, 1996.

Farson, 1975

Farson, Daniel, *The Man Who Wrote Dracula—A Biography of Bram Stoker*. London: Michael Joseph, 1975.

Murray, 2004

Murray, Paul. *From the Shadow of Dracula: A Life of Bram Stoker*. London: Jonathan Cape, 2004.

Annotated editions of *Dracula*

Byron, 1998

Byron, Glennis. *Bram Stoker's Dracula*. Peterborough, Ontario: Broadview Press, 1998.

Klinger, 2008

Klinger, Leslie. *The New Annotated Dracula*. New York: W. W. Norton, 2008.

Leatherdale, 1998 a

Leatherdale, Clive. *Dracula Unearthed*. Westcliff-on-Sea, UK: Desert Island Books, 1998.

McNally & Florescu, 1979

McNally, Raymond, and Florescu, Radu, ed. *The Essential "Dracula": A Completely Illustrated and Annotated Edition of Bram Stoker's Classic Novel*. New York: Mayflower, 1979.

Roos, 2012

Roos, Hans C. de. *The Ultimate Dracula*. München: Moonlake Editions, 2012.

Wolf, 1975/1993

Wolf, Leonard. ed. *The Essential Dracula*. New York: Clarkson N. Potter, 1975, followed by *The Essential Dracula: The Definitive Annotated Edition*. Penguin, 1993.

Sources relating to Transylvania, Moldavia & Wallachia used by Bram Stoker

Boner, 1865

Boner, Charles. *Transylvania—Its Products and Its People*. London: Longmans, Green, Reader, and Dyer, 1865.

Crosse, 1878

Crosse, Andrew F. *Round about the Carpathians*. London: Blackwood, 1878.

Gerard, 1885

Gerard, Emily. *Transylvanian Superstitions*, in *The Nineteenth Century*, July 1885, pp. 130-150.

Johnson, 1885

Johnson, E. C., *On the Track of The Crescent, Erratic notes from the Piræus to Pesth*. London: Hurst and Blackett, 1885.

Mazuchelli, 1881   Mazuchelli, Nina Elizabeth. *Magyarland*, London: Sampson Low, 1881.

Wilkinson, 1820   Wilkinson, William. *An Account of the Principalities of Wallachia and Moldavia*. London: Longman, Hurst, Reese, Orme and Brown, 1820.

DRACULA SCHOLARSHIP

Browning & Picart, 2011   Browning, John Edgar, and Picart, Caroline Joan. *Dracula in Visual Media*. Jefferson, N.C.: McFarland & Co. Pub., 2011

Crişan, 2013   Crişan, Marius-Mircea. *The Birth of the Dracula Myth: Bram Stoker's Transylvania*. Bucharest: Pro Universitaria, 2013.

Dalby, 1986   Dalby, Richard, ed. *A Bram Stoker Omnibus*. London: Foulsham 1986.

Dalby, 1993   Dalby, Richard. *Makt Myrkranna—Powers of Darkness*, in *Bram Stoker Journal* #5, 1993, pp. 2-8.

Davies, 1997   Davies, Bernard. *Inspirations, Imitations and In-Jokes in Stoker's Dracula*, in Miller, 1998, pp. 131-137.

Haining, 1987   Haining, Peter. *The Dracula Scrapbook,* Stanford: Longmeadow, 1987.

Hughes, 1997   Hughes, William. *Bram Stoker (Abraham Stoker), 1847-1912, A Bibliography*. Victorian Research Guide 25, University of Queensland, Australia, 1997.

Leatherdale, 1998 b   Leatherdale, Clive. *Stoker's Banana Skins,* in *Dracula: The Shade and the Shadow*, Ed. Elizabeth Miller, 1998, pp. 128-153.

McNally & Florescu, 1994   McNally, Raymond, and Florescu, Radu, eds. *In Search of Dracula: The History of Dracula and Vampires*. New York: Houghton, Mifflin & Co., 1994.

Miller, 1998   Miller, Elizabeth, ed. *The Shade and the Shadow*, proceedings of the *Dracula Conference* at Los Angeles in August 1997. Westcliff-on-Sea, Essex, UK: Desert Island Books, 1998.

Miller, 2006   Miller, Elizabeth. *Dracula—Sense & Nonsense* (2nd edition). Westcliff-on-Sea, Essex, UK: Desert Island Books, 2006.

Miller, 2009   Miller, Elizabeth, ed. *Bram Stoker's Dracula—A Documentary Journey into Vampire Country and the Dracula Phenomenon*. New York: Pegasus Books, 2009.

Skal, 2004   Skal, David J. *Hollywood Gothic: The Tangled Web of Dracula from Novel to Stage to Screen*. Revised edition. New York: Faber and Faber, 2004.

Storey, 2012

Storey, Neil. *The Dracula Secrets: Jack the Ripper and the Darkest Sources of Bram Stoker*. Stroud, Gloucestershire, History Press, 2012.

Sources relating to Icelandic, Norse and Germanic culture, history & literature

Ásmundsson, 1899

Ásmundarsson (Ásmundsson), Valdimar. *Saga Gísla Súrssonar*, Vol. I & II. Reykjavik: Kristjansson, 1899.

Bellows, 1936

Lokasenna (Loki's Wrangling), from the *Poetic Edda*, transl. Henry Adam Bellows. Princeton: Princeton University Press, 1936.

Bjarnason, 2004

Bjarnason, Bjarni. *Systkinabaekurnur—Kristnihaldi undir Jökli & Drakúla*, in *Lesbók Morgunblaðsins* of 17 January 2004, pp. 4-5.

Booss, 1984

Booss, Claire, ed. *Scandinavian Folk & Fairy Tales*. New York: Gramercy, 1984.

Boyer, 1994

Boyer, Régis. *La mort chez les anciens Scandinaves*. Paris: Les belles lettres, 1994.

Cutrer, 2012

Cutrer, Robert E. *The Wilderness of Dragons. The Reception of Dragons in Thirteenth Century Iceland*. MA thesis, Háskóli Íslands, Medieval Icelandic Studies, Sept. 2012.

Dagsdóttir, 2001

Dagsdóttir, Úlfhildur. *Blóðþyrstir Berserkir,* in *Lesbók Morgunblaðsins* of 21 April 2001, pp. 10-11.

Driscoll, 2008

Driscoll, Matthew James. *A New Edition of the Fornaldarsögur Norðurlanda: Some Basic Questions*. Copenhagen, 2008, online at driscoll .dk/docs/driscoll-new_edition.pdf.

Erlendsson, 1852

Erlendsson, H. *Fjórar riddarasögur*. Reykjavik, E. Þórðarsyni, 1852.

Fiske, 1983

Fiske, Willard. *Bréf Willards Fiskes til Islendinga*, in: *Arbók Landsbókasafn Islands*, Nýrflokkur 8, year 1982 (publ. 1983), pp. 28-68. Editor: Nanna Ólafsdóttir. Translations: Finnbogi Guðmundsson.

Gering, 1897

Gering, Hugo. *Eyrbyggja Saga*. Halle a.d. Saale: Max Niemeyer, 1897.

Grimm, 1828

Grimm, Jacob. *Deutsche Rechtsalterthümer*. Göttingen: In der Dieterichschen Buchhandlung, 1828.

Grimm, 1854

Grimm, Jacob. *Deutsche Mythologie*. Zweiter Band. Göttingen: In der Dieterichschen Buchhandlung, 1854 (Third edition).

Grimm, 1883

Grimm, Jacob. *Teutonic Mythology*. Volume III. Transl. from the fourth edition by James Stallybrass. London: Bell & Sons, 1883.

Gudmundsdóttir, 2007 — Gudmundsdóttir, Adalheidur. *The Werewolf in Medieval Icelandic Literature*, in: *Journal of English and Germanic Philology*, Vol.106:3, 2007.

Haugen, 1992 — Haugen, Einar. Review of: *Íslensk málhreinsun: Sögulegt yfirlit [Icelandic Language Purification: Historical Survey]* by Kjartan G. Ottosson, in: *Language in Society* Vol. 21, No. 2 (Jun., 1992), pp. 336-345, Cambridge University Press.

Jakobsson, 2011 — Jakobsson, Ármann. *Vampires and Watchmen: Categorizing the Mediaeval Icelandic Undead*, in *Journal of English and Germanic Philology*—July 2011.

Jakobsson & Halfdanarson, 2016 — Jakobsson, Sverrir and Halfdanarson, Gudmundur. *Historical Dictionary of Iceland.* Lanham, Maryland: Rowman & Littfield, 2016 (third edition).

Jónsson, 2011 — Jónsson, Ásgeir ed. *Makt Myrkranna—saga af Drakúla greifa.* Reykjavik: Bókafélagið, 2011.

Karlsson, 2000 — Karlsson, Gunnar. *Iceland's 1100 Years: The History of a Marginal Society.* London: Hurst & Co., 2000.

Keyser, 1854 — Keyser, Rudolph. *The Religion of the Northmen.* New York: Norton, 1854.

Larsen, 2006 — Larsen, Svanfríður. *Af erlendri rót: þýðingar í blöðum og tímaritum á íslensku 1874-1910. Studia Islandica,* Issue 59, 2006.

Laxness, 1919 — Laxness, Halldór. *Barn náttúrunnar*, 1919, quoted from snara.is.

Laxness, 1975 — Laxness, Halldór. *Í túninu heima, part I.* Reykjavik: Helgafell, 1975.

Laxness, 2005 — Laxness, Halldór. *Kristnihaldi undir Jökli, 1968 / Under the Glacier*, transl. Magnús Magnússon. New York: Vintage International Ed./Random House, 2005.

Magnússon, 2010 — Magnússon, Sigurður Gylfi. *Wasteland with Words: A Social History of Iceland.* London: Reaktion Books, 2010.

Matthíasdóttir, 2013 — Matthíasdóttir, Magnea J. *Eldhúsreyfarar og stofustáss—Könnunarferð um fjölkerfi íslenskra þýðinga.* Reykjavik: Háskóli Íslands, January 2013.

Milroy, 1966-69 — Milroy, James. *The Story of Ætternisstapi in Gautrek's Saga*, in *Saga-Book of the Viking Society*, London University College, Vol. XVII, 1966-69.

N. N., 1911 — N. N. *Sagan af Starkaði Stórvirkssyni.* Winnipeg: Ottenson, 1911.

Ólafsson, 2002 — Ólafsson. Davíð. *Sagas in Handwritten and Printed Books in 19th century Iceland.* Contribution to the conference publication on Sagas and Societies—Conference at Borgarnes, Iceland, 2002.

Pálsson & Edwards, 1976 — Attributed to: Snorri Sturluson. *Egil's Saga*, around 1240. Transl. by Pálsson, Hermann and Edwards, Paul. Harmondsworth: Penguin, 1976. Icelandic text on sagadb.org/egils_saga.

Rafn, 1829

Rafn, C. C. *Fornaldar Sögur Nordrlanda (eftir gomlum handritum)*. Copenhagen: Popp, 1829.

Rask & Afzelius, 1812

Rask, Rasmus Kristian and Afzelius, Arvid August. *Edda Saemundar hinns froda: Collectio carminum veterum Scaldorum Saemundiana*, Holmiæ (Stockholm), 1812.

Stephany, 2006

Stephany, Timothy J. *Lady of the Elves: The Great Germanic Goddess*. Rochester, NY: Rochester Institute of Technology, 2006.

Sæmundsson, 2004

Sæmundsson, Matthías. *Viðar. Héðinn, Bríet, Valdimar og Laufey*. Reykjavík: JPV-útgáfa, 2004.

Thorkelsdóttir, 2012

Thorkelsdóttir, Eva Dögg Diego. *Makt myrkranna: Sagan af Drakúla greifa - Rýnt í þýðingu Valdimars Ásmundssonar á Dracula eftir Bram Stoker*. Paper written for Háskoli Íslands, Nr. ÞÝÐ003M—Þýðingasaga.

Thorsteinsson, 1857

Thorsteinsson, Steingrímur. *Þúsund og ein nótt* (Icelandic translation of the *Arabian Nights*). Copenhagen: Sveinsson, 4 Vol., 1857-1864

Further translations mentioned in this footnote:

•Aldine Edition, based on the 1811 translation by Jonathan Scott. London: Pickering & Chatto, 1890.

•Burton, Richard. *The Book of the Thousand Nights and a Night*. First edition of 1885-8 in ten volumes. Supplemental edition in six volumes bound in seven parts. Printed by the Burton Club For Private Subscribers Only.

•Lane, Edward William. *The Arabian Nights' Entertainments*. Boston: Little, Brown & Co., 1853

•*Arabische Erzählungen* zum ersten Male aus dem arabischen Urtext treu übersetzt von Dr. Gustav Weil. First German translation from the Arabic by Dr. Gustav Weil. Stuttgart/Pforzheim: Verlag der Classiker, 1839-1841.

Wilda, 1842

Wilda, Wilhelm E. *Strafrecht der Germanen*. Halle: Schwetschke & Sohn, 1842.

Wisén, 1872

Wisén, Theodor. *Homiliu-bok. Isländska homilier efter en handskrift från tolfte århundradet*. Lund: Gleerup, 1872.

Dictionaries explaining pre-modern meanings of Icelandic vocabulary

Cleasby / Vigfússon, 1874   Vigfússon, Guðbrandur. *An Icelandic-English Dictionary, based on the MS. Collections of the Late Richard Cleasby*. Oxford: O.U.P./ Clarendon Press, 1874.

Jonsson, 1863   Jonsson, Erik. *Oldnordisk Ordbog*. Copenhagen: J. D. Qvist, 1863.

Köbler, 2003   Köbler, Gerhard. *Altnordisches Wörterbuch*. Gießen, 2014, 4th edition—online edition, at www.koeblergerhard.de/anwbhinw.html

Zoëga, 1910   Zoëga, Geir T. *A Concise Dictionary of Old Icelandic*. Oxford: O.U.P./Clarendon Press, 1910.

Zoëga, 1922   Zoëga, Geir T. *Icelandic-English Dictionary*. Reykjavik: Kristjánsson, 1922 (2nd edition)

Various sources

Allen, 1997   Allen, Vivien. *Hall Caine: Portrait of a Victorian Romancier*. Sheffield: Sheffield Academic Press, 1997.

Blaufarb, 2008   Blaufarb, Rafe, ed. *Napoleon: Symbol for an Age, A Brief History with Documents*. New York: Bedford/St. Martin's, 2008.

Bonaparte, 1935   Bonaparte, Napoleon. *Les lettres ardentes de Napoléon à Joséphine* (1796-1797). Paris: Éditions Beer, 1935.

Burke, 1832   Burke, John. *A General and Heraldic Dictionary of the Peerage and Baronetage of the British Empire*, Vol. 2. pp. 516-518. London: Henry Colburn and Richard Bently, 1832. Here: pp. 516-518.

Burke, 1869   Burke, Sir Bernard. *A genealogical and heraldic dictionary of the peerage and baronetage of the British Empire*. London: Harrison, 1869.

Caine, 1908   Caine, Hall. *My Story*. London: Heinemann, 1908.

Coleman, 1888   Coleman, John. *Players and Playwrights I have Known*, in 2 Vols. London: Chatto & Windus, 1888.

Coleman, 1904   Coleman, John. *Fifty Years of an Actor's Life*, in 2 Vols. London: Hutchinson & Co., 1904.

Debrett, 1840   Debrett, John. *Debrett's Peerage of England, Scotland, and Ireland, revised, corrected and continued by G.W. Collen*. London: William Pickering, 1840.

Gordon, 2002   Gordon, R. Michael. *The Thames Torso Murders of Victorian London*. Jefferson (NC): McFarland & Company, 2002.

Maines, 1999   Maines, Rachel F. *The Technology of Orgasm— 'Hysteria', the Vibrator, and Women's Sexual Satisfaction*. Baltimore, MD: Johns Hopkins University Press, 1999.

Müller, 1902	Müller, Max. *The life and letters of the Right Honourable Friedrich Max Müller;* ed. by his wife G. A. M. (Georgina Adelaide Müller), in two Volumes. London: Longmans, Green, 1902.
Myers et al., 1886	Myers, Frederic, Gurney, Edmund and Podmore, Frank. *Phantasms of the Living*. London: Trübner, 1886.
Renterghem, 2009	Van Renterghem, Tonny. *De Laatste Huzaar*. Schoorl, NL: Uitgeverij Conserve, 2009.
Sardou & Moreau, 1894	Sardou, Victorien and Moreau, Émile *Madame Sans-Gêne*. Paris: Albin Michel, 1912 (nouvelle édition). French premiere: 27 October 1893.
Sardou/Bond, 1895	Bond, Curtis, transl. *Madame Sans-Gêne—Historial Romance of The Revolution, the Consulate and the Empire*, by Victorien Sardou, in collaboration with Émile Moreau and Edmond Lepelletier. New York: Drallop Publishing, 1895 (translated from the French novelized version).
Sardou/Heller, 1895	*Madame Sans-Gêne—A Historical Romance*—founded on the play by Victorien Sardou—translated from the French by Louie R. Heller. New York: Hurst & Co., 1895 (novel, based on the play).
Sardou/Lepelletier, 1894-95	Lepelletier, Edmond *Madame Sans-Gêne: roman tiré de la pièce de MM. Victorien Sardou, Émile Moreau*. Paris: À la librairie illustrée, 1894-95.
Spicer, n.d.	Spicer, Gerard. *The Thames Torso Murders of 1887-89,* n.d., online at casebook .org/dissertations/thames-torso-murders.html.
Terry, 1909	Terry, Ellen. *The Story of My Life—Recollections and Reflections*. New York: Doubleday, Page & Co., 1909.
Tsernátony, 1902	Tsernátony, Julius, *Das Bistritz-Naßoder Komitat,* in: *Hungary, Volume VI—Das Südöstliche Ungarn—Siebenbürgen und die benachbarten Berggebiete,* as part of the series *Die österreichisch-ungarische Monarchie in Wort und Bild*. Vienna: Kaiserlich-Königlichen Hof- und Staatsdruckerei, 1902, reprinted in Zach, Krista, Ed., *Siebenbürgen in Wort und Bild*. Schriften zur Landeskunde Siebenbürgens, Köln: Böhlau Verlag, 2004.
Twain, 1893	Twain, Mark (Clemens Langhorn). *The £1,000,000 Bank Note and Other New Stories.* London: Chatto & Windus, 1893. Here quoted from the first Canadian edition: Toronto: The Musson Book Company Ltd, n.d.
Twain/Fishkin, 2006	Twain, Mark (Clemens Langhorn). *Is He Dead? A Comedy in Three Acts,* edited by Fishkin, Shelley Fisher. California University Press, 2006.
Twain/Leary, 1969	Leary, Lewis, ed. *Mark Twain's Correspondence with Henry Huttleston Rogers*, 1893-1909. California University Press, 1969.

Warren, 2003   Warren, Louis. *Buffalo Bill Meets Dracula: William F. Cody, Bram Stoker and the Wild West Roots of the Vampire Myth*. Presentation at Buffalo Bill Historical Center, 2003.

Warren, 2005   Warren, Louis. *Buffalo Bill's America: William Cody and the Wild West Show*. New York: Alfred A. Knopf, 2005.

"Waters," 1863   "Waters." *Autobiography of an English Detective*. London: Maxwell, 1863.

West, 1991   West, Trevor. *The Bold Collegians: The Development of Sport in Trinity College, Dublin*. Dublin: Lilliput Press, 1991.

ONLINE SOURCES

Finishing this translation and research project within a year would not have been possible without the help of the Internet. This goes for the textual basis itself—the facsimiles of *Fjallkonan* and the purchase of copies of the first edition—as well as for the initial communication with the National and University Library of Iceland, the Reykjavik City Library, with Ásgeir Jónsson and the various Icelandic archives I consulted. The same applies for the cooperation with my co-authors Dacre Stoker and John Edgar Browning in the US, with my co-editor Lounette Loubser in South Africa and with all Icelandic volunteers who participated in this network—parts of the text being worked on in Munich, Bremen, New York, Reykjavik and Paris, in Denmark and Saudi Arabia simultaneously. Furthermore, the use of online dictionaries—snara.is, ordabók.is, dict.cc, en.wiktionary.org, leo.org—and the inflection database of the Árni Magnússon Institute for Icelandic Studies considerably sped up the translation process. For all kinds of background questions, I not only consulted Wikipedia—which cannot be praised enough—but also dozens of other web pages, dealing with such various subjects such as the glass-harmonica, Napoleon's love letters, Scandinavian folklore, the Whitechapel murders, daylight hours in Transylvania and Iceland, political riots, evolution theory, aristocratic titles, lunar phases, etc. In order not to inflate the footnotes any further, I have abstained from quoting sources for every snippet of information. Should any of this information prove to be inaccurate, the responsibility remains with me.